THE FOURTH HORSEMAN

Other Books by Alan E. Nourse

Intern *(by Doctor X)*

The Practice

Inside the Mayo Clinic

The Family Medical Guide

The Outdoorsman's Medical Guide

THE FOURTH HORSEMAN

ALAN E. NOURSE

1817

HARPER & ROW, PUBLISHERS, New York
Cambridge, Philadelphia, San Francisco, London
Mexico City, São Paulo, Sydney

 For information address Harper & Row, Publishers, Inc., 10 East 53rd Street, New York, N.Y. 10022. Published simultaneously in Canada by Fitzhenry & Whiteside Limited, Toronto.

FIRST EDITION

Designer: Sidney Feinberg

Library of Congress Cataloging in Publication Data

Nourse, Alan Edward.
The fourth horseman.
I. Title.
PS3564.08F6 1983 813'.54 81-48056
ISBN 0-06-038034-9

---

83 84 85 86 87 10 9 8 7 6 5 4 3 2 1

Contents

PART I

THE SPARK

1

Pamela Tate found the first one lying on the dusty trail just below the saddle leading up into Nada Lake. It was a tiny, helpless little thing, on its back in the dirt—a golden-sided ground squirrel, seldom seen in these northern Washington State latitudes. It lay very still, with no sign of life whatever.

Instinctively Pam reached down and touched it, turned it over on its soft tummy. It was a stupid thing to do, she knew that, but she couldn't stop herself, the poor sad creature. Then she saw it wasn't quite dead. Painfully it crept forward in the dust several inches before collapsing, a tiny streak of blood trailing from its mouth. This time when it stopped it didn't move again.

After a moment Pam nudged it off the trail into the brush with the edge of her boot. *Caught by a hawk,* she thought, *and then dropped for something bigger. Hawks will do that sometimes.* She adjusted her pack and started on up the trail toward the saddle, momentarily hating hawks and all their kind. For all her wilderness experience, she had never fully made peace with the cold-eyed law of kill and be killed that prevailed in these rugged mountains. Ground squirrels ate nuts and seeds and hurt nothing at all while hawks tore and rended helpless flesh and blood and bone—and where was the justice to that? There wasn't any justice, no justice at all.

It was only 7:30 in the morning, but the trail was steep and getting steeper, and the sun was already hot. Pam felt sweat trickling down her shirt and standing out in beads on her forehead. She was a small woman, barely five foot two, with light bones and a deceptively delicate, fragile-looking structure. In truth Pam Tate, for all her dainty appearance, was solid muscle. She carried the forty-pound pack on her back like a rucksack, and after four steep uphill miles this morning her step was still springy. She was quick as well as strong, and sure-footed as a mountain goat, in the peak of physical condition. She had to be, to patrol this great complex of high mountain trails through the Enchantment Lakes Wilderness Area day after day on foot, carrying her food and shelter on her back—it built muscles women weren't supposed to have. She had once threatened to throw Frank out of bed—all six feet four and 250 pounds of him. He'd looked at her and grinned, lying there like a lump, challenging her to try. She didn't, of course, he was far too nice *in* bed—but she knew damned well she could do it anytime she chose.

In the shade of the saddle she stopped for a minute, pulled off her floppy green Forest Service hat and fanned herself with it. Her hair was red-brown and straight, cut just short of the thin gold earrings in her ears, her face even, almost plain, except for a tipped-up nose and very level, calm gray eyes. Not far now, she thought, to her first rest stop. This particular route up into the seven-thousand-foot Enchantment Basin went in three stages: the climb up a million steep switchbacks from the Icicle River far below, finally reaching Nada Lake; a second climb up a rocky trail leading high above Nada to the Snow Lakes, eight difficult miles in; and the final dismal scramble up the Snow Lake Wall, more goat path than trail, into the fantastic wonderland that lay at the top.

Some got no farther than Nada, a long, narrow sapphire-blue lake lying deep and cold in a cut between towering forested crags on either side. Nada itself was sublimely beautiful, with a dozen campsites set in forested areas well above the shoreline. Other hikers went on to the Snow Lakes the first day, to stop overnight before assaulting the Wall. The rugged ones made the whole twelve miles to the top in one day. But Pam had other things to do besides hiking. Three camps along Nada were breaking up as she arrived, and she stopped by each one briefly, checking automatically for discarded trash, garbage thrown in the lake, unburied waste, illegal fires. One party of eight teen-agers were boisterous but harmless enough; the other two camps were single couples minding their own business and desiring others to mind theirs, typical visitors to the Enchantments who came to these parts for solitude, not company. All the campers queried her about recent weather conditions "on top" and she answered them as well as she could: a little rain midafternoons, morning and evening sun, warm in daytime but chilly to downright cold at night. Fishing? She didn't fish, but she'd seen lots of nice trout caught, mostly with small gray or black flies.

She was hiking along the trail around Nada toward her usual rest stop when she saw the second ground squirrel. Only sharp eyes could have picked this one up, lying in some bracken at the edge of the trail. It was quite dead, the blood around its nose caked and dusty. *Damned busy hawk,* she thought as she peered down at it. *Too busy.* This time she found a stick and pushed the creature deeper into the brush, well away from the trail. Then she pulled a small pad of paper from her blouse pocket and scribbled a note with the date before she went on.

Her rest stop was at a place just a hundred yards before the trail broke away from the forest around Nada and started up the sharp, rocky trail across an ancient rockslide, climbing up toward the Snows. It was a magic glen of ancient towering cedars, deeply shaded and cool. A tiny stream tumbled down from the heights here to empty into the lake a dozen yards away. Pam dropped her pack to the ground, dipped water with her little tin cup and drank deeply. There was a refreshing downdraft from the cliffs above; flies and mosquitoes seldom came here. She flopped down near the creek with her back to a huge log, munched a bite or two of chocolate and leaned back, relaxing totally.

She thought of the ground squirrels—*Have to tell Frank*—and that turned her thoughts to Frank, as they so often did these days. A sweet guy, Frank, a really sweet, gentle, lovable man. A whole man in every sense of the word—if only he wouldn't push her so hard, right now. They'd met the first week in June when she'd just arrived at the Wenatchee station for a summer's work on the fire crew. Something had happened swiftly between them—first fondness, then affection, then, as natural as eating, love and lovemaking. Within two weeks they were living together in the second-story apartment she had found, spending every nonworking hour together. She had had the strong impression, at first, that Frank was decidedly marriage-shy, and that was fine with her. Yet it was Frank who drove her to grab this wilderness patrol job when it came open, knowing it would take her away three to four days a week by herself, alone to think and not be pressed. Loving and living with a man was one thing, but engagement and marriage now? So soon? She wasn't ready for that.

Frank had pressed harder, lovingly and inarguably insistent. At least an engagement, he had demanded, and finally she had agreed—

but not a formal engagement with notices in the papers and rings and all the ties that bind. Just a pledge between the two of them. Her fingers went to the tiny star-sapphire pendant on a white-gold chain around her neck, Frank's alternative to an engagement ring, and she thought once again, sleepily, what a silly fool she was making of herself. *Any woman in her right mind would grab a guy like that and never let go.*

For a few moments she dozed, maybe dreamed a little. Then she was vaguely aware of someone coming up the trail from the direction she had come. A small solitary figure. *Just a kid out hiking* was her first thought—but then she looked again.

It was a boy, hardly eight or nine years old, his dirty blond hair matted and snarled down to his shoulders, half hiding his face. He was filthy, his face and arms and legs caked with grime, his clothing little more than rancid brown rags hanging around his skinny chest and waist. He was totally barefoot and carried a thick walking stick with a tattered bandana bag tied at the top. As he came near, Pam caught a wave of rank animal odor so overpowering it make her wince.

The boy saw the creek and threw himself to the ground, sinking his face in the water. He drank and drank, with frantic grunting sounds. Finally he stood back up, brushed his mouth with his dirty hand, spit into the creek and only then looked straight at Pam.

His face was vile—the most evil, hateful human face she had ever seen. A little boy's face, but corrupted, the eyes mockingly cruel. A face straight out of hell. Then, before she could get her breath, he moved past her, trudging on up the trail toward the rockslide.

For a moment she sat transfixed, fighting down nausea. Then, as the boy disappeared beyond the trees, she jumped to her feet. The kid was barefoot—and going out on those hot, sharp rocks—She let out a shout and charged up the trail after him, reached the bend, stared up the straight rocky trail.

The trail was empty. It couldn't be, there was no place he could have gone, but no one was in sight. Not a soul. Nothing. She turned back to her pack, rubbing her forehead. She must have dreamed him. She must have gone completely out for a couple of minutes and dreamed him. Sure, she'd seen some weird people on the trail, but nobody like *that* before. Yek! She went to pick up her pack again, and then saw the third dead ground squirrel lying near the creek a few inches from where her leg had been resting.

The trail up to the Snow Lakes always seemed longer and harder than it really was, a sharp, climbing trail up across the face of a steep rockslide, then a long switchback climbing still higher, totally without shade and baking hot in the sun, shoulder-high bushes in places filled with mosquitoes and biting black flies. A single tiny creek trickling down the rocks offered a pause for a cold drink, then on up through rock outcroppings until she reached the long, cool forested corridor at the top that led down to the Snows. Lower Snow lay off to the left, shaded and shallow; Upper Snow to the right, a large lake with many bays, and with cliffs rising straight upward a thousand feet to the Enchantment Basin to the north and west.

She reached the Snows by 10:00 A.M. and found her favorite campsite, on a trail through the rocks on the north side, shielded from the rest of the lake by a high rocky point. There was work to do, so she pitched her tent and stored her pack inside without any loss of time. First she made the mile-long trek down the south side of the lake, past all the campsites, carrying just a small rucksack, pausing to talk to this or that camper, making a mental census of how many had gone up into the basin that morning. A dozen people were around the lake, some pleasant and talkative, some more silent, uncommunicative. Returning by noon, she fired up her little stove, made a cup of tea and munched on salami and cheese for lunch. Then she went back along the trail to the section that needed work. There was a place where a creek meandered down from the mountain to the south, spreading out into a swampy area, now just boggy because of the dry weather but filled with devil's club and wild blackberry all the same, a knee-deep sump in wetter weather. She found where the trail crew had been working with chain saws a week before, dropping five-inch lodgepole pines and bucking them into eight-foot lengths to be used to build a log trail over the swamp. Pam found her own cache of tools stored nearby: a huge machete, a Pulaski with its sharp adz blade on one side and ax on the other, with a file for sharpening it, a hammer and a big bag of six-inch galvanized spikes. She set to work, chopping out roots with the Pulaski, laying short logs for supports, splitting out support stays and driving them into the mud with a heavy rock she found, then setting in the eight-foot lengths of lodgepole and fixing them together with toenailed spikes and anchoring them to the supports with more spikes. It was hot work and slow; by 6:30 P.M. she only had sixteen feet of log trail in place, still not properly secured all the way around, but enough for use. She stored her tools away again and headed back to her camp, ready to quit for the day.

A headache had come on late in the afternoon, and her right wrist and left ankle were itching inexplicably, a fact that only reached her consciousness when she had scratched at them for half an hour. She squeezed her eyes shut, trying to drive off the headache, but it persisted, to her disgust—she *never* had headaches. Back at camp, secluded from view of the rest of the lake, she stripped naked and plunged into a deep blue pool by the rock, felt the icy water bite her scalp and underarms and breasts and groin. God it was cold! but good, good to get the dirt and sweat off. She used a tiny turkish towel to dry off, then lay naked on the rock to catch the dying sun's warmth, hoping to shake off the headache—but it didn't go away.

She was dressed in her woollies for the night, starting up her little gas stove to cook macaroni and cheese for dinner when she saw the smoke billowing up from the far side of the lake. Open campfire. *The bastards,* she thought, *they just won't read signs, will they?* Since the dip in the lake her chest felt tight and she was coughing repeatedly, as though something in her chest needed to come up but wouldn't. She pulled on her outer clothes, stuck her citation book in her pocket and started off toward the illegal fire, still coughing.

It was halfway around the lake, an enormous crowd of campers, twenty that she could count and who could guess how many more? Their tents were down on the very lakeshore, and a huge wood fire was blazing on a rock. Half a dozen people stood around the fire, including a large, beefy man with a .38 Special pistol on a belt around his waist. He turned to confront her as she walked into the campfire circle.

"What are you planning to shoot?" she asked, pointing to the pistol.

"Rabbits," the man said.

"There aren't any rabbits this high," Pam said. "And the squirrels, ground squirrels and marmots are all protected."

"So I'll shoot chipmunks," the man said.

"That's pretty big game for a man." Pam looked at the blaze. "Quite a fire you've got there."

"Say, who the hell are you?"

"Forest Service. Wilderness Patrol," Pam said.

"So why don't you piss off, lady? We don't need you around here."

"You've got an illegal fire going here."

"What do you mean, illegal fire?"

The headache was pounding behind her eyes. "I mean there's a fire closure in this area," she said irritably. "These woods are tinder-dry, they can go off like dynamite with one little spark. Fires were closed out a month ago; there's a clear notice at every trailhead and dozens more tacked up all over the place, including that tree over there: no fires except camp stoves."

The man laughed and looked at his companions. "So the girlie is going to make us put out our fire. How about that, guys?"

Suddenly Pam was tired of all this. She stepped up very close to the big man with the pistol, looking up into his face. For a moment she was wracked with coughing, but fumbled her citation book out of her pocket. "Mister, I don't care what you do with your fire," she said when her voice came back. "What's your name?"

"Jack B. Nimble. What's yours?"

"Okay." She glanced at a pack near the fire with a stenciled name and address on it. "That says Robert B. Comstock, 314 Sand Way, Canon City, Colorado. That's good enough for me; let Mr. Comstock carry the load." She was writing in her citation book. "You have an illegal fire, Mr. Comstock or whoever you are. That's point number one. You have at least twenty people in this one camp, where the legal limit is eight to one campsite. That's point number two. You've got a camp directly on the shore of the lake, when the Wilderness Law at the trailhead specifies one hundred feet back at a minimum. That's point number three. Now you can take your three citations and pay the judge a nice fat fine for each one, or you can break up this cozy mess and set up legal camps. Take your choice. I don't care what you do—but I'll be checking."

She ripped off a copy of the triple citation and shoved it into the man's paw. Then she turned and started back up the trail toward her campsite, coughing and coughing as she went. Behind her there was a flurry of activity; she heard the big man rumble, "For Christ sake, get that fire out and strike those tents. Goddam meddling bastards . . ." Pam went on, scratching her wrist and ankle almost raw as she went. They'd probably trim up their camp, at least halfway, she reflected. They usually did. But aside from that, she was appalled at herself. Seldom if ever was she so imperative and abrupt about a violation. The whole idea had always been voluntary compliance, not the force of law. If it hadn't been for this damned headache, she would have handled it far more smoothly. . . .

Back at camp she cooked up dinner, then found she had no appetite for it. She just didn't *feel* good. She really just wanted to get into bed and sleep forever, but the force of habit was strong. First she brought out the small notebook from her pack, pulled out the notes from her breast pocket, propped up her flashlight and made her day's log entry in her small, cramped handwriting. The three dead ground squirrels, the strange dirty boy at Nada Lake, the trail-mending work, the unpleasant crowd she had just encountered around the lake. Finally, inexplicably exhausted and still coughing every few moments, she took a couple of ampicillin caps, her cure-all for everything, crawled into her sleeping bag still dogged by her headache, and dreamed nightmares.

To her amazement, she didn't wake up until after eight the next morning—more than three hours late, for her. Her head still throbbed and her cough seemed deeper as she crawled out of the tent, stiff and sore. Breakfast was out of the question, the very thought turned her stomach, and she had to get going, there was a lot to do today when she got up to the top. Something nagged at her subliminally as she struck her tent and stuffed her pack—her armpits and groin were aching fiercely. *Flu? In August? Good God. That's all I need right now.* She took two more ampicillin, struggled into her pack and started around the lake to the beginning of the climb.

The Comstock party, broken up and moved back from the lake, was just stirring as she went past; three or four of them glared at her. At the far end of the lake she stopped at the feeder creek for water, suddenly unbearably thirsty. From the place where it crossed the creek the trail led back, rising and falling, through a deeply wooded canyon floor, then abruptly started up, and up, and up. Her usual time to the top in the cool of early morning was about an hour, but starting up now after nine, she knew she wouldn't make it that fast. The mist was already off the lake and a hot sun was baking down—*Great on those rocks up higher.* To top it off, the headache and the coughing slowed her down. Every time her pulse topped a hundred her head started pounding until she tripped or lurched or walked into a tree. Each coughing spell made her stop for a minute to get her wind, so she couldn't set a pace. She pushed doggedly on, finally giving up on pace and stopping to rest for five minutes out of every fifteen as other hikers came up behind her and passed her.

From time to time she could see the white water of the creek plunging down cliff and canyon from Lake Vivian, the first of the Enchantment Lakes high above. About a third of the way up, the trail switched out to the creek near a beautiful series of crystal pools, usually her first two-minute rest stop. This time she dumped her pack like an elephant off her back and sank down on a log, not even looking at the creek.

Abruptly, she realized she was shaking. She couldn't hold her hands or legs still, and her teeth were chattering so fiercely she could hear them. She was suddenly icy cold, frigid, nearly shaking herself off the log, shaking too hard to grip her arms across her chest. *Chills. That means fever, high fever, that's what the first-aid book says. Heat stroke? Impossible, her neck and forehead were still wet with sweat.* She sat shaking for fifteen minutes until gradually, gradually, the chills subsided and she felt a little better. She shouldered the pack and started slowly up again.

Two hours later, still nowhere near the top, she had another chill, worse and longer than the first. This time a spasm of coughing wouldn't seem to stop until she was totally breathless, and left red streaks on her handkerchief. There seemed to be a trace of a bad odor on her breath that she couldn't get away from. Perils of the wilderness didn't scare Pam Tate, she knew what they were and what to do about them, but perils of the body were something else. Suddenly she was frightened, wishing very much that Frank were here, wishing she were up on top of this rockpile and not still a third of the way down. For the first time she thought of dumping her pack and going on without it—but that was irrational. She had to have the pack, up on top. She started on.

It was almost 2:00 P.M. when she finally reached the open granite slabs that led up into the pocket where Lake Vivian lay, a cool, deep, green lake, clear as fine emerald, surrounded by scrub pine and larch and great rocky outcroppings, Mt. Temple rising like a vast granite crenellated castle behind it. She didn't pause there. She barely even glanced at the sublime beauty of the place, then crossed the outlet creek and up the rock trail that climbed five hundred more feet into a saddle and down into Lancelot, the lake where she usually camped. Several camps were already set up on the long, rocky point that extended out into Lancelot, but nobody was at the far end of the point, and nobody had taken "her own" campsite near the tiny fairy pond surrounded by stunted pink heather and twisted gray weatherbeaten larch. The place she sought had a wind-shelter of rocks, good drainage from the coarse sand of the tent site, a rock "table" for her camp stove.

She dumped her pack and sank down on the sandy ground. For a long time she did nothing at all, chilling and chilling, head and body aching fiercely. Her armpits and groin felt sore as boils—there seemed to be huge lumps there now, soft and mushy and agonizingly painful to touch. She stripped off her blouse, saw great black-and-blue welts where the pack straps had pressed, and more on her legs where the boots had rubbed.

She staggered to her feet, somehow got her tent out and raised, coughing repeatedly and bringing up great foul-smelling clumps of red-streaked stuff with each paroxysm. All thoughts of doing anything that day were pushed aside—she had to rest, get her breath somehow, get this aching and chilling to stop. While she worked, reality began to fade in and out, as though there really *were* enchantment up here. At one point, as she struggled mightily to get her sleeping bag lofted and into the tent, a half-hour job, she thought Frank was there and she was talking to him, but she never could focus on him. At another point she thought she was still down at the Snow Lakes, camped near the deep swimming pond, and went wandering off looking for it, then had to search and search to find her way back.

Finally the tent was ready. To keep a grip on things and fight away the phantom ideas flooding her mind now, she found her notebook and pencil and with hands still shaking started to scribble her short daily log. She knew what she was writing didn't make any sense, she'd already written about the Comstocks before, and she'd worked on the Snow Lakes trail yesterday, not today, but she plunged on. At one point, without any conscious intent, she found herself writing a love letter to Frank, a *real* love letter, pouring out all the things she felt but had never really been able to say to him, but the scrawl got so bad even she couldn't read it and somehow there was blood on the bottom of the page, so she threw it aside and crawled into the tent, aching all over and coughing until she was breathless.

She slept and woke and slept, repeatedly awakened by the coughing. At one point she took some pills from a little bottle, ampicillin and aspirin, she thought—had to be, there wasn't anything else there. Presently it was dark and she slept again, fitfully. . . .

Hours later she woke, suffocating and hardly able to move. The tent stank like a sewer and her body was baking. Desperately she tore open her sleeping bag. She screamed out as she moved an arm—something warm and slimy was draining down from the mushy lump in her armpit. She began coughing again, and found some dark, wet, sticky stuff pouring from her mouth and running down her chin and breast, soaking into the down bag around her. Her scream was choked off by the gurgling sound of more coughing. With a supreme effort she twisted her head down to the tent entrance, choking, suffocating, smothering, frantic for air. She wrenched the tent open and got herself halfway out. *Oh, God, Frank,* she thought, *help me. . . .* She inched a little bit more out of the tent before she collapsed, unable to move.

She died two hideous hours later, at 2:15 in the morning, facedown in a little pile of coarse granite sand.

2

In Brookdale, Connecticut, on the night Pam Tate died, Jack Dillman was standing in the bathroom putting the finishing touches on his second shave of the day when his wife banged on the door. "You planning to stay in there all night?" she called. "We're already half an hour late."

Jack opened the door. "Just finished," he said, and raised his eyebrows. Carmen was wearing a silky dress of bright scarlet, cut deep between her breasts. "Wow," Jack said. "You going on the prowl tonight?"

"Always prepared," Carmen said. She turned her head when he bent to kiss her. "Careful, you'll muss my hair."

"Gonna give Hal a big thrill, I suppose."

"He's always responsive, the poor silly ass. And he's the host."

"He's silly enough, all right," Jack said sourly. "He wouldn't know what to do if you dropped it in his lap."

Carmen turned businesslike eyes to the mirror, retouching her makeup. "Then I might have to teach him," she said. "If you didn't hate him so much, it wouldn't be near as much fun."

Actually, Jack reflected as they drove the half-mile to the party, he didn't hate Hal Parker at all. The guy was stupid, and an awful bore, for all his money, but nothing you couldn't put up with one evening a week. And he doubted that Carmen was serious about Hal anyway—just about anybody else would do as well. Not that it mattered too much anyhow, he reflected. He had learned to make a sort of peace with that years ago.

All the same, Jack thought, it wouldn't hurt to give Hal Parker a little jolt this evening, just to remind him that the goodies didn't necessarily come free, so he began considering what kind of a jolt might do it. Trouble was, with a guy like Hal, it took quite some kind of jolt to get through at all.

3

At Grizzly Creek, Montana, on the night Pam Tate died, Harry Slencik came into the cabin late, his arms and legs caked with mud, and tossed his ten-gallon hat onto the elkhorn rack over the fireplace with a sigh. "Well, speaking of good news," he said to his wife, "I think the irrigation pump's quit."

Amy Slencik looked up from the pan of frying chicken. "Aw, Harry, come on. We just *bought* it last spring."

"It ain't pumpin' water."

"But it's *got* to." The woman's alarm was real and intense. "Harry, it was 110 out in that sun today, and the dirt in the garden is bone-dry. Another day or two and everything we planted will be down the tube."

"What we need is some rain," Harry said.

"Rain, hell! We aren't going to have any rain now until the snow flies, and you know it. What we need is those spuds out there." She sat down with him at the little kitchen table. "Harry, with that underground wiring contract you've got going there in Bozeman, we're in right up to the neck. Every dime we've got is tied up in that job. You've got payrolls to meet every Friday and cash to pay for materials, and meanwhile the damned city waits six months to pay off your invoices. We couldn't borrow another ten bucks at the bank right now even if we wanted to pay their interest rates. So what do you think we're going to *eat* this fall? We need those spuds."

"I know, I know." Harry sighed. "I'll take the pump apart tomorrow, see if I can find what's wrong with it. Either something's jammed in the intake pipe or one of the impellers has gone squat. But I'll get it fixed."

"Well, you'd better. And we'd better get some venison this fall, too. Both of us. Unless you want to eat nothing but chicken all winter." She gave him a little shove. "Now go get yourself a short one. Dinner'll be ready in fifteen minutes."

Harry poured a little whiskey and walked out on the stoop of the cabin looking out on the creek. He could probably fix the pump, or cook up some other way to irrigate the garden while they were back in town. He could also worry about the undergrounding contract, damndest mess he'd ever gotten himself into, but he didn't want to think about that, right now. That's why they came over here to the creek as often as they could, to get things like that off his mind. Sometimes he felt like just dumping the damned business, maybe turn it over to the two boys, he was getting too old for that kind of hassle all the time. Bag it all and just come over here and settle down and grow a garden and raise a steer and a hog and take it easy. *Maybe not such a bad idea at that,* he thought. *Not such a bad idea at all.*

4

In Indianapolis, Indiana, on the night Pamela Tate died, a small blond woman with hair caught back in kewpie-doll ponytails stood up with an audible snort of disgust and marched out of the press conference, leaving the man from Sealey Labs droning on and on behind her. Once outside the conference room she unhooked the press pass from her blouse and gave it one final look before dropping it in the trash can. In addition to PRESS, the badge said: SALLY GRINSTONE—PHILADELPHIA INQUIRER in large red letters.

And so much for casting your bread upon the water, Sally thought sourly. *All that plane fare blown, a day's work blown, a perfectly good dinner date blown—well, crappio! You should have known better than to bother with a Sealey Labs press conference anyway. Should have known that anything Sealey produced would be sleazy in some way—but you never learn, do you, Sal? Especially when you think you smell blood . . .*

Another reporter followed on her heels, finally caught up. "Heard all you could stand?" he asked her, with a wry grin.

"You'd better guess. All they've got to promote is one more garden variety of arthritis drug, and they're hyping it up to the moon. And not one word about the Australian studies, even though they sponsored them and paid for them."

"Australian studies?"

Sally Grinstone glanced up at the man, her green eyes suddenly penetrating. "Haven't done your homework, eh, Saul? Well, I should make you do it, but I'm too kindhearted. Anyway, this is too small for me to get excited about. You want a story? You can have it free. Just check out Heinz and Faber's work in the *Acta Scandinavica* back in 1979, and the Australian team's report in our own *Immunology* in late '84 and '85. See what those people turned up about this 'safe' little arthritis drug that Sealey Labs is hyping now—press conference with the great Mancini himself, their top production man. And when you get finished, remember that you owe Sally Grinstone a stroke sometime when she needs it. . . ."

5

At the Centers for Disease Control in Atlanta, Georgia, on the night Pam Tate died, Dr. Ted Bettendorf was sitting late at his desk staring angrily at the bundle of papers in his hand. *Damn those people!* he thought for the twentieth time in an hour. *Damn them! They just can't let well enough alone. . . .*

He'd been hearing rumors about the request for weeks now, and he'd done his best to discourage it, unofficially, but now here it was on paper, demanding an official, appealable yes or no answer from him. They wanted to tie up the Hot Lab for the next four solid months—his own people—and tonight he had to think up some completely supportable reason to turn them down.

An hour earlier, just before she left for the evening, Mandy had brought him the sheaf of papers—the research protocol and formal applications. She had paused at the door, looking back at him. "Ted—this work they want to do is a bad scene, isn't it?"

"Yes, of course it's a bad scene."

"Do you have to decide tonight?"

"Better than next week."

"Can I help you? Do you want me to stay?"

He looked up at her. "No. Thanks, but no. I'm the one that has to do it. Nobody else."

After she'd left, he stretched his long, skinny legs under the desk, ran his fingers through his thick, graying hair. He'd be sixty-one next week, and sometimes he thought he was getting too old for the hassle, as Administrator of the Uncommon Diseases section at the CDC. Leprosy. Plague. Rabies. Anthrax. Half a dozen other living horrors. And smallpox. He'd thought he could put that on the back burner a few years ago when the disease was officially declared extinct on earth by the WHO. But now his own people wanted to use the Hot Lab to play around with smallpox again. . . .

Momentarily he turned his thoughts to the Hot Lab itself—that fantastically beautiful, fantastically secure laboratory-within-a-laboratory-within-a-laboratory, occupying a whole building to itself a few hundred yards from his office, a place for the safe study of the deadliest of all microorganisms ever let loose on the face of the planet—one of the half-dozen such totally safe laboratories in existence in the world. It was here in his Hot Lab that the Lassa fever virus had been pinned down after it first made its deadly appearance on the Gold Coast of Africa in 1976. It was here also that the Marburg virus, another merciless slaughterer from Africa, had met its nemesis in a six-month crash-study program. Variant strains of *Yersinia* had been studied here, off and on; work had been done here on the human diploid vaccine for rabies, the new chloroquine-resistant strains of *Plasmodium* that had made incurable malaria another new horror story in the world, the N43-B lymphoma virus with its strange cross-relationship with multiple sclerosis . . .

And now they wanted to play with smallpox again. A disease dead and gone, only four laboratory repositories of the live, wild virus remaining on earth, one of them here, deep in a quadruple-locked vault in the CDC, maintained only for possible future needs or scientific study. And that, of course, was what his people were asking for—use of the Hot Lab for further scientific study.

Ted Bettendorf knew without the slightest doubt that his answer had to be no. The question was: why? The reason had to be plausible—scientifically supportable—or they could challenge him in a court appeal, and very well might. But the only argument he could think of at the moment was that the program would tie up the Hot Lab for one-third of a year, which meant it couldn't be used for anything else once the program was started. This smallpox research was not critical to human life, right now—but something critical could turn up at any moment. . . .

He squirmed, searched through other reports. He knew of nothing. A human rabies case, fatal, from New Mexico, transmitted by bat guano in a cave. Two hundred and seventy-three new cases of leprosy identified in the last twelve months, a stable, steady growth of that disease each year for the past six years, much of it imported with refugees, nothing yet to become alarmed about. A sharp upsurge in new pulmonary tuberculosis in the slums, a hundred percent consistent with the continuing cutback in welfare funds. An oddly shifting pattern for Rocky Mountain spotted fever, more cases in the southeastern states than in the West—but other than things like that, nothing to hang his hat on.

Well, he thought suddenly, it really didn't have to be decided tonight. By the rules, he had fourteen days to respond to this request, and he would by God take fourteen days this one time. Tomorrow he would set Mandy to searching for *something* he could use. *Maybe tonight somebody is dying of something that will make a difference,* he thought wryly. A reach, perhaps, but there you were. Ted Bettendorf threw the sheaf of papers on his desk, scribbled a brief note on the paper in front of him and climbed wearily to his feet. *In the words of the immortal Willis McCawber, Esq., he thought, "Something will turn up. . . ."*

6

In another CDC office in Atlanta, Georgia, on the night Pam Tate died, Dr. Carlos Quintana was still dictating correspondence at 8:30 P.M. when Monique came in with a foot-high stack of folders in her arms. "You're going to hate me for this," she said.

"Impossible," Carlos said firmly. "Nothing you could do could create such a situation. But why are you still here?"

"Because you need this stuff for your report on that Legionella outbreak in Kansas City," she said. "It's all microbiology, and it's going to take you three weeks just to analyze it, unless you persuade me to leave my microscope and come do it for you. And Ted is going to be breathing down your neck in one week, because that's when he wants your report, wrapped up and finished."

"Yes, I know." The young man came around the desk as she dumped the pile of folders there. He placed his hand on her hip and kissed her gently. She was a striking woman: long slender legs, blond hair, an even, intelligent face, deep breasts. *Fantastically competent behind that microscope,* he thought. *And elsewhere.* He leafed through the first few folders. "Splendid excuse for working late tonight," he murmured. "Who could argue with one of Ted's deadlines?"

"You aren't going to like what you find here," Monique said.

"No? Why not?"

"Because you are a nitpicking perfectionist, my friend, who spent almost two weeks out there trying to tie up that mini-epidemic in a nice, neat scientific package—but there's nothing remotely neat about this lab data that you need to support your case. The truth is, it's one big indecisive mess. My people did the best they could with the stuff your people shipped us, but Jesus, Carlos . . ."

The young doctor laughed. "My dear, you worry about the damndest things. Believe me, somewhere in your pile of data here I will find the answers I need. For now, all I'm worried about, since I'm obviously going to have to work so late, is where we should have dinner. Barron's, would you think?"

She looked at the darkly handsome young man, realizing that he was laughing at her—as usual. "Do you really think that's wise, so soon again?"

He shrugged elaborately. *"Por qué no?"*

"*Porque* Angela is going to get wise one of these days."

"My dear, Angela was wise the day she was born. Don't worry yourself. So. It's Barron's, then?"

She nodded finally. *"Sí,"* she said. *"Cómo no?"*

7

In the black south-side ghetto of Chicago, on the night Pam Tate died, Sidonia Harper lay on her cot in her second-story tenement room, staring into the darkness long after she should have been sleeping.

It was amazing, Siddie thought, what you could tell just from the sounds and smells that came to your room. Here, in the summer heat, there was no hiding from the rank garbage smell that came billowing up from the fire-escape alley outside her window. No fresh air ever penetrated here—you didn't expect it to. In the darkness outside she could hear others, sitting out on the metal steps above and below—talking, smoking, now and then laughing, a beer can clattering down onto the alley pavement, a giggling discussion of the weatherbeaten tomcats patrolling the overflowing trash cans. Somewhere else in the building a party was going on, with shrieks and whoops and the thrumming of punk-rock music. And somewhere, inevitably, somebody was cooking cabbage, adding its reek to the fetid garbage stench. Siddie knew them all by their sounds and smells—but there was no way she could go out to join them.

It had been a long day for Siddie. The Man from social services had come today, like he'd said he would, to bring her his answer, like he'd said he would, and the answer was no. There wasn't going to be any banister-lift to carry her and her wheelchair down from this second-story flat to the ground floor below. There wasn't any money for that, the Man said. Everything had been cut back, so they had to do without the frills. A banister-lift wasn't a matter of life or death, the Man had pointed out. And after all, she did have her chair. It wasn't as if she had to stay in bed all the time.

So there she was, she thought, good old no-frills Siddie, taking it on the jaw again. Maybe once a week, if she was lucky, she or her mother could get a couple of the boys from upstairs to carry her down the long flight to the ground floor, along with her chair, so she could have an hour—a whole hour!—of freedom from this tiny second-floor prison. The rest of the time—well, this was home, baby, and this was where she stayed.

She stirred, got her arms under her, and laboriously shifted the upper half of her body over from one side of the cot to the other for a while. Some eighteen-year-old girls might have wept at the news the Man had brought today, but not Sidonia Harper. There was a dogged toughness about her that made even her mother wonder sometimes. As soon as she'd heard what the Man had to say, she'd started revising her thinking about more freedom, making peace with the denial. She'd learned how to make peace with a lot of things since that awful night two years before when she'd gone through the fire-escape rail and down to the concrete alley below. . . .

So there wouldn't be any lift to carry her chair down. Well, that was all right. Someday, she thought, things were going to be different and she wasn't going to need any lift.

8

On a mountainside north of Leavenworth, Washington, on the night after Pamela Tate died, Frank Barrington reached the uppermost corner of the 160-acre controlled-burn area about four-thirty in the morning and turned west along the firebreak line his crew had been busy digging for the past three weeks. He turned to survey the vast burned-out area below him, parts of it still flaming, other parts billowing dense clouds of acrid smoke, and nodded in satisfaction. Here and there above the firebreak line, in the thick forest along the ridge of Rattlesnake Mountain, he could see spot fires smoldering, but they didn't worry him. If the crew could get them before the sun got too much higher in the sky, they had this slash burn made.

Down the line toward him a big girl came trudging along, a huge black water pack on her back, hard hat down over her ears. She was even grimier than Frank was, smeared from top to toe with ashes and soot. She looked very tired. "Ho, Becky," Frank said as she stopped to wipe sweat off her forehead.

"Hi," the girl said. "Larry finally got that tanker pump working again, so we've got some water up here at last. Where do you want us to put it?"

"Those spot fires up there," Frank said. "I'll get Billy and Sue up here to help you. How does it look farther over?"

"Not too bad," the girl said. "There was a flare-up over beyond that granite rockfall that scared me a couple of hours ago; I thought it was going to jump the line, but only a few sparks went over." She sighed wearily. "I'm just glad we finally got the bugger burned, that's all. Before we had a lightning storm and the whole mountainside went up."

The "bugger" was 160 acres of heaped-up piles of small logs, stumps, branches and other debris left over from a logging operation two years before, baked tinder-dry by long seasons of hot summer sun and no rain—a terrible forest-fire hazard in these steep Cascade mountains until it could safely be burned out. The problem was finding the chance: after watching closely for three weeks, it had not been until 8:30 the previous evening that the humidity had finally gotten high enough to make a controlled burn possible, and Frank and his crew had made their move. As Fire Boss, it had been his responsibility to coordinate the whole operation—send out the lighting crews to touch off the heaps of rubble, keep the tanker trucks rolling to supply the pumps carrying water through hoses high up the mountainside, patrol the firelines himself for spot fires and bring in crewmen where they were needed. Now, nine hours later the acute danger was over as long as the wind didn't come up, but it would be another ten hours of mop-up before any of the crew could leave. *Damned logging companies,* he thought. *They love to get their greedy hands on those logs—but they can't be bothered with a decent cleanup. Forest Service has to do that.*

His walkie-talkie crackled and he took it off his belt. "Frank? Larry here," a tinny voice sounded. "How's it doin'?"

"Looks pretty good so far," Frank said.

"It looked great from down here. Seen anything?"

"I jumped a big bull elk about an hour ago, right up here in all that smoke."

"Smoke don't bother those big guys any," Larry said. He paused. Then: "Frank, the Super just called. Wants you back down at the office."

Frank blinked at the walkie-talkie. "In Leavenworth? When?"

"Like right now. That's what he said."

"Hey, man, I've got a slash burn going. I can't just walk off and take a twenty-mile drive."

"I'm supposed to relieve you," Larry said. "He wants you down there fast."

The burn was still far too hot to pick his way through it, and it took Frank half an hour to get down the outside fireline to the place where the pickups were parked. He looked at Larry, already shouldering the Fire Boss's pack, but Larry just spread his hands and shrugged. As Frank started his pickup down the rough mountain road toward the highway to Leavenworth, he grew more and more apprehensive. *Nobody hauls a man off a burn like this,* he thought, *unless there's a real bastard of a fire going somewhere else.* He didn't have the only first-attack fire crew in the Wenatchee District, for God's sake—but if something else wasn't burning, why would the Super be in his office at 5:30 in the morning?

Forty minutes later Frank stalked into the little Leavenworth Ranger Station, filthy and reeking, and stuck his head in the door of the Super's office. "Hey, man, what's going on? You got a big fire somewhere?"

"No, no. Nothing like that." The Super was a small, wiry, balding man of about sixty with blue eyes and a gentle face. "Nothing like that at all. Come on in, have a seat." He waited until Frank settled his huge bulk onto a frail office chair, his face quite unreadable. "That burn doing all right up there?" he asked.

Frank frowned. "Of course it is. You talked to Larry, you know it's going fine. You didn't call me off to ask me that."

"No, that's true. I didn't." The Super avoided Frank's eyes, fiddled with a marking pen on his desk. Then he took a deep breath. "Frank, I understand that you've been close to Pamela Tate this summer, is that right?"

Frank looked at the man. "You might say that."

"Maybe very close," the Super said.

"We're engaged to be married," Frank said. "Is that close enough?" He sat forward and stared at his boss, frowning. "Why? What about Pam? She's on patrol up in the Enchantments right now. She's not due back until tomorrow afternoon."

"Did she seem sick in any way when you saw her last? Before she started up there this time?"

"Lord, no," Frank said. "She was healthy as I am. Say, what the hell is this, anyway? Is something wrong with Pam?"

"I'm afraid Pam ran into some trouble on this patrol," the Super said quietly. "I thought you'd better know."

Frank was on his feet, towering over the desk. "What kind of trouble, up there? A bear? There hasn't been a grizzly up there since we shot that old sow eight years ago."

"It wasn't a bear, it was something else. A hiker found her lying half in and half out of her tent about noon yesterday and packed all the way out to report it. We sent Doc Edmonds and two of the trail crew up there in a chopper last night the minute we got word. They brought her out. Just got down an hour ago. They dropped her pack and tent over at her apartment." The Super paused. "She—she looked like she'd been worked over with a ball bat."

"Great God. Nobody ever assaults anybody up in a place like that! But at least she's healthy as a horse. She'll mend." Frank turned for the door. "Where is she now? Wenatchee General? I've got to see her."

"Frank, you don't understand. Pam's dead. She was dead when the hiker found her. We brought out her body."

The big man stood frozen by the door for long seconds. Then in horrible slow motion he raised a huge clenched fist and drove it smashing into the wall by the door, once, twice, three times, until the plaster crumbled. "You aren't lying to me?" he said finally. "This isn't some kind of lousy joke?"

"I don't make that kind of joke," the Super said, "and I'm not lying. I'm as sick about it as you are." His voice broke momentarily. "I don't know what happened up there, Frank, but whatever it was, it was something foul. Doc Edmonds should still be there at the morgue in Wenatchee. He may have some answers by the time you get there, if you want to go down."

He didn't know how he got there, his vision frozen down to a tunnel, his mind frozen, his emotions frozen. He didn't even know where the morgue in Wenatchee was located, but presently he found it, a long, gray, antiseptic-smelling room with two bare stainless-steel tables and white bathroom tiles on the floor dipping down to two metal drains. A bank of big filelike drawers along one side of the room, with red tags on the doors. At the end of the room was a small office-laboratory with glass windows looking out onto the morgue room. He saw Dr. Harry Edmonds there, writing on a long yellow legal pad. The doctor, thin and bearded and fortyish, came out to meet him. "Frank, I'm sorry as hell about this. . . ."

Frank shook his head. "Nothing you did."

"If there's anything I can do . . ."

"Yes. You can tell me what happened."

Doc spread his hands. "It looks like pneumonia, plain and simple. She'd been dead about ten hours when the hiker found her on Wednesday. That's about all I can tell you."

"*Pneumoniu!* I can't believe it. Doc, I was up at four Monday morning, helping her stuff her pack for that patrol. She wasn't sick then, not even a little. She hasn't been sick all summer, and she was in absolutely prime physical shape on Monday morning. Now you tell me what kind of pneumonia cuts somebody like that down in *forty-eight hours or less?*"

"I don't know. Sometimes an atypical bug turns up."

"Did you take any tests?"

"I took a sputum smear and stained it. It just showed a gram-negative rod, looked a lot like an ordinary colon bacillus except it didn't take the stain very well. But some strains of *E. coli* can be murder when they get into the lung."

"What about cultures?"

Doc sighed. "I plated out the sputum, of course, and some lung tissue, and some blood. But I'm not sure anything will grow, it was almost thirty hours post-mortem before we even got the stuff in an incubator. The X rays were pretty plain, though." He pulled out films and stuck them up on a viewer. "I took these with a portable machine. Even post-mortem you can tell there was no functioning lung tissue at all. Solid beefsteak. And my physical exam confirmed it—no air movement at all."

"But so fast . . ." Frank groped for something to say. "What about the autopsy?"

"No legal permission. Her only family is her father. We contacted his engineering office in New York. He's down in the jungle in southern India somewhere, designing artesian wells. There aren't any phones, no way to reach him."

"What about the Coroner?"

"He's satisfied there was no foul play. Won't issue the order."

"Look, I was engaged to that girl," Frank said angrily. "Maybe not officially, exactly, but I was. Let *me* give permission for an autopsy."

"That wouldn't satisfy a judge, Frank. I'm sorry. But that reminds me." He picked up a small box from the office desk and handed it to Frank. "I think you ought to have these, legal or not."

The box contained two plain gold earrings and a small star-sapphire pendant on a white-gold chain. There was a brownish smudge on the oval surface of the blue stone. Frank worked consciously to control his shaking hands as he tucked the box in his pocket. "I want to see her, Doc."

The doctor's tired eyes met his straight on. "I don't think you do, Frank, believe me. Not really."

"I've got to."

The doctor walked over to one of the drawers in the wall and drew it out full length. He pulled down the gray plastic cover and turned his back. A long moment later Frank turned away too, his face as gray as the plastic. "Those welts."

"She may have taken a fall in the rocks. We don't know."

"She walked on rocks like a goat."

Doc shrugged. "Just lying dead on the hard ground can leave welts on the skin, Frank."

"All over her body?" Frank turned to the man. "Okay," he said finally. "You're writing your report in there? Will you do me a favor and run off a copy for me? Just—unofficially?"

"Sure, Frank. I know she was somebody special." Doc looked at him closely. "Where are you going now?"

"Home."

"Do you want a sedative? A little Valium?"

"No thanks. I've got a real great sedative at home."

Frank Barrington drove back slowly to Leavenworth in his beat-up old pickup, his mind twisting, for the first time beginning to grasp the horrible enormity of what had happened. *Pneumonia. Maybe took a fall on the rocks. Worked over with a ball bat. Lying dead on the hard ground. And all this in less than forty-eight hours.*

It was all nonsense. There was something else, something else altogether. Something more vicious than any of that.

Frank Barrington walked into the hot little second-floor apartment about two in the afternoon, exhausted and drained. The blow had hit him too hard, too suddenly, too unbelievably to cope with it adequately; he had to back off and give his mind time to adjust. Stop thinking for a while. He went into the kitchen, poured half a glass of whiskey and drank it neat, then poured more over some ice and sat down in the deep chair in the living room. He seldom drank much, ordinarily; he liked to have his head and body working right, but this was something different.

He looked around at the little place, with so much of her about it, as if she were just in the next room. He could hear her banging pots out in the little kitchen alcove, swearing at the secondhand electric stove that wouldn't heat till she turned it up high, lighting candles on the table for romantic glow over a scorched gourmet dinner, handing him the pot if he dared to say a word. Sometimes bold in bed, sometimes like a frightened doe, guarding herself, hesitating, undecided whether to stand fast or bolt. The only woman in his life that he had ever totally, desperately, hopelessly loved, and now gone. *In forty-eight short hours.*

Surrounded by ghosts and bitterness, feeling the whiskey bite, he nodded in the chair, dozed off. When he started awake later it was almost dark and the phone was ringing. It was the Super. "Are you okay, Frank?"

"I'll make it. Thanks."

"Why don't you just bag it tomorrow, get your feet back under you? Larry can finish the mop-up on Rattlesnake. I can always give you a call if something bad breaks loose."

If something bad breaks loose! "I think I'll do that," Frank said. "Thanks again."

"Well, I just wanted to check," the Super said. "Doc was going to bring you a copy of his report on his way out to his ranch, but he's not feeling very good, so he's staying in town. Matter of fact Barney Block, one of the trail crew that went up in the chopper, isn't feeling so hot either. That must have been quite a shock."

Yeah. Quite a shock. Frank muttered something appropriate and hung up the phone. *Quite one hell of a shock.* He sat back in the chair, pushed the stale whiskey and water aside. Then, in the dying light, his eyes fell on Pam's green backpack propped against the wall. Beside it was a rolled-up tent with an aluminum support sticking out.

He threw all the lights on, pulled out the tent and unrolled it. He wrinkled his nose and stepped back—it smelled like a dead rat. Inside it the walls and floor were stained and smeared with stiff, brownish stuff. Holding his head aside, Frank grabbed it all up and dragged it in to the bathtub, began running hot water and turned on the exhaust fan.

Then, carefully, he went through her pack. No clues there, except that practically nothing was used. Extra clothes and extra socks untouched, the little white-gas camp stove still almost full, a bundle of freeze-dried food unopened. Poncho, crampons, rope—all emergency equipment. A dozen other ordinary things.

A little notebook fell out on the floor, together with a pad of Forest Service citations. He picked up the notebook. Her personal log book, sort of a private diary she kept of odd or unusual things she saw or thought of on her patrol trips. She'd never let him read it. Told him once that *her* idea of "odd or unusual" might upset his balance. Now he leafed through it quickly, found last Monday's date, began to skim through the day's entry in her tight, cramped hand. Early start from Icicle River, hot morning, three dead ground squirrels . . .

A chill went up his back and he took the notebook over to a desk, sat down where the light was good, began reading it closely, word for word. Three dead ground squirrels on the trail, one below Nada, one right at the lake, one on the approach to the Snow Lakes. Something weird about a dirty barefoot kid going up the trail; she'd tried to stop him and he vanished. Thought maybe she dreamed him. *Dreamed him?* Trail work at Upper Snow all day, headache and cough by evening. Nasty crowd across the lake with three camping violations, man armed with a .38 pistol. They started squaring away when she threatened citations, but with ugly grace. But she thought maybe she gave the big guy the flu, at least, with all of her coughing. . . .

Three dead ground squirrels.

The next day was a terrible scrawl, he could barely make it out at all. Written at Lancelot—that was where the Super said they'd found her. Sick all day, chills and fever, coughing, violent headache. Four hours to make it up to Vivian, another two to Lancelot—Christ, she *must* have been sick. The rest of the afternoon making camp. Handwriting even more scribbly. And then, before it all degenerated into delirium, there was something written to *him,* as surely as if she had been writing him the letter she had never written, and he read the words, and all the held-back grief finally caught up with him, and tears were pouring down his cheeks, and he buried his face in his hands and sobbed.

After a while it eased up, and he pushed himself back away from the desk and stared stupidly around him. The answer had come while he was weeping. He knew now what had killed Pam Tate.

The job now was to prove it, and then figure out what to do about it. He went back to her pack again, dug out the little personal bag, found her medicine bottle. He knew what she carried there. Some ampicillin gone, maybe three or four doses, and a few aspirin. He picked up the citation book, found the smudged carbon of a ticket she had written, somebody Comstock from Canon City, Colorado. He dialed for long-distance information, got a number to match the name, direct-dialed it. The distant phone rang and rang, but nobody answered.

He turned the lights out, sat back in the chair, rubbing his forehead in the darkness for a long while. The question was: what to do now? Call the Super and tell him what he was thinking? Sure, and get treated like you were some kind of nut. A dangerous nut—you don't wave *that* flag around unless you have solid, inarguable medical proof, and all he had to go on was a gut-deep hunch. *And that's not good enough, man. You've got to build a case. All you'll have is panic and bad trouble if you don't. You need proof. Support of some kind, real support. . .*

Support. He thought about that for a long while. There was something poking up from the bottom of his mind, something down in Oregon months and months ago—what was it? He knew Shel Siegler down in Deschutes National Forest; Shel had been his boss for a while up here when he had first joined the Forest Service, working trails, after the medical-school thing had fallen apart. A great joker, Shel, but very sharp. Suddenly something jelled in Frank's mind, the right question to be asking, and he sat up straight. He checked a number in Bend, Oregon, and dialed the phone. Moments later he heard Shel Siegler's nasal Brooklyn voice on the line. "Frank, you old son of a bitch! Long time no hear. How they hangin'?"

"Pretty low, right now," Frank said.

"Oh, yeah? Well, you don't want to let 'em drag in the dust. The Super handin' you a heap of shit or something?"

"No, no, it's personal. But Shel, I've got a funny question to ask you."

"Yeah, that's all I get these days, is funny questions. You'd think I was Henny Youngman or somethin'. So what's your funny question?"

Frank braced himself. "I wonder if you guys down there have taken a dead rodent count in Deschutes lately."

There was a long, long silence. When Shel finally spoke there was no trace of humor in his voice. "Odd that you should ask," he said. "Why?"

"I need to know, Shel."

"Okay, Frank, this is off the record, you got that? Okay. We've been doing dead rodent counts every week for the last six months. The counts have been high, and getting higher every week. Frankly, some of us are scared, and we don't quite know what to do about it."

"Have you had any actual plague?"

"Three cases, down in Sisters, about six months ago. First cases in Oregon in years. All three of them died before we had time to get a diagnosis."

"What kind of plague?"

"Pneumonic. All we could do was send sputum samples and a couple of dead squirrels—talk about a nightmare, baggin' *them* up—down to Atlanta, Centers for Disease Control. They pinned the diagnosis, very much post-mortem. I mean, those people went like a brush fire. So CDC sent a guy named Quintana up here, Mexican chap, and he looked around a bit and said, 'Very interesting, don't pat any ground squirrels,' and caught a plane back to Atlanta. Of course, like he said, he didn't have anything to work with, the cases were all six feet under long before he got here, and we didn't have any tissue samples for him. Our medical people wrote it off as some weird kind of pneumonia at first and didn't even take cultures, since the people were dead, and no new cases were turning up, and Quintana was a busy man, so you couldn't blame him going back to Atlanta. Nice guy, in fact, but he was just in and out. Suggested we start doing dead rodent counts, so we did." Siegler paused. "Now, why all the questions? You got some cases up there?"

"Just one," Frank said. "So far."

"What does the Super have to say?"

"He doesn't even know. I'm not so damned sure *I* know, not sure enough to get the whole state of Washington stirred up. What I need is some hard data about what's going on in the woods."

"Well, shit, man," Shel Siegler said. "Don't just talk to me. Get hold of—what's his name?—Kessler in the Humboldt in northern Nevada and Tad Okito down in the Big Sur. Then there's Murph Miller over in the Salmon in Idaho, and Don Whitney up in the Kootenai. Get on the horn and *find out* what's going on in the woods. It may be pretty raw data, but if we've got dead rodents down here and you've got a funny case up there, even just one, somebody better find out what's happening. Keep me posted, and if you need any help, any way at all, give me a buzz, okay? And Frank . . ." The man paused. "Did you have any contact with that case up there?"

Frank sighed. "You might say so."

"Then take some medicine. Don't wait to get hit in the head."

Frank set the phone down and found that his hand was shaking. Dead rodents in Deschutes, lots of them, and three cases of plague. Nobody had done a rodent count up here since that rabbit hunter from Ellensburg died eight years ago. Everybody had thought it was tularemia and only confirmed bubonic plague on autopsy later. They'd counted dead rodents like mad then, for a while, and found nothing. All of the Forest Service had plague shots and ate a lot of some antibiotic that was supposed to stop it, and the press—he flinched. Talk about whipping a dead horse. From the press reports, you'd have thought the Forest Service deliberately *planted* that case of plague just to spite the tourist industry.

The fact was that isolated cases of plague had been turning up in the West for years, and more in the last decade or so—a dozen or more cases a year scattered here and there, mostly in the Southwest. The disease was kept alive by flea-ridden wild rodents—squirrels, chipmunks, ground squirrels, marmots, even prairie dogs and gophers. A tiny percentage of those creatures were always infected, dying, passing the infected fleas on to other rodents, ever since the plague had turned up in San Francisco in 1900, transported from Hong Kong by way of Hawaii. *Endemic* was the word they used for it, a quiet ground fire of infection smoldering in the wilderness, never moving very fast or very far, just waiting. And the only humans ever infected were those rare, unfortunate individuals unlucky enough to happen to be bitten by an infected flea. . . .

And Pam? Was that what she had been? One of those twenty million-to-one victims of sheer, blind bad luck? His Pam? Frank stared into the darkness, refusing to accept it. There had to be something more. *So fast, so incredibly fast. To cut down a superbly healthy girl in less than forty-eight hours? Too terribly fast to believe. No infection known to man moves that fast. What ghastly kind of plague could do that?*

He got on the phone again, working on the names Shel Siegler had suggested, adding some others that he could think of. Every call he made was met with caution, great hesitation—why did he want to know? Cautious himself now, he evolved a cover story: no cause for alarm, but he'd run into some high dead rodent counts up here in the Wenatchee. He just wondered if maybe others had too. It was flimsy, but it had to do. Very guarded responses from half a dozen. But from those who answered at all, a sort of consensus: there were dead rodents around, more than normal. At one place in California and another in Colorado, quite a few more.

Frank walked into the bathroom and found the old shoe box of pill bottles he kept on a linen shelf. *What was that stuff they handed out to us when that rabbit hunter died? Chloro something. Great big bottle. Chloramphenicol.* He still had half a bottle full of the white capsules with the gray-blue bands around them. The typing on the yellowed label said *Take two four times a day,* with a double dose to start with. Probably way outdated, he thought, but maybe better than nothing. He looked at the tent in the bathtub and took four capsules with a glass of water.

He found a piece of cold chicken in the refrigerator and ate it with some milk. Then, back at the desk, he tried the Colorado number again. There was still no answer. He sat in the darkened room staring at the wall for a long, long time, his mind racing. *Twenty people or more in the camping party—where are they now? In what mortal danger?* He felt as if his mind would explode with the thing he was considering. Moment by moment the pressure became more unbearable.

Finally he stirred. He knew he could not sit there a moment longer—he had to *move, do* something. He couldn't bear the thought of facing the Super or Doc Edmonds again just now. They knew what had happened, they could put things together with just a nudge from him. *But none of those Colorado people know. . . .*

His decision finally made, he dialed a Seattle phone number. Then he took a pad and pencil out and wrote a brief note to the Super. I THINK PAM TATE DIED OF PLAGUE. CHECK WITH DOC EDMONDS ABOUT THOSE CULTURES. DEAD RODENT COUNTS HIGH THROUGHOUT WEST. PAM WAS SICK WHEN SHE CAME IN CONTACT WITH THOSE COLORADO CAMPERS. AM FLYING DOWN TO CHECK THEM OUT. WILL PHONE IN TWO OR THREE DAYS.

He sealed the note in an envelope with the Super's name, locked the house and fired up his old pickup. It was 2:00 A.M. He stopped by the Forest Service office and stuck the envelope in the mail slot. Then he turned the car north toward Stevens Pass and the road to Sea-Tac airport.

PART II

BRUSH FIRES

9

It was 2:00 A.M. when Dr. Ed O'Hara jolted awake and groped for the ringing telephone. He recognized the young, anxious voice instantly. "Ed? I've got a guy down here in the emergency room with something funny going on with his chest. I'd sure like you to come take a look at him."

"What kind of 'something funny'?" Ed growled.

"Well, it looks like pneumonia."

"That's funny?"

"No, but I think he's got heart failure too."

Ed sighed. "A lot of old geezers get heart failure with their pneumonia," he said.

"Yeah, but this guy's only seventeen. Can you come take a look?"

The older doctor got dressed and started driving down toward the Rampart Valley Community Hospital. *Damnation,* he thought as he stopped at the town's only stoplight, invariably red. *I knew I should never have left that kid alone in the ER until I'd seen him in action a little bit more.* Some of these Family Practice residents were dynamite in a crisis, he reflected, and some of them just fell apart. Pete Whitehead was showing signs of being the falling-apart kind.

Ed pulled into the ambulance entrance of the hospital, a handsome modern structure, fifty patient beds, including an eight-bed maternity ward and birthing rooms in an adjacent building, a fully equipped emergency room, intensive-care facilities and a good basic lab with twenty-four-hour coverage. The building was about the only handsome thing there was in Rampart Valley, Colorado, he reflected, what with the lead mines, the zinc mines, the uranium mines, and every hill in sight scarred and ravaged by years of mining operations. It had taken Ed O'Hara years of prodding to get the other doctors and the people of the town galvanized into building this hospital, and it was a pearl of its kind, saving the local people hundreds of eighty-mile round trips down to Colorado Springs for medical care each year. To Ed O'Hara it was the most beautiful structure in the world.

Pete Whitehead met him at the emergency-room door, looking very young and very nervous. Quite the picture of the proper young doctor, Ed thought, with his crisp white knee-length clinical coat and the stethoscope tucked into a side pocket on that hot summer night, but the illusion faded as he kept tugging uncertainly at his wispy mustache and looking back over his shoulder. As Ed walked in, wearing his "Here today, Gone to Maui" T-shirt and a pair of shorts and sandals, he heard somebody coughing up a storm in one of the draped cubicles to the rear of the ER. "Okay," he said to the young doctor. "Now what the hell's going on that you've got to call me out at two in the morning?"

"Well, this kid came in just before dinnertime this evening, and I didn't know whether to believe his story or not." Dr. Whitehead tugged at his mustache. "He was just a drop-in, said he was driving down from the airport in Denver to Canon City and couldn't go any farther because he was coughing so much and his head ached so bad. Said he could hardly see to drive. Seems like he'd been up north somewhere with a big crowd on a camping trip this past week, and then all of a sudden everybody started getting sick. Three of them died—"

"Died!" Suddenly Ed O'Hara blinked awake.

"That's what he said."

"Died of what?"

"I'm not just sure. Pneumonia, it sounded like. They'd begun packing down the mountain when they started getting sick, and they tried to get the three worst ones to some hospital in Seattle, but all three were dead on arrival. At least I *think* that's what he said, the story was getting pretty garbled. I gather that he was getting sick too, and somehow lost contact with the rest of the party and just took a cab to the airport and flew back to Denver on the ticket he had in his pocket. Stopped here because he couldn't go any farther."

"So what did you do?"

The young doctor took a deep breath. "Well, I examined him and took a chest X ray—he had consolidation in both lungs, looked like double lobar pneumonia, but he wasn't cyanotic yet, just coughing like mad, so I took a culture and smear of his sputum and ran a fast gram's stain on the smear, but the bug sure wasn't pneumococcus or anything else gram-positive. All I could see was gram-negative rods. Of course, I plated out the culture and put it in the incubator, but he was getting worse in a hurry, coughing more than ever, getting up some blood, and I didn't think we had time to wait around for a culture, so I started him on gentamycin and clindocin."

Ed nodded. "On the premise that it was some kind of atypical *E. coli,* I suppose."

"Right. I hoped the antibiotic might hit it, but it hasn't done anything yet that I can see. And then about an hour ago he started bringing up lots of blood and getting very short of breath and cyanotic, so I had Miss Towne and a couple of the LPNs help me get him on the respirator back there—his temp had gone up from 101 to 105 in three hours—and that was when I found out he had a pulse rate of 240 and damned little blood pressure at all, and I decided I'd better call you."

"Good thinking," Ed said sourly. "Well, let's take a look at him."

They took a look. The youth was coughing weakly in the respirator; otherwise he was barely responding at all. When Ed stopped the machine and bent to listen to his chest, the patient burst into an explosive paroxysm of coughing, spraying Ed's face and T-shirt with blood and splattering Peter Whitehead's white lab coat with red-streaked sputum. Ed wrinkled his nose. "God, what a stench. You don't suppose he's got a lung abscess, do you? Ho—wait a minute."

The doctor had been stripping down the youth's gown when he saw the purple hemorrhagic welts on the arms and chest. He felt under the armpits. "Did you feel these lumps?"

"Uh, lumps?"

"Yeah, under his arms. Groin, too. Did he have these welts when you first saw him?"

"Uh, not like that."

Ed O'Hara's face was gray when he came out of the cubicle. "Let me see those slides you made."

The young doctor tagged along behind as Ed headed for the little emergency-room lab. "I'm afraid they aren't the greatest slides, Ed. They just didn't seem to take the stain worth a darn . . ."

"Don't worry, just show me the slides." Ed adjusted the microscope and stared down through the oil-immersion lens, a muddy-looking field filled with pus cells and red cells and debris, rod-shaped bacteria all over the place, but barely pink and barely visible, certainly not the sharp red-staining appearance of *E. coli* organisms.

"I hope I didn't do something wrong," Whitehead said nervously, tugging his mustache.

Ed looked up. "Son, you did everything you knew how to do and did it just exactly right. Now I need to know if you did one other thing. Did you save the original sputum specimen?"

"Yes. It's in the incubator."

"Great. Have we got any Wilson's stain around here?"

"Wilson's stain? There's Wright's and Giemsa . . ."

"Giemsa might do, but Wilson's would be better." Ed rooted around on a shelf. "Yeah, Wilson's. You heat-fixed that first slide?"

"Yes."

"Then make another just like it and I'll stain it."

Moments later he was staring down at a newly stained slide, filled with bacteria, far more distinct and sharply defined. "Take a good look."

Peter looked and looked. "They're rods, all right, but they've got a little spot of chromatin in each end. They sort of look like closed safety pins . . ."

"Right," Ed said. "They're the murderer."

"What do you mean?"

"I mean we've got a dead man back there on that cot. He was probably beyond help before he even walked in here. He's got a couple of hours left, no more. And we're liable to be dead men, too, if we don't move fast." Ed looked at the bloody smear on his T-shirt and the brown splattering on Pete's white coat and swallowed hard. "First of all, get those nurses down here, the ones who helped you with the respirator. Get them *off the hospital floor* and get a list of every patient they've been near since they were down here—or anyone else they've contacted. Tell Miss Towne to open up the pharmacy and bring down all the streptomycin and chloramphenicol we've got, and I hope to Christ we've got quite a lot. Meanwhile, lock the doors to this place and don't let *anybody* in until we can get some help—God! You, me, the whole emergency room, the respirator, those nurses, the patients, all contaminated. We're going to have to close this place down. A whole fine modern hospital turned into a pesthole in eight hours flat by that little bug that looks like a safety pin . . ."

"What is it?"

"*Yersinia pestis.* The kid's got plague pneumonia, and he's blowing it around with every breath he takes. *Now get going,* fast, and then come back. I'll have some other things for you to do when you get that all taken care of."

"But what are *you* going to do?"

"First I'm going to make a couple of calls, to the State Department of Public Health and then to the Centers for Disease Control in Atlanta to find out what you do when you've got a live case of plague pneumonia that's contaminated a whole community hospital." Ed took a deep breath. "Then I'm going to start feeding streptomycin to everybody in sight—if we have enough on hand—and then I think I'm going to pray for a while. We're liable to need all the help we can get, before long."

10

Carmen Dillman had martinis already made when Jack came down from his studio around five, paint still on his fingertips. "Did you get that dust jacket finished?" she said.

"Finally."

"Do you like it?"

Jack made a face. "Alonzo will like it, and that's all I care about. It's part of a series layout, so it's nice exposure." Jack took half a martini down at a gulp. "I'll take it with me down to the city tomorrow and see what else he has stacked up for me."

"And lunch with Jocelyn, I suppose," Carmen said.

"Sure, why not? She hands me a lot of artwork to do. And I have to see that aerospace client of hers, too. That sounds like a nice fee—all kinds of fancy color work for their annual report."

Carmen nodded glumly, staring at her cocktail in silence. Jack watched her closely for a moment. "So what's the problem?" he said finally. "You know I go down there on Tuesdays. Why so gloomy about it?"

"Jack, I saw a rat in the backyard this morning."

"Oh yeah? You're crazy. We haven't had a rat here in Brookdale since the town council passed those sanitation ordinances ten years ago—and started enforcing them. You must have seen a squirrel."

"It was a rat," Carmen insisted. "I saw it come out of the woodshed and cross the backyard toward the house. It was a foot long, and black, with a pointy nose and a long naked tail. I grabbed a broom and ran outside. By then it was running along the foundation of the house, and then it just disappeared. I think it went in the basement."

"And where was Dummy all this time?"

"The cat? Asleep on the sofa. Where else?"

Jack poured himself more martini and stared soberly at his wife. She could have been right, of course. The rats used to come up from the river, years ago, when the restaurants in town were still leaving big cans of garbage open in the back alleys. He could remember seeing them dart across the road in his headlights now and then. But then people began to complain, and the County Health Department climbed all over the town council, and there was a big extermination program and the lids went onto the garbage cans and the disposal trucks started coming daily instead of once a week, and pretty soon the rats all disappeared . . .

No, he thought, *it was a squirrel she saw, or maybe a woodchuck, they're all over the place these days. But just the same . . .* "Tell you what," he said. "Why don't you get Dummy off her ass and put her down in the basement for the night? If we've got a rat down there, she'll get it. And listen, for God's sake: don't go chasing rats with a broom anymore, okay? They can be vicious when you corner them."

11

"Who was that on the phone?" Amy Slencik said as she came into the cabin on Grizzly Creek with an armful of beets from the garden.

"That was my job foreman," Harry said sourly. "He says Ted Smith has pulled his crew off the underground wiring job."

"He's *what?*"

"Pulled out. Disappeared in the night. His boys came in and hauled off their backhoes and trucks about midnight. No sign of them in town today. Said they were losin' money, so I could just go suck rocks."

"But Harry, Ted *bid* that trenching job! He signed a contract with you."

"So what's a contract? He's *gone.* Am I supposed to chase him to California? I can't even hold up his last week's payroll—he's got it already."

"Well, you can sue the bastard," Amy said.

"I could if I was rich—but I haven't got time or money to sue him. What I've got to do is get those trenches dug, somehow. You can't lay underground without trenches. Goddamned bastard." Harry walked over to the cabin window. "Well, at least I got your irrigation pump going again."

"I know. And just in time. What was wrong?"

"Dead pack rat in the intake pipe. Plugged it up tight. Don't ask me how he got in there, the foot valve was just fine, but there he was, inside."

"Well, I'm glad it wasn't the whole pump," Amy said.

"That's for sure." Harry nodded. "Pack rats I can live with. People like Ted Smith are something else." He stared down the creek toward the place where old Doc Chamberlain's cabin was located, a hundred yards downstream in the cottonwoods. "I keep thinking we should just dump the construction company and retire out here full time. Show those bastards that somebody else can walk off a job too. Doc was talking about the same thing last summer, just taking up full-time residence here on the creek and let things in town go hang. Maybe we ought to talk to him again one of these days and see what he thinks right now. Maybe go down and buy him a drink tonight."

12

The house Frank Barrington was looking for was down a long canyon road outside the town of Canon City, Colorado, at the very end of a string of cheap builders' houses as alike as ugly ducklings in a row. Frank eased the little rented Ford down the steep road, watching the house numbers closely. Near the very end of the road a little yellow house had a yard sign that said COMSTOCK on a plastic board pressed to make it look like wood.

Frank turned into the driveway and snapped off the motor. The place looked deserted—no car in the drive, garage open and empty, drapes across the front windows. *Well, that figures,* Frank thought glumly. He had gotten a 7:00 A.M. flight from Sea-Tac to Denver, then boarded a local puddle jumper south to Colorado Springs, arriving around 2:00 P.M. Mountain Time. Four times en route he had tried the Comstock number, twice in Seattle, twice in Denver, with no response. By the time he'd rented the car and started south to Canon City to find the place itself, he was pretty sure it was going to be a big waste of time, but he had to try. It was the one connection with Pam that he could pin down: a name and address on a Forest Service citation.

He got out of the car, walked up on the porch and pushed the doorbell, heard the dingdong noise inside. He pushed it twice more, waiting, then banged on the door with his fist. Nothing. Finally he walked around the house, looked into a kitchen window at the back. Nothing alive in there. An open box of cake mix sitting on the counter. A mixing bowl with a beater, tipped back, the blades covered with something thick and white. Some dirty dishes in the sink, and a microwave oven, still turned on . . . *somebody left in a hurry . . .*

Starting back for the car, Frank saw a white-haired man standing on the neighboring porch, staring at him. "You looking for something, buddy?"

"I'm looking for Comstock," Frank said. "Robert Comstock."

"You ain't going to find him," the man said. "He ain't here."

"So I see. Do you know where he went?"

"Couldn't rightly tell you, buddy." The man looked at him closely. "You didn't hear about that? He's dead."

"Dead of what?"

"Pneumonia, so they say. Got sick up there in Seattle and just turned up his toes. Same with two or three of the others."

Frank walked over to the man, not sure he'd heard right. "You say Comstock *died* in Seattle? *This* Robert Comstock?"

"It was on the TV just this morning."

"Look, this is very important," Frank said. "He had about twenty people with him up there. They were camping, right? Do you know if any of the others have come back?"

"Well, sure, I think Art Toomey's kid, Pete, got back, and—say, who the hell are you, anyway?"

"Forest Service." Frank held out his government ID with his picture on it. "I'm checking out that camping party."

"You aren't planning to make trouble, are you?"

"Well, no, I'm trying to keep people *out* of trouble, and I need to know what happened up there."

"Well, you could check with Pete Toomey, they live up on Avondale Street, you can get the number out of the phone book. Then there were Ted and Vi Thompson and a couple of people from Colorado Springs . . ." The man went on to name half a dozen others, with their addresses or general locations.

Frank thanked him and got back into the car. Exhausted as he was, he felt an urgency to get going down the list that afternoon. It was no easy job. Canon City, thirty-five miles south of Colorado Springs, boasted only about 12,000 people, but it was a rural sprawl of a town, spread for miles across a flat basin surrounded by rough sandstone hogbacks and outcroppings to the north and south and the rising Rockies to the west. Frank checked a local map in a gas station, then drove a couple of miles west of town and turned right up Skyline Drive for a high view back at the town for general orientation. Then, back in town, he started searching out the streets and houses. The rental car was a lemon, a clutch that slipped on grades and brakes that grabbed so badly he nearly flew through the windshield whenever he touched them. Nor were the people he was looking for, when he began finding them, much more cooperative. Mostly they looked vaguely frightened, closed up like clams or slammed their doors in his face the moment he mentioned Comstock or the camping party.

Pete Toomey, the first one that he actually located, was sick in bed with a "bad cold," his mother said, and she wouldn't let Frank see him; the doctor told her, she said, to take him to the emergency room at the local hospital if he got any worse, and in any event, he wasn't in condition to talk to *anybody* right then. Ted and Vi Thompson, in a little cottage on the far side of town, cut him off in midsentence and slammed the door hard; when he persisted at the doorbell, Ted returned with a double-barreled twenty-gauge and told Frank, past a privacy chain, exactly how many seconds he had to pack into his car and get out of there. Two other tries were equally unproductive—one not home, with no response to repeated telephone calls, the other a house he couldn't find at all until he discovered that the town had two streets with the same name on opposite sides of the valley and he had wasted an hour searching up and down the wrong one.

By then it was eight o'clock in the evening, and Frank was beginning to see things at the side of the road that weren't there. *No point going on without rest,* he thought, *got to have a clear mind, at least, just in case one of these people decides to break down and talk for a change.* He found a room in town at the Sky Valley Motel, walked down the main street to a steak house for food and then returned to the motel and fell asleep on the bed with his clothes still on.

It was not until three the next afternoon that Frank finally struck pay dirt. Jerry Courtenay was just getting home from work as Frank drove up to the little house tucked away in the hills above the town. Jerry was a small, bright-eyed, wiry man driving a plumber's van. He looked at Frank's Forest Service ID, and then at Frank, and nodded briefly. Yes, he was one of the group that just got back from the Enchantments. Yes, it was the group Comstock had organized, and no, he wouldn't mind talking to Frank about what had happened up there if he thought it would do any good. "Goddamned awful about Bob and those others," he muttered. "I don't know what hit 'em, but something sure did." He led Frank into the house, introduced his wife and a small son. "Beer?" Frank nodded, and the man tossed him one. "Just let me change my clothes," he said.

A few minutes later Jerry sank down in a living-room chair with his own beer. "So what do you want to know, exactly?"

"Everything that happened up there," Frank said.

"If I knew what happened I'd sure tell you, but I don't," Courtenay said. "All I really know is that one minute everything was going great up there, beautiful country, the whole crowd of us were having a ball, and then the next minute it seemed like everything turned to shit."

"There were twenty of you?"

"Twenty-one in all. Bob Comstock had his group all lined up, and then he found out we were thinking of going up a week later, and we knew some of his crowd pretty well, so we decided to go up together. We all took the same flight to Seattle, and then got the bus over the mountains to Leavenworth and started up the trail next morning. We drifted in to Upper Snow Lake about five in the afternoon and decided to call it a day."

"You see anybody odd along the way?"

"Well, there was this lady cop from the Forest Service came into our camp about six-thirty and climbed all over us. Bunch of laws we'd never heard of before . . ."

"It's a Wilderness Area. You didn't see the rules posted down at the trailhead?"

"Well, no. I mean, we'd had a few beers in the morning before we started out, and the kids were all over the place, and we didn't hardly see anything. Anyway, this girl came over and made us put out our fire and break up our camp and all that stuff. Seems like they coulda put up some bigger signs or something. And hell, the fire was right out on the rocks, it wasn't gonna start anything burning."

Frank nodded patiently. Suddenly, with an agonizing pang, he could see Pam walking over there in her little green hat and taking on this crowd of twenty-one people without a second thought, looking up at them and saying, "Look, folks, these are what the rules are and this is how it's going to be done," and then jolly well seeing to it that it was. "Did you notice anything peculiar about the girl?" Frank said.

"Well, she was just a tiny little thing, kinda risky to be wandering around up there all by herself, I thought, but she wasn't takin' any crap, she read the riot act and that was that. We started putting the fire out and she headed back toward her camp. Had a bad cold, though, she did. Got to coughing there by the fire and couldn't hardly stop. Matter of fact, I remember hearing her coughing all night long, clear across the lake."

"You didn't see her in the morning?"

"No, she was gone before we even got up." Courtenay produced two more beers. "We broke our camp around noon and started around the lake and up that steep path toward Lake Vivian. Lousy trail, straight up, you'd of thought we was mountain goats, and it must have been a hundred in the shade by then. I thought I was gonna die with that backpack on, before we got to the top."

"You didn't see any other people that looked—odd?"

"Hell, yes, there was plenty of them." Jerry shook his head. "Let me tell you, you got some weird hikers in that part of the country. People came charging up that trail at a dead run, like their lives depended on getting up there in thirty minutes flat. I swear to God, white-haired old ladies were catching up to us and passing us by, going uphill. I don't know what they were trying to prove. But no, there wasn't anybody you'd call exactly odd." The man was silent a moment, ruminating. "Except for one real strange one that we saw. There was this kid coming up the trail while we were resting by the creek and soaking our feet. Just a young kid, was all, but mean-looking, and he was barefoot—I mean, no boots at all—and that trail was nothing but sharp rocks."

"This was a boy?" Frank asked.

"Right. Maybe eight or nine years old. Scruffy little bastard, too, looked like he hadn't had a bath in a month. He had a long stick with a bandana bag tied to the top. Soon as he saw the creek he flopped down and started drinking like a pig. When he finally got up he gave us all a filthy look and started on up the trail. Didn't say one word, and we never saw him again."

"Well, I guess it takes all kinds," Frank said. "So what did you do then?"

"When we finally got to the top? We found a couple of good campsites in a meadow up above the second lake, that place where the creek comes wandering through before it drops off down the rocks, you know? So we set up our camps, and some of the kids went down to the second lake for a swim—we were plenty heated up, by then."

"You didn't see her up there on top?"

"Not a sign of her. So the kids went swimming and a couple of us started rigging our fly rods—and then all of a sudden everything all fell apart. Bob Comstock and his niece Janie Austin got sick."

"Sick," Frank repeated. "Like how, exactly?"

"It was like they'd come down with a bad cold and a fever," Courtenay said, "only it started up all of a sudden like somebody'd thrown a switch. They both crawled into their tents for a nap, and then Bob started chilling, said he felt like he was burning up. Then next thing they were coughing up a storm, the two of them, and aching so bad they could hardly move. By dinnertime two others were coming down with the same damned thing, and a fifth one wasn't feeling very good." The man shrugged helplessly. "Hell, we didn't know what to do, never got sick on a camping trip before. We gave them some aspirin and they just threw it right up. Couldn't hold any dinner down, either. We figured we'd just let 'em sweat it out for the night and start back down next day if they didn't feel any better—but then about midnight Bob started coughing up blood, said he couldn't hardly breathe, and we could *hear* Janie bubbling in her chest, and the rest of us began to get scared, decided we'd better get them down to some help then and there without waiting for daylight . . ."

Jerry Courtenay got himself another beer. "I guess you'd say we sort of panicked then," he went on. "It seemed like I was kind of in charge, with Bob knocked out of it, and all I could think was we needed a doctor. So I told everybody to forget their gear, just get on their boots and jackets and grab their flashlights—and we started down." He sighed. "Believe me, picking our way down through those rocks in the dark was something else, and the trail down the wall was damn near impossible. Terry Gilman hauled Bob along by draping an arm over his shoulder until Bob's legs give out, and then another of the boys took his other arm and they fairly dragged him. Had to do the same thing with Janie before long, and then two other sick ones started to give out. I was the strongest hiker, so when we finally got down to Snow Lakes I took off ahead at a dead run in order to get to the bottom and get an ambulance up to meet the others at the trailhead. I swear I nearly broke my leg three times, falling over windfalls and roots; there wasn't much moonlight through the trees, and the one or two camps with somebody still up gave me lots of great advice but no help, so I just kept on going. When I finally did get down and found a phone, I tried the Ranger Station first, and finally got somebody, but they were no damned help—"

"How do you mean?"

"Well, no offense meant, but it was kind of strange. I mean, those guys are usually pretty gung ho when somebody's in trouble, you take it for granted they'll help you, but this guy I got on the phone was definitely not gung ho about anything. Said all their vehicles were in service at the moment, and anyway they didn't have any night crew, and I should just call the ambulance and get these people moved to a hospital when they got down. He didn't even want to take my name, as if he might have to do something if he wrote it down."

Frank nodded sourly. "I suppose I can see it," he said. "So you called an ambulance?"

"Finally got one from Wenatchee, packed the five sick ones in as soon as they got down. Terry and Peter Toomey rode along with them, and the rest of us followed in cars."

"To Wenatchee General?"

"No. To Harborview in Seattle. We figured we should be close to Sea-Tac airport, since we figured we'd be shipping those sick ones home just as soon as possible. Well, things don't always work out the way you figure. Bob was dead by the time we reached the hospital—he must have died about the time they hit Interstate 5 north of Seattle. Janie lasted about three hours after arrival and a third one died twelve hours later. The fourth one, the Edstom kid, went into intensive care and started to rally. He may well still be there, for all I know, his dad came up from Boulder to relieve me so I could get the other kids home. In fact, I didn't learn much at all, the docs at Harborview were very close-mouthed about everything, said they'd caught a 'typical pneumonia' or something like that."

"*A*typical pneumonia," Frank murmured.

"Well, whatever it was. They sure didn't want any publicity. I started rounding people up to get them home, and then we couldn't find Terry Gilman, he didn't show at the airport when he was supposed to. Far as I can tell, he just got on a flight for Denver on his own and took off, Continental had his used ticket—but he never got home to Colorado Springs."

"This was the one who had his arm around Comstock all the way down the trail?"

"Right. I suppose he'll show, sooner or later. He's kind of a crazy kid anyway." The man looked up at Frank. "So that's all I know, and I don't understand it. Do you?"

"I'm not sure," Frank said. "It looks like you people got hit with a very vicious infection. You may have gotten it from the patrol girl—I happen to know she was very sick when she came over to your camp that night." Frank looked at the little plumber. "The trouble is, I'm not sure it's all over yet, as far as your crowd is concerned. The boy you call Peter Toomey is sick in bed at home here in Canon City. If you should happen to turn up with a chest cold or a fever, you should get to the best hospital there is here and do it fast. What *I* need is more detail about the others—the names, addresses and phone numbers of every one of them that was up there with you—and it might help if you'd call them all before I reach them and tell them to talk to me. So far all I've gotten is slammed doors. Then if I find out anything, I'll try to let you know."

Frank pulled a pad and pen from his pocket and started writing as Jerry Courtenay began reciting names.

Six hours later, with the long summer twilight finally fading to darkness over the mountains, Frank Barrington returned to his little motel room and unloaded his pockets of a dozen scribbled, crumpled note sheets. Though he hadn't eaten since breakfast, the thought of food turned his stomach. What he did need was a drink, so he pulled a bottle of bourbon out of his suitcase, poured a glassful, cut it with a little cold water and threw himself onto the lumpy bed. As his hand quit shaking and his stomach settled down a little, he sat staring into the gathering darkness of the room, reviewing the results of his fact-finding mission, since he'd left Jerry Courtenay.

He had made just five contacts from Jerry's list so far, and already he was appalled. Four dead for sure, from that one party of twenty-one people. That included the missing Terry Gilman, who had died in the emergency room of the Rampart Valley Community Hospital up north of Colorado Springs—Terry's parents had just gotten word as Frank walked in the door. Three more here in Canon City were actively infected with something. Maybe the one left behind at Harborview in Seattle had made it and maybe he hadn't—there was no one at his address.

And how many more were already sick or getting sick? He didn't know. He wasn't a doctor, either, and there was no way to guess whether the picture of contagion he was piecing together made medical sense or not. One thing was certain: nobody else in Canon City was piecing that picture together, at least not yet—and that was what was *really* scary. . . .

He knew he had to talk to somebody, somebody who could help, somebody who knew something. Even if it made *him* look like a meddling ass, he had to unload what he was thinking to somebody. *And the horrible part was that Pam must have been the spark. Whatever it was that hit her, she must have passed it on at least to Comstock and the girl. Maybe they infected others in their party in turn—if whatever it was moved just ungodly fast—*

And then he thought of something else, and sat bolt upright on the bed, sweating. If Pam had infected Comstock, who else had she infected? What was it the Super had said when Frank called him after going through Pam's diary? Something about Doc Edmonds not feeling well? And the other two who had helped him bring Pam out? With his heart pounding, Frank leaped across the bed to the telephone, got the operator, rang the Super's home number in Leavenworth. . . .

It rang ten times before the Super answered. "Oh, Frank? I was wondering when you'd call. Are you okay? Well, *that's* something, at least." His voice sounded strained and distant. "You're in Canon City, Colorado, you say? Wherever that is. Checking out that camping party." There was a long, long pause. "Did you know that three of them died at Harborview? Big ruckus up here. Fourth one's just hanging on by his fingernails. Nobody's sure what's doing it, it's *weird.* How are those people down there?"

Frank told him, briefly. Then: "How is Doc Edmonds doing?"

"Doc? Oh, he's gone, of course." The Super sounded very strange, almost out of contact. "Dead. Night before last. So is Fred, the guy who flew the chopper in to get Pam, and Barney, who went along to help bring her down. Both dead. The public-health people called in the Centers for Disease Control, but they keep insisting that it isn't plague. They say it couldn't be, it doesn't act like plague. It's moving too fast, with too much person-to-person spread, bypassing the fleas altogether—you know what I mean?"

"Well—sort of," Frank said.

"They think it's some new, unidentified bug, don't know *what* it is, exactly, but they think it's definitely not plague. Plague just doesn't move that fast. . . ."

They talked a little more, but the Super was definitely not with it, he sounded half delirious, drifting in and out of coherence, so Frank promised to call back next morning, and then signed off. He got another drink, trying to puzzle out what the Super had said. *If not plague, then what else?* he thought. *Not that it matters much, it's killing people like plague. And speaking of that, shouldn't I keep taking those little white capsules?* He got up, took two more in the bathroom, then paced the floor.

It was plague, it had to be, and he needed *help,* not just incoherence. On impulse, he picked up the telephone again, got long-distance information and then placed a call to Atlanta.

He got a woman on the line and started to tell her where he was and what he wanted, but she cut him off abruptly and gave him another party. This one, another woman, at least listened; she even asked him to spell his name. "You say you have information on cases of plague in Canon City, Colorado? Are these cases you're treating, Doctor?"

"I'm not a doctor. I'm a forester."

"A forester?" Vague confusion. "I think you'd better talk to our Chief in the Uncommon Diseases section, Mr. Barrington. One moment . . ."

It was a long moment; he almost thought they'd been cut off. Then a deep voice came on the line. "Ted Bettendorf here. Plague, you say? In Canon City? That's just south of Springs, isn't it? Yes, I've got it here. And you say you've been tracing a party of twenty-odd people who've been exposed?" A long pause. Then, very carefully: "That—doesn't really seem very likely, Mr. Barrington. We haven't had but two or three confirmed cases of plague in Colorado in the last five years, and to have twenty people suddenly involved out of the blue with a flea-vector disease doesn't add up—uh, hold it a minute! Did you say that the contacts were made in *Washington State?* Okay, there has certainly been some puzzling illness going on up there, we are still digging it out—but these people are now in Colorado, you say? And that's where you are right now?" Another long pause, longer than the last. Then: "Mr. Barrington, I think I'd very much like to have you talk to our Dr. Quintana. He's had a great deal of field experience with plague."

"Fine. Put him on," Frank said.

"I can't. He's in flight right now to Denver. There's a case he's checking out up north of Colorado Springs, and you could contact him while he's out there. I can reach him and have him call you if you have a number."

"Any hour," Frank said. "I'll be here." He gave the motel room number and hung up. It didn't occur to him right then to wonder what the Chief of the Uncommon Diseases section was doing in his office at two-thirty in the morning, Atlanta time.

He sat down on a chair, staring at the blank TV screen across the room. *First Pam. Then Comstock and his niece. Then Doc Edmonds and the chopper crew. Terry Gilman. Peter Toomey. Two others in Seattle, maybe more, and now Christ alone might know how many more down here. All in four days.*

Something was happening, he reflected. Something fast. Something bad. Something big, far bigger than just Pam. And it had to be some sort of plague, it couldn't be anything else.

As he sat in the gloom, trying to grapple with the reality of what was happening, his eye fell on a Gideon Bible on the bedside stand. Something stirred then, deep in his mind. He remembered reading something in there once, years before, when they'd had that plague scare with the rabbit hunter. What was it? Something about horsemen. There were four of them—yes, of course. Heralds of the end of the world. He'd seen pictures, too; sometimes they were depicted riding wild-eyed, hellish unicorns. The first one was Conquest, riding a white horse. The second was War, on a blood-red horse, the third, Famine, on a black horse. . . .

And the fourth? He racked his memory. Somewhere there in the Revelation of St. John the Divine, the most hideous horseman of them all . . .

He picked up the Bible, searched through the back end of it. Yes. sixth chapter of Revelation, seventh verse:

> *And when he had opened the fourth seal, I heard the voice of the fourth beast say, Come and see. And I looked, and behold a pale horse; and his name that sat on him was Death, and Hell followed with him.*

Death. Pestilence. Plague. Mounting his pale steed, digging in the great spurs, leaping forth at full gallop and sweeping across the land. Two thousand years ago they knew him, and knew what he meant, Frank thought. Long before that, they knew him well. And now, he thought, now, in modern day when it couldn't happen, it was beginning again.

Impossible! But impossible or not, here, today, the Horseman had mounted his pale beast, with hell following after.

13

In the early morning heat of Atlanta in August, Dr. Ted Bettendorf stopped to pick up the folder of Telex reports from Communications on the first floor of the CDC building annex and then, ignoring the elevator, walked up the fire stairs to his second-floor office, leafing through the folder as he went. He was a long, lean, cadaverous man with iron-gray hair and a face like Boris Karloff, a quiet, soft-spoken, unflappable man who always looked amazingly fresh and crisp even on days, like this one, when he had spent the whole night before sweating out an alert. At the front desk he nodded a good morning to Mandy, who kept his office running, and ducked into the small, book-lined inner sanctum he maintained for himself in the back.

The Telexes were from the offices of the Washington State Epidemiologist in the Smith Tower in Seattle, and Ted skimmed them, hoping for the detail he was waiting for, not finding it, and finally went through the reports line by line. He had a thoroughly bad feeling about these incidents in Seattle and now, it was beginning to appear, in Colorado as well, and all interconnected. *Pamela Tate, Wilderness Patrol, Enchantment Lakes Wilderness Area in western Washington.* There was not much mystery about *that* one, Ted reflected, except for the almost unbelievable swiftness with which it hit. It was *Yersinia,* plain and simple, confirmed by the cultures done in Wenatchee, now being repeated in Seattle, and she was an almost classical index case for plague. High in those western mountains the rodents were there, and the fleas were there, and she was there; there was even some mention here of confirmed contact with dead rodents. He didn't know quite how they'd gotten *that* little item but he was very sure they weren't making up fairy tales. It just closed the circle nicely. The girl died of plague, obviously, pneumonic, and the doctor and the chopper crew were contaminated, and *that* made sense. The others, turning up at Harborview in Seattle, didn't, at least not from the data *he* had. He pulled at his lower lip. . . .

With a conscious effort he pushed the Seattle cases aside in his mind and went back to Pamela Tate again, to the little snag in that story, the place where the circle didn't quite close.

It was the timing. It was too fast. Carlos had remarked on that before he took off for Denver—it was all far too fast. It didn't fit the classical picture of plague. *Unless there is something else very unclassical involved . . .*

He sat back, letting his mind wander for a moment. If it didn't fit the classical rules, it did fit, in a way, Ted Bettendorf's own private concept of this ancient and terrible disease. His personal picture, unproven but perfectly reasonable, evolved from his own long years of studying and writing about the *pestis*. Only now the microbiologists and geneticists were coming up with exactly the pieces he needed to fill the holes in his picture, the missing pieces that had hung up the progress of the scholarly work he had been writing, the thick bundles of manuscript piled on the shelves behind him. . . .

Pamela Tate was only one of multimillions that this ugly Thing, this pestilential disease, had slaughtered down through the ages in its murderous fight for survival on Planet Earth. She was not even the first in modern times to be struck down. But just suppose, Ted reflected, that she really *were* the first human being to suffer the effects of some slight change in an ancient pattern of survival, some tiny interior genetic change in the organism, almost undetectable, occurring by blind chance, triggered by the natural radiation in the earth, or some happenstance direct-hit by a cosmic ray, or just by the organism's natural tendency to shift its genetic arrangement spontaneously. Suppose that somehow, for some reason or no reason, three tiny amino acid fragments on a certain spiral of DNA had gotten displaced, maybe traded places with three different amino acid fragments, while three others dropped off altogether, and the change somehow improved the survival qualities of that one organism over its brothers, led to slightly different infective qualities given precisely the right host—and suppose the change was then passed on to successive generations. It could be so simple, and so deadly. A minor step in an evolutionary chain that made one organism and all its progeny subtly and horribly more capable of survival—and murder. The organism wouldn't know or care—it couldn't, for it had no sentience. All it had was an implacable, mindless need to survive. . . .

Ted ran a hand through his thick gray hair and pursed his lips. Sheer speculation, of course, but the notion was sobering—and from his own studies, he was convinced there was supporting evidence from history. One thing was certain: the organism of plague was a tough survivor from way back. Nobody knew when it had first made its appearance on earth—surely long before the beginning of recorded history. Probably it had evolved geological ages ago in the warm, salty seas at the same time that other one-celled creatures first appeared. Maybe many bacteria evolved at the same time—nobody knew for sure. But unlike other free-living, motile protozoan water creatures, unlike the algae and *Euglena* and diatoms and other free-living one-celled plants, the bacteria were never free, complete forms of plant life. They were always cripples. They needed help. They mostly depended on decay for their nourishment. Many became useful symbiotes with other life forms: they released nutrients and fixed nitrogen from dead matter for plants and animals to use. They fermented rock into sand and then soil so that the land plants and animals could survive. They were the garbage men of the planet, busy seeing that nothing was wasted in the great cycle of evolving life.

Many were benign and helpful, but not all. Some attacked and destroyed living things—and these survived along with all the rest, tiny capsules of death, crippled and malignant half-cells. They too grew and evolved, Ted thought, and now millions of years later they were still picking their hosts, their favorite victims, destroying life in order to survive, and creating jobs for people like him. . . .

From the best accounts he knew, that ugly Thing that had slaughtered Pamela Tate first made its appearance in recorded human history in the ancient city of Athens in 753 B.C. One day in that unhappy year, without warning, people in a great and civilized city began dying. Many people, and many rats. No one then saw any connection. For the people, the dying was horrible: fever, prostration, great purple-black welts appearing under the skin, huge festering painful lumps of swollen flesh appearing in the armpits and neck and groin and finally, after days of agony, a death that must have been a welcome relief. They called it "The Pestilence" or "The Death" in those days, and if The Pestilence was really caused by angry gods, as the people believed, the gods must have been appeased because The Death finally went away. And none too soon, either. Ten thousand people died in that wave of Death, and since the mighty Athens of those days probably had no more than thirty thousand inhabitants, as much as a third of the population was wiped out. Another third suffered the infection and recovered. Including, of course, some of the rats. And the fleas that fed upon the rats.

Whatever the exact numbers—they varied with the source, Ted knew—The Pestilence had vanished as suddenly as it had come, and remained quiescent for centuries. It was next recorded in Rome in A.D. 103. It was Rome at the height of its glory, a city of 1.5 million people, largest of all cities of the ancient world. The Rome of those days was remembered down through history for its excellent supply of pure water, and its fine sewers for the disposal of human waste. But for garbage disposal and other matters of everyday hygiene, Ted reflected, not so much could be said. The common man of Rome in those days lived in filth, along with the rats. Even the kitchens of the nobles were filthy and rat-ridden.

When the disease struck Rome, perhaps the same disease of Athens, perhaps something slightly different, it struck with ferocious violence, devouring five thousand human lives a day. The sheer logistics of disposing of all those corpses in that huge city must have been staggering in itself. And the death toll went on for months, perhaps years, no two accounts agreed. Then, once again, it stopped for a while—but by that time another name had been coined for the murderer. A name that said it all: *The Plague.*

It recurred repeatedly in parts of Italy in succeeding centuries. With the fall of Rome, records became obscure. In the tenth and eleventh centuries Italian coastal cities recognized that the dread death-dealer often arrived by ship. Boats were required to hold offshore for a *quarantine*—a period of forty days—before anybody or anything was allowed to come ashore; as a result, some of those cities escaped The Death.

Despite all this, in the 1300s, The Plague struck hard and fast in Mediterranean regions and began moving inexorably north and west in a long, slow, murderous sweep across Europe and Asia. In those days, in the very depths of the Dark Ages, there were few cities large enough to speak of. Most people lived in villages and hamlets clustered around the manor houses or castles of local lords for protection. Nobody had the slightest concept of personal cleanliness or public hygiene. "Lest one think it a romantic time to have lived," Ted had once told a lecture audience, "bear in mind that everyone had lice and everyone had fleas—rats, dogs, cats and humans. The average life expectancy for a new baby in those days was about thirty years." As The Plague struck these villages, one by one, the widely rumored symptoms began appearing: fever, shock, huge black draining sores in the neck and groin, followed by convulsions and death, or—in some cases—a long, painful convalescence leading to recovery. No patterns of spread were recognized; people accused the physicians of the day of spreading the disease in order to fatten their purses, despite the fact that they were dying faster than the patients they tended. And in that great epidemic, a new twist seemed to appear: some victims, after a few days of illness, suddenly began burning up with fever, coughing fiercely and hemorrhaging from the lung. This so-called "pneumonic" form of The Plague terminated in death within two or three days and killed as many as eighty-five percent of its victims—and, for the first time, direct spread of infection from one person to another was clearly recognized.

Of course The Plague spread panic wherever it struck. People boarded themselves up in their houses to keep it out—and died inside. Bodies of the dead were stacked like cordwood at the crossroads to be burned or just left to fester and decompose. The stench of rotting bodies clung over whole villages. Dwellers in castles and fortresses pulled up their drawbridges to protect themselves from the horror outside, only to be found, sometimes years later, all dead *inside* the walls, mostly from Plague, but many from starvation or thirst because people were too terrified to come out. Certainly in those superstitious days The Death was considered the work of Satan, but the spread of the disease was slow and sporadic. Nobody traveled very far or fast in those days, and the march of The Pestilence was measured in years as first one village was hit, then another. Some were missed altogether by some stroke of fantastic good luck; others were wiped out almost totally. The slow march of Plague across the continent took 150 years or more that time, and when it was all over, it had proved to be the most vicious Pestilence in all human history, leaving some twenty-four million people dead in its wake—one-quarter of the entire population of Europe.

Slow as it was, that great Plague had been more virulent, more deadly, than any that had preceded it. All the accounts and records Ted had ever read confirmed that. But why? Had there been some tiny, seemingly insignificant genetic change then, too? Some rearrangement of atoms on a strand of DNA? No way to tell, of course, but earlier plagues, horrible as they were, had been a laugh compared to what that one had been.

Finally it had seemed to burn itself out, reappearing only sporadically, here and there, over the next two hundred years. Then, abruptly, London was struck in 1665—that crowded, huddled, jam-packed, filthy city of 500,000, built on the banks of the oily Thames with its piers and docks and warehouses and rats and fleas. Plague swept the city then like a giant scythe—sixty-eight thousand dead in a single year. The following year a sort of Providence intervened: the Great London Fire gutted four-fifths of the city, burning out millions of rats and their breeding places at the same time. It was an awful remedy—but never again was there a major outbreak of plague in that city.

Just over two hundred years later, in 1894, Hong Kong was struck with epidemic Plague. Things had changed during those two hundred years, Ted reflected. The concept of scientific observation had emerged, and now it was known that rats and Plague were inextricably interrelated. Get rid of the rats and The Plague slowed and stopped. Bacteria had been discovered, and were known to cause infectious diseases of all kinds. Though the organism that caused Plague had not yet been isolated or observed, it was assumed to exist, and was given a name: *Pasteurella pestis* after the great French pioneer of microbiology, Louis Pasteur. Then in 1894 two different men—a Japanese named Shibasaburo Kitazato, and a Swiss, Alexandre Émile Yersin, separately isolated a slender, poorly staining rodlike bacillus from blood and tissue of Plague victims—the organism causing The Plague. Ultimately its name was changed to *Yersinia pestis*.

Identifying the ancient killer did not stop it, however. In the late 1890s it swept from Hong Kong to the cities and opium dens and brothels of the South China Coast—Canton, Foochow, Shanghai—killing fifteen million people. It moved south across tropical Asia—Singapore, Bangkok, Rangoon—and plunged into India, where ten million people died in a single year. And in Bombay, amid festering heaps of dead bodies, another obscure scientist finally closed the link of causation. *Yersinia pestis* was primarily a disease of rats, afflicting the ubiquitous black Norway rat in particular, but other rodents as well. Fleas living on an infected rat drank its infected blood; when the rat died, the fleas abandoned the corpse, found another rat and injected their bacteria-laden vomit into the new victim when they bit. And when rats weren't handy as a new host, those infected fleas found humans instead, and the humans grew feverish and shocky, with huge festering buboes developing in their armpits and neck and groin, and developed massive purple skin hemorrhages as the infection progressed to septicemia, or coughed blood as it reached the lung. And when they died, their infected fleas went on to bite other humans.

Fortunately, there were no airplanes in 1894, Ted Bettendorf thought. If there had been, that vast pandemic of Plague might never have been stopped. Ships were far slower, with far fewer ports of call. Ships from Hong Kong brought The Plague from the Far East to Philadelphia, New York and San Francisco, especially San Francisco. Public health measures stopped it at the docks in each of those places, but plague-bearing rats abandoned ship all the same. Some of those rats, unwelcome in the city, made their way into the hills and forests surrounding San Francisco, and then to the Sierra Nevada, their fleas infecting forest rodents as they went—chipmunks, ground squirrels, marmots. A reservoir of plague-in-waiting built up in those creatures, far from human habitation, a reservoir of "sylvan plague" which slowly, slowly spread north to the Cascades and east to the Rockies, and south through the Sangre de Cristos.

From then on, a few cases of human plague had begun to appear in the western United States each year. Isolated cases, a dozen or so one year, three or four the next. Year by year, Ted Bettendorf's section on Uncommon Diseases at the Centers for Disease Control, a branch of the United States Public Health Service, monitored those cases, kept a watchful eye on them, ever alert to the subsurface danger that existed. A child playing with a sick chipmunk on a California camping trip. A Mexican woman near Nogales living in a house infested with rats. Two boys in New Mexico cutting off the flea-ridden pelt of a dead coyote they found in the hills. The cases were sporadic, individual, almost always related to rats, rodents or fleas. Often diagnosed far too late, and very deadly—three-quarters of those victims died. But slow-moving, never really catching fire. *Over the years,* Ted thought, *we've been lucky. That Horseman, called Death, has been in no hurry.*

He got up, walked to the window and stared out at the flowering Atlanta trees, fresh and green in the morning sun. *Yes, on balance, we've been lucky. But now, something alarmingly new.* A brush fire of cases from the mountains of Washington. Maybe more than one brush fire, in more than one place. Too many cases, too fast and too deadly—and the connection with rats and rodents and fleas seemed terribly tenuous. Was it just the sylvan plague they knew? Or something slightly—and murderously—different? This was the question he had sent Dr. Carlos Quintana west to answer, winging his way from Atlanta to the western mountains for the second time in six months. *The right man for the job, Carlos Quintana—an odd, uneasy, little man, the perfect plague hunter, his mind stirring with an ancient, irra-*

tional cultural awareness of the imminent presence of Death—

A buzzer on his desk sounded. He took the phone, heard Mandy's voice. "Ted, are you operational?"

"Right. Bring 'em on."

"The President caught an item about that Seattle thing on the morning newscast. He wants to talk to you. Can you stand by at ten-oh-three?"

"Sure. Break in on anybody but Carlos."

"And the Secretary wants a briefing too. He'll be on-line in four minutes."

Ted Bettendorf sighed, loosened his necktie and settled down to the phone.

14

"La Muerte," the dark-haired man muttered, twisting in the cramped airplane seat and pushing the maps aside.

The woman beside him blinked awake. "Hm?"

"The Death," Carlos Quintana translated. "The word is feminine in Spanish—isn't that interesting? There are some weird cultural reasons for that, but I won't bore you. Well, she may be female, but she isn't any lady. A lady at least would wear a deceptive fragrance, and this particular sweetheart can't be bothered. She stinks from here to Chihuahua and back."

Monique gave him a level look. "Honey, you're dog tired. Why don't you just lean back and sleep till we get to Denver?"

"Look, I was tired before we started, and I'm going to be a lot more tired before we finish. And how am I supposed to sleep? I keep looking at these maps and the more I look at them, the more this whole business stinks. There's a great big gap in the picture somewhere. We just aren't getting the whole story."

"So what do you think is missing?" Monique said.

The engines rumbled and the plane lurched in some choppy air as it approached the escarpment of the Rockies. Carlos, who hated flying, clutched his seatbelt and hoped he wouldn't be violently ill right in front of this beautiful, talented woman. When the flight settled down again, he looked at her. "You mean you can't see the gap?"

"Not really. We're certainly dealing with plague, that's clear enough from those first cultures we've run in the Atlanta lab. They just confirm what Seattle and Fort Collins have reported. It's plague all right. A lot more plague than there ought to be."

Quintana snorted. "You might say so," he said. "But where are the rats? Where are the fleas? Doesn't that strike you odd? All this data piling in about a sudden, plaguelike illness, but not one word about rats or fleas."

"We'll find the rats and fleas," Monique said firmly. "They'll be there, don't worry. They always are."

"Maybe so," Carlos said uneasily, "but the pattern's all wrong. Look here." He flattened the maps out on their laps. "We've got the index case way up here in the Northwest, the girl died in the wilderness. Not down in a hospital, mind you. Out in the woods somewhere. She's got to be the index case, because everybody who came close to her has also died. We've got eleven cases so far in the Northwest alone, confirmed or suspicious, nine of them dead, and the Shoeleather Boys up there, along with the State Health Department, have pinned every one of them down to her. God knows what the count's going to be by the time we get to Denver. But no rats, and no fleas. Okay, now look here." The dark-haired doctor shuffled maps again. "We've also got this disaster at this little hospital in Rampart Valley, Colorado. That place was apparently contaminated from top to bottom in about three hours. A very sharp doc there pinned it down, thank God, and got everybody in sight taking prophylactic antibiotics, and even at that we already have five dead out of there by last count, according to our people in Fort Collins, and still no rats, no fleas. . . ."

Monique pulled on her lower lip, frowning. "What did that doctor use there? Tetracycline?"

"For the antibiotic? No. Streptomycin and chloramphenicol, together. Full therapeutic doses."

"*Both?* And five people still died? But Carlos, that's weird. Those drugs *stop Yersinia.* Unless he started the drugs so late—"

"He started them within an hour after he identified the bug under the microscope, you can't get much faster than that, and the people still died. So maybe you see what I mean about somehow not having the whole story?"

"I'm beginning to see."

"Well, I'm not quite clear yet just *where* that Rampart Valley case came from, but if a bunch of people have brought some plague down from the Northwest to central Colorado, and it's acting like this, we may just have a mess on our hands. Ted said the state of Colorado is already frantic about a publicity leak. This is the peak of their tourist season and one little news story could kill them." Carlos pushed the maps aside with a sigh. "I just hope Ted has gotten things organized out here by the time we arrive. Who are we supposed to meet in Denver? You have that list?"

Monique unfolded a memo sheet. "First there's Roger Salmon from our CDC base in Fort Collins. He's supposed to meet us at the airport in Denver. He's coordinating things, Ted said, already has a crew of Epidemic Intelligence Service people gathered in from Seattle, San Francisco and Mullin, Idaho—"

"Experienced people, I hope," Carlos said.

"Ted said they may be pretty green, but they've got good shoes. Then there'll also be a man up from Albuquerque, name of Bob Romano."

"Right, I've worked with him. Knows what he's doing in a field investigation." Carlos scratched his head. "There was somebody else Ted mentioned just as we left, a funny one, but he thought it might be important. Something about some other town. Somebody named Barringer . . . Farringer. . . ?"

"Barrington," Monique said. "He's a forester."

"A *what?*"

"He takes care of trees. In the wilderness. He works for the Forest Service."

"So what are we going to learn from him?"

"I don't know," Monique said. "Maybe something about rats and fleas." Carlos glanced at her sharply, and she shrugged. "One thing, though—Ted said he was living with the first girl before she died."

"Ah, so." Carlos nodded. "In that case, I certainly *will* want to see him, and early on, too. I think maybe you'd better stick around for some of these first meetings, my dear. You're going to need the background as much as we are. And then I think you're going to have your work cut out for you when you get to Fort Collins."

"So do I," Monique said soberly. "If these little bugs they've been collecting for me are as nasty as they sound, we're going to need a full-scale hot microbiology lab to play with them. We are, that is, if we want to find out how these *Yersinia* are different from ordinary plague bugs—and how to stop them. . . ."

15

Like ships passing in the night, the Boeing 747 carrying Chet Benoliel south from Denver to Atlanta whispered past the Eastern DC-10 carrying Carlos Quintana north from Atlanta to Denver a little bit before midnight. Neither man had ever met the other. Neither one would have wanted to.

Chet squirmed in his seat in the almost empty first-class cabin, trying somehow to get comfortable. A large-boned, beefy man of thirty-five, he was not built for air travel, and this trip had been a disaster from beginning to end. First that god-awful bush flight by Lear Jet across the north slope into Kotzebue; the ten hours' wait there, in the heat and mosquitoes and the stink of rotting fish, for the Wienie-Bird flight down to Anchorage and on to Seattle; and the fast briefing meeting with Carey at Sea-Tac before he ran to catch the Continental flight to Denver, rush-rush all the way. And then, to top it off, that goddamned kid they'd planted right beside him in the first class Denver flight, because they'd overbooked the coach section and the kid said he was sick—acted it, too, for God's sake, coughing in his face all the way to Denver and gasping like a fish out of water—he should sue that goddamned airline for dumping that kind of company in his lap, practically. Then fourteen hours' bloody delay in Denver getting aboard this crate—*fourteen hours*—just because some crazies had called the airport and said a bomb was on board, and the airline didn't have another seat unbooked for the next two days. He'd almost called for a company plane, but decided he'd better not. There wasn't any emergency, after all; the meeting in Savannah wasn't scheduled until day after tomorrow and the board was very picky about any exotic spending right now.

Chet coughed, trying to clear a frog from his throat that just wouldn't go away. All the sitting in airports and airplanes had made his muscles ache—his neck, his back, his legs. He'd put down quite a few double Scotches during the layover in Denver—nothing else to do, for God's sake—and his head was throbbing on account of it. Well, maybe a hair of the dog—he flagged the tall black stewardess for a double Scotch and sipped away at it, staring out the window at the darkness.

At least, he reflected, the meeting in Savannah was going to be worth every minute of the nasty trip. Ever since he'd first started with Sundown Explorations, ten years ago, he'd been waiting for a chance to really gig those Big Oil Bastards and now at last the time had come. Sundown had always been a little outfit. A very sharp outfit, what Chet liked to think of as Quality—but being small, they'd always had to pick up the crumbs after the Big Bastards had finished stuffing themselves. Take what the Big Boys couldn't be bothered with, lick their plates after them and pretend to like it. Well, no more—all that was going to change. Because by great good fortune and some clever detective work, Sundown now had the goods on the Big Bastards involved in that Upper Yukon Shelf ripoff, clear proof of the biggest exploration fraud that had ever been pulled in an industry where fraud was a way of life. A word from Sundown could blow the lid off the whole stinking mess and cost those Big Bastards multibillions in taxes, multibillions in penalties, multibillions in consumer reimbursements.

Of course, Sundown had no intention of blowing the whistle on anybody. They had the goods locked away in seventeen different strongboxes. They also had that whole south Wyoming field locked up tight, proven solid-gold, to provide for cash flow and security. All they had to do was go to a meeting in Savannah and tell those Big Oil Bastards just how things were going to be cut up. Give them plenty of time to think it over—maybe forty-eight hours. All the time they'd need to figure out how badly they wanted to make Sundown rich.

"You don't have to sell them anything, or ask for anything, or substantiate anything," Carey had told him at their hasty meeting in the VIP lounge at Sea-Tac airport a few hours before. "You're just the bright-eyed boy bringing them the information we promised; other than that, you don't know nothin'. Your company just wants to make sure they have this information before they make any important policy decisions on the Yukon Shelf, that's all. And if a single one of them looks cross-eyed at you, you get up and walk out. If anybody says one word you don't like, you say 'Thank you, gentlemen,' and leave, right then—and you don't go back. We've got them by the balls this time, Chet. All you've got to do in Savannah is acquaint them with that fact. We'll do the twisting from this end."

Chet coughed suddenly and explosively, choking on his drink and knocking it onto the floor. When the black stewardess stooped down to clean it up, he leaned very close, pretending to help, suddenly aware of her light fragrance. *Might just make a play for this little honey,* he thought, *if I could get her to go on to Savannah with me. Talk about nice. And I haven't been laid for a week.* He coughed again. When she brought him a new drink he tried to engage her in a little light chitchat, but she didn't seem to rise to the fly. *Oh, well, the hell with her. Plenty more where I'm going, and once the meeting's over, there'll be plenty of time for fun and games.* He thought of the condo at Hilton Head, the big pool and the golf course and the lush company suite on the twelfth floor, and that sweet little beauty he'd met in Savannah the last time he'd been there. Maybe he'd give her a jingle after the meeting and see if she had some spare time. They usually had some time for a weekend at that condo, with its high ocean view, and the best goddam food they'd ever eaten, and all the booze and snow they could ever hope for, and a little high-quality entertainment thrown in—he shifted in his seat in anticipation. Matter of fact, maybe he'd call that girl tonight, after he'd gotten a little sleep and before all the suckers started turning up for the meeting. They could just buzz off to the condo for dinner and a few hours to get reacquainted. He coughed again and pulled on his drink, beginning to feel downright feverish.

In Atlanta, however, Chet's connecting Delta flight to Savannah turned out to be overbooked, and he was bumped onto a flight that left forty minutes later. By oddest coincidence, the tall black stewardess rode in the seat he'd had reserved as she deadheaded home to Savannah. *Serve the fat bastard right to have to sit and wait a while,* she thought bitterly. He was just one too many white men mentally undressing her in the past forty-eight hours. *Let him sit and rub his crotch,* she thought. And coughing right in her face, too. The girl shivered. You'd think even a slob like that would try to do something about his breath.

In Savannah the black stewardess caught the limo to the DeSoto Hilton, then walked south along Bull Street in the hot morning sun, through the three graceful plazas to Forsyth Park. From there she angled west into the maze of scruffy tenements toward home—the sad, noisome, rat-infested home she'd been trying to escape for something like a million years, and had never quite made it.

16

The flashbulbs and photofloods hit Carlos full-face the minute he stepped off the plane at Stapleton International Airport in Denver—POW!—and he realized instantly that he should have been prepared for it, and like a damned naked baby, he wasn't. A microphone was shoved into his face, brandished by a wild-looking female. "Dr. Carlos Quintana, CDC?" Yes, yes. "Marge Callum, JTLM-TV News, Denver. Dr. Quintana, what can you tell us about the Black Plague epidemic that's hitting people, down in Rampart Valley?" Epidemic? My God, woman, what epidemic? There isn't any epidemic—"Well, there's plague been reported down there, hasn't there?" A few cases of plaguelike illness have turned up, yes. It hasn't been precisely identified—"But people have been dying from it, haven't they?" It's true a few victims have succumbed in an isolated area, but I assure you it's completely under control—"Well, if that isn't an epidemic, how would you define the word *epidemic,* Doctor?" I wouldn't, right now, ma'am, I'm trying to get down there to get some information about it—"Aren't you the Black Plague expert at the CDC, Doctor?" ***sigh***I'm just a working epidemiologist, ma'am, nothing more, and I've got a job to do if you'll just please let me get past, here—"Well, Doctor, I'm sure you're very modest, but we have some viewers who would like to know the facts about what's going on with this disease." So would I, ma'am. That's why I'm here, to dig out some facts, but so far I haven't made it out of the airport—"Well, let me tell you right now, Doctor, our viewers are going to recognize a cover-up when they see one. . . ."

Somewhere beyond all the lights and gabbling reporters he spotted Dr. Roger Salmon from the Fort Collins, Colorado, CDC unit, tall, white-haired, horn-rimmed glasses, moving toward him with a couple of burly airport guards on either side. Carlos grabbed Monique by the arm, ducked under the mikes and started plowing through the crowd toward Salmon as fast as his slight wiry frame could manage, sensing bitterly that he'd blown it with that reporter, but not knowing what else he could have done. Trouble was, he never could manage to hold on to his temper or watch his acid tongue; all he'd been taught about handling inquiries gently, instilling confidence, making positive and comforting statements that didn't sound evasive—all that always seemed to vanish every time he faced one of these hawks with a microphone trying to put words in his mouth. As he moved, with Monique in his wake, other microphones appeared, other bald, unanswerable questions came at him, but he just shook his head and plowed on. At last he reached Salmon, and the guards helped them break free of the pack.

"Sorry that happened," Roger said. "They promised us they'd bring the plane in at an alternate gate and announce it just at the last minute, but then they already had a plane there, and we were screwed."

"Never mind, just get us somewhere else." Carlos nodded gratefully to the airport guards. "Almost anyplace else will do."

"Well . . ." Roger Salmon hesitated. "We've been changing our plans by the minute. There's nothing to do here in Denver, nor Rampart Valley either—I've got a dozen people working down there. We need to go to Canon City, south of Colorado Springs. We've really got trouble down there." The man looked very tired and very nervous. "If you aren't completely pooped out, I've got an army chopper waiting for us. We can leave right now."

"You've got plague in this Canon City?"

"Twenty new cases in the last twelve hours."

Carlos pursed his lips. "Any rats?" he said. "Any fleas?"

"I wouldn't know—but there's a guy down there who's been doing a lot of legwork for us—"

"That would be our forester friend, I think," Carlos said. "The first one I want to talk to when we get there."

17

In Bozeman, Montana, Harry Slencik walked out on the porch of his little town house and looked at the elderly man sipping beer there. "Hey, Ben," he said, "did you see that six P.M. newscast last night on Channel 5?"

Dr. Ben Chamberlain scratched his grizzled beard. "Don't watch TV much anymore, Harry. Same old crap, day after day. I just kinda eased out of it."

"Well, they said there's some kind of Black Plague going on down in Colorado."

"Oh, yeah?" Ben shrugged. "They always have a case or two every summer."

"But twenty-eight cases in a week? Amy says we ought to be payin' attention."

The old doctor laughed. "Twenty-eight cases I don't believe, Harry. Far as I know, there haven't been twenty-eight plague cases in the West in a single year since the 1890s." The doctor took another sip of beer. "And as for Amy, you can tell her I said we've had plague up in those hills above Grizzly Creek since long before we ever built our cabins out there."

"You're kiddin'!" Harry stared at him.

"Not a bit," Ben said. "Plague doesn't hit people, primarily. Never has. It's a disease of rodents, and it's passed on from one to the next by the fleas that live on 'em. The fleas drink infected blood from the rodent, and when the rodent dies of the infection, the fleas go to another rodent, and vomit up some infected blood while they're biting the new rodent, and *it* gets infected. People only get it when too many rodents die and the fleas have to look for something else to bite. People will do in a pinch, but the fleas would rather have the rodents."

"But we don't have any rats up in those hills near our cabins," Harry protested.

"Not city rats, no. But we've got pack rats around all the time, trying to get into the cabins in winter. They're just native wood rats, is all they are. And then there's the squirrels, and chipmunks, and ground squirrels, maybe rabbits, marmots up in the higher country. There was a case down in New Mexico a few years ago when a couple of kids got fleabites from a dead coyote and came down with plague—I read about it in a journal."

"Then why aren't people just dropping dead all over the place up there?"

"Not that many people around, that's all. I mean, who's wandering around up there, ordinarily? Maybe a logger now and then, cruising timber. A few mushroom pickers in the spring, a few hunters in the fall, maybe a backpacker going through on one of the trails, a fisherman here and there. But it's big country. The odds of any one person actually contacting it are very small."

"Then how did it get there?"

"Just growed, I guess. Came in by boat from China around the turn of the century. Rats from the boats infected some wild rodents in the hills and it started spreading, very slowly. By now we've got low-grade sylvan plague, sort of endemic, in every state west of the Rockies and maybe even as far east as Kansas or Nebraska. But we don't have to worry, Harry. It takes *people* to get the plague moving, even when it's around. In fact, if you want to get away from it, you just get away from people. And that was why we built those places up on Grizzly Creek in the first place, wasn't it? To get away from people?"

"I suppose," Harry conceded. "But I tell you, Ben, if that Amy doesn't quit going into a panic every time she watches the news on TV, I'm going to have to belt her one . . ."

18

It was almost 4:00 A.M.—7:00 Atlanta time—by the time Carlos and Monique were checked into the discreet separate rooms Roger Salmon had arranged for them in the new Holiday Inn just south of Colorado Springs. "That's an hour's drive from Canon City, but you'll need some rest before you go down there, and facilities are better here." On the way down Roger had briefed them on the status quo in Rampart Valley and the thoroughly disturbing developments in Canon City—new cases turning up all over down there, an infection that was moving too fast, far too fast, an atypical pattern even for something as volatile as plague. "The first cases down there obviously came from the camping party up in Washington," Roger told them, "but these last ones have got to be secondary cases. Denver is getting very nervous about a major panic down here, and the TV newscasters obviously smell a very juicy scare story. We've got to get a handle on this thing very soon or we're going to be in deep trouble. . . ."

Yes, but get a handle on what, exactly? Carlos wondered. He had hoped to get a few hours' sleep before Frank Barrington came pounding on his door—Roger had already contacted the man and set up an early morning meeting—but sleep proved elusive considering the sort of yawning chasm Carlos found himself staring into. Then, just as he was dozing off about 6:00 A.M. the phone jangled and he discovered that Denver was not the only place that was getting nervous. It was Ted Bettendorf on the phone from Atlanta, and his usually calm voice sounded just a little ragged. "Carlos, what in *hell* did you tell those TV people in Denver last night?"

"Tell them? I told them nothing. *Nada. Nichts. Gornish.*"

"Have you seen the morning ABC newscast? They quote you as saying we have a major epidemic in central Colorado, with uncounted people sick or dead, and we don't know whether we can control it or not—Jesus, Carlos, they just went on and on."

"Holy Mother of—" Carlos leaped out of bed. "They didn't actually *show* me saying any of those things, did they?"

"No, you were just on the screen. This was all some woman's voice-over commentary."

"Well, they just made it up, that's all. All I told them, on camera or off, was that there were a few sick people we were investigating, and that everything was under control. I followed the rule book on Contacts with the Press the best I could, but you know what those people do when they want a story—"

"Look, I don't know *what* you told them," Bettendorf said, "and you probably don't either, but I know what *I* just got told. I just had the President on the line, the third day straight now, and he caught that morning newscast, and he was fit to be tied. Demanded to know what was going on out there that he didn't know about. He was very upset, babbling something about panic in the streets during his administration and people dinging the Governor of Colorado to declare the whole state a disaster area, and how all he needs right now is a nice big public-health mess that we can't control, right out in the middle of a major western state—well, you get the picture."

"Okay," Carlos said, "the next newshawk that comes around I'll shoot on sight. Meanwhile, I need about six hours to find out what floats out here and what doesn't, and I'll be back to you."

He hung up, got dressed and went down to the coffee shop for some breakfast. Monique was already there. "Couldn't sleep," she said. "They're ready for me up at Fort Collins anytime you say. I've already got them started setting up a Hot Lab so we can handle the samples they've been collecting. I get the shakes every time I think about what I may find."

"Yeah, well, everybody else has got the shakes, too, right up to the President, but we've got some work to do before you take off. This Barrington guy will be here at seven, for openers."

Frank met them in the lobby as he came in off the street, the little Chicano doctor and the tall willowy blonde. There were quick introductions, and then Carlos led them to a small conference room. Frank glanced at Monique, wondered fleetingly how any woman that beautiful could want to spend her time rooting around in a bacteriology lab. But once in the room he turned his attention to Carlos. "So you're the troubleshooter from CDC," he said. "I just hope to hell you're going to be able to stop this damned thing."

"Stop it?" Carlos made an elaborate gesture. "Of course I'm going to stop it. Why do you think I'm here?"

"Whatever it was that hit Pam Tate may not be so easy to stop."

"Pam Tate? Ah, yes." Carlos's face fell. "The unfortunate young woman. Your fiancée, I understand, and maybe a key to the puzzle." He looked up at Frank. "Look, my large friend, I was being facetious, and it was in bad taste. I apologize. No, I most certainly am not going to be able to stop this damned thing, not in any sense of wiping it out. Nobody yet has managed to wipe it out in four thousand years of recorded history, and I don't really think I'm going to be the lucky fellow. With a few good breaks and a lot of help from Monique and a lot of others I'm hoping at best to nail down this particular outbreak long enough to learn something about it and keep it from turning into a real mess. But I'm going to need those breaks, because something very strange is going on."

"That's for certain," Frank said. "If it's really plague, it's been moving like lightning."

"And you've been in Canon City?" Carlos said. "Tracing down contacts?"

"And finding a lot of sick people," Frank said. "Here, I brought everything with me."

He handed a large bundle of note sheets to Carlos. The little doctor sat down at the table and went through them carefully, page by page. Then he went through them again. "Remarkable," he murmured. "You just came down from Washington on your own and started in on this?"

"I had to do something, and I knew that Pam had had contact with these people."

"Remarkable," Carlos repeated. "You've done this kind of work before?"

"Not really. But it seemed pretty common-sense to me. You find somebody sick with a contagious disease, you try to trace back to find out who he got it from, and then trace ahead to see who he might have given it to."

"Yeah. Where I come from we call it epidemiology," Carlos said wryly. "You've had no medical training at all?"

"I had two years in medical school, four or five years ago, before I had to drop out."

Carlos looked up. "Oh, really? What happened? If I'm not too nosy."

"Nothing terrible. My father came down with a bad cancer. Somebody had to mind the farm, and I was elected. By the time he died, we had to sell out to meet debts and expenses, and by then the idea of being a doctor had kind of lost its charm anyway—I'd seen enough for a lifetime, with Dad. A spot with the Forest Service came open and I grabbed it."

"Well, this is very good work you've done down here. It's going to give us a running start, and I want you to stick around, if you can. But right now the burning question is what happened to Pam Tate—and how in hell it could have happened."

"You mean so fast?"

"Exactly," Carlos said. "Ordinarily an infectious disease behaves in certain characteristic ways that you learn to recognize. That's one of the ways that you tell Disease A from Disease B. Of course, Monique's little bacteria cultures are a big help, too—but clinical patterns may be more important. Take leprosy, for instance—an infectious disease that normally spreads directly from person to person, but only after long-standing, very close physical contact with someone who's infected. Even after the organism invades the new victim, it often takes from five to fifteen *years* of incubation before it really starts to move. It's a deadly disease, all right, but very slow, very indolent. Plague has a characteristic pattern, too, but it's totally different from leprosy. Plague doesn't normally spread from person to person. The usual pattern is Rat gets sick, Flea bites Rat, Flea bites Man, Man gets sick. Then once the organism gets in the human body by this complex infective chain, it normally takes some three to five days to grow in there before fever or any other signs of illness appear." The doctor looked up at Frank. "Compared to leprosy, it's really explosive, it's so fast, but we're still talking about three to five *days* as a sort of minimum. Not twelve *hours*. Not even forty-eight hours. Which brings us to your Pamela Tate and the absolutely incredible report I have on her from our Shoeleather men up there."

"Pam Tate went fast," Frank said.

"If the story's true," Carlos said, "she went faster than I ever *heard* of anybody going, with plague. Look at the timing. From the story I have, she started up that mountain in full good health about four A.M. on a Monday morning. By Monday evening she was symptomatic—coughing, feverish, feeling sick. By then she was actually spreading infection to others by casual respiratory contact—it was the only contact she had with these Colorado people. By sometime on Tuesday—Day Two—up at Lancelot Lake, she was violently ill, and she died of pneumonic plague sometime before dawn of Day Three, and other people later contracted virulent infection just from contact with her body." Carlos sighed. "Well, my friend, for classical plague that story just doesn't hang together. Some vital piece is missing. I'm hoping you can fill it in."

Frank shook his head. "The story you just outlined is exactly what happened. Except that she did have contact with some dead rodents that first day."

The doctor looked up. "How do you know that?"

"She wrote it in her log. The little journal she kept." Frank produced Pam's notebook from his pocket.

Carlos took it to a window, opened it in the bright morning sunlight and began reading, very slowly, very carefully, stopping now and then to take notes of his own. After a long while he handed it back to Frank. "Well, there are the rats and the fleas, as far as Pam was concerned. Amazing. But she couldn't have passed the fleas on to all those other people. To one or two of them, maybe, but not all of them." He got up and paced for a moment. "You know, this business about the dirty, ragged boy is very strange."

"I can't make any sense out of that," Frank said.

"Oh, I can," Carlos said. "That's why it's so strange. One of the oldest persisting folk tales in history involves some kind of a demon-creature who always appeared just before the plague. The story turns up again and again. Ted Bettendorf, my boss in Atlanta and a major scholar of plague, has written papers about it. As far back as 100 A.D. Apollonius of Tyana was writing that the plague in Asia Minor was always preceded by the appearance in crowded places of a man whose eyes flashed fire—how about that? Philostratus, his biographer, confirmed the story five hundred years later. And then there was a thirteenth-century text—Ted has actually seen this one—written by some medieval chronicler called Gunther of Brandenburg who wrote, 'Never yet has the plague come but one has first seen a ragged, stinking boy who drank like a dog from the village well and then passed on. . . .'"

"You don't actually *believe* that, do you?" Frank said.

"Please. Of course I believe it. I mean, I believe it was believed. True or not—I couldn't say."

"I don't believe it," Frank said.

"Ah, well. Would you believe in the Day of the Dead in old *México?* No, you probably wouldn't. Little candy skulls with your name on them. But *I* do." Carlos shrugged eloquently. "There's the difference between you and me. But let's come back to the present. Tell me about this town you live in, this Leavenworth, Washington. No connection with the prison, I presume?"

"No, it's just a little mountain village. The town fathers prettied it up with an Alpine Village theme a few years ago—Swiss false fronts on the main street, German names, knackwurst for breakfast, all that sort of stuff. Turned it into a modest tourist attraction, very beautiful location at the foot of the mountains, good fishing, and it's close to a lot of trailheads leading to the Central Cascades."

"Nice and clean? Good sanitary facilities?"

"They work overtime at it. Clean and pretty as a Dutch girl's nose."

"No rats around, I suppose."

"Well, sometimes pack rats get into people's attics in the winter," Frank said.

"No, I don't mean pack rats. I mean the big brown rats with the long naked tails." Carlos held his hands apart. "The big humpbacked bastards that measure two feet from nose to tail tip and hang around alleys and sewers and waterfronts."

Frank shook his head. "I've never seen one of those there. I'm not sure I've ever seen one in my life."

"Count your blessings," Carlos said. "What about the place you and Pam were living? An old building?"

"Brand-new. The builder couldn't sell it because of interest rates, so he gave us a break on the rent for an upstairs apartment."

"No mice around?"

"No."

"Did Pam have a cat?"

"Matter of fact, she hated them. We didn't have a dog, either. We just weren't around the place enough to keep a dog, especially with the summer work load."

Monique, busy taking notes, looked up. "Any birds? Budgies, parakeets?"

"No birds."

Carlos chewed on his thumb, then took a deep breath. "Okay, my large friend, now I have to crowd you a little—but it's critically important. You said Pam was in peak physical condition that Monday morning when she started up the mountain. Perfectly healthy in every way. How did you know that?"

Frank flushed. "She sure seemed to be in pretty good shape the night before."

"Okay, like specifically."

"Hell, man, you can't take a woman like that to bed without knowing whether she's sick or not," Frank exploded. "You could tell in a million ways. We were very, very close. We were fine-tuned to each other, mentally and physically. Her job demanded top physical conditioning or she just couldn't have hacked it. What's more, she was one of these people who had to be really high on what she was doing or she tended to droop, and she wasn't doing any drooping." Frank took a deep breath. "Everything I remember about her that night and morning spelled exuberant good health to me. That morning, as usual, she got out of bed like she was shot from a cannon when the alarm went off. Then she decided I was too slow crawling out, so she got hold of a foot and started pulling. There was a little horseplay, a little wordplay, a little light fooling around, but I finally let her win and rolled out and started helping her stuff her pack. Well, Doctor, that is not a picture of a woman who's *sick*."

"No," Carlos said gloomily, "I guess it isn't. But what about earlier? What were you two doing two or three days before that particular morning?"

"The Thursday before, she came down from the Enchantments over Asgard Pass into Colchuck Lake and down Eight Mile Creek to the road. Caught a ride, so she got home a little earlier than usual. We'd finagled three days off at the same time, so we went to Wenatchee for dinner and a show, stayed over with some friends, and then went to a country auction on Friday. She found some cheap kitchen cabinets that caught her eye, so we hauled them home and spent the rest of the weekend refinishing them. That was about it."

Carlos regarded the big forester for a long moment. "Could something possibly have happened to Pam on that previous trip, before she came out on Thursday? Dead rodents or anything like that?"

"Not that I know of," Frank said. "She was a sharp girl. If anything had happened, she'd have put it in her logbook, and probably told me as well. She didn't say anything, and when I checked back through the book later I found nothing."

"There were no breaks in her skin that you know of? No scratches? Sores? Flea bites?"

"I guarantee you, she didn't have any flea bites."

Carlos sighed and walked across to rub Monique's shoulder. "Well, there you are, my dear," he said. "You see why I'm nervous."

"Yes," she said. "I certainly see."

"A whole chain of infections, all moving far too fast, with a very high ratio of direct person-to-person contact. No rats, and no fleas in between. And most if not all of these cases traceable to a single totally impossible index case. You know what that adds up to, God help us."

Monique sighed and nodded. "An atypical variant. A wild one that writes its own ticket."

"Well, pinning *that* down is up to you at Fort Collins," Carlos said. "You've got plenty of samples to work on."

"Yes, but they're old samples. Run a bug like that through a few successive culture plates and you don't know *what* you've got."

"Don't worry, the Shoeleather Boys will get you enough new samples. And Frank and I are going out tomorrow to find some of these dead rodents he's been talking about. We'll bring you some fresh meat."

19

Chet Benoliel knew he should have passed up the date, let the girl wait until she got tired and went home, and just forgotten about it. He knew that before he even left the hotel to pick her up, but he pushed it out of his mind. By the time he had checked into his room at the DeSoto Hilton in Savannah that morning he was thoroughly sick, coughing almost constantly, baking under that furious overhead sun and suffocating in the swamplike humidity steaming up from the river. To top it off, the air conditioner in his room wasn't working and he was just too sick to call the manager and scream about it—which, for Chet Benoliel, was pretty sick. But Chet had made up his mind that he was going to make it with Shari that night, after that stewardess had given him the chill, and when it came to some things, Chet tended to be very stubborn, not to say downright stupid.

He had thought some sleep might help, and collapsed fully clothed on the hotel-room bed, but eight hours' sleep didn't seem to be the answer. He woke about 5:00 P.M. pouring sweat, with the afternoon sun beating in his window and the room like an oven. He took a belt from the Scotch bottle in his bag, coughed for three minutes until he got his breath, and then sloshed his face down with cold water in the bathroom. Then he took a long cold shower. His hands were shaking as he sat on the bed and dialed Shari's number at work to be sure she'd be free for the evening. *Not that she wouldn't—unless she had an awfully short memory.*

Shari was free, all right, no question about that. Shari was a waitress at the Seafood Express down on River Street, and though the boss didn't like it too much, the job gave her plenty of chances to meet well-heeled young businessmen looking for some plain and fancy evening entertainment. Usually she kept it strictly to after-hours, but not with Chet Baby. She may not have been the brightest twenty-two-year-old working girl in Savannah, she thought, but she wasn't a total idiot. She remembered the last time Chet was in town, three months ago—that great big pool, the palace of a condo, everything clean and neat, and Chet himself. She'd actually enjoyed it, he was one pile-drivin' man, all night long with hardly a rest. And when she got home, she'd found that what he'd stuck in her purse wasn't a couple hundred like she thought, but a thousand-dollar bill with that beautiful picture of Clever Groveland or whoever he was on it.

After Chet's call, Shari talked DeeDee into covering the rest of her shift, and a few minutes later headed the few blocks home to her messy little walk-up flat. She bathed in the washbowl (somebody was using the shower down the hall, naturally—*But there'll be that swimming pool anyway*) and made it back to the bar a few doors up from the Seafood Express to wait for Chet.

He was driving a T-Bird, like the last time, but he didn't look so sharp this time, his eyes all bloodshot, coughing a lot and spitting out the window. He kissed her when she got in the car, and it seemed to her his breath smelled funny, but he explained why he looked so ragged—the long plane flight, hardly any sleep, a little too much to drink. He turned the car north across the bridge and up the highway toward Hilton Head just as the sun was dropping behind the trees, leaving shadows across the road and bringing a little coolness. Shari relaxed a little. She tried to make some friendly conversation, but Chet didn't seem too responsive. Just didn't feel top rate, he said, but then a couple of drinks and a little TLC would take care of that. He took a pull from his silver flask and offered it to her. She took a stiff drink, and then another, before handing it back. *This could be a tough evening. . . .*

They were rounding a curve through a grove of trees when Chet swerved sharp right, almost going off the shoulder into the ditch, to miss a figure walking toward them down the middle of the road. Shari had a brief glimpse of a skinny, raggedy kid, feet bare, hair tangled. Chet fought the car back on the road, then slowed and looked over his shoulder. "Did you see that bastard? Right in the middle. We could have ditched this thing!"

"I saw."

"Goddamn fool! I oughta go back and whip his ass."

"Aw, come on, honey. Let's go on to that nice place and forget him. Let somebody else wipe up the road with him."

"He'd damn well deserve it, too."

The place at Hilton Head was exactly as she remembered it—high ceilings, beautiful rooms, rich carpeting, a well-stocked bar and an enormous bed. Chet was coughing more than before, but he mixed stiff drinks for both of them, raw whiskey over ice. When he brought Shari hers he put his arms around her, tried to kiss her, and she turned her face away. "Honey, that business on the road kinda scared me, I need to settle down a little." She sipped the drink. "Why don't we try the pool first? Freshen up from all this sticky heat. And I brought my sexiest suit, too. Here, I'll show you what I mean."

She showed him. While he lay back on the bed, she slowly stripped down to the buff, poured herself more drink and then twisted and tugged into the sheer black bikini. Chet disappeared into the bathroom to put on his trunks, and they headed for the pool elevator together.

The pool turned out to be a bad idea, for Chet. Shari went in like a nymph, laughing and urging him to catch her, but the minute he hit the water he was in trouble. Suddenly he couldn't breathe; the slightest movement was an impossible effort, and a strangling spasm of coughing came and wouldn't go away. He floundered to the edge somehow and hung on, waiting for the coughing to stop, waiting for strength enough to get out of there. Finally he found a ladder, lunged out and collapsed on the poolside. She was up on the diving board now, large breasts and slim body and tight buttocks on full display, but he couldn't even *look* at her. His breath wouldn't come, and then suddenly, still dripping from the pool, he was chilling, shaking so violently he could barely make it to the poolside chair and sit staring stupidly at the water.

Sometime later he stopped chilling and she was there beside him, bending over him. "Honey, are you okay?"

"Yeah."

"You aren't sick?"

"No, no, no," he gasped. "I'll be all right. Just gotta get warm."

"Let's go on up. You look sick."

She half supported him to the elevator, opened the door with his key when he couldn't hold his hand still enough and somehow got him over to the bed. He collapsed on his back, panting. "You need to see a doctor, honey," Shari said.

"Nah, screw the doctor. It's just that damned swimming that got me."

She sat on the edge of the bed, looking down at him, for once in her life completely at a loss. His hand came up to her breast. "Chet, honey, maybe you need to rest a little while. . . ."

"Don't wanna rest," he gasped. He pulled her down, started to kiss her, and then began chilling again more violently than before.

"Maybe if we get those wet old trunks off," Shari said. She untied the string, tugged them down and off him and barely stifled a scream.

He had a huge purple welt on the side of his penis, as if somebody had kicked him. Higher up, in the groin, she saw an angry purple lump the size of a plum, with a gray spot on top for all the world like a huge boil about to burst.

Quite suddenly Chet sat upright with his hand over his mouth and bolted past her into the john, stark naked. She heard him vomiting again and again; then the sound evolved into ragged coughing and gasping. It went on for a long time. Then, finally it stopped.

She sat dead still on the edge of the bed, looking at the half-open bathroom door, and listening, listening. There was no further sound. "Chet, honey?" Still no sound. She walked to the bathroom and looked in.

He was kneeling over the toilet bowl, blood splattered all over his face and chest and the tile floor. The bowl itself was full of bright crimson clotted stuff. His head and shoulders were ash-gray. She took one shoulder, tried to raise him up, but he just slid sideways onto the floor, banging his face on the toilet bowl as he went.

He wasn't breathing, and it didn't look like he was going to start again, either. An intensely practical girl, Shari dismissed the hulk on the floor. *No help for him. But Jesus! What if somebody walks in here? What if somebody phones, expecting him to answer?* She walked back into the bedroom, licking her lips. *Nobody saw us come in, and there was nobody else in the pool.* Moving fast, she went through his pants, tossed the car keys and his wallet on the bed. *Good, I can park the T-Bird on a downtown street with the keys in it, and when the bulls find it they'll call Hertz.* She stripped off her bikini, stuffed it in her purse and put on the blouse and slacks she'd come in. She needed to go to the john, but she decided that could wait. Finally, she stripped all the cash from his wallet, $2,420, and stuffed the wad into her bra. With a final look around, she peeked out into the corridor, closed the door and headed for the elevator and the parking lot.

An hour later she left the car parked at the corner of Oglethorpe and Broad in downtown Savannah after wiping away prints, and hurried to her flat a few blocks away. It was only 10:30 P.M., and she was afraid she'd meet somebody who knew her coming in, but all she did was startle a huge rat on the stair. It disappeared into a hole in the wall. Once inside her room, she took a long drink raw from the gin bottle and collapsed on her bed. *Home again,* she thought. Thank Christ for that. *Home and safe,* she thought.

20

During the next week Dr. Carlos Quintana and a growing army of epidemiologists and other CDC personnel put in grueling twenty-hour days trying to define and control the brush fires of plaguelike illness that now centered in Canon City, Colorado, but were also springing up elsewhere in a long arc stretching from Chihuahua State to the south, up through mountain villages in New Mexico, through Colorado and north into Wyoming, almost all traceable directly or indirectly to somebody in that first ill-fated camping party. Many of the workers were the Shoeleather Boys Carlos liked to refer to—members of the Epidemic Intelligence Service, many of them experienced epidemiologists, but more merely recruits-in-training, working out of offices all over the West and shipped in because Canon City was where they were needed. Their job was staggering and wildly varied: tabulating and interviewing each new individual case of plague, meticulously listing all possible contacts that might have occurred while the victims were infectious, then painstakingly tracking down each of those contacts—and their contacts—and *their* contacts—to New York, to Anchorage, to Hong Kong, to literally anyplace in the world, in order to gather information, urge medical observation and, when necessary, prescribe prophylactic antibiotics. Since every plague victim had dozens, sometimes hundreds, of potential contacts, and since each one had to be traced out individually, the reason for the Centers for Disease Control's unofficial insignia—a shoe sole with a hole in it—was soon painfully apparent in Canon City and environs. To make matters worse, the EIS workers were made fully aware that the patterns that might ordinarily govern the spread of plague might not apply—that failure to account for any rodent or flea exposure, for instance, did not in any way mean that a possible contact could be considered safe. This plague was heavily loaded with cases of plague pneumonia, a form of the infection easily spread from person to person.

With the enormous amount of data they were collecting, it was easy for these workers to imagine that they were covering everything and forget that multitudes of contacts like Chet Benoliel might be slipping through their nets. With the sheer magnitude of the task created by first twenty, or twenty-three, or thirty cases of plague, it was easy to be fooled into thinking that pages and reams of raw data somehow equaled accomplishment, and to imagine they were really getting somewhere when the fact was they were merely getting buried in figures.

In addition to the Shoeleather Boys, some elite specialists came in, setting up shop either at the Fort Collins CDC installation, at the Colorado Springs motel headquarters or in Canon City itself: chemists, microbiologists to work with Monique, nurses, physicians, public health advisers to work with the local doctors, veterinarians, entomologists, rodent-control experts to help assess local rat populations, live-trap the rats and send their fleas up for examination and bacteriological culture—the list of jobs to be done seemed virtually endless.

That first day Carlos called a council of war to establish and discuss certain basic ground rules. "We can't assume that we're dealing with plague the way the textbooks describe it, or the way any of you may have encountered it before," he said as the workers crowded into the small Holiday Inn conference room. "We've got to assume that anyone who's had direct or indirect contact with a proven infected person is in mortal danger, and we simply don't dare sit around and watch what happens. We have to move as soon as we have a presumptive history."

"But we can't treat somebody who isn't sick, can we?" one worker asked.

"In this situation we may have to. So far it looks like ninety percent of the people who have developed symptoms have been dying no matter what was done. That's one hell of a mortality rate, and I don't think we can fool around waiting for a laboratory diagnosis."

"Why didn't the antibiotics stop it, up at Rampart Valley?"

"Maybe just too slow," Carlos said. "It takes any antibiotic three hours or more to reach an effective blood level, unless it's given intravenously, and then another twenty-four hours for the antibiotic to knock down enough of the invading bacteria to slow the attack. Here we have an organism that seems to move like greased lightning. Maybe it just walks right over the antibiotic. Maybe there's already an overwhelming bacteremia before symptoms really begin to show up. Or maybe the bug just isn't very sensitive to the antibiotics we've been using. Until Monique can define the organism better, up at Fort Collins, we aren't going to have answers—but meantime, we've got to do something, and as long as the outbreak is small and localized enough,

I think that means full-dose antibiotic prophylaxis for every person with any suspicion of contact."

There was a general discussion of that. What antibiotic to use? Tetracycline alone? Carlos shook his head. "We've got to hit it harder than that." Streptomycin, then? Better hold the streptomycin for people with symptoms, we don't want everybody in Colorado going deaf. Well, that leaves chloramphenicol—in quantity. But where are we going to get enough? Nobody stocks that drug in quantity. "True, the local supply is low," Carlos said, "but Parke-Davis says they can get us a whopping big supply straight into Canon City by noon tomorrow. I talked to them this morning."

"Why not use broadside vaccination?" a young woman asked. "There *is* a plague vaccine, isn't there?"

"Yes, there *is* a vaccine, such as it is, and every one of you people are going to take it, too—but that's really about the weakest weapon we've got. For one thing, it takes three or four weeks to build up an antibody level, so it's not going to stop anything that's moving fast *right now*. Even then, at best, the vaccine is only about forty to sixty percent effective in the field, depending on the particular microstrain of *Yersinia* we're dealing with. It's a killed-bacteria vaccine, and like the cholera vaccine, it may not be worth too much of a curse when you really need it. And as for broadsiding it into everybody around, hoo boy! Just this one little town would put a dent in the national stockpile of the stuff. We could have more made in a hurry, but you're talking about weeks or months of lead time. We'll use the vaccine for health workers, yes, but for a broadside weapon here, forget it."

The workers went on their way, gathering their data. Carlos dispatched Monique north to the Fort Collins CDC installation up near Estes Park by army helicopter with instructions to move as fast as possible—" Until you've got this bug pinned down in all dimensions, we're really flying blind down here." With her on her way, he worked far into the night with Roger Salmon and Bob Romano from Albuquerque getting the Canon City fieldwork organized and moving.

Next morning at daybreak he and Frank Barrington, now officially on loan to the CDC from the Forest Service after a little high-level interdepartment finagling, took off to the forested slopes to the west of Canon City in a little Forest Service Jeep Frank had commandeered, carrying a large, oddly shaped bag that Carlos hoisted into the back end, in search of dead rodents. As Frank turned up a steep canyon road through scrub pine and bramble, he said, "The whole concept of dead rodent counts really evolved from the fact that you don't ordinarily find any dead rodents in the wild."

"None at all?" Carlos said.

"Not very often. For one thing, most wild rodents never die a natural death. They're caught and killed by predators—hawks, eagles, coyotes, weasels, martens—and immediately eaten. The few that do die on the ground are devoured within hours by those same predators and a few others—ravens, buzzards, bobcats. Even a cougar won't turn his back on a nice, crunchy one-bite meal if he finds one. So the only time you find any dead rodents around to speak of is when there's been an overwhelming kill of rodents by something that doesn't immediately eat them."

"I see," Carlos said thoughtfully. "But how do you find them when they *are* there? Just walk out in the woods and look around?"

Frank shook his head. "Not quite. Your best bet is to cruise a line, follow a compass course through likely country for so many miles, watching for anything you see along your way. Then you run a second line, parallel to it, and then a third, and then extrapolate for a square-mileage area. Much the same way that we counted tussock moths on Douglas fir up in Washington and Oregon some years ago when they were killing so many trees—you couldn't go out and count each moth. Or the way the Game Department estimates how many deer there are in a given area."

"You mean you walk a line through the woods for so far, and count the deer you see, and then multiply it by some factor?"

Frank laughed. "You wouldn't get much of an answer that way. I mean, you might see some deer, but your extrapolated number wouldn't mean anything. Even the most crafty hunter in the world going through the woods is going to spook a lot of the deer off ahead of him without ever seeing them, and walk right past a whole lot more that he also never sees. No, to estimate the deer in an area, you have to look for something that can't just sneak away while you're looking."

"So what do you count if you don't count deer?"

"You count piles of droppings. Fresh piles that don't look more than twenty-four hours old. They tell you beyond question that the deer have been there, and roughly how many, whether you see any deer or not. You'll see what I mean, up ahead here. But what we're going to be looking for are dead rodents, and they'll either be just freshly dead, or they'll be gone."

He picked an area of pine timber interspersed with dense patches of buck brush, running along a ridge with a long, gentle rise. Carlos packed the large bag he'd brought over his shoulder; Frank carried a day pack. They plodded, climbed, scrambled and sweated for four long hours as the August sun got higher and hotter, trying a multitude of areas, and finding nothing. "Maybe we'd better go higher," Frank concluded as they finally made their way back to the Jeep. "There may just be too many scavengers at this level. You're game to keep going?"

"Oh, yes. Yes. We've got to do this."

A few miles higher into the mountains hardly seemed any better, except that there was less brush and bramble underfoot. Sometime after noon, discouraged, they stopped for lunch in a little grove of pines, sitting on a downed log to munch their sandwiches. Flies buzzed and the warm air was rich with pine resin. Carlos looked drowsy and disheveled. Then Frank said, "Speak of the devil," and pointed.

Twenty feet away from them a sick chipmunk was struggling feebly in the dusty turf a few feet from cover. "He's not quite gone," Frank said, "but he's getting there."

He started to his feet, but Carlos caught his wrist with an iron grip. "Just stay put," he said. "I'll take care of this."

Watching the chipmunk constantly, Carlos opened his bag and brought out the oddest assortment of equipment Frank had ever seen: a large, heavy-gauge polyethylene bag with a strange-looking tie around the top, a pair of shoulder-length rubber gloves, and a long pair of collapsible tongs that looked like stainless steel. Carlos opened the polybag and set it on the ground near the barely moving creature, keeping well away from it. Then he stripped on the long gloves and pulled the tong handles out to full length, about a yard or more. Very quietly he edged toward the chipmunk, tongs in his right hand. Then he extended the pincers to either side of the rodent and snapped them together sharply, crushing the creature with clinical precision. He lifted it into the open mouth of the polybag and brought the bag top closed with the tongs. Then he tossed them well aside and backed away. "Matches in my breast pocket," he told Frank.

Frank, who had been staring at him, bemused, fished the matches out and handed them to him. Approaching the bag, Carlos struck a match to the tie around the top. Frank saw something flare and run around the bag top, puffing black smoke, exactly like a long fuse on a firecracker. When the thing stopped Carlos went forward again and peered critically at the bag.

"Fine," he said. He moved the bag and tongs twenty feet away from where the chipmunk had been. "Now, you'll find a bottle of murky-looking soup there in my bag, Frank. Toss it to me."

Carlos caught the bottle, sloshed the long gloves liberally, then treated the tongs the same way before collapsing the handles again. At last he pulled off the gloves and stowed them and the tongs in another plastic bag, which he also heat-sealed. Finally he took another deep breath and sat down on the log with a wan smile. Frank saw that his hands were trembling.

"Now, what the *hell* was all that about?" Frank said.

Carlos looked up, startled. "About?"

"All the hocus-pocus."

The little doctor shrugged. "Look, my large friend. A flea can jump four feet or more if it feels like it. That chipmunk's fleas could be carrying some very nasty customers around with them—I didn't want them jumping on *me*. If you want to go up and fondle the next little beast, that's *your* problem. Not me, thanks."

"Sorry," Frank said. "But that's a pretty fancy setup."

"A couple of our EIS recruits down in New Mexico worked the system out, mostly for collecting trapped rats, to minimize any possibility of getting a plague-infected fleabite. It's not foolproof, but it beats bagging them up bare-handed. You think you could work the system?"

Frank nodded. "If you'll run through it again and explain exactly why I'm doing what."

"Good. We'd better get back to town now, but I'll give you a lesson with a catnip mouse tonight."

"You want me to look for more of these?"

Carlos nodded. "I can't spend more time up here, I've got things to do down in town, but we need as many dead rodents as you can find in the next few days. Take a crew with you, but you handle the dead ones. Try to get them from different places, high and low elevation, north and south. You know where to look, you be in charge. But believe me, this is no game—it's critical. Our little friend in the bag here could be a major key."

21

As the battle was joined, those first few days, there were far more troubles than triumphs for Carlos and his crew of workers. Four new cases were spotted in Canon City the first two days; three of them were dead of pneumonic plague within forty-eight hours despite swift and vigorous antibiotic treatment, while the fourth lingered on in a coma, with spiking fever and chills. ("A brain abscess, maybe? Those sputum plates and blood cultures are *clean*.") Out of the blue, two cases were reported in Gunnison, 120 miles to the west, no identifiable contact with Canon City, EIS people raking over reports item by item and finding nothing, and then another case down in Walsenburg, a town located between a north and south segment of the San Isabel National Forest, again with no identifiable contacts. "Brush fires," Carlos said, shaking his head and staring at the reports. "Brush fires, all over. Where are they coming from?" and teams were dispatched to both places in hopes of stopping the spread. City fathers in Pueblo were vocally alarmed, Colorado Springs officials next to irrational, the State Attorney General's office in Denver very, very quietly investigating the possible legal ramifications of imposing selective roadblocks on certain state, county and local highways without precisely declaring a state of emergency and scaring everybody in Colorado to death. . . .

Then, late in the week, JTLM-TV News Denver laid its little egg, and the fat was really in the fire. Under the able guidance of announcer Marge Callum and a team of cameramen and reporters, and despite all CDC efforts to maintain a news brown-out, JTLM-TV News preempted Thursday-night primetime to air their own thirty-minute special, engagingly entitled "Plague in Colorado" and done with all the stops pulled out. They had everything possible in it and much, much more. There were shots and stills of the Enchantment Lakes Plateau in the Washington Cascades and shots of a Forest Service chopper in the air, ostensibly hauling Pam Tate's body out. Somehow or other they had gotten footage of the interior of the Harborview Hospital morgue in Seattle, with four early victims on view on their slabs, the shots made all the more grisly due to the graininess and bad quality of the black-and-white film—it looked like the ovens at Buchenwald. Next they focused on the Rampart Valley Community Hospital, still closed up tight, featuring a hair-raising through-the-window interview with the young doctor there, apparently filmed after he was good and sick but somewhat before he died. And then, homing in on Canon City, there were interviews with parents and friends of victims, with vivid descriptions of how the infection struck and killed. For wrap-up, a scathing attack on the "do-nothing attitude" of the Centers for Disease Control, a rousing "citizens' call" for action, a demand that Canon City be isolated completely "to see that this horror does not move beyond its boundaries. . . ."

The show had impact, all right. The town councilmen of Canon City howled exploitation, while the ACLU screamed foul at the very suggestion of isolating a community—"This is not medieval Italy"—and the CDC people in Canon City gritted their teeth and very carefully refrained from responding at all, much as they might have liked to, on orders from Carlos Quintana, who held the fatalistic conviction, reinforced by long and bitter experience, that howling at JTLM-TV News Denver would be considerably less fruitful than howling at the moon—and a great deal more dangerous to their mission.

In Atlanta, Ted Bettendorf fielded the howls officially and—unlike Carlos—decided that action was demanded. Within an hour of the broadcast he had a senior PR man on a plane for Denver with three legal men in tow, their major mission to abort any reruns of the show that might be planned. Then, after a half-hour phone conference with the Secretary HHS in Washington, Ted got an assistant commissioner of the FCC on the line. "Damon, for God's sake! This kind of broadcast has got to stop, this is absolutely intolerable. We can't work with this kind of light in our faces."

"Ted, I can certainly sympathize, I guess the show was a little raw, but I don't know what we can do about it. We can't precensor those producers, you know."

"Maybe not," Bettendorf said, "but you can knock them across the room later, can't you? This is a clear and present public danger, what they're doing. They didn't bother to check one single fact. They've taken a few cases of infection in one isolated region and blown it up into a raging epidemic."

The FCC man was vastly apologetic. "I'll do anything that's legal, Ted, you know we want to cooperate with you guys, but the laws are pretty tight."

"Well, you can keep the damned thing off the air elsewhere, can't you? It's not prior censorship once it's been shown."

"We can't block it unless the station voluntarily pulls it, Ted. The freedom-of-speech people are watching us like hawks these days, and believe me, you're going to have more press, not less, if you try to get rough. Why don't you have your man out there just pat the producer's ass and see if he can't talk him into cooperating?"

The PR man didn't do any ass-patting when he arrived in Denver. The show's producer and the station manager of JTLM-TV were both intransigent. They weren't the public conscience; they didn't care if the special was less than precisely accurate in fact or implication; and they scoffed at the notion that false or distorted data in a TV show might threaten human lives. Let the CDC worry about that, that was what they were paid for. JTLM-TV had sponsors to worry about, and they happened to have some great footage, the script was a real heart-tugger, great TV, viewed by twenty-four percent of the audience on the Boulder–Denver–Colorado Springs–Pueblo axis, and they already had it scheduled for rerun on primetime Saturday night. Biggest hit they'd ever produced, and the networks were interested. . . . The PR man and his lawyers walked out of there in mid-tirade, heading across town to the federal courthouse, but knowing already that the chance of getting a restraining order or injunction was practically zero on the kind of evidence they were authorized to supply, and there were reporters to face at the courthouse too. . . .

The effect on the people in Canon City was immediate—and ominous. Before the broadcast, in this mountain-foothills town of twelve thousand souls, people had realized there was a medical problem and that some people had died, but life had gone on much as usual just the same. There was a lot of local gossip going around; people had commiserated with the families who had been hit, and pursed their lips at the idea that the State of Washington would export this sort of thing; they had watched the teams of CDC people coming and going, and cooperated with them in their investigation; there was an almost touching esprit de corps about it all—nothing this big had happened in Canon City, Colorado, since the train had derailed over the Royal Gorge thirty years ago—and when the town officials passed the word that anyone who had had any contact with any sick person should report to the Fremont County Health Department to be interviewed and receive preventive medicine to take, they queued up dutifully, congratulating themselves and everybody else that Something Was Being Done. For most of them, it was an excitement that was around them but not quite touching them.

JTLM-TV changed all that.

The broadcast brought the horror home to the very people who were, they actually heard for the first time, living at the center of the horror. Pneumonia was pneumonia, but the Black Plague, proclaimed baldly on the television like those horrible medieval epidemics, was something else. Within a day of the broadcast, Canon City, Colorado, took on the aspect of a ghost town. The Mayor and the local police, succumbing to panic, spread notices urging everyone to stay home, to stay in, to go nowhere except in an emergency. The Shoeleather Boys now had to pursue their contacts; they met with locked and bolted doors and had to conduct interviews through cracked-open windows. Business doors slammed shut as the local radio station—the only one many Canon City radios would pick up—repeated feckless and largely useless advice, over and over and over, every hour on the hour. One supermarket remained opened to sell "emergency supplies," but few customers were bold enough to go shopping; they lived from their pantry shelves instead. Streets were deserted except for an occasional rattletrap pickup truck going by. Only the small local hospital and doctors' clinic remained busy, crowded with people suddenly terrified of *every* ache and pain.

Meanwhile, plague continued to surface—two new cases here, three there—all too often appearing among contacts of earlier victims who had been seen by EIS workers and were already taking full doses of prophylactic antibiotics. Carlos Quintana was slightly cheered that a few of these people were only developing the bubonic form of the disease, with raging fevers and circulatory collapse and swollen, painful, draining glands but none of the devastating respiratory symptoms—"But not many of them," he reported to Ted Bettendorf, "not nearly enough. The balance is all wrong." People wore face masks, supplied for free at the Public Library in Canon City, when they went out; others wore bandanas over their faces like western-movie bandits. Nobody knew if either did any good.

On the third night after the broadcast, at 2:30 A.M., the manager of the local bank and one of Canon City's social and business pillars packed his wife and two children and dog and stereo set into the back end of his van and took off down the highway for parts unknown, leaving the house lights on and the doors banging and all of their furniture right where it was. The protective antibiotic they all had been taking was left on a bathroom shelf, an unfortunate oversight. By morning the whole town knew they were gone. Rumor had it that they had headed down toward Texas, but despite this, and very suddenly, Getting Out Of There seemed to be an idea whose time had come. By noon an alarming assortment of cars, vans, trucks, pickups, Jeeps and even tractors began moving out of town in all directions, first a few, then a steady stream, by nightfall a deluge. Carlos and his people pleaded, the local radio station pleaded, the town councilmen pleaded—the ones who hadn't left—but people kept on moving. The State Patrol set up hasty roadblocks to try to screen the outflow, in the midst of one of the torrential summer thunderstorms that swept in from the plains that afternoon; the roadblocks obstructed things somewhat but did not stop the movement because even the State patrol was not sure that they could legally block traffic indefinitely, and in the face of outraged challenges didn't quite dare stop someone from going through in a legally licensed vehicle. In the midst of one roadblock, in a narrow gap between the sandstone hills west of Canon City on the road toward the Royal Gorge, a superannuated farm truck piled high with household goods overturned across both lanes of the highway, effectively blocking traffic from *both* directions and trapping a whole caravan of rubberneckers who had been coming from the west to have a look (from behind closed car windows) firsthand at the "Plague City." The net result could not have been a greater mess if a chunk of road had been blocked by a mudslide; there were cars in ditches, cars backed into each other, trucks driven halfway up hillsides and turned over, people screaming at each other from car windows, patrol cars with blue flashers blinking, helplessly entrapped in the middle of the mess, patrolmen wandering past each other in opposite directions waving their arms and shouting bullhorn orders that nobody whosoever paid any attention to, children and dogs and a few chickens running wild underfoot. . . . Carlos Quintana got a survey look at it all from a Forest Service chopper that made a couple of low sweeps over the scene of carnage, and nodded his head glumly. "It figures," he said, "it's all part of the pattern. And it hasn't even started yet. Get me back to town, okay? I've got work to do."

22

In their second-story tenement in south Chicago, Sidonia Harper and her mother watched the nationwide network rebroadcast of the JTLM-TV show on their ancient black-and-white set, Sidonia from her wheelchair in the living room, her mother from the adjoining kitchen. When it was over the girl sat clutching her arms across her breast, hearing the summer sounds coming in the screenless window, shaking her head. "That's no good," she said finally. "That's no good for anybody."

"Ain't nothin' to worry about," her mother said, putting down her cooking spoon. "That's way out west there."

"They said it was rats that caused it," Sidonia said.

"I think them's *western* rats," her mother said dubiously.

"Don't matter where the rats are," Siddie said. She waved her hand toward the window. "You ever look down in that alley, just when it gettin' dark? Got rats all over down there. Come in the door at night, up the stairs. You seen 'em well as I have."

"Honey, we can't do nothin' about *them* rats. They always been there. What you worryin' about?"

"Don't have to have 'em," Sidonia said. "Nasty things, gnawed Miz Berry's baby's ears off. We could get rid of them."

"How?"

"Man come around, over in the block where Jerry live, over near the park. Gov'mint man, talked to everybody in the block. Laid out traps and poison down in the basements, long as people promise to pick up their garbage, clean up the trash a little. Used gas in one of the empty buildings, killed a lot of rats. Man said they keep workin' at it, they gon' be a rat-free block pretty soon. Lots of blocks already that way. Why not this one?"

Her mother laughed. "Ain't no man been around here, honey."

"Maybe we ought to get 'em."

"Well, you work on it, Siddie. Maybe you can get a gov'mint man to come round. No harm tryin', I suppose."

The girl looked at her mother retiring back to the kitchen, a long, level look her mother didn't see. Then she wheeled her chair over to the window and gazed down to the darkening street. "Maybe I will," she said, too quiet for her mother to hear. "Maybe just do that. Lots of things people think you can't do, you can do all right." She looked down at her withered legs. "Lots of things."

23

Yersinia pestis was the name Monique Jenrette best knew it by. Textbooks described it as a poorly staining gram-negative rod-shaped bacillus fatally pathogenic to certain rodents, certain other mammals, and man. Unlike the viruses, *Yersinia* was not an obligate parasite—it did not require living cells in which to propagate. It would grow and multiply quite vigorously in cell-free dilutions of blood plasma, on certain nutrient agar plates, or in various pH-controlled sugar or peptide solutions. Stained with Wilson's stain, a special preparation from which the organism took up staining pigment more readily than from others, it looked like a pale, slightly bent rod with bits of genetic material staining more heavily in each end, thus appearing under the microscope lens rather like a tiny closed safety pin.

All this, of course, you could learn from any textbook. Monique Jenrette was concerned about things you could not find in any textbook.

In the special Hot Lab she was charged with setting up and supervising at the CDC installation in Fort Collins in northern Colorado—a rigidly structured, high-security lab designed for the safe propagation and study of violently dangerous bacterial organisms. She was joined by a team of microbiologists flown in from Stanford and the University of Washington, people thoroughly skilled in bacteriologic techniques. Three of them were particularly experienced in recombinant DNA studies with gram-negative bacilli, one of them a prominent Nobel Prize contender for his work pioneering techniques to recombine the genetic material in certain harmless coliform bacilli to make them produce gamma-interferons, growth hormone, Hepatitis B vaccine antigen and multiple sclerosis neutralizing factor. None except Monique had any particular personal experience working with *Yersinia pestis,* and none had more than a nodding acquaintance with high-security Hot Lab procedures.

The materials they had to work with, at first, were none of the best: cultures taken from early victims, mostly in Washington State and a few later ones from Colorado, that had been old when originally flown to the lab in Atlanta for confirmation and now had been plated and replated waiting for somebody to come and do something with them. Many bacterial strains, having been grown and regrown through repeated reculturings, would typically begin losing certain of their characteristics, changing themselves, altering their behavior, especially "frail" bacteria such as *Yersinia* strains. Under Monique's guidance the team at Fort Collins did what they could do in studying bacteria from these cultures, plating them against antibiotics, performing various fermentation tests and agglutination tests to identify genetic characteristics, undertaking animal inoculations to document infection patterns and virulence, but for all their care, the results were unpredictable, varying from specimen to specimen from the same culture, sometimes positive, sometimes negative, sometimes indeterminate. They worked in a specially sealed, specially ventilated wing of a lab building, scrubbed, gowned, masked and gloved under the full aseptic precautions of any surgeon in an operating room about to perform open-heart surgery; inside the lab they did their work in a long, sealed, transparent tunnel, using built-in shoulder-length rubber gloves to manipulate specimens, nutrient tubes, culture plates, incubator trays, equipment for enzyme and protein assays and so forth. Death was afoot inside that sealed transparent tunnel, invisible and treacherous and silent and very final; there must be no possible way for any trace of it to escape while they studied the unnatural quality of it.

Those first studies were suggestive, perhaps, but maddeningly inconclusive. Monique knew full well that hundreds, perhaps thousands, of people were going to have their lives altered by what might be discovered in that sealed transparent tunnel; at the very least they had to find out what it was those people were dealing with; at the most, her work here might reveal to her colleagues what they might best do. But she couldn't commit them to widespread action on the basis of inconclusive data. From time to time, like maybe about once every hour during those first few sixteen-hour days, she wished that she were working in the absolutely fail-safe, microbiologically flawless Maximum Security Lab in Atlanta, a sterile room within a sterile room within a sterile room, confining Death from any possible escape within a nest of laboratories built like a nest of boxes—but perhaps, she consoled herself, that would be overkill when dealing with a mere antibiotic-vulnerable bacterium. Maxi had been built for studying and manipulating the truly terrifying and world-threatening viral killers: the Lassa fever virus, the Marburg virus, the hideous Argentine bovine encephalitis virus that turned ninety-eight percent of its human victims into turnips in forty-eight hours—all virulently infective new viral agents with largely unknown spread characteristics, staggeringly high mortality rates, no vaccine whatever and no known treatment. But if *Yersinia pestis* was really so much less frightening, so much more benign than those wild viral bastards, then why was she suddenly breaking out in sweats and having waking nightmare fantasies every time she walked into this lab?

On her third day there the first chipmunk arrived by special courier, reaching her not terribly long after having been bagged by Carlos and Frank in the wild. *Fresh meat, indeed.* Well, Monique was ready for it. The bag went into a separate, sealed tank in the sealed, transparent tunnel, relieved of the outer transportation bag, which itself was sent down the belt to the autoclave and thence to the incinerator. The polybag inside was filled with fleas no longer interested in the dead, cold rodent hulk they had once inhabited; they were hopping about on its nose and eyes, on its belly, and swarming around on the inside of the bag. Telephone conversations ensued with some rather specialized people in Atlanta to figure the best agent to use under Hot Lab circumstances in order to kill eggs as well as fleas, to get them all, but as dead as possible. A nonflammable gas was chosen and applied to the polybag in a pressure-cooker affair, capable of permeating the capture bag without opening it. Two hours should be plenty of time, but let's give it three just the same. Endless minutes spent waiting out the time; Monique broke scrub and paced the adjoining corridor for a while, nervous as a cat, smoking one of her rare cigarettes—*God forbid this job should drive me back to that foolishness again.* Finally, after a full three hours the cooker was opened, the bag opened in the long transparent tunnel, and a million dead fleas collected, six million eggs, totaling about a half-tablespoon of specimen. The dead fleas and eggs crushed in a special nonporous quartz-crystal device. Half of the material was placed in a special holding broth for later use, the rest divided in hundreds of aliquots for initial plating and culturing that had been so carefully planned.

Then, finally, there was the chipmunk itself. Body fluids cultured—blood, urine, lymph, spinal fluid, using microcollection techniques devised by one of the UW men. Cultures from organs and tissues—lymph glands, liver, kidney, fascia, muscle, lung—yes, by all means, lung—even eye vitreous. Into the incubator. Labeling, numbering, computer-keying, working furiously, then waiting. Hurrying again, then waiting. Out for a bite of dinner that nobody felt like eating. Then waiting again.

Within six hours they knew that the fleas were teeming with very live *Yersinia.* That meant the chipmunk was too. *But what kind of Yersinia? What nature of deadly beast?* Monique huddled with the others for a final hour, reviewing once again the protocol, the order and urgency of studies they could start tomorrow when growth would be far enough advanced to start working, *really* working, determining once again who would be responsible for what so that not a waking hour would be wasted.

Teeming with Yersinia. Monique went back to her motel room, sweat-soaked, drenched from the skin out, underwear, outer clothes, hair, forehead. *Teeming.* She took a fast shower and fell into bed and dreamed of an imaginary Pamela Tate she had never met. Her last conscious thought before sleeping was: *Soon we will know.*

Each day brought new rodent specimens to process. On the third day, while the first answers they sought were still cooking—Monique profoundly hoped—in nutrient flasks, with the computer programmed and ready to handle an expanding volume of microbiological genetic data when finally it was ready, Frank Barrington appeared to hand deliver yet another specimen, a golden-sided ground squirrel in one of Carlos's bags, catching Monique just as she was leaving the lab for the evening. "I've been walking ridges and gullies for five days now," he said, "up in the mountains, watching the ground, and I decided a break would be a smart idea."

"Oh, good," Monique said. She took the bag, peered at it. "Where is this one from? It's important we have samples from a wide area."

"Each one has been from a different region. We got this one about noon today from the Red Feather Lakes area just a few miles north of here, near the Wyoming border."

"Ah, so. And I thought you'd come all the way up from Canon City just to see me." She smiled at him. "You're staying over tonight?"

"Right. Then tomorrow we'll hit the lower reaches of Estes Park."

"Sounds good. And what's going on down south? I've barely heard from Carlos since I got here."

Frank spread his hands. "They're going crazy down there. New cases in seven different communities so far, including Colorado Springs, but mostly in Canon City. Twenty new ones just yesterday, the last I heard. It's getting way ahead of them just trying to track down new contacts, and Carlos is looking kind of gray. Parke-Davis doesn't seem to believe the amount of chloramphenicol he wants, they keep shipping half-orders, and he's using streptomycin on suspect cases now, right from the first." The forester shrugged his big shoulders. "They're short on data, that's the real problem. They're floundering around blind, don't really know what they're dealing with." He looked at her. "You'd better realize they're waiting for you to pull a rabbit out of the hat up here."

"I know." she sighed. "But I can't create answers overnight. And right now, if I don't get out of this place for a few hours and forget about this whole hideous thing, I'm going to start smashing windows and climbing walls. Look, this little fellow in the bag here has to be taken care of right away, that's four hours' work at least, but maybe I can sweet-talk the guys from Stanford into doing it for me. Let me drop it in their laps and go back to change, and then you take me out to dinner—would that be nice?"

Frank hadn't planned it that way, uncertain as he was of her lab hours or the demands on her time, but he had certainly thought often enough of this tall, oddly beautiful girl with the violet eyes and red-blond hair, as he had walked the ridges and searched the ground for his quarry. Certainly Monique was as totally different from Pam as night from day, and the wound of Pam's loss was far too raw and immediate for him to turn his mind seriously to anything but the pain and emptiness. Yet there were odd moments when Monique's expressions and gestures and way of speaking evoked Pam as sharply and bitterly as Pam herself had; justification or not, he somehow felt that Pam would approve this slender, hard-driving woman—at least approve what she was doing and the intensity she was bringing to the job. So Frank was both pleased and relieved at Monique's proposal, pleased at the prospect of her evening company, half relieved that she had made the first move—*as Pam would have done.* He agreed to pick her up at her motel room in an hour, and then departed for his own simple lodgings out at the edge of town to shower and shave and dress. When he arrived to pick her up she was still in a slip, doing interesting things to her hair, but she waved him toward an ice bucket and some good bourbon and he settled down to an hour's contemplative wait. "You won't mind in the end, I betcha," she shouted through the bathroom door. "I haven't worn anything but jeans and a T-shirt for a solid week, and I'm damned if I'm going out looking raggy, so just drink up and be patient. . . ."

She did not, in the end, look raggy; she looked almost painfully lovely. They took Frank's Forest Service Jeep, found a modest but respectable steak house in town, and ordered another drink before tackling the menu. Frank lifted his glass and touched hers. "Eat, drink and be merry," he said.

She winced. "Any more of that, and I get up and leave," she said. "Graveyard humor I can't take right now. Nor lab talk. Nor plague talk."

"Sorry. Really. I just wasn't thinking."

They talked about other things, inconsequential things, new-acquaintance things, as the meal came and went. She clearly wanted to talk, and he let her, sensing the sharp undercurrent of tension in her voice. *She's tight as a wire,* he thought, *tight to the breaking point—from what? From what she's fearing that I don't know enough to fear?* He guided the talk to herself, who she was, where she had come from. Two more different people might never have been found, except that both were rebels in their own odd ways. Monique Jenrette, only child of a wealthy New Orleans architect representing very old money, sent to a highly selective finishing school for Young Southern Ladies in Baton Rouge. They had nearly finished her then and there, but she had been pretty resilient even then. Bowing to her father, she had spent a year at Smith as an English major, where she lost a little of her thick New Orleans drawl and acquired a thoroughly curious overlay of Back Bay Massachusetts nasal that she never entirely weeded out—together with a bitter hatred of northern winters. Perversely, then, she had transferred to Duke, sweet-talking her father into tolerating it if not liking it, and graduated magna cum laude in biological sciences. Well, medical school was at least *respectable,* and she had gone on to Emory in Atlanta with medicine in mind, but an uncanny knack for thinking her way through complex and labyrinthine biochemical problems and then finding insanely simple, practical laboratory techniques for solving them, got her sidetracked from the medical mainstream within a year and a half. She had never really wanted to palpate bellies and examine tonsils; what she came to want was to find ways to make microorganisms do what she told them to do and nothing else, and she soon was concentrating her total attention on the arcane and mysterious world of cutting-edge microbiology. For her Ph.D. thesis she had worked two additional years to compare the natural mutational behavior of three exotic families of bacteria, among them the family of *Yersinia.* With that accomplished, and with a small but growing reputation for somewhat outré thinking about bacterial genetics and mutations, and a positive flair for creative laboratory techniques, she had left the multicolored stone walls of Emory to move six blocks up the street to the Centers for Disease Control, with their microbiological laboratories unequaled anywhere in the world, and their endless succession of microbiological problems to be solved.

Through all this, of course, Monique being Monique, there had been men, two of them almost serious enough for her to have thought of marriage, but not *quite* serious enough, with neither man quite capable of accepting the notion that this rather frail-looking, willowy girl might have a will of iron and a driving ambition and an acknowledged national name in a field of science they could barely understand at all, so nothing ultimately happened. *And then, of course, there was Carlos. Yes indeed, Carlos.*

Frank Barrington contributed bits of his background as Monique's torrents of words slowed, a simpler and briefer background and a total counterpoint except for the common thread of an abortive entry into medical school years before. Only son of a self-educated farmer, born and raised on a wheat ranch in the Palouse country of southeastern Washington. Taught to read at the age of four at his mother's knee, with freedom of the rather surprising family library that made up for the lack of any public or school library whatever anywhere within reach. Long hours and days and months and years in the blazing sun, helping tend the farm; attendance at a tiny one-room grade school taught by a teacher with a tiny one-room mind, then on to a slightly-less-tiny high school, created to grant obligatory diplomas, but nothing to trigger a hungry mind beyond the books at home.

The natural science of field and stream, heritage of any farm boy, had appealed to Frank early and led to a solid interest in biology and, later, medicine. He started college in a forestry major, graduated in a zoology major, and moved on to medicine, uncertain that he wanted it but willing to try. Family tragedy broke that up: his mother's sudden and shocking death from pneumonia, and then, in the same year, the pancreatic cancer that took his father, the loss of the farm, of all funds, and of the ambition for medicine. . . .

A forest fire in Idaho late that terrible year triggered something else. Frank went over as a volunteer to help fight the blaze and spent two weeks digging fire lines, hauling hoses, filling tank trucks from natural springs and breathing smoke and ash. As a result, he was offered a job with the Forest Service the next summer on a first-strike fire crew, and that work blossomed into a full-time appointment. He went back for night courses in forest management, evolving a strong conservationist attitude toward the local logging practices that somebody in the Forest Service in western Washington liked; there was room there for someone willing to fight for real, rational management of the forests and to oppose the pressures to cut them all down as fast as possible and ship the logs to Japan. In the logging industry he wouldn't have lasted long; in the Forest Service there was a chance to be heard as he entered into what he clearly conceived might be a lifelong battle.

Monique had listened closely as they devoured their steaks, skipped dessert, sipped coffee and finished their wine. He touched only briefly on the direction his work had been taking him in the time he had free from slash fires—for example, his plans for simple but supremely logical small-scale studies to document the permanent environment-changing effects of logging at the forest-desert margin. "Where the forest in the foothills comes down in fingers into semiarid land, there isn't enough water for any recovery if the trees are taken," he said. "The ones that are there are scrubby, hardly worth harvesting, but they may be hundreds of years old, marginally surviving because they have enormously deep tap roots and themselves hold water in the soil. Cut them out, and little ones will never grow back, and the desert will creep up the mountainside, acre by acre. I can't do anything big with it, of course. But with luck and a little work I can maybe get a few reports published in *Science,* small-scale studies, and maybe catch somebody's attention."

"And Pam fit into that plan," Monique said.

"Oh, yes. She fit into the whole Forest Service kind of life." Frank was silent for a moment. "Lots of women wouldn't. There's no money in it, ever, and you're off and away three-quarters of the time, and there are—very real hazards." He grimaced.

"I'm sorry," Monique said, touching his hand across the table. "I shouldn't have mentioned it."

"It doesn't bother me that much. Not now. It already seems like a long, long time ago."

"The mind's a remarkable mechanism. It works like lightning to protect itself from too much pain. Sometimes it works almost indecently fast. But then, sometimes remembering and talking can help."

"Maybe. There's not that much to talk about, with Pam. She turned up out of nowhere, one day, and then she disappeared, like the girl in the Keats poem. We only had three months together, not even that—what can you say about three months? That for me it was a whole other lifetime? A sort of dream world, come and gone? Maybe so, but that lifetime is over. It's not ever coming back. End of story." He looked up at her sharply. "Not for you, of course. You do have your Carlos."

Monique glanced aside. "Yes, I have my Carlos, and he is a very lovely man, sweet and gentle and smart and capable, a man any woman could love. And Carlos is also very, very married to a proud and exquisitely beautiful woman from a proud upper-class Mexican family, and his background is so deeply entrenched in him that that marriage is never going to change. Carlos behaves himself in the way the men in his culture are permitted to behave, and his wife conducts herself in the way such wives are required to conduct themselves, and that is that. Another dream world." She gave Frank's hand a squeeze and pushed her chair back from the table. "Why don't we go see the sights before it's totally dark out there?"

He drove the Jeep toward the setting sun along the valley floor, then turned west on a road into the steeply rising mountains. Half an hour later they found a turnout on a high viewpoint ridge. To the west the sun was setting behind the high peaks of the Rockies in Estes Park, splattering the sky and clouds with reds and oranges and pinks and yellows and blues and blacks as an evening thunderstorm came billowing up. To the south and east the lights of Fort Collins were coming on in multicolors, the freeway strip to the east a shimmering golden necklace.

They got out of the car and walked out on a promontory to take in the panorama. There was a chill breeze from the west; Monique shivered in her summery dress and Frank slipped his down jacket over her shoulders and held it in place with his arm. "You're still not relaxing," he said.

"I can't," she said after a long silence. "I can't get away from that lab. The world looks so beautiful from up here, but I have to work with ugliness."

"You don't have to. You could go back home and marry a rich New Orleans lawyer and be a society lady."

She gave him a brief look. "I'm not precisely a lady. And New Orleans society is a screaming bore. So are most rich New Orleans lawyers. Anyway, I can't run away from what I'm doing—not now. I'm really into it up to my ears, and there you are."

"You personally?"

"Somebody personally has got to do it. I'm equipped, and I'm on the spot. People are dropping dead while I fool around with culture plates. We need to know which way this evil wind is blowing, and I haven't got the answers yet." She shivered in spite of the jacket. "Let's go back, Frank."

They drove in silence back to town. Her place was a second-story room with an outside entrance. He opened her door and turned and kissed her, tentatively. She returned a different kiss, long and deep and yielding. When he started to turn away she said, "Frank Barrington, don't you dare walk away from me tonight."

He looked down at her pale face, the wide-set, frightened eyes looking up at him like a doe terrified at the approaching fireline, and he couldn't move.

Suddenly her arms were around him, clinging to him fiercely, and her face was buried in his chest and he realized she was weeping. "Hey, hey," he said gently, stroking her hair. "Take it easy—"

"I can't take it easy, Frank. I'm scared. You just don't know how scared I am." She looked up, holding him with her eyes. "Stay and help me not be scared tonight."

24

The really sick people in the poverty ghettos of the great cities never find their way to the free clinics and charity wards for examination and treatment. Those places are packed with the ones who have the minor or nonexistent aches and pains, the ones with nothing whatever else to do, who look forward to the daily or biweekly clinic visit as a major social event and grand diversion from dullness. For the really sick ones, the desperately ill, these places are torment. The crowded corridors, the hard benches lining the walls, the endless waits while their eligibility numbers are transmitted and approved, the longer waits for the nurse, the doctor, the laboratory, the X ray, the other doctor, the third and fourth and fifth doctors—these things they know are in store for them are literally more than they can stand. They stay home in bed, the desperately ill, unexamined and untreated, getting sicker, and if they die, well, after all, they could have gone to the clinic, couldn't they? But since they didn't, that's one less we have to be bothered with. . . .

For Althea Willis, the tall black cabin attendant on the flight from Denver to Atlanta, things might conceivably have been different, but they weren't. The culture and background and habit she could not escape defeated her in the end. Her contract with Eastern Airlines provided her not only a modest salary, much of which she had salted away for later college expenses, but also an excellent prepaid private health-care plan. When she became ill, she could have gone to any private physician in Savannah. She *knew* she could have done that, but she didn't. It would have meant no expense to her, and only a modest wait for the doctor, and she knew that too, but she didn't go. For one thing, it all came on so terribly fast she couldn't believe what was happening. One hour she felt fine. An hour later she was feverish and chilling, the next hour delirious. And the sicker she became, the more her buried, bone-deep ghetto background rose up to control her mind and body. The modern, liberated Althea Willis she thought she had become vanished from sight in the first few hours of trial. The old Althea Willis went to bed and took age-old remedies her frightened sisters brought her, and grew violently sicker.

When she finally died and lay in state in a ragged bed in a shambling, rotting frame house in center-city Savannah, neighbors and friends and curious acquaintances by the dozens came through to pay their respects and to grieve with her mother, and then pass on and go back to their own ragtag frame tenements west of Forsythe Park, until at last the long black car of the funeral director, one of their own, came to take her away, and no one thought for a minute that anything different might have happened.

25

And throughout those first five days, six days, seven days, in Colorado, as the growing list of sick was counted and contacts were relentlessly traced down, and isolation techniques were tightened, and word of some kind, any kind, was awaited from Fort Collins, Carlos Quintana moved through it all like a thin omnipresent wraith, working eighteen-hour days, looking grayer every day and somehow keeping in daily personal contact with virtually every one of the hundred-odd people who were working with him now. He was a ramrod, demanding hard, perfectionist labor, but he was a gentle ramrod, ready with a wry grin or a word of encouragement whenever he sensed the need of it. He wanted results, not fights, and he did not make the tempting mistake of blaming his crew for the steadily climbing count of newly infected cases, up well over 150 in the first week alone and still climbing, including five of his own people. The mortality rate was over eighty-three percent among those first cases, a horrendous figure that only barely began leveling off as they poured in all the antibiotic resources they had available. He maintained to each of his workers the same repeated point, made over and over again, relentlessly: don't look at the short term, it had a terrible start on us, but we're surely closing the gap. The work we're doing now will catch up if we do it well and meticulously and thoroughly, it *has* to catch up, and the thing will peak and begin to drop off, and new data will help with that when we have it. Keep digging. . . .

Yet through it all there was an odd, fatalistic air about Carlos Quintana that others could sense but not quite identify. True, he breathed confidence that this present battle would be contained sooner or later—but he was clearly under no illusions but that other and worse battles would face them at other times and other places. It was not just his long professional acquaintance with the history of the black killer facing him here; far more, it was his own, personal, deep-grained cultural heritage—an ever-present awareness of the imminent presence of death.

Carlos Quintana came from hardy Spanish and Indian stock, traceable back for well over three hundred years by the omniscient eye of family tradition, although no written records had ever been kept. In the time of the Great Depression his father had been thrown back across the Rio Grande four separate times before he finally managed to evade the American Federales long enough to reach quiet, unpatrolled saguaro desert and walk to Tucson and thence, on foot or swinging aboard ranch trucks, on east to Albuquerque where family friends sequestered him long enough to teach him rudimentary English. At the time, it had seemed an odd direction to go. If Emiliano Quintana had been an ordinary Mexican peasant or farm worker, he would have made his way west to join the California *braceros,* or northwest to the orchards of Oregon and Washington, or northeast to the big Kansas harvests, and lived in an eight-by-eight-foot box without a toilet and worked for peppercorn wages when work was there and starved when it wasn't, living only one tiny bit better than any Mexican peasant or farm worker might live below the border.

But Emiliano Quintana was not an ordinary peasant or farm worker. He was a city boy from a Chihuahua slum who had, in his own city, with much hustling and fighting for jobs and reading of manuals, become a singularly excellent seat-of-the-pants truck mechanic. He left Chihuahua only when he could not advance further because the boss's son, and his nephew, and his son-in-law were all in line for the good jobs—but it was Emiliano who had made the truck motors purr, not those others. In Albuquerque his friends found him a job of sorts, a bottom-rung grease monkey at a truck stop, but soon he was full mechanic, and presently shop foreman. One day his boss, well pleased with a mechanic who could make trucks purr the way he could, and not wishing to have him deported, withheld $100 from his pay, and spoke to a certain man in Albuquerque who quite swiftly produced perfectly legal naturalization papers for Emiliano—and then the boss raised his pay to help cover the cost.

Only then did Emiliano Quintana return briefly to Mexico, to the city of Chihuahua, to formally court and marry a beautiful woman with large, dark eyes, daughter of a respectable Mexican family, and bring her back to Albuquerque with him. With her, *muy macho,* he conceived three sons—Carlos, Jesús, Ramón—before an endless string of daughters appeared, and all three boys had their mother's large, dark eyes and handsome good looks, and their father's patient drive and willingness to work. They were that commonplace anomaly in the Southwest, the totally American family with ninety-five percent Mexican characteristics. Their food, their religion and their mores were straight from Old México. They spoke Spanish exclusively in the home, but never outside it, and the boys all grew up with perfect

English. They lived in a small modest home in an acceptable part of the city, and saved money, and celebrated the Day of the Dead with illegal firecrackers and little skull-shaped candies and cookies made with loving care, and like all Mexican families, death was part of their thinking, always nearby, always imminent.

Carlos was the scholar among the boys, bright and interested and energetic, passing through grade school and high school like a breeze, then on to the University of New Mexico to study biology. When the time came for application to medical school, he could not quite meet the academic level of the prime candidates, he had sown too many wild oats in college instead of studying—but suddenly (and inexplicably, to his father, who could not understand such things) his status as a Mexican-American worked in his favor: at precisely the right time, certain government regulations left the medical school at the University of Iowa suddenly, desperately searching for one live Mexican-American applicant, never mind his grade-point average as long as he was breathing—and Carlos went to medical school.

The rest followed naturally. The wild oats were over, and he led his class. A growing inclination toward epidemiology carried him on. An internship in the Public Health Service followed, with work in the Epidemic Intelligence Service—one of the Shoeleather Boys. A job with the CDC came next, and presently a special interest in plague, partly because he was fascinated by the disease and partly because nine-tenths of the cases that appeared each year turned up in New Mexico and Arizona among Spanish-speaking people, and he could speak Spanish. He found a strange satisfaction in his encounters with plague, in unmasking it, fighting it, stopping it, in case after case after case. But always, entrenched in his mind and never far from the surface, was a clear recognition that plague was *La Muerte,* death on horseback, and however hard you fought it, it was never going away. . . .

26

Council of war. On the eighth day after Carlos and Monique's arrival in Colorado, they met with their top people at the Fort Collins CDC installation, purposely trying to keep the meeting small and elite enough that data could be digested swiftly and firm operative plans agreed on without delay. Monique was there with all of her crew except the two who were on duty then and there in the lab. Carlos brought two of his top Shoeleather lieutenants, representatives of the Denver and Colorado Springs city/county health departments' epidemiological staffs, a Parke-Davis official who had flown west to try to unsnarl the supply problem with the chloramphenicol, a couple of others. Frank Barrington's presence was a little anomalous, but then his position had been a little anomalous right from the start, and he had proven himself far too useful not to have him around. Carlos had taken one look at Frank and Monique talking quietly and intensely, heads together over coffee in the conference room, and thought whatever thoughts that single look had led him to think, and raised his eyebrows to himself, and kept his mouth shut. Roger Salmon, the project coordinator at Fort Collins, was on the phone to Atlanta a little overlong, but as soon as he joined the group, Carlos nodded and stood up. "Okay, I have the Canon City figures up to last night. Do you want the figures first, or do you want Monique's report first?"

"Let's hear Monique first," the coordinator said. "She may help us make more sense out of the figures." There was a murmur of assent around the room.

"Okay, my dear, you have the floor."

Monique looked exhausted, her face pale, her hair done back carelessly in a bun. "Well, I have good news and bad news," she said. "The good news is that the whole state of Colorado isn't infected yet. The bad news is that it has to be some sort of miracle that it isn't."

"Better enlarge on that," Roger Salmon said.

"Of course. First of all, just to dispel any lingering doubts, the organism we are dealing with is definitely *Yersinia pestis,* and the infection is plague. There simply isn't any question about that. We have some twenty-three separate biochemical and genetic markers we can use to identify the genus *Yersinia* and an additional eleven markers to put the cross hairs on the species *pestis*. Granted, you *never* hit all of these markers with any given strain. We'll accept fourteen or fifteen markers as proof of *Yersinia,* for example; this strain exhibits nineteen. Seven or more *pestis* markers are pretty definite proof of species; here we have eight, so we're dealing with a strain of *pestis.* The problem is that we also have half a dozen additional and totally bizarre species markers that don't match anything we've ever encountered before."

"Which means what?" Carlos asked.

"Which means we are dealing with a wild mutant," Monique said. "A strain of plague organism that has undergone a natural genetic change, and almost certainly a very major change."

"So we need to know what change, precisely, and in what directions," Carlos said.

"Yes. Well, I have some answers there, and you're not going to like them." Monique took a piece of chalk to the blackboard. "It's not exactly news anymore that practically any microorganism can undergo mutation or genetic change under certain circumstances. There are a million different mechanisms. A piece of DNA can break off and not get repaired, or get stuck back on incorrectly. Genes can be obliterated or replicated and stuck on in triplicate or just about anything you can imagine. Whole pieces of chromosome can get stuck back on the wrong base, or get teamed up into threesomes. Well over ninety-nine percent of all such mutational changes are going to be dead ends—they're strictly nonsurvival, either leaving the organism fatally vulnerable to its environment or preventing reproduction in some way so the mutation hits a brick wall and dies."

Monique went back to her chair. "Some organisms do this sort of thing more than others. Certain viruses mutate like mad, but they're simple to figure out. Bacteria are more complex. Some, like the tuberculosis bacilli, don't mutate much at all. The red-bugs killing Alaskan Eskimos today are virtually identical genetically to the ones that killed Mimi in *La Bohème* ninety years ago." Monique paused. "Unfortunately, most of the *Yersinia* group, including the *pestis* or plague organism, tend to mutate constantly. That's why no one strain exhibits all the identifying markers—some have lost some markers, while others have gained new ones we haven't identified yet. The point is, they *change.*"

"Why them and not others?" one of the public-health men asked.

"This we don't know. We can do things in the laboratory to *make* them change, but that's not what we're talking about. Some changes come about as a result of natural selection in the face of a hostile environment—that's why so few staph strains can be touched by penicillin anymore, and why we have so many penicillin-resistant gonococci around today. Maybe the *Yersinia* are extraordinarily sensitive to natural radiation. Maybe they have certain genes that *direct* mutation in a random fashion. It hasn't been studied enough to know. We just know they do change, sort of constantly."

"Then why aren't we constantly having bizarre new strains turning up in epidemics?"

"Probably because most of the changes aren't that big. How can I put it? We could say that *Yersinia* mutations fall into two classes: minor and major. A minor mutation, most common by far, may cause no detectable change in the organism's behavior at all, or at least no change that makes any difference. Say there's a minor DNA rearrangement, involving just one tiny bit of a strand, and all it does is alter the nature of some minor enzyme system, so the organism only makes two-thirds as much of that enzyme as formerly. So maybe all we would notice would be that that strain of organism, inoculated into a variety of sugar solutions, only seems to ferment two-thirds as much galactose as it used to. Same fermentation as before in all the other sugars, but the galactose consistently less. All right, this is a new marker; it tells us there's been a mutation that affects the amount of galactose-fermenting enzyme—but so what? It doesn't change the behavior of the organism in any way that matters to us. We can't even tell for sure if it's a survival or nonsurvival change for the organism."

"We'd worry, though, if the mutation altered an enzyme system in a way that makes the organism more resistant to chloramphenicol, wouldn't we?" Carlos said.

"Right. We'd call that a major mutation, because it would bother us as epidemiologists. A mutation that helps a plague organism survive and resist an antibiotic—that's a major mutation, as far as we're concerned. It could just be an enzyme change, or a co-enzyme change, or a vitamin change, or a dozen other things, but it could mean trouble. Another mutation might alter the biochemical toughness of the organism, enable it to survive and reproduce better in a marginal environment, so it's harder to kill. Still another kind might affect virulence—the ability to cause disease, the seriousness of the disease, the incubation period it needs once it's invaded a host. With *Yersinia pestis*, any such change could be exceedingly dangerous."

"So what do we have down in Canon City?" Carlos asked.

Monique took a deep breath. "We've got an organism that's jumped the fence," she said. "From what we can see, there are two or three major changes back to back—changes involving a whole sequence of genes. This bug is still plague, but it's different from any plague bug we've ever dealt with before. It's incredibly virulent—it gets in under body defenses so fast that there's already a raging septicemia before normal defense mechanisms even get the word that there's been an invasion. I know it's ridiculous to talk about an incubation period of only twelve hours before the infection is entrenched, but that's what we're looking at. There is some toxin produced that breaks down cell walls directly and converts normal intracellular protoplasm into a fantastic growth medium for this organism. You know what a staph organism can do to a bowlful of unrefrigerated chicken salad in about six hours. It can turn it into a bowlful of poison—except that the staph bug and its poison just give you a few hours of diarrhea. This plague bug invades soft tissues, invades the blood, invades the lymph and lymph glands, and starts ruining capillaries all over the body, all in a matter of hours. Worse yet, it thromboses capillaries in the lungs very early, jams them up tight, and then begins suppurating, eating right through the lung tissue itself and creating a fast-moving pneumonia. Ordinary plague only takes this pneumonic form in about fifteen percent or less of cases. This bug goes pneumonic in over eighty-five percent of our test animals, and I think Carlos will confirm that it's doing that in humans too. It also follows the classical pattern of spread: infected rodent to flea to uninfected rodent—or to man, if the flea gets to him first—but once the man is infected, the course of disease is still likely to go to pneumonic infection, which means *direct respiratory spread, person-to-person.* That's what hit that Comstock crowd so fast, and that's what's hitting everybody else."

"But what's wrong with the antibiotics?" the Denver public-health man burst out. "Chloramphenicol and streptomycin should stop plague, by my book, once you pin it down, but they're not working here. Are you saying it's just the timing? The bug is moving too fast?"

"I wish that were all," Monique said, "but it's not just the timing. This bug shows only about twenty-eight percent sensitivity to streptomycin, seventeen percent to chloramphenicol and none whatever to tetracycline—our three major antibiotics against plague. Those figures have to represent mutation; they're far, far lower than anything in our previous plague experience. In plain language, those drugs are not going to help very much, even if we could get them into patients early enough. With pneumonic disease spreading from person to person, and with modern air-travel patterns, an unsuspecting contact could be across the country—or across the ocean—before he begins to get symptoms, and have nothing to help him when he does." Monique pushed a wisp of hair away from her face and looked around. "It's not a pretty picture. And if you ask me how a mutated organism like this can turn up in Washington State and almost simultaneously in wild rodents in central Colorado, I can't tell you how, but it's done so. The earliest samples from up in Washington State show precisely the same mutation pattern as fresh samples from wild rodents down here in Colorado. Well, when you've eliminated the impossible, whatever is left has to be true. It just defies belief that identical, highly complex mutations of this sort could have occurred simultaneously, without any connection, in two such widely separated areas. Scientifically, it just couldn't happen. It *had* to spread by way of rodents and fleas. The only possible answer is that it's been spreading like wildfire through the sylvan rodent population, incredibly fast, for some unknown period of time and just never surfaced in a human case until Pamela Tate came along."

"But if it's spreading that fast in wild rodents," one of the EIS girls said, "what's it going to do when it hits city rats?"

"Maybe they won't be susceptible," somebody else said.

"They're susceptible," Monique said. "We've already run tests." She looked around at the group, most of whom were staring at her glumly. "Carlos will brief you later and individually on rat control and where that fits in. I've got just a little more here on the microbiology. So far I've been telling you all the bad things I could think of, because we're dealing with something quite malignantly different from classical plague, something that could get totally out of control very fast if we don't slam it hard right now. But we do have a couple of bright spots in the picture. For one thing, our existing plague vaccine, which is a simple killed-bacteria vaccine, seems to give reasonably effective protection against this bug. It's only about sixty percent effective ten days after the first inoculation, but it's better than nothing, and we've pulled in enough from western state stockpiles to cover anyone with any contact with patients. So if you aren't covered yet, check with

Carlos and get covered. The other thing is antibiotics. Streptomycin and chloramphenicol are at least *somewhat* effective, and people can eat them like popcorn if need be, for prophylaxis. We'll have some nerve deafness from the streptomycin, and there's a certain statistical risk of bone-marrow depression in those who take the chloramphenicol—but they're all we've got right now. Maybe not for long, though. Ted Bettendorf has shipped us samples of a dozen new antibiotics still under development by various drug companies, and we've already started sensitivities. One of them, from Sealey Labs, looks very good on preliminaries. That's Sealey 3147—Ted said it's a close cousin to tetracycline, and on our first sensitivity plates, this mutant bug is *extremely* vulnerable to it, and it looks like it may stop it cold in test animals. There's a Mr. Mancini from Sealey Labs on his way here now to check our preliminaries; he'll be checking with you, Carlos, to expedite a clinical supply if preliminaries hold up and toxicity is low. That drug may save the day for us. Now that's about all I've got to report."

A buzz of conversation, then, when Monique had finished. A flurry of questions, mostly for background and detail. A pro forma request for dissenting opinions from the others on her team, with none forthcoming. Finally Carlos stood up. "Well, my friends, now it's our turn. I'm going to start by briefing you on how it is out in the real world in Canon City, Colorado, and about a dozen other brush-fire sites in four states. Then we're going to sit down and brainstorm exactly what we're going to do to break this thing in half wherever it's turned up."

With Carlos at the head of the table, they turned to the disease at hand.

27

After the Fort Collins council, one thing was frightfully clear: they were no longer fighting brush fires. They were facing a major conflagration that required a massive and vigorous field operation to break it, and once the real nature of the fight was defined, the battle moved fast. The goals and motivations were all just right: faced with a mutant plague, they had to stop it fast and they had to stop it cold, because every one of them knew without any reminder from Carlos that the only way they would stop it at all would be while it was small and localized. Excise a small nest of cancer cells early in the tumor's life and you can kill the cancer; let it spread beyond its immediate confines and you have lost the fight most bitterly.

The battle plan, in its essence, was simple and straightforward: *localize, isolate, inoculate, medicate, tabulate.* In its execution, it was a staggering task. In many places in the world, it might have been easy: the government would declare martial law, order out the army, tanks, sten guns and armored cars to block all roads and highways: airports would be shut down; rough men would pull citizens' IDs; curfews would be declared, orders of command given out and the region blockaded within twenty-four hours. So it could be in some places, but not in south-central Colorado: in a real sense the price of freedom is—freedom. Carlos and his people did the best they could within the limits of established law. All Wilderness Areas and National Forests in the region were closed by Forest Service edict (the timber companies screamed, but the wives of the loggers did not). All secondary roads were blockaded by the State Patrol on grounds of local emergency and traffic on major highways was stopped and screened to discourage the ingress of tourists and sightseers and the egress of possibly infected people. It was not a matter of law or force but of reasonable persuasion, and it mostly worked; word got out about three-hour delays at the roadblocks and dissuaded many; and at each roadblock a team of CDC Shoeleather Boys were on hand with vaccine for immunization and antibiotics for prophylaxis, however unsatisfactory these agents may have been.

In times of crisis a single voice of sweet reason can counteract panic, and help of a vital nature came from one unexpected direction—the local Canon City newspaper, with a public-information campaign that was just at that time beginning to make itself felt through the person of thirty-three-year-old Terry Linder. For the past five years Linder had been the editor of the Canon City *Record,* circulation 14,300 copies, a weekly tabloid that served many of the small communities that had been stricken. Linder dealt only with local news, generally, since the Denver papers reached everybody anyway, but this did not minimize his stature as a responsible reporter. He was a large man in a small job, quietly and competently bringing his readers news and editorial opinion of interest to *them,* and his quiet writings were known, liked and *believed* throughout the region. Infuriated beyond words by the destructive TV spectacular that had broken earlier, Terry had spent a long evening with Carlos Quintana over a bottle of middling good whiskey, and then had gone to his typewriter and quietly and calmly written a long discussion of the truth of the situation for his circulation to read. When Carlos saw it, he had leaped into the air and clicked his heels: it was *exactly* what was needed—a sober, true account of the real risks, the real dangers, the useful precautions people could take, the folly of trying to flee, the work the CDC was *really* doing. Carlos urged Terry to print off twenty thousand extra copies of the page with the story on it and gave handfuls to his Shoeleather Boys to distribute far and wide. Immediately Terry wrote an update, and then the CDC subsidized a special issue with a more detailed report and again helped distribute an extra printing. People all over southern Colorado stood outside their post-office windows to read it; banks in the region had it prominently posted, as well as all the supermarkets, hardware stores and grade schools.

Terry Linder wrote only one more update, a week later, off press just after the Fort Collins meeting and just as the campaign began in full strength. It was a voice crying in the wilderness, a voice of reason that people read and listened to. By then the wire services were picking out sections of this material, far superior to the sorry stuff their own reporters were providing, and publishing it in far-flung national newspapers; and then one wire service, at least, headlined a small supplementary item, datelined Canon City, Colorado, when Terry Linder died painfully in his bed of the bubonic form of plague in the middle of the third week of the affliction.

Other steps of the campaign moved into full swing. Stockpiles of plague vaccine from throughout the West, never in too great supply, came in by special plane. Sources in the East were also tapped, and the manufacturers, with considerable reluctance and at special-order price guarantees, agreed to step up production, using the plague bacteria strains they had on hand. There was never enough to go around, so Carlos and Roger Salmon each day determined a priority list—who should get what from the amount available that day, who should wait until the batch turned up from San Diego tomorrow (well, they *promised* tomorrow, but then the day before they promised today)—while Ted Bettendorf in Atlanta spent hours and days on the telephone trying to spring more from health agencies that suddenly and inexplicably wanted to keep what little supply they had at *home*. . . . The antibiotic supply, by that time, was a little better in hand; Parke-Davis was pulling in chloramphenicol from all over Mexico, where it was far more heavily used than in the States; streptomycin continued to arrive from all corners; and there were so many cartons, crates and hampers full of useless tetracycline that everybody kept tripping over them.

As for the new antibiotic, identified only as Sealey 3147, Carlos had a jubilant call from Monique toward the end of the week. "Carlos, baby, we've got a *weapon!* This Sealey stuff is dynamite. It stops this bug cold on the plates and it stops it in the animals. Effective blood levels in twelve hours on oral doses, and it seems to be deadly to the bug. If it's started within two or three hours of onset of fever, recovery rate is over fifty percent, and I think it'll be even better if we start it earlier."

"And how deadly is it to the animals?" Carlos said.

"You mean toxicity? Nothing that we've been able to see; it looks as harmless as aspirin. Sealey's production man, Mancini, has been hanging over my shoulder, and he and Ted have gotten a special experimental-use order cleared with the FDA. Ted says we should go with it if you agree—use will be up to you—so Mancini is on his way down there to set things up with you."

Mr. Mancini arrived in Canon City that night, a short, heavy, black-haired man with yellow eyes and lips twisted into a perpetual snarl around a set of badly protuberant teeth. He was accompanied by an even shorter, rounder man with a gray face and a gray suit, gray hat and gray tie to match. Mancini introduced himself, obviously ill at ease, obviously not wishing to be where he was at that moment nor anywhere near it. "Vice-President, Production, Sealey Labs," he said. "You're Quintana, I take it." Carlos acknowledged the fact. Mancini waved a thumb at his globular gray shadow. "This is Lunch, legal staff. Untested drug, liability problems, you know how it is. Okay, your woman in Fort Collins says you want supplies of 3147, experimental protocol. How much do you want?"

Carlos told him how much, for openers. "Then it'll depend on what happens. We're in up to the neck here, and the old drugs don't work. If this one does, we're going to *need* it."

Mancini scowled. "We're not in production, you know. We pulled this off the shelf because Bettendorf asked us to shake our sleeves.

Totally untested beyond routine screenings. If we gear up, it'll cost money."

"Then it'll cost money," Carlos said.

"Okay, as long as you understand." Mancini started to turn away.

"Records," said Mr. Lunch.

"Yes, there's that," Mancini said. "We'll need copies of all your clinical records, patient names, histories, doses, responses, side effects. Can't waste a good clinical test, with the FDA to fight later."

"All right, we'll get you the records," Carlos said. "Just get the drug out here. Air freight to Denver and our chopper will pick it up—"

"Shipping cost," said Mr. Lunch.

"Yes, you bear the air-freight cost FOB Indianapolis."

Carlos's fingers began twitching. "Shipping costs. Anything else?"

"Limitations," said Mr. Lunch.

"I nearly forgot," said Mr. Mancini, presenting a sheaf of papers. "A few FDA restrictions under the experimental-use protocol. Maybe you can iron them out."

The restrictions, as it turned out, ran to four legal-sized pages, spelling out a series of special extenuating circumstances under which the new drug could and could not be used—circumstances Carlos found so extremely limiting as to be ridiculous to try to cope with in a swift, hard-fought field campaign against a deadly killer, and he spent most of that night and half the next day on the telephone off and on to Bettendorf in Atlanta and the FDA people in Washington and half a dozen others concerned before finally gaining permission for him personally (but no one else) to dispense the drug according to his own best judgment over and above the restrictions and limitations of the experimental protocol when he determined that it was necessary. Mancini had a small stock of the drug on hand in Canon City within twenty-four hours, with more to follow as soon as possible, while he and Mr. Lunch remained on hand and underfoot to monitor its use, and Carlos, soberly mindful of the limb the CDC had been forced out upon, reserved the supply solely for those persons actively and unmistakably ill with the plague. It seemed, on the basis of first experience, that Sealey 3147 might not prove to be quite the clinical triumph it had appeared to be in Monique's laboratory; most people who took it became violently nauseated after the second or third dose, and it made people's hair come out by the handful, and it seemed, in some cases, to interfere, to some degree, with visual acuity—but it also seemed, on the basis of initial field data, to turn advanced cases of plague around where nothing else would, at least in some cases. At any rate, Carlos reflected, it was—well—a *weapon*. . . .

Field stations were established. Carlos commandeered time on the local radio station, and soon lines of people were forming at the field stations for vaccine or prophylactic antibiotics or both. It was twenty-hour-a-day work for everybody, and there were questions, because the campaign became a focus of national television and news coverage, and inevitably questions were raised, irrelevant questions mostly, but questions just the same. Nor did the campaign escape international attention. The British press was restrained and sympathetic, but British customs began quietly but firmly checking all American passport holders to determine what prospective enterers had been in Colorado, checking those for vaccine and prophylactic medication and determining closely where they were going and for how long. Reuters reported a terse preliminary report from Tass that a plague outbreak had been confirmed in Denver (incorrect, but close enough for Tass); a later Tass report, in much greater detail, charged that the outbreak was confirmed "by informed sources" to have resulted from leakage of the organism from a huge stockpile of bacteriological warfare agents illegally maintained by the United States government in underground vaults in the central Rocky Mountains. Carlos read the reports and sighed and answered questions and moved like a scourge from field station to field station, looking for holes, finding holes, plugging holes, like a dike with too, too many leaks in it, and snatching each morning's tabulations of new cases discovered, contacts covered, old cases dead, old cases still surviving, cases medicated with what, contacts vaccinated and when, contacts not vaccinated and why not, plotting the graphs, watching for the sign he was watching for, watching for everything, anything that would tell him what he wanted to know, talking to Atlanta, talking to Denver, talking to New York. . . .

Through it all Frank Barrington worked as Carlos's ex officio first lieutenant, learning skills strange and unnatural to a forester: how to autoclave old-fashioned glass syringes from time to time when the current supply of plastic throwaways gave out; how to give subcutaneous injections without arousing the ire of the injectee; how to do brief physical examinations for evidence of lymphadenopathy or subcutaneous hemorrhage; how to run statistical analyses of raw data and apply the appropriate statistical rules and calculate standard deviations; how to drive cases of pharmaceuticals in the back of a pickup over rocky, rutted mountain roads without smashing every package in the load; how to face a wire-service reporter and talk as if he were a doctor and make the reporter believe it—a dozen diverse activities including ringing hundreds of doorbells and transporting thousands of people to the field centers when necessary. On three occasions when materials had to go to Fort Collins to Monique's attention, Frank elected himself chief courier, rather peremptorily, leaving Carlos staring thoughtfully at him as he went out the door, but Carlos—perhaps curiously—did not argue this self-appointment.

A week passed and the upward curve of the statistics continued to climb. Nothing seemed to be happening, and bit by bit the tension and long hours and the incessant drive, drive, drive, began to wear through Carlos's implacable calm and good cheer; more and more he became snappish, irritable, impatient with the holes that had to be plugged. There were times of brooding, as though his built-in fatalism was slowly closing in on him like a shroud, until he shook it off and got moving again. He told himself it was still too early, that all they were doing couldn't show effect overnight, but something mocking in his mind kept saying, *You started too late, you didn't move fast enough,* and he found no way to argue. Two days into the next week after the Fort Collins meetings, there was still no pattern—nor in three days, nor in four days. Mr. Mancini and Mr. Lunch did not add to his general peace of mind; they hung about the wings like a pair of ever-patient vultures. Mr. Mancini spoke only to Carlos, and then very seldom indeed; Mr. Lunch spoke to no one, not even Mr. Mancini, but maintained a gray globular presence—until one day both of them vanished, without preamble, and Carlos heaved an enormous sigh, as if a staggering weight had been lifted from his back, and moved on. . . .

Then, just after 3:00 A.M. on the fifth day of the second week, the young intern who was handling the raw tabulations broke Carlos out of a dead sleep and thrust papers into his hand. "I couldn't wait," he said. "I just finished them."

The new case figures were the same as for the day before. For the first day since the beginning they weren't higher than the day before. In addition, old case survivals were up a whisker—more known victims had survived longer after onset of symptoms than any previous day.

Carlos whooped and hugged the young man. "Go home to bed. Let me go over these. It could be a fluke, there's always a bobble in the curve now and then. But let me just study them. You go to bed."

He was up the rest of the night, too excited to sleep. He went over the figures, paced the floor. It could mean—*Yes, yes, it could, but it's more likely a fluke. You can't make a federal case out of one day's raw figures. But if it were—*

The next day he haunted the headquarters field station, where the raw data filtered in, unable to tear himself away to check—or indeed think—about anything else. This time he worked with the intern and half a dozen others in an atmosphere of growing excitement, although he had said nothing and warned the intern not to. They wrapped up the raw figures by midnight, waiting for final data from Pineville and McCardle, and Las Madres down in New Mexico. And this time there was a drop in new case reports, small but real, and a larger rise in case survival.

At 1:30 in the morning Carlos and the intern drove to Colorado Springs to an all-night steak house and each had a huge steak. "Don't say a word," Carlos told the youngster, almost unable to contain himself. "Just keep your mouth shut one more day. It's like it was with the old vacuum-tube computers—you could never trust them. What they told you once from some data was very likely wrong. What they told you twice could still be wrong. But what they told you three times was true. One more day."

They ate in silence. Then the intern said, "Something I've never understood. Why didn't it take off up in Seattle or Wenatchee the way it took off here?"

Carlos threw up his hands. "Who can say? Not enough cases and contacts, probably. Nearly everybody the girl, the index case, infected, came down here. The few that were nailed from her were identified, and good isolation techniques were used. But basically, it had to be a matter of numbers. Even with a virulent mutant bug like this one you need a certain threshold number of cases for it to perpetuate itself and move. Somehow, they didn't cross the threshold—the flash point—up there. I don't know why. Sheer blind luck, maybe. . . ."

Next day, again, the vigil. Word was out that something was up, something was about to break, and a large number of people began drifting to the headquarters station, more and more as midnight approached. Carlos checked and double-checked the tabulated figures, and the figures told him three times. He went out to the waiting team members, his hands trembling with excitement. "Okay, my friends, this is official: we've crested. The figures confirm it. We've broken the back of this bastard, and you can all take the credit."

There was no cheering, just one huge collective sigh. The fight had been too hard and bitter, the enemy too murderous, to cheer. The people turned to each other, talking quietly. *"However,"* Carlos said, and they stopped talking. "This does not mean we can quit. It means we work harder than ever. The mop-up is the toughest part, and here it has to be very thorough. Okay? Get some rest and tomorrow we'll arrange things to see the mop-up gets done exactly right."

He left them then, and went into another room and telephoned triumph to Ted Bettendorf in Atlanta.

28

The excitement was palpable the next day as Sally Grinstone flew down to Colorado Springs from Denver in a plane carrying a whole squadron of CDC people coming in to relieve some of the ones who had been running a long string of twenty-two-hour days in Canon City. It was from them that she learned that the main headquarters in this plague fight was in Canon City, not Colorado Springs, and that one Dr. Carlos Quintana was the man to see for a news story, if there was going to be any story. It was also from the relief workers that she learned that Terry Linder was dead, subliminally the *real* reason she'd decided to come out here at all—God, that man should win a posthumous Pulitzer for those plague stories he wrote, the greatest piece of medical reporting she'd seen in half a lifetime, and that was not excluding her own. . . . And finally it was from the relief workers that she learned that a new antibiotic drug had surfaced just in time in Canon City, and helped the CDC people finally pull the fat out of the fire down there, or so the rumor went. Having picked their brains by the time they had reached Colorado Springs, Sally crowded her luck still farther and cadged a ride down to Canon City with several of the CDC crowd in a rented Chevy, and thus arrived half a day sooner than she had expected.

Not that it did her any good, in the long run. Wherever Dr. Carlos Quintana might have been, he was not immediately available, and he wasn't holding press conferences nor giving exclusives to investigative reporters from the Philadelphia *Inquirer,* especially female reporters. In fact, one of his aides made it quite clear that Dr. Quintana currently had a thing going about reporters, especially female reporters; he'd already locked horns with one during this current Colorado plague business and was definitely taking the attitude of once burned, twice shy.

Well, Sally reflected, it wasn't the first time she'd run into a stone wall. She did get to talk to a dozen or so of the Shoeleather crowd who had been working with the good doctor there, and pulled out enough background from a few of them to make at least a back-page or supplement story—maybe a good retrospective summary piece, if it really was true that things out here were finally coming under control. . . .

It was all very workaday and ordinary for Sally Grinstone, and she gave it half a day's time and then headed back toward Denver in disgust. And indeed, the trip might have been a total loss, from her viewpoint, except for that flight back to Denver, when she happened to trip over the foot of a heavyset man in a gray suit with a heavy black five-o'clock shadow—a man whose grim face, even at her fleeting glance, seemed strangely familiar; in fact she'd seen it very recently in some other place—where was it? And then it clinked down in place: *Mancini. Indianapolis and a drug-company press conference. Production man from Sealey Labs.* And then the obvious question: *Why here?* with no answer forthcoming. And beneath that unanswered question a less obvious but plainly disquieting thought: *God. If those plague fighters are counting on Mancini and Sealey Labs for anything what-so-ever, the fat could really be in the fire. . . .*

29

There was one thing to be said: nobody quit. The crest of an epidemic was just that, the high point, the point of control or containment. The campaign continued full force, as if the brush fire were in full flame, despite the now-encouraging word carried on national radio and television. A week after the crest Monique and a couple of her people came down from Fort Collins and joined Carlos and Frank and Roger Salmon and a few of the public-health people and they all went out for an evening's bash, but it was a restrained sort of bash, and that was about all the celebration there was. New cases were dropping very swiftly to the zero line; projections said it would be another month before the whole thing was past and gone. Monique had asked Atlanta, and received the go-ahead, to stay at Fort Collins long enough to pursue her study of the mutant organism with the setup she had, and long enough for Atlanta to prepare the Maximum Security Lab down there for her to use when she came back, especially for new antibiotic testing *in vivo* in rodents and small primates. Frank, his usefulness fast drawing to an end, had negotiated a transfer to a Rocky Mountain regional Forest Service unit to monitor dead rodents and to train and dispatch personnel to other forested areas to try to determine the spread of the mutant *Yersinia* in the wild. And Carlos was replaced by a junior CDC man from Atlanta so he could go back for several weeks' debriefing and preparation of a detailed report of this first major skirmish with plague in the United States since 1904.

Mopping up. It was great to have hit it and killed it right here. Mopping up was an anticlimax.

The next day, Carlos's last one in Colorado before he caught the evening plane from Denver to Atlanta, he ran into Frank in one of the field stations, clearing out some of his personal gear. "You going today too?" Carlos said.

"Right. I'll be stationed at Golden, just out of Denver."

"Well, I wish you luck," Carlos said. "You've been one hell of a help, and it's been a bitter fight."

"Not my kind of a fight, if I had a choice," Frank said.

"Nor anybody else's kind of a fight. All dirty. But when you have to, you fight that kind of fight." Carlos looked up at the big man. "So now you're going to Golden, and I'm leaving tonight. And I hope and trust that you will be taking very special care of Monique."

Frank turned sharply. "Don't worry," he said. "Look, Carlos, believe me, I'm sorry about—what happened up there."

Carlos blinked at him. "You're sorry? Whatever for?"

"For moving in on you, there. Believe me, I wasn't trying to crowd you out, personally. There didn't seem to be anything I could do, it just happened."

"Ah." Carlos looked at him quizzically. "It was just—what would you call it? . . . Fate, maybe? In the stars, so to speak?"

"Well, maybe. In a way. Only I don't think you believe that."

Carlos smiled. "I merely believe you don't know too much about women, my friend. Not that Monique is not a very exceptional woman in every imaginable way, because I truly believe she is. But at the root of it all, she is a woman."

Frank frowned. "What do you mean?"

"I mean that Monique is a very crafty and skillful engineer of her own best interest. And let me tell you something, my friend, before you begin to get angry with me. I have known Monique for a long time, and I truly believe that she is one of those rare people who can often foresee certain broad aspects of the future. If I believed in ESP, which I do not, I would say that she was very definitely prescient. I think she has in the past foreseen times and events in the future that I could not foresee. And being a woman, she instinctively moves in the directions she foresees as best for her. And I think she has known for some time that something is happening, and she is going to need a man to help and protect her, a man to cleave to, and she knows that I am not that man, because she knows that I have, shall we say, obligations. So much for Fate—and for your apology for what *you* have done. I hold no grudge. Just keep her well and closely as long as she will be kept, that's all I ask. . . ."

Later, as the plane rose high above Denver, heading east, Carlos thought again of his oddly stiff conversation with Frank before they had clasped hands and taken leave. *She knows that I am not that man, because she knows that I have, shall we say, obligations.* Yes, of course—but she knew all that before. Long before. *So what else might she have foreseen?* He turned aside from the thought, listened to the motors roar, bone weary, too weary to think. He had a double bourbon, savored it in the first real moment of relaxation he had had in over six weeks, ate one bite of the dry sandwich offered for a midnight snack, dozed for a couple of hours. Awakening, he was disoriented—where could the plane be? Over what city, what village? Somewhere over Missouri, the cabin attendant told him when he finally attracted her attention, St. Louis far to the northeast. He ordered another double bourbon, then sipped it as he took out pencil and paper and began outlining the lengthy report he would inevitably be called upon to write. A vicious outbreak of plague, sudden and unexpected, now broken. The work his people had done to accomplish that. He scribbled on. Summer nights were short, flying east. It was clear dawn as the plane began its descent into Atlanta. There would be no wife to meet him there, he disapproved of wives meeting airplanes. Good Spanish wives stayed home, they did not meet their husbands in public airports. A swift pass by the baggage port, a taxi, and soon enough he would be home to greet his wife, to have a meal, to rest and rest and rest before reporting for duty. . . .

Up the ramp and through the crowds, heading for the baggage claim, when someone took his arm and he found Ted Bettendorf beside him, tall and gaunt and gray, his face haggard. "Carlos, thank God. I was afraid you might have dawdled somewhere."

"Dawdled?"

"Never mind. We've got to get you down to Delta Gate 24 in ten minutes and it's twenty minutes' walk in this antediluvian airport." Bettendorf flagged another CDC man. "Call down and hold that plane, and then be sure his baggage gets aboard—"

Carlos stopped dead. "Hold it. What's this Delta Gate 24 business? Where are you packing me off to? I am dead on my feet, man, I haven't seen my wife, my family. . . ."

"Easy," Ted broke in. "It's necessary. I'm sorry, but there's nothing else we can do."

"About what?"

"There's plague in Savannah. Lots of it, and all over. Five days ago there was one identified case, one single case. Today we have over thirty confirmed and about two thousand suspected. We're shipping you to Savannah with all the support we can scramble. That's about what."

Carlos walked along with him, benumbed, unable to grapple the man's words, down ramps, down escalators, up stairs, down corridors toward the Delta Airlines gates, and for the first time in his life Carlos Quintana was fully, consciously and crushingly aware of the full ugly weight of the imminent presence of Death.

PART III

SAVANNAH IS BURNING!

30

Savannah, Georgia—pearl of the southeastern seaboard. Stately, graceful, beautiful Savannah, most gracious of all the antebellum cities of the South. The first, deepest and most lasting impression upon visitors is the sense of otherworldly grace: streets deeply shaded from summer's heat by tall, subtropical trees; whole blocks and miles of splendid ancient mansions, well painted and restored, many dating back to the 1700s; rich greens of foliage and flashing blue of sky of a drowsy afternoon; and the quiet restfulness of the flowered, shaded landscaped plazas. A sizzling, steamy Savannah, in these late summer days, yet an overall sense of coolness and long sweet drinks and sumptuous food and gracious living in the Old City spreading south from the busy riverfront.

James Oglethorpe, surveyor and architect and gentleman of England, was the leader of the Georgia colony and founder of this first truly successful southern colonial settlement. Wily and far-seeing, he chose a site for the city several miles inland from the coast, safe from the hurricanes that occasionally struck, yet near the spreading coastal plain with soil so rich for the husbandry of cotton. He sited Savannah on the southern bank of a broad channel of the Savannah River, which then divided into many estuaries on its way on out to the sea, some of which were navigable for the ships that came in for the rice and indigo for England and later, for the cotton bales for the textile mills to the north. The climate was paradise for Englanders, hot and steamy in the summer, springlike in winter, with the southern sun prevailing all year round. A flat lowland terrain, of course—no rolling moors, no highlands—but what could you ask of a warm coastal plain?

Oglethorpe himself designed the city in detail before a stick of wood was laid. The design was unique and brilliantly imaginative: a settlement planned around forty-three large, handsome plazas, each to form an island of green in the heart of the city. Twenty-eight of those plazas actually were built and still existed at the time when Carlos Quintana came to Savannah, forming green oases every few blocks, with the main thoroughfares dividing to go around them. Each plaza was planted differently, yet each was now set with tall, ancient thick-leafed trees, shrubs and flower beds; each had a central monument, crisscrossed walkways of old brick, and iron benches; some boasted fountains of cool water. A slow, stately traffic passed around those plazas in the old days; now fast-moving cars squealed their tires and geared down for the corners, but the plazas remained islands of quiet delight and Savannah was a city for walkers. On each plaza Olgethorpe had provided space for a public building on one side and space for a church on another. In the remaining spaces, and on the streets between the plazas were erected the fine town houses of the wealthy burghers and plantation owners of Savannah, the cotton factors and the traders, great three-and-four-story houses of brick and frame, the outsides handsomely kept, the interiors finished with oaken parquet floors and dark glossy walnut paneling, vast dining rooms, reception halls, master bedrooms. Household slaves were quartered in the lower regions of the houses, field slaves on the outlying plantations.

In those early days of the Old South Savannah waxed and grew prosperous. The ultimate source of wealth lay in the two-mile-long row of huge brick cotton warehouses built along the riverfront in an arching curve. These mammoth buildings, with their foot-thick brick walls and iron reinforcements, their iron lattice supports for each weight-bearing floor, were footed at river level and rose up four, five or six stories in front of the riverbank escarpment rising behind them. In the space between buildings and riverbank, a strange arrangement of haphazard ramps, narrow stone staircases, driveways, tunnels and bridgeways were built, so that each floor of each warehouse building could somehow be reached from behind with carts laden with baled cotton. One of those buildings had the first approximation of an elevator to be built in America (it was still there when Carlos arrived in Savannah)—an open wooden platform held plumb by iron poles and run up and down from floor to floor on a crude ratchet powered by an enormous hand-turned wheel. That elevator was an exception, however; most of the cotton was hauled to successive floors and stored by way of the ups and downs and burrows and bridgeways of Factor's Walk, the name given the ramp system on account of the cotton buyers and traders and brokers who worked there, directing what cotton should go where, for what ship and what market. Sometimes donkeys dragged the carts of cotton bales up the ramps and bridgeways for storage; sometimes slave teams hauled them. And by the end of each harvest the warehouses were stuffed and crammed with cotton bales and dirt and dust and rats.

Then when the ships came, the waterfront swarmed with black slaves pouring sweat in the murderous sun, loading deep holds with bales of cotton bound for England and France and Norwalk and New Haven and New Hampshire, and what wasn't sold was stored for later sale, and the rats scrambled for scraps and invaded the slave quarters and plundered the wharves and docks for food and dug their grottoes in the beams and supports and cubbyholes of Factor's Walk and moved up into the city only when times were lean. And the city of Savannah itself grew rich and beautiful (at least to the fortunate) and complacent, a languid, flourishing flower of the Southland.

A terrible war changed all that: the War of the Rebellion, according to arrogant Yankee invaders, the War for Southern Independence, according to the Confederate gentry, an ordeal by fire according to history, the Civil War. There came a time late in that war when General William T. Sherman's Union Army, having utterly destroyed Atlanta, marched eastward across Georgia and South Carolina toward the sea, burning everything in its path. It was perhaps the world's first cold-eyed experiment in Total War, not War against an Army but War against a People, since no one needed that land, and there was no significant defense for the cities in Sherman's path. His purpose was to break the back of a People, once and for all, to strike such terror that resistance everywhere would melt. Flames and long rifle fire and mocking songs from Sherman's men: *Peas, peas, peas, peas, eatin' goober peas; goodness, how delicious, eatin' goober peas!* while the Union men scorched crops and pillaged larders and the defenders starved on rotten peanuts. One by one, in that sweep toward the sea, the cities and towns and villages of Georgia were sacked and burned, one by one by one.

It was almost Christmas of 1864 when Sherman approached Savannah, literally sniffing the salt air, but at Savannah something different happened. The city fathers approached him in the field under appropriate guarantees. They did not want their beautiful city burned, and to spare it that fate they offered to yield the city and everything in it without dispute or bloodshed. Sherman himself could have the finest mansion in the city for his residence and headquarters. And if that were not enough, he could have those two miles of riverfront warehouses—stuffed with cotton.

General Sherman was no fool. Fire would burn cotton as well as wood. Thanks to the northern blockade, the cotton here was piled high, while the North was starving for cotton. That year, as a Christmas present, General Sherman presented President Lincoln the intact city of Savannah—and several hundred thousand bales of cotton. The price to the city was high—but Savannah did not burn.

The old days of languid prosperity never came back, of course. With the slaves gone and the plantations ruined, cotton production moved to the plains farther west, where machinery could do the work. Railroads and Mississippi riverboats carried the bales north, and northern ports transshipped it. Savannah's warehouses stood empty; Factor's Walk fell quiet. The stately old mansions stood empty, too, quietly decaying. Freed slaves came to live in huge board-windowed tenements forming a vast ghetto around the Old City. For almost a century Savannah was dormant, a quiet sleepy out-of-the-way backwater town on the Georgia coast, forgotten by time. But bit by bit other industry came, drawn by low taxes and plentiful labor. People of wealth and taste began buying up the old mansions for peppercorn prices and then restoring them. Factor's Walk came alive again as architects and lawyers established offices in the upper stories of the warehouses; riverfront levels were developed into boutiques, craft shops, pleasant restaurants and bistros. Hotels came in, and tourists, and the city grew—now a city of 300,000 souls, Carlos Quintana learned, when he arrived late that steaming morning in early September, totally exhausted by the long flight from Denver and the long struggle in Colorado, to help Savannah face an ordeal nobody in the city had ever even dreamed of. Beautiful Savannah did not burn in 1864—but now the conflagration was riding nigh on a pale horse.

31

In Canon City, Colorado, Madge Miller, twenty-nine-year-old housewife, got out of bed on yet another bright September morning and looked out at the brilliant sunshine as though peering through an ever-darkening screen.

It wasn't that she couldn't see, exactly. The images were quite sharp and clear—that tree, that street, that pickup driving by—but the total light, day by day, was receding to a dim twilight. A week ago colors were largely gone, as though a color print, fully developed, were unaccountably darkening and fading and turning to black and white. The change had been going on for two weeks now, ever since she had begun pulling out of the plague infection that had nearly killed her. The doctor had a name for what was going on, *retinitis pigmentosa,* he called it, where cells in the retina slowly collect an abnormal pigment and cease to respond to light. There was nothing to be done, he'd told her. Maybe it was just a temporary reaction to the new medicine they'd given her for the plague—and after all, she *had* survived when a lot of others hadn't, he'd said. Probably it wouldn't last, he'd said. Maybe it would just go away, pretty soon; but then, again, maybe it wouldn't. He really didn't know.

And meantime, Madge Miller couldn't drink her morning coffee, either. She slopped it all over the table trying to get the cup to her mouth. Along with the dimming of her vision, her hands had begun to shake. Not when she rested them in her lap, they were just fine then. It was only when she started to move them, to reach for something—then they started shaking, and shook worse and worse the closer she got to what she was reaching for. An intention tremor, the doctor called it, and he didn't know what caused that, either. It was a little like Parkinson's disease, he said, but he didn't think it was that. She was awfully young to get Parkinson's disease. It would probably go away, he assured her, he didn't see any reason it wouldn't, but if it got any worse, he'd have her try some L-Dopa and see if that helped any. Meanwhile, she could use one of those plastic straws to drink her coffee with and probably do okay—*And to pour the coffee, doctor? Can I do that with a straw? Or sign checks? Or wash dishes? Or change the baby? Or stroke Jerry to get him hard these days when he's almost scared to come near me? Can I do these things with a plastic straw?*

Madge Miller stared out at the dark sunny street for a long time, her hands at rest at her sides. The medicine had saved her from a fast, dirty death, all right—she knew that. But now, for the first time, she was beginning to wonder what, exactly, she had won. . . .

32

It was abundantly clear to Carlos Quintana that the major problem in Savannah, when the plague first appeared there, had been that the index of suspicion was appallingly low. There was simply nobody there who had thought of it quickly enough. Cholera would have been nailed down in twenty-four hours, typhoid fever in forty-eight. Yellow fever, certainly, who could miss that? Malaria—of course. But *plague?* Preposterous. Of course, they'd heard reports of the trouble out in Colorado or Wyoming or someplace, but that was the sort of low-grade endemic sylvan plague from wild rodents that kept turning up in those remote parts all the time, wasn't it? A sort of a local flare-up, out there, they assumed, and who paid attention to patches from a TV scare story? As for Savannah, they hadn't had a case of plague there since—since—since when? Hell, they hadn't *ever* had a case of plague there. Period.

Index of suspicion has always been a vital factor when it comes to making an obscure diagnosis. As Carlos pointed out later to Jack Cheney, "It's really very simple—you have to think of it to diagnose it. A doctor in this country is *never* going to think of loa-loa when his patient complains about something crawling around under his skin. There isn't any loa-loa in North America, that I ever heard of. He's not going to think of yaws when a patient turns up with a festering leg ulcer, either—he's going to think of varicose veins. And before the Vietnam refugees started coming over, most local docs would have missed primary leprosy until their patients' fingers dropped off. You think of things that are familiar and likely, you don't think of things that just don't *happen*. . . ."

Whatever the reason, Carlos saw clearly, the reality of plague in Savannah had been missed for far too long. He arrived on the scene much too late for any hope of tracing elements and events back to their index sources; it would have been folly to have tried. But if he had made up a scenario out of whole cloth, the things that had actually happened would have fit into his imaginary screenplay with uncanny accuracy.

The truth was that the dance of death Chet Benoliel had triggered in Savannah some three weeks before had played to an indifferent audience at first. Two men from Sundown Explorations, Inc., wisely dispatched to Savannah to back Chet up at that critical oil-executive meeting at the Hyatt, had found Chet's body at the Hilton Head condominium after he had failed to make any appearance at all at the appointed time. They had found his clothes and the car-rental packet in his hotel room, and figured that Hilton Head was where he had gone. They'd expected to find him stoned giddy and shacked up with a whore; when they found him alone and dead instead, it shook them up a little, and they checked with the home office fast. After considerable hasty debate, they followed orders and turned things over to the local constabulary. The investigation was perfunctory; he'd been rolled but not knifed, and it didn't really look like homicide. The local coroner wrote it off as bilateral lobar pneumonia with pulmonary hemorrhage—reasonably close, without benefit of autopsy, but still half a light-year away from the answer. The coroner released the body to a Savannah mortuary, where he was cremated and buried in some inexpensive niche somewhere, courtesy of Sundown Explorations, Inc., who sent a bunch of flowers to his mother in Cincinnati and thanked the Almighty that they'd had wit enough to send backup men to nail down that meeting. All told, including the two backup men, two police, a detective, a doctor, a coroner, a mortician and sundry ambulance attendants and hotel clerks, Chet Benoliel had exposed a total of nineteen people to a virulent bacteria before they got him tucked away, all nineteen of them in a state of wide-open susceptibility.

Shari Adams did much better. After ditching the car and getting a few hours sleep, Shari had turned up for the dinner shift at the restaurant feeling vaguely unwell, a state she chalked up to her unsettling experience the evening before. Since things were slow, she went home early and straight to bed. That night she had trouble with the bedbugs in her mattress again, quite a bit of trouble, to judge from the bites she found on her legs and arms. It was an old story—she'd been fighting these "bedbugs" in her mattress for months, every time she sprayed the damned things they just went away for a day or two and then they were right back again, which was not really surprising considering that they were actually not bedbugs at all, but the fleas which she shared with the rats which she knew subliminally were always around the place and which, at the moment, were sharing her mattress with her, scuttling out of their warm, cozy nest inside and into the baseboards whenever she got into bed, just waiting for her to leave again for them to return. They were large, black Norway rats, the kind that were thriving in swarms all around the riverfront area despite Savannah's vigorous rodent-control program, and their fleas were largely indifferent to the species they bit, man or *Rattus,* as long as whatever they bit had blood in it.

The second morning Shari almost didn't go to work. She felt feverish, and she was coughing—but she was down for the lunch shift that day, and the boss had been getting nasty about her absences, and it was too good a source for paying dates to let the job go, so she dragged herself out of bed, gave the mattress another spray with bug killer and went to work. All day long she was coughing—into the hand that carried the plates, into her sleeve, into a clean napkin that she swiftly replaced on a fresh-set table, into the other waitresses' faces, into the customers' faces, into the food—coughing, coughing, coughing. She waited on a total of thirty-seven people on that shift as well as coming in close contact with the boss, the boss's wife, seven other waitresses and everybody in the kitchen. She was chilling and spitting some blood by the time she got off and dragged her way home, completely forgetting the after-hours date she had made with the young visiting tennis pro at lunchtime—too bad. He'd thought himself pretty lucky when she'd coyly agreed to the date, and he would never know how fantastically lucky he was that he'd leaned down to pick up his napkin just as she started to cough in his face. . . .

Shari was not remembering much of anything by the time she got to her room and flopped into bed in her bra and panties, leaving her uniform on the floor where it fell. She was shaking and burning at the same time, so constantly thirsty she brought a pitcher of water to the bedside and emptied it in an hour, coughing and panting and pouring sweat. She slept a little, waking up to horrible nightmares. About two o'clock she dropped off for an hour and a half but woke up shaking violently and nearly suffocating. Delirious by now, she wasn't entirely certain where she was; something in her mind urged her to go tell her boss she couldn't come to work in the morning. Finally, at 3:30 A.M.

she pulled herself out of bed and started out the door into the hall and fled down the stairs in a final feverish fugue.

In the warm outdoor air she made her way down to the riverfront, still wearing the bra and panties, but the restaurant was closed when she got there. A car swinging around a curve on River Drive nearly struck her, then squealed to a stop as the occupants saw her lurching up the street. Terrified, she fled up a narrow file between warehouse buildings, up a steep stone stairway barely wide enough to permit passage, onto a dark middle-level ramp of Factor's Walk. Thinking she heard shouts and footsteps behind her, she rushed on up the ramp, ducked through a stone passageway to a place where another up ramp passed through a tunnel to higher ground. Stumbling over garbage and trash in the way, she reached a point where she thought she could leap up onto the next higher ramp directly, failing to notice the heavy, rusty overhead davit that once had lifted cotton bales from the loaded wagons and lowered them onto handcarts for transfer into the warehouse. She leaped and struck the davit with her forehead and crumpled down into a trash-filled crevice between the ramps, two feet wide and five feet deep. Four rats scuttled out from under her as she fell and struck bottom; they waited until they saw that she did not stir before returning to their hidey-hole. Of course no one had been shouting or following her, but it didn't matter to Shari anymore. A secretary making her way up the ramps toward her job at an architect's office found her at eight in the morning, lying in the crevice in her bra and panties with one arm upraised, her skin blotched and mottled with purple. In her short and terminal illness, Shari Adams had left behind her no fewer than fifty seriously contaminated people, a contaminated room in a tenement lodging house and a random selection of very sick rats.

Nobody recognized Shari Adams as an index case of plague, any more than they recognized Chet Benoliel or Althea Willis as anything but normal, if sad and untimely, deaths. Downtown cops spotted Shari in the morgue as a familiar part-time hooker who worked out of the Seafood Express down on River Street; they knew her well enough from the string of minor arrests that had always left Shari free on the street but invariably poorer. "Musta run into somebody she couldn't handle," one of the cops remarked after a glance at the bruised and battered body. "But then, they're always on the thin edge, those babes."

Nor did anybody see anything odd a week later, at the beginning of a late summer heatwave, when a whole scattering of hemorrhagic pneumonia cases began to surface here and there throughout the city, no particular area, except that more seemed to come from the River Street area and the west side of Forsythe Park than elsewhere. Bacterial pneumonia isn't generally reported—nor even noticed much—unless somebody later reviews the death certificates. It was not until some local doctors and nurses and hospital personnel began succumbing that the Public Health Department in Chatham County, Georgia, already short-staffed because everybody had fled the steamy coastal area on vacation, began to realize that they had a very real epidemic of something very nasty on their hands and began wondering for the first time just what it might be. And only then, after the original coals had already spread into a hundred smoldering pockets of fire, did the culture plates and fermentation tubes and the immunofluorescent assays begin to spell plague in large red letters, and the Chatham County Public Health Director, Jack Cheney, begin figuring out what had *really* happened and came up with the astounding statistics that had greeted Carlos on his arrival: that probably-identified cases of plague had leaped from two or three cases on one day to more than five hundred on the next—and the health workers who had been frantically called back from their vacations began trickling reluctantly back to the city and found themselves facing a nightmare.

Dr. Jack Cheney had a crash planning session already set up when Carlos and his team from CDC arrived—top people from the Health Department, the President of the Chatham County Medical Society, people from the Mayor's office in charge of public relations, the chief of police, two dozen other people. It was early in the morning; Carlos had had just two hours' sleep, and felt bleary and strangely out of touch with reality. He soon found the others were too, only more so. "Okay, folks," he started off, "let's begin with some basics. As I was coming in here I heard somebody say that our first job would be to keep this thing from getting out of control. Well, it's already far past that point. From the figures Dr. Cheney has shown me, we're already dealing with an epidemic disease that is badly out of control, by definition. It's here, it's moving fast, and nobody is controlling it. And with the head start it's got, it's going to be a lot worse before we get a handle on it, no matter how fast we move or what we do."

There was muttering in the room, city leaders eyeing each other, sounds of skepticism. Damned doom-singer from Atlanta coming down here—"Do you really think it's going to be all that bad?" somebody asked.

"If this outbreak is related to the one in Colorado," Carlos said, "it's going to be worse than anything you ever dreamed of. That's one of the first things we've got to find out. Out there we had wide-open spaces, low population density. Here people are packed in cheek by jowl. If it's the same mutant organism here, we're in serious trouble. . . ."

More mutters, and louder—*They really don't believe it,* Carlos thought as he burrowed into the planning, trying to force people to be convinced that there was real trouble afoot. Protection for the health workers was a first and obvious step, but Jack Cheney hadn't even started planning for that. Only fifty doses of the old protective vaccine in the whole city, the big companies like Merck and Lilly were both working on a vaccine specifically for the mutant strain, but no guessing when it would be ready. No stockpile at all of the new Sealey antibiotic drug to use for treating people who had been hit—*Just have to get Ted Bettendorf to work blasting that loose, and use the chloramphenicol and streptomycin we have as a stopgap. . . .*

A long, hard day of planning with people who didn't really believe what was happening. Time spent urging Jack Cheney to get some kind of microbiology lab working—*Monique, where are you now when we need you?* A long, hard fight with the local hospital administrators to square away plans for one hospital for plague victims alone—Did you say a whole *hospital?*—and finally settling on the big Civic Center Performing Arts Pavillion to use as an emergency hospital to handle as many victims as possible, with Jack Cheney directing the setup. A long, hard fight with the city police and State Patrol, trying to plan some way of controlling people and activities without imposing a *de facto* martial law, which absolutely *nobody* wanted to try to impose on a hot, frightened city like Savannah. A long, hard fight with the communications people, trying to plan some fail-safe method for getting official notices and vital information out to the most people the fastest. In fact, a long, hard fight with practically everybody there, right down to the rodent-control people, who couldn't or wouldn't seriously believe that Carlos was, indeed, planning to go after the rats with as much dispatch and vigor as possible. . . .

He plowed through it all, through the whole long, grinding morning and late into the afternoon, arguing and cajoling and warning and pleading, and above all, planning the direction of battle. About four-thirty Jack cornered Carlos with some updated figures on probable cases to date, looking sober-eyed and white around the mouth. "I've finally got a team going that's taking this seriously," he said, "and I'm afraid that figure of five hundred cases I quoted you this morning should be closer to two thousand. Christ alone knows how many unreported penumonia deaths there were in the same period. But if these figures are even close, it has to be your mutant bug that's doing it."

"Yes, it's the Colorado bug," Carlos agreed.

"Well, I'll keep them digging and get them onto suspicious septicemias as well. I assume you *do* want them to keep on digging. . . ."

Carlos smiled and clapped the man on the arm, sensing at least one solid ally who was beginning to come alive. "If I had to guess, I'd guess the real figure is almost double the numbers you've got there, early on like this. Later on, the proportion will flip-flop, when people get scared and start blaming every runny nose on plague. But yes, by all means keep your people working, Jack, and you stick around, too. We've got a night's work ahead of us trying to coordinate this mess into some kind of rational program. . . ."

By late afternoon it was blindingly clear to Carlos that he was going to have to tackle the medical-supply problem at once, and head-on. Preventive vaccine and antibiotic drugs were both going to be utterly essential, and the sooner he knew how much of each was on the way the better. First he spent an hour on Jack Cheney's office phone trying to reach the right people at Lilly and Merck and the other vaccine-manufacturing outlets. Oh, yes, they assured him, production was continuing on batches of the old vaccine, and they could round up pretty good stockpiles within a few days—well, at least within a few weeks. As for the new vaccine being made from the mutant *Yersinia* strain, Carlos encountered nothing but evasions and vaguenesses from the vaccine makers. That first test batch had been totally consumed in Canon City, and no one could seem to say whether more was being actively processed or not. No one could even seem to tell him if the drug houses had consulted with the FDA on emergency-production protocols—or even intended to. Carlos finally threw down the phone in exasperation, recognizing determined, obdurate stonewalling when it walked up and kicked him. *Bettendorf is just going to have to get on this,* he thought. *I can't spend the next week talking to a bunch of nitwits who are not going to tell me anything whatsoever until the sky falls in. . . .*

Vaccine, of course, was the major weapon to create immunity and prevent people from becoming infected at all. Antibiotics with which to treat the ones already sick, the ones exposed and never immunized—which was to say, virtually the entire mass of population—was another matter altogether. One of Carlos's team of CDC people already had a rundown of drugs immediately available, size of the stockpiles, some tentative plans for additional shipments. Carlos leafed through the report, went back through it again and then looked up. "This is all just delightful," he said, "but what about the new Sealey 3147 antibiotic?"

"You mean the new drug you were testing out in Colorado?"

"Yes, of course."

The young man blinked at him. "Well—you heard about the side effects, didn't you?"

"I know it made a lot of people throw up," Carlos said. "But it also stopped the plague infection, and one bad side effect of this plague infection is sudden death. . . ."

"Well, I just talked to Atlanta ten minutes ago," the young man said, "and *I* heard there wasn't going to *be* any more 3147. They said that Sealey was withdrawing it."

"Good Christ." Carlos turned back to the telephone, got a line open and finally made connection with Ted Bettendorf's office. "Ted, for God's sake, what's going on with my drug supply?" he wailed. "I can't get *any* information out of the vaccine people—"

"Neither can I," Ted Bettendorf said. "They're playing that new vaccine very close to the vest, and I can't make them budge."

"Well, what do they *want?*"

"They want three months' worth of testing, plain and simple," Ted said. "They're scared of the new vaccine, and they're scared of what's going on, and they want to cover their asses. And the way people have been suing everybody in sight for bad vaccine results, you really can't blame them. I'm working on it, but I don't see a breakthrough at this point."

"Then what about the Sealey antibiotic?" Carlos demanded. "What's *their* problem?"

"That's a little hard to say." Ted paused for a long moment. "There's something funny going on there. All of a sudden Sealey is very upset about those side effects out in Canon City."

"You mean the vomiting?"

"More than that. The later side effects. Vision disturbances and tremors."

"Well, I saw a little of that," Carlos admitted, "but who says it was the drug? Monique ran all kinds of tests at Fort Collins—biochemical tests, *in vitro* tests, multiple animal studies. She found no problems at all, and we gave the stuff in quantity to over three hundred people."

"Well, a couple dozen of those people have checked in with late side effects, and more are turning up all the time. It's not the sort of medicine we want to scatter broadside into the population unless we have to. The strange thing is that our lab people here have repeated Monique's test studies right down to the letter and have gotten *bad* results with the Sealey drug. Clearcut evidence of neurotoxicity, including a roomful of Parkinsonian guinea pigs."

"You really think Monique could have screwed up on something like that?"

"I don't know what to think," Ted said. "But all of a sudden Sealey Labs are pulling back. They want to take it back to the lab, and ordinarily I wouldn't argue with them."

"Well, God damn it, they're cutting off my right leg," Carlos snapped, "and the vaccine people are gnawing on the other one. What the hell am I supposed to stand on? This *isn't* 'ordinarily,' Ted, it's a long old way from 'ordinarily.' We've got a live disease in this town. I need a preventive vaccine, and I need an antibiotic that kills the germ, and I need both of them *fast*. Now, somebody has got to break those things loose for me somehow, and if that means using some political heat, then let's fire up the stove."

Muttering Spanish vulgarities under his breath, Carlos retired the phone and glared up at a startled-looking CDC aide. Carlos looked sheepish. "So now we'll see," he muttered. "Let's go find Jack Cheney. We've got a night's work to do."

33

The meeting took place on a hot, steamy morning in early September, a gummy, sticky day with barely a breath of heavy air moving off the Potomac—*one hell of a day for major policy decisions,* Ted Bettendorf thought as he loosened his shirt collar under his tie. He and Mandy had flown up from Atlanta very early that morning, using the plane flight for a final review of the drug-utilization statistics from Canon City, figures Mandy had spent all week rooting out since Carlos never had had time to complete a final report. It had taken Ted most of that week to get the meeting set up; there had been distinct reluctance in Washington to bite the bullet that had to be bitten, and Ted had had to exhaust every other possible approach before the thing could be brought out on the table officially. He had stuck to it because he had to. Carlos *had* to have the Sealey drug one way or another, and fast, and it didn't really look as bad from the toxicity standpoint as the earliest figures had suggested. Bad enough, God knows, but not intolerably bad. . . .

They'd made Washington in time for a two-hour wall-banging session with Larson, an Undersecretary for Public Health in the Department of Health and Human Services, and then he had taken them over to the paneled White House meeting room in plenty of time for the 11:17 A.M. appointment—the Boss from HHS could come over later if it turned out that she were needed. A representative from the Food and Drug Administration was already there, a man named Tarnisher, and Ted's heart sank—from many previous scrambles, Ted knew him to be a typically useless FDA functionary, possessed of impeccable biomedical credentials and an absolutely fantastic inability to come up with a really clean-cut recommendation about anything whatsoever. *Well, we shall overcome, just the same.* . . . The other party present was John Mancini, Vice-President in charge of Production at Sealey Labs, a short, broad man Ted had talked to endlessly on the phone but never had met, built rather along the lines of a granite headstone or a Mexican pig, Ted thought, *not somebody you'd want to run into on the road at any high velocity.* . . . Mancini was flanked by a round, gray person named Lunch, who carried a briefcase, and a couple of others who kept to the background and took notes. And then, punctual to the second, the President, looking cool and relaxed on this fearsome hot morning, his smile engaging as ever, his California tan resplendent. "Now, then, gentlemen, let's get to it. Appreciate your coming out this morning, John. Can't be any hotter than Indianapolis, eh? You've met Bob Larson from Health and Human Services? Ted Bettendorf from CDC in Atlanta?" The President looked at Larson. "You got an answer on the vaccine thing, right?"

"They'll bend the testing protocol a little if Tarnisher will send them a letter. That'll speed things up a little."

"Hear that, Ted? I told you you were worrying too much. Now, about the antibiotic—Bob, why don't you lead off?"

Larson nodded. "To be brief, we've got a bit of a problem with this thing going on in Savannah."

"Terrible thing," Mancini said. "I trust you people have got your thumb on it by now."

"Not exactly," Ted Bettendorf said. "As you may have gathered from the newscasts."

"But with a little help from your people, John, we're quite sure we can," the President added.

Mr. Lunch whispered into Mancini's ear, and the Sealey man nodded. "Of course, of course. Anything we can do—within our rather severe limitations."

"Specifically," Bettendorf said, "we need to expedite a field supply of Sealey 3147."

Mancini frowned. "Dr. Bettendorf, I'm aware that you seem to have a great deal of interest in 3147, and this may perhaps be unfortunate. You're aware, of course, that the drug is still very much investigational—that is to say, experimental." (Whisper, whisper from Mr. Lunch.) "Make that *highly* experimental. You people know that—yet we seem to be encountering unprecedented pressure to turn this substance loose on a city of three hundred thousand people."

"John," the President said, "I understand the circumstances are extraordinary."

"But there are other antibiotics for controlling *Yersinia.* Streptomycin, chloramphenicol—why not use them?"

"Because they don't work very well against this new strain of *Yersinia,*" Bettendorf said. "That's why. We used 3147 in Colorado, and it worked."

"That's delightful, but we also have a question of toxicity, some rather unfortunate long-term side effects. I can't imagine the FDA authorizing mass distribution at this point."

"Well, now . . ." The FDA man coughed. "Dr. Bettendorf's figures don't seem so alarming. With the administration's support, there are possibly some ways we could, um, authorize more, um, widespread clinical testing, even in the field—"

"In a city of three hundred thousand people?"

"Well, um, we'd have to review this very carefully, of course, exercise very close controls—"

"You're not going to make any friends turning Savannah into an experimental drug farm, Mr. Tarnisher," Mancini said. "But assuming you're not interested in making friends, let's get down to cases: could you get me formal approval of a clinical testing protocol for

3147 down there within, say, forty-eight hours?"

"Well, now—there'd be a great deal of red tape to be cut through, but—I—I—" Tarnisher glanced nervously at the President. "I'm sure it could be done if we had a great deal of cooperation on all sides."

"Fine, then that settles it," the President said, beaming and rising from his chair.

"Not quite," Mancini said. "From Sealey's point of view it doesn't settle a thing."

"What's the problem, John?"

"Liability."

"But surely if you have authority from the legally constituted Federal regulating agencies—"

"Oh, that would be *nice,* but it really doesn't even approach the problem. That's why I drew Mr. Tarnisher into a commitment, which my associate Mr. Lunch here has duly noted down—I wanted to demonstrate how completely irrelevant government regulations are to the question. There's no problem providing the drug—we already have a considerable quantity in stockpile. But the problems of making it available are formidable. Dr. Bettendorf can confirm the difficulty of obtaining truly informed consent from any of the people who might receive this drug—under conditions of plague and panic. How's that?" He bent down to Mr. Lunch. "Oh, yes, a *legally ironclad* informed consent that would hold up anytime anybody might come back to us anytime in the future."

Bob Larson cleared his throat. "These are not ordinary circumstances, Mr. Mancini. We're talking about a large number of people dying."

"Ah, yes, I know, and believe me, we'd like nothing better than to be more outreaching to those people. There was a time when people recognized that even the best of medications might occasionally have unfortunate side effects for some. That was simply considered the price we all paid to have the medication available for the vast number who might benefit, with no thought of making somebody pay when a bad effect did occur. Well, those were the days of innocence, gentlemen. Today Sealey Labs is being sued for alleged damages a forty-year-old man now claims to be suffering because the company may have manufactured a medicine that his *mother* took for excessive weight gain on two occasions while she was carrying him. He doesn't even know what company made the medicine; all he can establish is that Sealey is one that *might* have made it. Yet on the basis of his claim, Sealey is now involved in a class-action suit demanding a total settlement of—what was that figure, Mr. Lunch?—$600 million. And if that case is decided in favor of the plaintiffs, as it may well be, regardless of any merit to the claim, you will not have to worry about Sealey Laboratories cluttering up the market with new antibiotics because Sealey Laboratories will be in receivership. And if that occurs, since Sealey is a privately held company, we will simply destroy our development records and retire to the Caribbean somewhere, out of reach of the court. Our new-development drugs will go to no one."

There was a long silence. Then Bob Larson said, "You couldn't license 3147 to be manufactured by some company less concerned about this problem? Perhaps someone abroad?"

"That wouldn't change things a whit. If we license it, we're liable. And we oppose licensing new-drug patents to *anybody* unless forced to do so."

"So what is it going to take to get 3147 to Savannah?" Ted Bettendorf asked.

"Not much," Mancini said. "Just legally binding indemnification of Sealey Laboratories against any and all claims that might arise—retroactive to Colorado, as Mr. Lunch insists. We must be held totally harmless, with absolute guarantees, in advance, or Sealey 3147 stays on the shelf."

"And I'm supposed to do this by executive order?" the President said. "No way."

"There are precedents. The Swine Flu business . . ."

"Yes, and now we know better. There's no way I could do this without an Act of Congress."

"Then there's no way Sealey could either," Mancini said, rising and gathering up his papers. "Plague or no plague."

After they had gone, Ted Bettendorf looked around. "Mr. President?"

"Mm?"

"We need that drug," Ted said. "How do we get an Act of Congress passed?"

34

In a small, expensive flat off Rittenhouse Square in Philadelphia, at two in the morning, Sally Grinstone suddenly sat bolt upright in bed, wide awake, staring into the darkness. "Just hold it a minute!" she said.

Her companion, still not recovered after a full hour, stirred beside her. "Whazzat?"

"Not you, dummy, go back to sleep. I've got to think."

Think she did, and never more clearly than when she'd just been laid. She lit a cigarette in the darkness, brushed a spark off her naked belly and clasped her arms around her knees. As an investigative reporter for the Philadelphia *Inquirer*, and a very good one indeed, Sally Grinstone was one of those rare people who survived almost exclusively on the product of her subconscious. She read voraciously and omnivorously and never forgot anything she read, watched innumerable movies, gorged on TV at all hours and talked to anybody who would hold still to be talked to. All the time, she was "shoving it into the garbage can," as she put it, and when her subconscious shoved something back out at two in the morning, she had long since learned to pay attention—because *this* was where the red meat was going to be found.

Sometimes, like now, she didn't know what she was after. Something was wrong with something she had seen or heard or read—so often, in the past her first clue to a really juicy morsel, but always hard to pin down. Something she'd read. Several hours earlier, before Teddie had gotten her turned on and distracted, she'd been reading about things going on in Savannah—God, what a mess! She'd been following this plague business extra closely since her trip out to Colorado, everything she could find about it, because she was dead-eye certain there was going to be a big story turn up there if she could just get hold of it. Sure as God wiped up the floor with reporters, there was going to be a big story there—but she couldn't see it yet. *So what was her head trying to tell her now?*

Every cell in Sally's chubby, bouncy little body told her it was something important. Something to do with the plague, that was sure. Medicine was her special bailiwick; she had a dozen major newsbreak exposés to her credit in that area, two of them had won prizes and brought cascades of indignant denial from the medical establishment and the government and supportive howls of indignation from her readers, and even, in one or two cases, some real prosecution and some real legislation, and man, was there going to be an exposé somewhere in this plague thing!

She hopped out of bed, naked and sweaty in the close air of the flat, and went into the little alcove office off the living room. Something she'd read or remembered, but not directly connected with Savannah. There'd been a meeting in Washington, at the White House—no statement from the President, just a Press Secretary's report. Sally rooted around on her desk, a four-inch-deep clutter of junk beside her typewriter. Yes, here it was, Bernie'd sent it over, dear guy, or she'd have missed it completely. The President, some underling from H_2S she'd never heard of before, an FDA advisor, and Mr. John Mancini—that was it! On the scene in Colorado, she'd seen him there, Vice-President in charge of production at Sealey Laboratories, Makers of Fine Pharmaceuticals, now in Washington talking to the President, flanked by a certain Mr. Lunch—ah, yes, she knew about Mr. Lunch from other sources. An indecisive meeting: the President urging FDA and H_2S and Mr. Mancini to get together and resolve their differences and find ways to get around some awkward testing regulations on new drugs, on an emergency basis, of course, in order to get a new antiplague antibiotic drug on line fast, because they needed it in quantity in Savannah yesterday, not tomorrow. Odd that the President was doing the urging personally, that was what he had H_2S around for in the first place, but that's what it said. Mancini's response was *very* indecisive for a drug man with a potential hot one on his hands. Some unfortunate problems, Mr. President. Some untoward side effects that turned up in preliminary animal testing made them very cautious about rushing into production—(Production? *Preliminary testing?* Wait a minute. They must have *done* their preliminary testing long since, they'd been using that drug on *people* in Colorado, from what CDC relief people had told her . . .). The President assuring Mancini of administration cooperation in any possible way to speed up resolving these problems—and then Mancini springing his trump: federal indemnification against all claims in perpetuity if they released the drug now in a "major population center," i.e., Savannah. An impossible demand, of course, what could the President say? More indecisive talk. End of report.

Sally lit a cigarette, frowning, and sat back in her desk chair. That was part of it, all right, but it wasn't that which set the bell jangling.

Damn strange story, though—why report it at all? Unless the President was setting up some brownie points against something coming up. But what *did* set the bell jangling? She turned on a fan to cool her skin a little and sat chain-smoking for almost an hour, poking through the garbage can, begging the old subconscious to spit out something else. They'd certainly used a new drug in Colorado, but not without "preliminary testing," far too much risk of side effects, even in an emergency. . . .

Side effects. Sally dove into a thick file and pulled out a very brief item from the Denver *Post.* Several people from the Canon City area were reporting progressive visual disturbances following recovery from the plague infection there. Similar but not identical to *retinitis pigmentosa.* Also, a few had associated intention tremors—yeah, she knew all about that, her granddad had Parkinsonism. Thought to be cerebral side effects of some kind of plague toxin among those who survived the infection. *Fine. But why did those people survive? Because they were fed a new antibiotic? If so, maybe the side effects were due to the antibiotic, not the infection. . . .*

Still there was a hole, something missing. She knew she'd seen something, several weeks ago. She tried key words to see if she could spring anything. Names. Places. Something in there was on the right track. . . .

Fort Collins. That was it, a dateline, someplace in northern Colorado. A TV newsclip that she'd seen, some woman from the CDC working there—what was her name? *Janrette?* Something like that—and they'd been testing a new antibiotic agent against the plague bug. What had hit Sally was how excited the woman had been, really high on this drug. They'd tested it against infected lab animals and it had been amazing, hit the bug hard and fast almost a hundred percent of the time, and *no side effects of any kind.* Safe as tetracycline, she'd said, two or three times. Half a dozen people in the lab there had taken it, too, to measure human blood levels and be sure of the no-side-effects bit. She'd recommended it for use in Canon City. . . .

Yes. That was it. Sally Grinstone sat back and smoked. That was what her subconscious had been worrying about and finally coughed up. First of all a splendid new drug, highly effective, a miracle drug right when they needed it. And then, suddenly, side effects, *nasty* side effects, people going blind, for God's sake, and Sealey Labs backing off from the President himself. . . .

Something stank.

Sally sat there a long time, more and more certain that something was wrong. She knew a little bit about drug testing. With any major toxic reaction, you either got it in the face right at the start, or you didn't get it at all, at least nothing big. Unless they had a bunch of blind Parkinsonian rats running around that lab in Fort Collins, Colorado, and just weren't talking about it. She looked at the telephone, started calculating the time difference to Denver—*Maybe they stay up late out there*—but shook her head. *That's no good. You can't go for blood over the phone, it doesn't work. . . .*

She heard Teddie padding out behind her, felt a touch on her shoulder, a kiss on her neck, a gentle hand cupping her breast.

"Honey?"

"Not now, sweet." Sally slipped to her feet. "Got to get some sleep. I've got a long trip tomorrow."

35

In cadence with the dull hoofbeats of the Horseman, plague moved relentlessly in on Savannah. At first people responded only slowly to Jack Cheney's public-health directives going out on the emergency Civil Defense radio and TV. For one thing, it was altogether too hot to pay attention; the scalding sun beat down every day in the longest, most merciless early September heat wave in recent memory, day after steaming day of 105-degree heat. Nobody stayed inside by the radio or TV in that kind of heat, especially in the long miles of stinking, heat-creaking frame tenements that stretched across the middle of the city, where air-conditioning was seldom to be found and then rarely, if ever, still working. There were few trees gracing those parts of the city, but the only breathable air was outdoors and the tenements themselves threw some shade, so people sat on their rickety porches, gazing at the heaps of trash and garbage in the vacant lots across the street, where the rats wended their way through their mazes of tunnels. When the afternoon thunderstorms would strike, the gutters would fill and overflow for a while and nobody would seem to notice how very many dead rats were washing down to the drainholes. And then, the storm's momentary coolness merely tantalizing, the streets would start steaming again in the afternoon sun and the dense, humid miasma of hot heavy air would press down upon them for the rest of the night.

The earliest response to the public-health warnings came, predictably, from the city's doctors, and they defined the problems that lay ahead. It came first from the crowded offices and free clinics in the vast tenement areas, then from the middle-class and upper-class doctor's offices and private clinics and group practices. Suddenly doctors everywhere were seeing a sharp influx of very sick people. Many became abruptly, devastatingly ill, spiking 105-degree fevers, shaking with chills, coughing and gasping and spitting into blood-filled handkerchiefs. Others—far fewer, but still some—were breathing all right but presenting more classical symptoms: septicemic shock and prostration; great ugly, swollen purple-black lumps under their arms and in the groin; nausea and sudden uncontrollable vomiting; all the marks of the raging toxicity as the bacteria spread and grew.

They knew what they were seeing, the doctors did, and they scrambled to get the vaccinations they had neglected to get a few days earlier for themselves and their nurses and receptionists—the old vaccine first and then, finally, finally, in a dribble that was earmarked first for medical workers only, a tiny supply of the new vaccine said to provide up to sixty percent protection from the mutated bacteria. But unfortunately, just knowing what they were dealing with didn't in itself tell the doctors what to do about it. Jack Cheney and his public-health crew, aided by Carlos Quintana's CDC team, mounted a major effort early on to reach every doctor, lay out ground rules for handling the sick, mailing them photocopied guide sheets, bulletins, updates, but still the Health Department switchboards were flooded twenty-four hours a day with thousands of calls asking for specific advice—calls for information, supplies, directions—the demand billowed in from all parts of the city. Most doctors and their nurses made some sort of attempt at establishing isolation techniques in their offices. They all worked in gloves and gowns, caps and masks, and—short of urgent emergencies—some of them turned away all the patients who *didn't* have plague and sent them home in order to spare them possible exposure. Some clapped surgical masks on everybody who walked in the door. But at best, all such impromptu efforts proved terribly imperfect. What was worse, antibiotics and vaccine could not be improvised, and soon the tiny stockpiles of these vital necessities began dwindling. When more new vaccine came in, it immediately went out to the public-health workers, the police, the five-hundred member rat squad hastily mobilizing a rat-control program to hit the major concentrations of the vermin and all others trying to fight the epidemic's ravages, including the garbage men.

Especially the garbage men.

Their humble role in the infinite scheme of things was suddenly transformed as they found themselves needed just as urgently as the doctors. The pressing problem was: what to do with an ever-increasing number of bodies? Patients who had walked into doctors' offices were found dead on the waiting-room floor—with nobody around to claim the bodies. At first, aid cars were called to pack them off to the county morgue—but soon the morgue had bodies stacked up like cordwood, without enough refrigeration, without even enough ice to hold them until they could be disposed of. Every mortuary in town was overfilled with bodies; the crematoria were working to capacity and glowing cherry-red from the heat and still falling far behind. Finally, one day, a long, sad line of bulldozers were spied making their way out the old highway to the west, toward a large unimproved tract of city-owned land, where they began scooping out a vast sanitary landfill disposal site. While the mortuaries and crematoria fought to meet the needs of the paying customers, this huge city excavation was prepared to take care of the poor.

Well, a mass grave and landfill five miles outside the city limits was all well and good, but it did not solve the logistics of getting the bodies out there, and it was here that the garbage men found themselves impressed into an unaccustomed role. In the ghetto areas there was no place to put the bodies at all, so the dead would lie in state in their tenement beds until the dark hours of the night. And then the cousins, or uncles, or husky sons of the victims, their activities mercifully concealed from light of day, would perform the rites of transport to an empty lot a block away, or an alley strewn with overflowing trash cans, or a readily opened storm sewer, and the corpses would be deposited. And of course the ancient bond of silence prevailed: nobody saw anything, nobody heard anything and nobody knew who had done what.

Thus with the Coroner and the Mayor both backed to the wall, the garbage men were summarily appointed to act as a city death patrol. At first one or two garbage trucks a day, then three or four a day, departed from their usual rounds to weave up and down the streets and alleys, their motors and cranks and lifts rumbling a mournful threnody, performing their strange collection rites, then rolling on out the Old Highway through the swampy flats to the sanitary fill, soon known as Five Mile Dump, to lower the bodies to their final rest. And on days when the bulldozers did not get the day's produce fully buried before sundown, the rats were there to help, soon expanding into the most enormous colony of sick rats in all the sovereign state of Georgia, but nobody paid attention to this for quite some time. . . .

It was at this point that the public response to the plague began to undergo a sharp and distinctive change. With bodies to be tripped over in the streets each morning, and with more and more families bereaved of one or two or more members, people for the first time began to grasp the true nature of the disaster that was upon them, and they began to follow blind instinct in seeking safety. Ancient gut-wisdom declared that the familiar was safer than the strange, home safer than elsewhere, inside safer than outside. All over the city of Savannah people abandoned their streets and porches and fled inside, closing and barring their doors, slamming their windows and emerging only when forced to emerge. They huddled inside in the stifling heat and the smell of death and waited for something to happen, and the plague in Savannah moved on to a different, more sinister phase.

36

"You say she's coming *here?*" Frank Barrington said when he arrived in Fort Collins about six o'clock that evening and Monique told him what she had planned.

"No, not here," Monique said, looking around the small furnished apartment. "We're going to meet her for a drink at Barnaby's. It shouldn't take very long, I hope, and then we can shake her loose and come back here for some nice chops for dinner." She hesitated. "I probably shouldn't have bothered you at all," she said. "It just seemed so odd to have her calling, just after that grim little note from Carlos about the mess in Savannah and the fight they're having with Sealey about that medicine. And you know more about Canon City than I do; all I did was run the tests up here and report what happened—"

Frank put a finger on her lips. "Stop apologizing. It's only eighty miles up here from Golden. I can drive that anytime, and I'm getting bored with this weekend visitation crap, anyway."

She smiled. "Bored with me?"

"Bored with being eighty miles away. I'm either going to get myself assigned up here or start commuting." He kissed her. "This woman that called . . . You say she's some kind of detective?"

"She's an investigative reporter, which is something else. She writes for the Philadelphia *Inquirer.* She called from Denver at seven-thirty this morning and she's turning up at Barnaby's in thirty minutes."

"So what does she want with *you?*"

Monique shrugged. "I'm not quite sure. Said she was checking some things about the Colorado outbreak, but she got very vague about just what." She saw Frank's cloudy expression and smiled. "Don't worry, sweet. We'll meet her and have a nice drink and play it close to the vest, and everything will be all right. I've dealt with these people before."

"If she acts like that TV woman," Frank said, "I'll break her arm."

As it turned out, Sally Grinstone was not quite the horsey, aggressive female newsperson Frank had been visualizing. Aside from a pair of very sharp and penetrating eyes, Sally Grinstone looked for all the world like an overchubby, slightly untidy teen-age kewpie sitting there in the booth at Barnaby's, sipping some colorless drink and chain-smoking cigarettes, her breasts quivering a little with every movement, her hair done up carelessly in an incredible double ponytail. Hardly anything *threatening* about her, Monique thought, except for the air of slightly spurious innocence. No tape recorder on the table, either, Monique noticed. "You're not taping this?" she said as she and Frank slid in across the table.

"No need to," Sally said. "This is just background, a couple of points to clear up. Doesn't even need to be on the record, if you'd rather not." She spread her hands. "I'm not even sure what I'm looking for, just yet—maybe you can tell me. You're Monique Janrette?"

"Jenrette," Monique said.

"That's right. I've seen quite a number of your papers," Sally said, and Monique had the sudden odd feeling that maybe this girl actually *had.* "Look, I'm here because some things have me puzzled and I hope maybe you can help me clear them up. You've heard about Sealey Lab's decision on their new antibiotic?"

"I've heard they're dragging their feet about supplying it," Monique said cautiously.

"They've pulled it out of production altogether, as of five P.M. yesterday," Sally said. "It was on all the wire services. They're calling back all outstanding supplies, including supplies for all experimental protocols." She leaned across the table. "Now what do you think of that?"

"I think it's very strange," Monique said. "If it's true."

"It's more than just strange," Sally said. "It's an outrage. Consider the timing. We've got a city like Savannah in terrible trouble right now, with Sealey 3147 the only drug in sight that might keep Savannah from turning into the disaster of the century—and now we find that Sealey is suddenly pulling out. We also know that Sealey has that drug boarded up with patents that nobody can break, so if Sealey doesn't make it, nobody does. Now what does that sound like to you, as a microbiologist with the CDC, at a time like this? Off the record, of course."

Monique sighed. "I don't like it, if that's what you mean—but maybe they have no choice. The drug hits this plague all right, but it also turns up side effects. If they're afraid of the liability—"

"Liability, hell," Sally Grinstone said scornfully.

"Well, what do you think they're after?"

Sally raised her thumb and forefinger and rubbed them together. "Scratch," she said. "Money. Nothing else. Money like you wouldn't believe. I smell blackmail like the stockyards breeze, a squeeze play that's going to make the oil sheiks look like two-bit shills at a carney." She gave Monique a cold look. "Add it up for yourself. When you've got something that a whole lot of people have to have in a hurry—or die—you don't just give it away, not if your name is Sealey. You squeeze it for everything it's worth. You lock it up and wait to see how many are *really* going to die before you set the price, that's all."

Monique took a deep breath. "Well, that's an interesting allegation," she said. "But why are you coming to me? You're certainly not going to *print* all that."

"No, I'd be crucified upside down. But maybe there's something here I *can* print. Something I can't quite get my hands on yet." Sally fixed her large eyes on Monique. "You're familiar with this drug. You ran tests on it before they used it down in Canon City, didn't you?"

"That's right." Monique exchanged glances with Frank. "We tested it here in the lab. Sealey provided a small supply through CDC in Atlanta. We didn't have much time—we already knew the regular antibiotics were not going to work well against the new organism, and we were getting desperate—but we did some very intensive testing."

"And you found it was good. Very good. I saw you on a late news clip on TV when your first results were in."

"The drug was absolutely great," Monique said. "We are getting up to ninety-seven percent kill of the organism with very low concentrations of the drug. I can hardly remember a new drug that looked so extremely good so early. Those tests suggested the stuff would stop infection cold in infected animals, assuming we could get high blood levels fast enough."

"Did that look like a problem?"

"No," Monique said, "but sometimes you just can't. Sometimes a drug is metabolized into something totally inactive just as fast as you stick it into a living system—or sometimes it's cleared so fast by the kidneys or liver that you never get an effective blood level. But when we used this on sick animals, it was just as active there as it was on the culture plates. The only animals we lost on it were the ones that were absolutely terminal before we started the drug. We were really excited—remember how excited we were, Frank? We thought we really had something to nail it to the wall."

"And no sign of side effects?" Sally said.

"No evidence whatever. When the earth-mold antibiotics are toxic, they usually show it in certain characteristic ways in rats or guinea pigs, and there wasn't any sign of trouble. Let me tell you: we were sure enough that it was clean, we had everybody in the lab up here taking therapeutic doses for over a week, more than twenty-five people, and we found no signs of toxicity. So finally we had enough left to send down to Carlos for field testing, and he used it in some desperation cases, people who were unquestionably going to die, and it stopped it, with no side effects. So we got FDA clearance to move with it on an emergency basis, and Sealey shipped us a good supply on an experimental protocol. Believe me, they weren't dragging their feet then—they were as excited as we were! They had Mancini, their production man, crawling all over the place. They even sent out that little chemist who developed the drug—what was his name, Frank? Tom Shipman? Funny little guy with horn-rimmed glasses—they sent him out to document our testing procedures so they could save time on their end. So we wrapped it all up in ribbons and they moved the drug into Canon City, and Carlos got started with it."

"And then it all fell apart," Sally Grinstone said.

"Well—" Monique muddled her drink. "I wouldn't say *that,* exactly. It worked, in the field, but—Frank, you were down there at the time. What the hell *did* happen?"

Frank scratched his chin. "It's hard to say, at this point," he said finally. "The drug worked, all right. It just didn't work anything like we thought it would, from Monique's reports from Fort Collins. It helped—it really *did* stop the plague—it just didn't do the job the way we'd hoped it would. You have to understand the pressure we were under. At first Carlos thought it was the dosage, and he jacked that up, but it didn't increase the effectiveness much. And then the late side effects began sneaking up on us, and they were pretty subtle, at first, and we didn't notice them until the outbreak was nearly over, but then all of a sudden they were very much there."

Sally sat chewing her thumb. "And how do you explain this?" she asked Monique. "A red-hot drug suddenly turning sour in a crisis?"

"I can't explain it," Monique said, "except that it sometimes happens. A new drug looks really special in early testing but then doesn't prove out when under extensive use, isn't as effective as it should be, or turns up some scary side effects, or something. It happens all the time."

"But *this* much difference?"

"Well—sometimes."

"In something as straightforward as bacteriocidal effects?"

"Sometimes." Monique spread her hands. "Remember the pressure. When it's some new drug you're trying out on multiple sclerosis or something like that, and it turns out to be a flop, you're naturally unhappy about it, but it's about what you anticipated—nobody really expected a barn-burner anyway, and those patients are very sadly accustomed to trying new drugs that don't work. But when you're dealing with a deadly thing like plague, and everybody's desperate, the failure of a promising new drug—even a half-failure, like this one—really hurts. Maybe all we're talking about is psychological. We expected miracles and we didn't get them."

"Hm." Sally Grinstone looked at Monique with those penetrating eyes. "Well, maybe. Anyway, I've tied you up for long enough already, and I've obviously got to dig deeper. Thanks for your time and your help. Believe it or not, I hope you're right, and they make the drug, and it stops things." She got up from the booth and tucked her bag strap over her shoulder. "By the way, what did you say that Sealey chemist's name was? Shipman? Yes, that was it. Tom Shipman."

37

From the time the bodies began to appear in the streets, a pall of silence fell over the city of Savannah. People, once indifferent, now were terrified, and they moved in off the streets. The wealthy fled to upper stories of their restored mansions and peered out the windows from behind heavy curtains and barred doors. Middle-class breadwinners crept out of their homes reluctantly, if at all, to go to work, until the businesses that employed them closed down. And housewives clung to their children in the depths of their neat little homes, hardly even daring to touch the telephone when it rang for fear it would bring bad tidings.

In the tenement flats it was worst of all. Dank little overcrowded rooms, the walls filled with fly nests, doors and windows slammed shut in the terrible heat, with only fans blowing over chunks of ice from the public Ice House for cooling. Day followed steaming hot day in grim succession as the sick and dying slowly but steadily increased in number.

For Carlos Quintana it was a time of agonizing frustration. It seemed that the larger his team of plague fighters became, the more totally at cross-purposes the battle seemed to be running. And as commander of the battle, Carlos found himself bogging down deeper and deeper trying to control the uncontrollable. None of the rules he long had known, believed in and practiced had any chance of working because none of them could be effectively applied.

Ted Bettendorf was an anchor in the storm—lean, gray, cadaverous, utterly unflappable, he was there on the phone to Carlos hourly if needed, night or day, listening, consulting, suggesting, in addition to the hours he spent on the phone to everywhere else. "God, you wouldn't believe the heat we're getting from Europe, from Russia, from Singapore, for God's sake," he groaned to Carlos one night. "You couldn't know, you don't want to know. From Mexico—Jesus!

You'd think we created this. One odd thing, though: suddenly Russia has let up on the accusations. They've gone a solid week without broadcasting any of that biological warfare crap."

"Did they have agents in Savannah?"

"Where didn't they have agents? Don't ask me, I don't know. All I know is that they certainly have plague, and at first it was all our fault, and now suddenly they've stopped screaming that we deliberately started it. Maybe they're just too busy fighting it to scream. Now, about those disposable syringes . . ."

At one point Ted went to Savannah for almost a week, moving about the city with Carlos and Jack Cheney, checking out the Big Hospital set up in the Performing Arts Pavillion, suggesting this approach, pondering that problem. The night he left he told Carlos: "I can't help you much, my friend. I'm still working on the drug supply and the vaccine, you know that. The situation here—well, you're as much on top of it as anybody could be."

"It isn't going to hold together, Ted."

"It will if you stay on top of it, Carlos. So stay on top. Jack will help."

"But the death toll, Ted. There's no end in sight, and I *can't fight without weapons. . . .*"

"You're fighting, Carlos. Keep fighting. I'll help you as much as possible." And Ted was off into the air to Atlanta, and Carlos went back to find Jack and spend another night trying to figure out what might help the next day.

The matter of the public broadcasts was one of the earliest and most flagrant examples of everything going wrong at once. Threatened by a deadly epidemic, people needed a constant, accurate, reliable source of information—yet the public broadcasts Carlos had originally tried to set up speedily degenerated into chaos. First an early tropical storm swept through, leaving the public information station standing in six feet of swampland water with no drainage. Then when the commercial stations stepped in to fill the gap, Carlos soon found that vital announcements were tucked into time-corners when most people were sleeping, or else were edited so heavily and creatively that the important part of most messages was lost altogether.

The problem was expanded by ten orders of magnitude by the simple fact that there were multitudes of messages to be passed on from a dozen different sources, and rather than coordinating efforts, each source shut its eyes to anyone else's needs and plunged ahead in its own private direction. This meant, of course, that information from one source was almost always in direct contradiction to instructions from other sources, but still were broadcast end-running on the same radio station.

The inevitable upshot was that virtually nothing got done properly, or in time, or even at all, and this was what tormented Carlos Quintana the most. A dribble of the new vaccine would reach the city, and a vaccination center would be manned at a certain location to provide at least minimal protection for certain groups of people living in certain areas of the city—and when the appointed time came, nobody appeared to be vaccinated. Why not, for God's sake? Word was out over all the radios—ah, but Doctor, the date was scrambled up. Everyone turned up *yesterday,* and of course there was no vaccine here yesterday. Attempts to distribute antibiotics in particularly high-incidence areas of the city came to similar ends. The actively ill would come, not the healthy family breadwinners as was planned—and the more chaotic the communications became, the less cooperative the people, crammed up in their hot, rancid little rooms, hiding from the street and the scourge, and watching helplessly as the scourge came right in after them.

Ultimately a less obvious—and far more dangerous—result began to appear as the chaos in communication continued: people who once had paid attention and tried to do things right began throwing up their hands, first merely impatient of the authorities, then resentful, and finally downright angry. They had enough on their hands just trying to cope, without the confused communications, so they began tuning it out and not listening at all. A pox on *me,* then a pox on *them,* was the growing attitude, and people began hardening into this posture more steadily day by day.

It was this attitude of desperate bloody-mindedness that was responsible, in large part, for the first real spark of violence to flare in the city when, two weeks into the plague, the great Central Ice House ran out of ice.

For many decades the four-story Ice House, occupying a full city block just south of the densest tenement area, had been as much an institution in the city of Savannah as the great antebellum mansions or Factor's Walk. People still remembered the horse-drawn ice wagons clip-clopping through the streets, dripping cold water from every crack, the iceman with the fearsome-looking tongs, the four-sided signs tucked up in the windows to indicate orders. Even today many tenement homes still had their old iceboxes standing ready and waiting, and although the horse-drawn wagon was a thing of the past, many a small black boy could still be seen any hot summer day, scuffing dust in the street and lugging a cardboard carton and a blanket, on his way to the Ice House.

During heat waves the ice was vital for far more than just food preservation. Air conditioning was all well and good for those who could afford it, but for the poor homes the universal substitute was a block of ice sitting in a large pan on the floor with a small electric fan blowing over it into your face.

Now, with fear of plague keeping people indoors, and with the longest, most murderous late-summer heat wave on record in Savannah, the Central Ice House was jammed daily from morning until night. For ice, at least, people would go out, however briefly, some walking, some driving, some parking and *then* walking, as queues to the ice delivery chutes grew longer. It was not a cheerful gathering of people at the Ice House those dismal days. Nobody wanted to be there. Everybody had news of death in his mouth, and little good to talk about. Little groups of kin would huddle together, muttering in private monosyllables. Moods were sullen, fights often broke out, and as the days passed, the prevailing attitude of bloody-mindedness took over more and more.

What exactly happened inside the Ice House on that particular day, nobody ever determined for sure. Whatever happened—some breakdown of superannuated, worn-out machinery—it happened all of a sudden at one o'clock of a blazing afternoon, when lineups for ice were at maximum, both at the truck-loading docks on the north side and the individual block-ice dispensers on the east side. There may have been two thousand hot, sullen people there at the critical time, or ten thousand—nobody knew—but however many, there was one weary woman who put her quarters into the dispenser slot, and shoved in the lever, and waited for the ice to come down the chute for her to take. . . .

And waited, as nothing happened. Ten other people at adjacent chutes had paid their money, too, and they also waited, complaining at the slow delivery, their impatient voices joining the rumble and snarl around them.

Then a loudspeaker boomed out overhead. "That's it, y'all. Ain't no more ice. No more ice today. Come back tomorrow."

Silence fell like a sodden blanket. Then: "No more ice? Man say no more ice—" and then, the enormity of it dawning: "No more ice today? Man, what you *mean,* no more ice?"

"Compressor's broke down. Cain't make no more. Now go home, come back tomorrow—"

"But my dollar's in that slot, man—"

"Cain't help that, lady. Closed up now. Come back to the office tomorrow and make an application and maybe you'll get it back. No more ice today—"

The anger and outrage in the crowd was palpable, a living thing. Then somebody was shouting, pointing toward the truck-loading docks. "Lookee there! Around there they got ice!"

The crowd split and surged around toward the docks. There a big eighteen-foot wooden panel truck was standing, filled to the scuppers with ice blocks. People swarmed toward it like ants to sugar. "That truck got ice! Let's get it!"

In a moment half a dozen men had climbed up the back of the truck, starting to dump the ice blocks off onto the dusty pavement. The driver started out of the truck cab, got a good look at the throng fast gathering around him and moved back inside. He shouted out the window: "I'm loaded up, man, I'm movin' out. Now *get!*"

The motor roared and the truck began slowly pressing away from the loading dock. A woman who had ducked under the rear wheels to retrieve an ice block was the first one crushed; others went down screaming in front of the cab and still the heavy-loaded truck inched forward. People climbed up on the running boards, trying to tear the doors open, but by now there was no stopping the driver; eyes glazed, he plowed on.

The truck was far too much to stop under power—but not too heavy to turn over. With the superhuman strength of built-up fury, people on both sides began rocking the truck. Somebody slashed a front tire, and the cab sagged on that side, the steering wheel spinning out of the driver's hands. Then the double rear tires went, and the top-heavy vehicle finally went over on its side with an enormous grinding crash, crushing ten more people as it fell.

Some people around the truck grabbed the ice and ran, but others swarmed up onto the loading dock into the Ice House itself. Three squad cars appeared as more people began pouring into the Ice House. The police took one look at the melee, the overturned truck, the bodies strewn on the ground, and radioed for the riot squad. The people storming the Ice House now had picked up any weapons they could lay their hands on—rocks, two-by-fours, ball bats and very sharp knives of all lengths and descriptions. Once inside they found long racks of needle-sharp ice hooks hanging along the walls, choice weapons for close infighting—and the search for ice began.

Of course, there wasn't any ice. The compressors were silent, the great rooms heavy with cold, dead air. Soon the screams and roars of pitched battle were heard up above; the more the mob couldn't find any ice, the angrier it became, the more vindictive and outraged—*They couldn't keep us in ice!*— And then a huge black man with wild eyes and an ice hook in each hand was standing up on a barrel and shouting, "You don't give us ice, we give you *fahr,* mon!" and piles of rubble were suddenly heaped up and fire was struck, and billows of black smoke poured out of the upper-story windows while people up above tried to scurry for escape.

Many didn't make it. The old dry wood of the interior went up like flares, the stairways were crammed and packed with struggling humanity, and the heat and smoke and collapsing brick walls got many of the rest. Fire sirens screamed as thousands poured out of the building to join the thousands more outside, all angry, all not giving a damn, venting the pent-up rage and fear of two long, unspeakably horrible weeks, and moving onto the surrounding blocks of buildings, smashing store windows, taking whatever they chose to take in lieu of ice, moving like a headless monster without direction.

The Central Ice House was a pyre before the firemen got hose water pumping. The police finally contained the riot within an eight-block perimeter around the Ice House, using shields and road blocks and riot guns and tear gas, and then waited all night and all the next day for the fire to burn itself out and people to crawl home again, such people as were left. Officials estimated eighteen hundred dead, unknown numbers injured or burned, and the Ice House a heap of smoldering rubble too hot to approach for four solid days.

Some of the people did get home, but something had happened to their minds in the meantime, and madness spread with news of the fire. Those who were there and those who merely heard were different people now, nursing their wounds and sharing their outrage, a people betrayed—*bereft of their ice*—and the plague descended even deeper into evil.

38

On the evening of the day the Ice House burned, Sally Grinstone was sitting at a remote table at the rear of the main dining room of the Chase Park Plaza Hotel in St. Louis, staring fixedly at a group of people dining just a few tables away. The object of Sally's attention was a small, balding young man with horn-rimmed glasses sitting near the center of the group. Certainly not a handsome man, Sally reflected, but not as unhandsome as she had feared; more than anything, she thought, he looked grossly unhappy, responding to the others' conversation in monosyllables, mostly concentrating on the dinner before him. And that, too, fit the picture. *Well,* Sally thought, *at least I've found him. Now it's just a matter of the right kind of contact. . . .*

Sally hardly looked like the same person who had been talking with Monique Jenrette and Frank Barrington just a few busy days before. She was done up in a formal cocktail dress just one thin whisker short of totally indecent, cut deep in front and back and worn without bra, black with no trim. She had left her twin ponytails with the hairdresser in the hotel basement, traded in for a short shag cut, and her owlish glasses were nowhere in evidence. True enough, she couldn't see a thing on the table, but that was okay with Sally; you could always order a steak and French fries without seeing the menu, and she could see the man in the horn-rimmed glasses just as clear as crystal glass, and that was what mattered right now. Of course, the big hotels didn't like having overdressed, underescorted young women they didn't know sitting alone in their dining rooms during big conventions; too many free-lancers killed things for the regular convention whores. The maître d' had given her a fishy stare when she appeared for dinner and let her cool her heels for thirty minutes while he seated couples and groups. At last, when she didn't go away, he sighed a silent sigh and led her back to a table the size of a cookie sheet in a remote back corner of the place and abandoned her to waiters who were scarcely any more interested; it had taken another thirty minutes just to get the drink she ordered—but in the meantime, luck of all luck, the little balding man had come in to the same dining area with his grim-looking dinner partners. *So fuck you, too,* Sally had muttered under her breath to the maître d'. *Thanks to the long wait, you've just handed me the game, you ass.*

To anyone but Sally Grinstone it might have seemed an impossible task that had faced her after she'd left Monique and Frank: to track down an obscure research chemist employed by a very large, very paranoid drug company in Indianapolis, identify him, somehow contact him in neutral territory, get acquainted with him, get him alone, and then, by hook or by crook, get him to talk about his work under circumstances that were such that the mere mention of the word *reporter* would make him slam shut like the Giant Clam of the Antilles upon encountering a bit of grit. And to accomplish all this *fast*—in three days, maybe four at the most. A formidable task indeed, for anyone else, but as it happened, Sally Grinstone was no slouch at her job. She had half a lifetime's worth of very firm connections in all kinds of unlikely places, connections she had diligently nurtured over the years. She knew what sort of questions had to be asked to spring what kind of information free; she knew the whole netherworld of muckraking like the back of her hand, understood the intricate politics of Finding Things Out, and she was not afraid of the telephone.

No, the task had not seemed impossible to her, certainly not at the beginning. Difficult, maybe, with some hellish time pressure, but that was nothing new. On her way back to her motel room after talking to Monique, Sally had stopped at a liquor store and bought half a gallon of cheap gin, three quarts of fake orange juice and two bags of ice. Back in her room she pulled the curtains tight, drew a soft chair up to the telephone and broke out a writing board, pen and legal pad. She stripped herself naked, wrapped an ice-cooled towel around her head, poured herself a long, stiff gin, and did something funny to the telephone wire. Then, with the phone jammed against her ear and the pad on her knee, she got to work.

She had telephoned and slept and scribbled notes, intermittently, all that night and all the next day. Many of her sources were night owls by choice and inclination. Many others happened to work all night, and many who didn't were willing to work for *her* all night anytime she whistled. After a dozen tries she finally connected with one of the latter a little after 1:00 A.M.—4:00 A.M. in Washington, D.C. "Merritt? Sally here. Been out on the town, I'll bet."

"Yeah, you might say; what's up?"

"Maybe a hot one, maybe not. I'm going to need some things mooee pronto. Can you call me back from your office?"

"Sure, Sal, gimme thirty minutes. What sort of things?" Sally told him. "Tom Shipman, huh? Shipman—sounds familiar. Antibiotics? Well, he's bound to be a member, so I should be able to flag him for you quick enough. Jingle the office in forty-five minutes."

When she did, Merritt said, "Hey, you got a busy boy hooked here. He's got a string of publications as long as your arm."

Sally snorted. "Some of these guys publish their birth certificates just to pad out the list."

"Well, this all looks like solid stuff. A long list of patents, too—all assigned to the company, of course."

"Okay, concentrate on the publications in the last three years," Sally said. "What's the main thrust?"

"Antibiotics almost exclusively, some of them new cell poisons for cancer—you know, chemotherapeutic agents. Almost all of them far too toxic. Hey, here's a weird one. He was fiddling around with an adriamycin derivative—that's one of the good ones—and he got a molecule that looked absolutely great against breast CA, but the drug carried this wild shocking purple color. He fed it to cancerous rats and they got well, but they turned bright purple and *stayed* purple. Patient acceptance nil. So he figured it had to be the optical properties of an acetyl group, the molecule sort of wrinkled up instead of wrinkling down like he thought it would, so he finally figured a way to get the acetyl group turned over at the same attachment, and that got rid of the color just fine. Got rid of the anticancer activity too. That one's back on the drawing boards."

"What about the antibiotics for infection?"

"Well, let's see." Long pause. "Most of them here are some new tetracycline derivatives he's been playing around with—God almighty, all kinds of them! He did three or four good review papers in that area about three years ago, plus a whole slew of technical reports—"

"Go pull them for me, will you? The major ones."

"Sure, I'll throw them in the mail before I leave."

"Don't mail them, Merritt. Read them to me."

"You mean right now, over the horn? God, Sal, who's paying this phone bill?"

"Ma Bell, dummy. Now go get 'em."

He got them, and read them, and Sally listened intently, picking them up on a pocket recorder held right near the earpiece while Merritt read. When he finally finished she blew him a kiss and sent him back to bed. "Oh, Merritt, listen. Put your head to work, will you? I may have to hit this guy, and he mustn't know it's press or it won't work. If you can think of anything, or find out anything that might help, let me know fast. How's his sex life? Will he sell? How deep does Sealey have him hooked? Absolutely any angle that might help, I need it, okay?"

"I'll work on it," Merritt said, and rang off. Good old Merritt, he *would* work on it, too, he had some funny sources and he'd never failed her yet, especially not since she'd saved him his ass and his eighty-grand job with one well-placed national news story, back at a time when he was caught in a real nut-crusher and needed some solid help.

On through the night and into the dawn, dialing, talking, replenishing her gin and orange juice, hour upon hour of the sort of intense, total concentration you had to use on a thing like this, and gradually the barest profile of the quarry began to fill out into a lifelike picture.

Thomas Eugene Shipman, age forty-two, Caucasian male, never married, a lifelong perennial bachelor. Five feet nine inches tall, 159 pounds. Male pattern baldness appearing at age twenty-three, now moderately advanced. Severe astigmatism, required thick corrective lenses; tried contacts but found they made him look like he had Graves' disease so he retired them and went back to the heavy horn-rims. Occupation: organic chemist (Ph.D.) with special interest in pharmaceuticals and an enviable reputation in antibiotic research and development.

Shipman was born in Shaker Heights, Ohio, son of an affluent neurosurgeon, his mother a debutante daughter of a family entrenched in the high-office politics of the state. Tom had been a small, sickly boy who learned early on to capitalize on his very sharp mind. Taken out of public school in fifth grade, when other boys began picking him apart and smashing his glasses as a routine prank, he found private school more protective, but still young Tom showed no great ability to select or hold good friends; his buddies were invariably the ones who depended on him for test answers but ignored him at other times. A sullen, unhappy child who soon learned to be arrogant of his knowledge because a very sharp mind was the one thing he had going for him.

From early years on there was paternal pressure to guide him into medicine, but young Tom detested the vaguenesses of biology, the apparent pointlessness of zoology, the uncertainties of physiology. Math was his forte when he left home for Andover Academy, with chemistry running a close second. Then, when he first encountered organic, that bewildering nightmare of carbon chemistry that left so many of his classmates far behind, he knew he had found his real métier. Quite aside from possessing a phenomenally acute memory, he had that type of mind that could conceive of organic molecules in living, three-dimensional depth and color, not merely as flat, inaccurate formulas on paper. With a near-perfect grade average behind him, he went into the Westinghouse Science Scholarship competition in his senior year with a crafty system of computer simulation for determining the spacial and rotational qualities of complex multiringed organic compounds, a system quite impressive for its uniqueness and imagination, and won first prize hands down, together with a full four-year scholarship in chemistry and an early acceptance at Yale.

During his undergraduate years he spent most of his time in an honors program doing what amounted to advanced graduate work in organic chemistry. Job offers started turning up from his sophomore year on, and much of his work began finding publication in the major chemical and engineering journals. After completing his Master's work he went straight on to doctoral work at Princeton, simply pursuing the avenues of research he had already set out for himself, before finally, armed with a Ph.D. at the age of twenty-three, he accepted a position at Merck, Sharpe and Dohme in their research and development laboratories, tackling the many divergent problems of synthesizing new drugs designed to have high potential as antibiotics active against infection but with very little evidence of toxicity that might spoil them for human use. It was work right up Tom Shipman's alley, playing games with theoretical molecules, taking them through endless permutations of various basic forms, altering them subtly again and again in the computer and in the lab, tabulating alterations in their activities, convinced that if he could find *what it was* in a molecule that altered its ability to destroy bacteria, he would have found the Rosetta stone to the endless search for really new antibiotics that consumed so much time and effort with such very spare results in those days.

Tailored to him or not, the job at Merck didn't last more than two years. Merck's R&D scene was, in good part, a team effort, whole squadrons of people tackling a given problem, and Tom Shipman was not a team person. He fretted about the wasted time and indifferent concern he discerned in the crew around him. You couldn't solve problems, in his view, by standing around telling jokes during endless coffee breaks and flirting endlessly with the cute little lab assistants and getting out of there at the stroke of five—and you couldn't solve problems sitting at your own lab bench with all that going on around you, either. Very soon Tom got permission to *start* his workday at five, when the others were leaving, bringing his dinner in a lunch box, and working on in silence and solitude until two or three in the morning. This didn't increase his popularity with his team, who regarded him as some new kind of nut and resented the volume of work that consistently poured off his desk; perversely, it even made his supervisors frown. Of course they liked his results well enough, and recognized his value, but when it came to promotion evaluations and such, reports of his superiors were filled with remarks such as "Does not relate well to laboratory staff," "Tends to be secretive" and "Doesn't fit in with cooperative ventures." And although small merit raises materialized from time to time, there was no talk of promotion.

Probably worse, from Tom Shipman's viewpoint, the company was an enormous, impersonal pharmaceutical organization with many other sharp and ambitious chemists on the payroll and Tom found himself a small frog in a large pond. Company policy did not lend itself to personal recognition of individual scientists, and although many papers originated on Tom Shipman's lab bench and made their way off his desk through the convoluted channels that led to eventual journal publication, his name rarely headed the list of authors on those papers and often never appeared at all. Others higher on the team would review the papers, edit a few sentences, alter a few remarks in the summary statements and then slap on their names as coauthors. Patents were the same: by the time the company lawyers got through with prospective patent applications, *everybody's* name would be involved, with his somewhere down at the bottom of the list, frequently misspelled. And thus it was that when some people from Sealey Labs, a much smaller firm engaged almost exclusively in antibiotic research, came around on a raiding party and offered Tom Shipman full autonomy in his own lab and full credit for his own papers and patents and twenty-five percent more salary than he was already making, he kissed the Merck matrix good-bye without a single pang.

It was from Sealey that the prodigious stream of Tom's papers that Merritt had referred to had come. It figured, Sally thought. The big outfits could afford to take a prospective winner, bury him in some obscure basement somewhere and then skim the cream off his work. A smaller outfit couldn't do that, and didn't want to. Sealey needed their man's name on those papers in bold prominence. Indeed, the more Sally Grinstone had rooted into it, the more it seemed that Sealey had needed—and had hoped to get—a very great deal from Tom Shipman. In Sally's mind now, the big question was: *What, precisely, had they gotten?*

By two o'clock the next afternoon, discouraged and half starving, Sally went out for a steak, still wracking her brains over that question. She had a picture of the man, all right, and she thought she saw a possible approach or two, but the picture seemed to end at Sealey's doors. She'd met people like this before: the brilliant, hopelessly immersed scientific workaholic who never did anything or thought about anything beyond his work (except that they always seemed to break from time to time, in some sort of a pattern—sex, booze, gambling, something). But it was what he had done at Sealey that she had to have, and she just didn't have it. The published papers offered hints, told her the general area of his work, but not the details. It was what he had done that *hadn't* been published that she needed.

She sat and devoured one steak and ordered another, raking her memory for possible contacts. There was no one at Sealey she could go near for information, not one soul—Sally put down her fork. *Wait a minute.* There was Jan Livewright, of course. Jan had detailed for Sealey for a while, promoted drugs to the doctors, back while Sally and she had been . . . Last she'd heard, Jan had moved on to Abbott Labs, but the detailers were a pretty thick crowd. Sally munched slowly on her steak. She hated like hell to foreclose on that particular mortgage, but she was beginning to feel desperate. . . .

Back at the motel, with the kind of eerie, prescient scent of blood in her nostrils that had become so familiar to Sally over the years that she had come to expect it, she struck gold. Jan Livewright didn't have any current knowledge of things going on at Sealey, but a guy she was dating had a friend who had worked there as a lab assistant in one of the labs until they'd abruptly fired him a week or so ago, for no apparent cause, and the friend was pissed. Jan would contact him, a chap named Bob King, and if Sal didn't hear to the contrary in thirty minutes, she could call him.

Sally prowled the room, gulped gin and orange juice, and at the stroke of the appointed minute she called. Yes, the man said, he'd heard from Jan. Yes, he'd been working for Sealey, and if he could just find some way to gig those bastards, he'd give his right arm for the chance. . . .

"I don't want to gig anyboody," Sally said. "All I want is some information. When did they lay you off?"

"Three weeks ago, when they closed down Tom Shipman's lab."

"Closed—did you say *closed down?*"

"That's right. One day I was there and the next day the lab was locked up tight and I was sent down to wash bottles in the production department. A week of that and they gave me the boot. Overstaffed, they said. Pick up your check."

"You're sure it was Shipman's lab?"

"I ought to know," the man said. "I was working there."

"But why close it down?"

Bob King didn't know. He'd thought Dr. Shipman was on the track of something very hot indeed, a new antibiotic. A real barn burner—at least everybody from the R&D people to the sales staff seemed to be excited about it, and all of a sudden, whoppo, they cut if off. Shipman himself? The man laughed. "You think *I* was pissed, you should have seen him. He was fit to be tied. Went around like a madman, banging on doors and screaming at people. They put him on some other project, a real dead-ender, some chemotherapeutic they'd had on the shelf for ten years because they couldn't get the glitches out of it, and I swear he was ready to kill somebody. But as for why they cut if off—I just plain don't know. Whatever the reason, they sure moved fast . . ."

Sally rang off and sat back, fairly quivering. It looked like the key, all right—but the key to what? She knew then she wouldn't get it from other people. Shipman himself was going to have to tell her, and it sounded like he might be ready to spill if only she could find a way to hit him. But how? Slowly, carefully, she went back over the heaps of notes she'd been making. Not much personal data here, not much to get hold of. Long work hours, lots of reading of chemical literature when he got home to his nice little three-room apartment in Indianapolis. Listened to lots of music, opera and classics, but didn't even own a TV set. Took most of his meals out, same little restaurant near his apartment, probably had the same dinner every night—she snorted. There had to be an approach—what could she do? Go take a job at Sealey and work it from there? Never, that would take far too much time and she knew now she had to move fast. What's more, if it was really something hot, the bastards might just shoot her. Go plant herself at his table at the restaurant? She'd just get thrown out. Follow him and see if he ever hit a bar? Time, time, time—even assuming he ever *did* hit a bar, which maybe he never did. Take the apartment next to his and scream for help? Oh, hell, Sally, come *on*—

The phone rang suddenly, and it was Roger Merritt at the American Chemical Society. "How's your digging coming along?"

"Twenty feet under and still going," Sally said sourly. "By now I know more about the guy than he does—but I can't find a fast way to touch him. I'd have to set something up for months, and I haven't *got* months."

"Have you got three days?"

"I might have—if I can convince a couple of editors that I'm going to bring them Sealey Labs on a platter."

"If you've got three days, I know how you can nail him. It just dawned on me ten minutes ago. There's an American Chemical Society regional meeting at the Chase Park Plaza in St. Louis starting tomorrow, two thousand chemists turning up there. Our registration file says Tom Shipman is going with a few others from Sealey."

Sally sat bolt upright. "Is he giving a paper?"

"Now that's a funny thing: he's not on the program. He almost always gives two or three papers at one of these confabs, but not a thing this time. The point is—I did a little confidential digging, and it seems that Shipman loosens up quite a bit at these big Chemical Society affairs. He hits the cocktail parties, and one source says he usually ends up very cozy with some unattached female before the conference is over. He never seems to follow up, it's just fun and games while the party's going, but you might find an opening there. I thought you'd like to know."

"Like to know! Roger, you're a one hundred percent doll. When this is all over, I'm coming down there and make you as happy as you've made me. Now I've got to ring off and get packing. Do you know his room number? Good. And Roger—get me a press registration, but have them give me an ordinary member's ID card, okay? See you later, dummy."

For a long moment she sat back and marveled—her prescient nose had been right. The rough part was over, and now she was on her own ground. *Fun and games while the party's going,* she thought, and tipped her glass in an imaginary toast.

Fun and games, indeed.

39

In Brookdale, Connecticut, on the day after the Ice House fire, Jack Dillman sat in a silent house in the cool of his upstairs studio and carefully airbrushed in the finishing touches on the dust-jacket layout he was just completing. He sat back, cocked his head and tilted the light over his shoulder onto the drawing board, started to add a final stroke, then shook his head and set the airbrush aside.

For a long time he looked at the artwork spread out before him. Then neatly, almost ceremonially, he began closing the paint pots and ink bottles, setting them back in their places, carefully cleaning the brushes and pen nibs before storing them away. It was almost five in the afternoon, and not a sound from down below all day. *"Shopping" again,* Jack thought sourly. *And later every time. Doesn't the bastard's wife ever walk in on them? Or where do they go?* Not that it mattered that much. With good old Hal Parker, one bed was as good as another.

Jack walked downstairs, made himself a drink, extra long and extra strong. *A job wrapped up calls for a celebration, he thought.* The house was very still and still smelled of Pine-Sol from yesterday's cleaning lady. An antiseptic smell, more like a clinic than a home. He drifted from room to room uneasily—she wasn't usually so damned late. As always, the thoughts drifted to his mind: *Bad traffic: suppose there was an accident? Maybe she didn't even carry her purse—who would they call?* He shrugged the thought aside, disgusted with himself for worrying. Finally he sat down in front of the Eye and flipped on the TV news.

Savannah, again, top of the evening. *God* was he sick of hearing about Savannah—why in hell didn't the Health Service get cracking and *do* something down there, for God's sake, instead of all this sackcloth-and-ashes stuff? Surely there was *something* they could do—

The screen caught his attention, a helicopter news clip—what the *hell?* Big fire, huge building going up, and rioting. The camera zoomed in on riot police behind portable shields, facing off a huge mob of angry black people—he watched, shaking his head. Then, after a while they went to something else, and he snapped off the set.

Thank God he wasn't down *there.* Riots and looting and nobody doing anything to help. But suppose it was here. If you were down there, you'd get *out,* sure, but here? Get out to where? He thought of some other film clips he'd seen last week, sick people sitting alone in empty houses down there, and long lines of garbage trucks heading out toward the swamps. . . .

People alone in empty houses. Suddenly the thought was not very nice, not nice at all, and he stirred, glanced out the front windows toward the driveway. Something like that happen here, you wouldn't want to be alone. *But suppose she'd decided she wasn't coming back?* Suddenly, faced with a possible reality, he felt a chill, bone deep, and sweat broke out on his forehead.

Another drink helped, but not too much. He was well into his third when she finally turned into the driveway.

40

For Carlos Quintana the first real hint of a breakthrough came four days after the Ice House fire. He had checked in early at the pro tem CDC headquarters, an old restored office building on Lafayette Street, to pore over the morning public-health reports—new cases reported, deaths, hospital reports, statistical data, the same old ever-worsening story that was grinding him into the ground day by day—when somebody called out, "Hey, Carlos, front and center! Your boss is here. . . ."

It was Ted Bettendorf in the flesh, looking tall and gaunt and gray and tired, with a cardboard parcel tucked under his arm and a cadaverous smile on his face. He looked around at the crowd of people milling in the room, manning telephones and desks, and then at Carlos buried under piles of papers and reports and readouts and raised his eyebrows. "You're looking a little ragged," he said mildly.

Carlos leaped up and swept papers off a chair onto the floor so Ted could sit down. "I'm feeling ragged. Hoo, boy, you might say so! Ragged isn't the word."

"What are you up to?"

"Same thing I was up to yesterday morning, and the morning before that, only it's a little worse every day. We're just now getting more firm casualty figures on that Ice House debacle—"

"Well, set that aside for a minute," Ted said. "I got you a present and decided I'd hand-deliver it." He handed the parcel to Carlos.

"What's this?"

"The new preventive vaccine. By special courier from Lilly's stockpile. I thought you'd be pleased to see it."

"You mean the new vaccine we can use to immunize people to this mutant organism so they don't get infected?"

"That's right. It's made from the mutated strain of plague organisms, right from Monique's original cultures. I've been twisting arms for all I was worth, and it takes forever to make—they only have tiny quantities of it finished—but Lilly's control people are finally satisfied that what they have tests out safe enough, at least for emergency use. The injections are painful, but the antibody titer against the bug is measurable in as little as a week. The bug is antigenic as hell—which means that people will have *some* immune protection from the bug within four or five days after receiving the vaccine."

"Wow!" Carlos sat straight up, his eyes bright, his mind already revising his immediate field plans. "Let me tell you, my thin friend, it's just about time. At least we can get some of our field workers protected, if there's enough here. How much are they sending? Just this little box?"

"No, no. They've been producing it all during the testing, and slow as it is to manufacture, they can let you have five thousand doses off the top of the pile. They should have them to you here by tomorrow morning. What's more, they have four other labs cooperating, making it under license, so there should be more very soon."

"Good. Most exceedingly good." Carlos paced excitedly. "We may even have a chance to do something good down here yet. Tell them to just get it to Savannah airport—we'll have a truck waiting. We're using one of the warehouses down on River Street, Factor's Walk to be exact, for storage supplies—hospital goods, pharmaceuticals, everything, right handy to the center of activities here. That'll do fine, and it's a fast shot in from the airport by freeway. Warehouse 14—have them mark that on the consignment, so we don't have some idiot truck driver hustling it all through the city streets." Carlos turned back to Ted, his face suddenly sober. "This will be great to protect some uninfected medical workers from future infection—if they stay clean long enough for the vaccine to build up an immunity—but what can we do for some twenty thousand people who are already infected and dropping dead for want of treatment? The vaccine won't help them. What we need is the new Sealey antibiotic, that 3147 stuff we used in Colorado."

"I've got help coming there too," Ted said. "I just got word this morning that Sealey Labs is going to release a supply of the 3147 antibiotic for you to use on people that you will certify have active plague. That stuff should be turning up here in just a few days."

"That's the same stuff we were using in Colorado?"

"Exactly. The antibiotic that Sealey's Mancini was talking about withdrawing because of its side effects."

"So what made them change their minds? Did you get an Act of Congress?"

"No Act of Congress. They've made some kind of funny deal with the administration—I don't know what it is, and I can't seem to find out—but they're springing a field supply of the stuff loose at a perfectly staggering price and with some kind of outrageous liability guarantee. As part of the deal, it's only for use under your direct control, and only here in Savannah, nowhere else."

Carlos sat staring at the older man. "What about the outlying areas we talked about on the phone yesterday? I mean, this movement out of the city we're beginning to see—"

"That'll be up to you to decide," Ted said. "On your own responsibility."

"I see." Carlos bit his lip. "Well, hanged for a sheep—what the hell, we've all got to die sometime, might as well go down in a blaze of glory. We'll worry about that when we hit it. At least we'll have something to work with—Christ! Tell them yes, a thousand times yes. Spring all of it you can pry loose and get it down here while there's still somebody around to treat. . . ."

For Carlos it was the first real ray of hope that had appeared since the Savannah plague had started. From the very start it had been a steady downhill progression from bad to worse, with the very worst possible always all too clearly in sight up ahead. It wasn't just that the chance to pull things together and establish control had been lost before they'd even started—as it most certainly had. It was the plain, blunt, agonizing fact that they had had so terribly little to work with, so little of anything that could help, so little that accomplished anything. And as night followed day, the situation had deteriorated step by step, without a single way in the world to prevent it.

Standard procedures had been of little help—it had never even remotely been a standard problem. From the very beginning, geographic containment of the plague had been the essential priority—and a totally unachievable goal. First of all, the disease had to be contained within the city, and disease-free areas of the city had to be identified and kept disease-free. Only then could disease-affected areas be identified, blocked off and treated in order to reduce plague areas to smaller and smaller segments. It was simple enough in principle: knock it down where it exists and don't let it spread. But how to achieve this? At every step of the way the "simple" principle had fallen apart. You needed tight civil control—but there was no way in the world to establish it. You needed resources, but the resources didn't exist. You needed an organized army of experienced field workers. You needed a million things you didn't have.

Nor did breaking the problem into segments prove any more fruitful. You needed rodent control immediately and desperately—but how to achieve it on a crash basis in a swarming, superheated city like Savannah? It was worse than useless to try to evacuate rat-infested tenement blocks and then kill the rats—the infected fleas would simply hop off the dying rats and lie in wait, fully virulent and ever more hungry, for the people to return, or the dogs, or the cats or anything else the fleas might feed on. To accomplish anything at all, the rat warrens first had to be sprayed to kill the fleas, and then sprayed again a week later, to hit the fleas' hatching nits. Meanwhile, the rats, not pleased at being sprayed, moved out of the target areas in droves, only to pick up new infected fleas in the adjacent unsprayed areas. The city's Rat Squad tried throwing up crude barriers to prevent this defeating migration, but the barriers were promptly torn down each night by the people *inside* who wanted the rats *outside;* some adventurous rats scaled the barriers like ladders, while others took to the sewers to turn up in other, disease-free portions of the city. An army of 100,000 experienced rat fighters working diligently night and day with unlimited resources and holding large segments of the population at gunpoint might conceivably have made some inroads into the problem—but a Rat Squad of five hundred volunteers with ten spray trucks and no real authority whatever to demand and obtain either obedience or compliance from an ever more sullen and surly populace were—literally—whipped before they started. The very best results they could manage were along the immediate waterfront where nobody actually lived except drunks and vagabonds, killing rats by the thousands and hoping forlornly that the fleas from those rats would not find their way to where people *did* live. And on the waterfront, those thousands of rats were the merest drop in the bucket. . . .

Holding down the disease in infested areas was equally unsuccessful. The tiny supplies of the old vaccine were used, but the effectiveness was barely noticeable as far as Carlos could tell from such muddled statistics as he could rally. Correct the figures for this and correct them for that and very soon you had corrected the life out of your data and you didn't know what was what. And further to this, another thing soon became certain: attempts to contain the plague within the city itself clearly were not working. Especially after the Ice House riot, people began leaving the city by the thousands. Some left in cars and pickups and flatbeds loaded with household goods and bedding and rats, often with one or two family members already sick and others fast on their way. Many, many more left the city on foot—mothers and fathers and barefoot kids straggling along the edge of the road, loaded up with nothing more than what they could carry on their backs or in crude two-wheel carts, drinking the mud-yellow ditchwater, eating peanuts and beans and sugar and what little else they could carry, easing the kids' hunger pangs with stale Twinkies stolen from neighborhood groceries as they passed.

Of course these people ran a gauntlet of roadblocks and deterrents. They were warned repeatedly to turn back, that there was nothing up ahead for them, that farmers were driving people off with pitchforks and shotguns—but what were a few state troopers and sheriff's deputies supposed to do, standing on top of their shiny squad cars and shouting into bullhorns as endless streams of ragged people kept coming down the road at them, pausing to mill around the obstructing squad cars and then shuffling down into the ditches to go around them and up onto the road beyond? What were they supposed to do—shoot them? There was no *law* that said they couldn't go down the road, and the long-promised National Guard hadn't turned up to help yet, at least they might have created a physical barrier, but even then the people would just have scattered out through the fields to go around, and who was going to be the first to shoot kids, for Christ sake?

The fact was that the plague had already and long since crept out to the surrounding villages and farms anyway. Farmers had hauled their trucks full of dried-up, drought-ruined produce into the city for whatever they could get for it, and came back home carrying an infinitely more spoiled cargo. Nobody had any idea how many sick, dying or dead there might be in these outlying areas because nobody out there wanted to bring their sick into the city, hearing what they'd heard, and the dead were disposed of in shallow graves dug just above ground-water level in remote corners of the back forty. Public-health investigators who tried to check the countryside were greeted by snarling dogs and no information. Meanwhile, the barn rats took their infected fleas on to neighboring farms, and people who hadn't even been near the city at all began falling ill.

Thus it was that the city refugees who headed away weren't really heading for the outlying farms and villages at all. Even if they hadn't believed the roadblock police, they had soon learned for themselves that the farmers *were* driving them off with pitchforks and shotguns. Those refugees raided what fields they could raid at night for whatever food they could find as they passed through, but they were not country folk anyway. Though they fled Savannah, they tended to bypass the incomprehensible terrors of the country in favor of the known terrors of the city, heading northward toward Augusta, east across South Carolina toward Charleston, south toward Albany, west toward Macon and Atlanta. And those and other cities, soon aware that they were coming—only a trickle now, but a trickle that could become a deluge later—were slamming their gates and hauling up their drawbridges like medieval fortresses.

Meanwhile, with no real authority yet established to *prevent* travel, and facing confused directives from a dozen different public-health and law-enforcement agencies, those who had the means to travel did so as they chose. Many truck drivers, more enterprising than sharp-witted, rolled their rigs wherever they wished whenever they felt like it, fighting like longshoremen for what dwindling cargo there was to be hauled into and out of Savannah, cash paid in advance. Some auto drivers were intimidated by the state troopers' roadblocks and threats and turned back, but others refused, and pitched battles at those bottlenecks became ever more frequent. The airlines serving Savannah and Atlanta were far too hungry for fares to come up with any coherent or responsible containment or quarantine policy, and the long-anticipated, long-expected, long-promised federal regulatory injunction on air and ground travel in and out of Savannah and Atlanta which Carlos had believed to be so utterly vital, and had spent days begging and pleading for, never quite seemed to materialize from the quagmire of conflicting directives, regulations, executive orders and proposed procedures emanating from the Corridors of Leadership to the north.

So containment had failed for so long already that it hardly made any difference anymore anyway. And without vaccine and drugs, even early containment could not have saved Savannah. *At least now,*

Carlos thought, *we will have weapons, maybe too few and too late, but something we can work with.* He dispatched Ted back to the airport by taxi, completed some calls, and then started on foot down Emery Street in the already hot September morning sun to find Jack Cheney in his improvised public-health field office in the big museum basement just across from the Big Hospital, as everyone was now calling the Performing Arts Pavillion. Jack had proven a solid ally in the battle, a man with a cool, reasonable, practical mind, trying from the beginning to coordinate his very real responsibilities as the Director of the Chatham County Public Health Department with Carlos's often very different responsibilities as emergency epidemiologist for the Centers for Disease Control. Sometimes Jack had said no when Carlos had said yes, sometimes they had fought it out, and sometimes Jack had prevailed, but throughout the growing horror they had come to respect each other, see each other's viewpoints, and—inevitably—become friends. Carlos knew that Jack would be as delighted as he was at the news of the imminent arrival of the vaccine and the S-3147 supplies. . . .

Dr. Cheney had already left the field station, Carlos was informed, he was probably over at the Big Hospital; so Carlos headed across traffic toward the vast building that had been raised a few years ago as a new center for Savannah's cultural life, now turned into an enormous receiving hospital and treatment center for plague victims, a modern-day equivalent of the medieval pesthouse. He was just about to start across the main thoroughfare to reach it when he stopped abruptly and cocked his head. Somewhere far to the south he could hear the distant rattling and popping of fireworks. Fourth of July? Nonsense, Labor Day was already past. Some Civil War hero's birthday? More rattling and popping and popping and popping.

Fireworks? He heard more of it, sporadically, as he saw a green light and dashed across the last traffic lane, narrowly missed by a rumbling truck. Rattle, pop, bang, all from the south side of the city. *Fireworks?* Fireworks, hell. Those were rifles and submachine guns he was hearing.

The sounds faded as he ducked inside the entry to the Big Hospital. He'd been here before, numerous times, but never could adjust to the sight that greeted him: the vast auditorium floor paved with row upon row of mats wrapped in white disposable paper sheets, each mat bearing a patient, some moving, some not, the heat and the stench and the noise of the place almost unbearable despite the great ventilators in the ceiling going full blast. Paper-clad, white-masked, rubber-gloved nurses and doctors and aides moving here and there along the narrow walkways, growing ever narrower as additional mats were shoved in, extending like a vast scene of carnage to the far, far end of the building. Carlos walked to the sterile bins near the door, slipped on mask and paper gown and gloves as he searched the upright figures for Jack Cheney and finally spotted him, halfway to the east wall of the place. He started across the floor toward his friend, sidestepping constantly to avoid stepping on a patient's leg flailed out into a walkway, somebody's arm flopped askew in his path. Fingers plucked at his pants legs as he walked. Paper garments clung to the patients, some half torn off. Here a man was coughing up great gouts of blood all over sheet and mat and floor around him. A woman, gray as putty, sat motionless except to slap at two flies that wanted to land on a crust of blood at her nostril. As Jack had told him a few days before, "We barely have time to take temperatures once a day, and get food out once a day, and haul away the dead ones. Nursing care? It's a travesty. We just do what we can. There's not enough time and not enough people."

Paradoxically, Jack was angry at the news about the vaccine and the Sealey drug coming. "The fucking bastards," he said. "*Now* they send us a teacup to fight back the ocean. Three weeks ago we might have had a chance of stopping this thing—but they had to spend those three weeks covering their asses. So now they've got their asses covered and the blood of all these people all over their hands—let's see how they put *that* into their goddam self-aggrandizing ads." He turned away, muttering to himself. "All the sweet little deer and chipmunks bouncing around the tree stumps—"

"Tree stumps?"

"You know what I mean. All the big, glossy look-how-good-we-are-planting-the-dear-little-trees ads the big timber companies publish in *Time,* make a clear-cut gouge in the forest look like some kind of paradise, while out in the real world they're turning whole beautiful mountainsides into rubble and slash, laying waste to the country. And oil companies telling you how *very* good they are while they busily rob the country blind. The drug companies are doing the same damned thing. . . ."

Carlos shook his head sadly. "Jack, my friend, you're just too much of a dreamer."

"I work day after day down in this hell-pit and you call me a *dreamer?*"

"Like a five-year-old kiddie. In your dream world the rights and wrongs are all very clear, and evil should be struck down without mercy. But in the real world these piddly thieveries don't count for too much, really. To me, what really counts right now, is that we're getting the vaccine and the drugs, finally, and maybe they'll give us a fighting chance, if we can just plan things right and work fast enough. They kept it from running away from us in Colorado—maybe they'll let us hold it here."

Jack shook his head. "And you call *me* a dreamer."

"In this one case, I prefer to be a dreamer. I dream that we're going to win."

"And the medicine? When does it get here?"

"Tonight. We'll store it down in Warehouse 14 if there's still room enough. Hell, we'll make room enough. Right now we need to get across the street and break out those master plans again and start fixing priorities and mobilizing personnel—"

Somewhere in the distance there was a vast muffled boom and the floor jolted under their feet. Carlos looked up, startled.

"Just a gas-station storage tank," Jack said, his face grim. "Or maybe a riot-squad ammo truck. They've been blowing things up out there ever since the Ice House fire. You mean you haven't heard it?"

"Not that I noticed—until this morning."

"Then you must be stone deaf. Half the streets in the center city are blockaded off. Goon squads with lead pipes and Berettas wandering around at night smashing store windows and looting. Now it's going on in the daytime too." Jack Cheney looked back over his shoulder at the vast expanse of sick and dying people sprawled across the floor of the great room. "Yes, I guess we'd damned well better get over there and make some plans while there's still something left of this city to save."

41

In the second-story tenement flat in south-side Chicago, Sidonia Harper heard her mother's footsteps coming up the stairs with the groceries, down the hall to the door and on into the kitchen. Siddie hunched down in her chair, facing the TV set, uneager for her mother to come in and complain about her watching that stuff—and this time, her mother didn't. Sidonia reached out and changed the channel to the beginning of another newscast, and leaned forward to watch it, absorbed. She'd been watching newscasts all day, all the things happening down in Georgia, the epidemic and the riots. It was like film clips she'd seen so many times before of one war front or another, hideous and hypnotizing, so horrible you couldn't take your eyes away from the screen. And sometimes, it seemed to her, those things took on far more reality in her life than her bed and her wheelchair and the dull, unchanging life that she lived. . . .

In the dim room she became aware that her baby sister Tessie had come into the room and settled down on the bare floor beside the right wheel of her chair. She shook her head and frowned—eight years old was too young to watch this sort of thing, people smashing windows and burning buildings and wandering the streets with two-by-four planks in their hands. "Tessie, get out of here. Go get a book to read. You shouldn't watch this stuff."

"Mamma's sick," Tessie said.

With her attention on the screen, it took a minute to get through. "What's that? What you sayin'?"

"I think Mamma's sick. She not cookin' dinner. She just sittin' on the bed."

Sidonia Harper snapped off the set and turned her wheelchair sharply to the door. "Mamma?" she called. She wheeled through, into her mother's bedroom.

Mamma was sitting on the edge of the bed, her shoes off, leaning forward, hands bracing herself on the edge of the mattress. Her eyes were closed and she seemed to be breathing hard.

"Mamma?"

Her mother's eyes held a baffled look when she opened them. "I'm feelin' poor, Siddie," she said. "Couldn't hardly make it up those stairs. Can't hardly breathe, right now." She looked at Sidonia as if she were having trouble focusing. "Best you get some supper for us, girl. I think I'm gettin' sick. You may have to do for us, for a day or two."

42

Fiddle-de-dee, fiddle-de-dee, the fly has married the bumblebee, Sally Grinstone thought, stretching luxuriantly in the darkness. Well, not hardly *married,* exactly, she reflected, that would be far beyond the call of duty, but close enough, close enough. She shifted in bed in the dark room, feeling immensely pleased with herself as she heard Tom Shipman snoring softly beside her, just a few inches north of her left ear. *Said the bee, said she, I'll live under your wing, and you'll never know that I carry a sting. . . .*

So far it had worked out beyond her fondest dreams. She had followed him from the hotel dining room, leaving exact change on the table, sans tip, and stuffing a half-eaten steak into her handbag as he got up to depart with the sour-faced men and the old crone who had accompanied him in. The best Sally had hoped for that evening was a look at the terrain, with the outside chance of a bar pickup later, she'd fully expected to have to sit through some of the next day's scientific sessions in order to catch his eye and nail his toe to the floor—but then, quite unexpectedly, the opportunity had presented and Sally Grinstone was nothing if not resourceful. Outside the dining room he had fallen behind the others to step into the newsstand off the lobby. Sally had followed, perusing the magazines side by side with him and selecting a copy of *Good Housekeeping* with just the slightest protrusion of her tongue. Then, as he turned away from the cash register, she collided with him, hard, tripping and collapsing at his feet with a little scream and dumping her handbag on the floor three feet away.

Profuse apologies, solicitude, assurances that she wasn't injured as he helped her to her feet, started brushing off the seductive dress, stopped rather abruptly and helped her retrieve the handbag instead, with sudden appreciative attention to her and the seductive dress and the convention name badge. "You're sure you're all right?"

"Oh, it's nothing, really, I'm just so clumsy—"

"No, I should look where I'm going." Pause. "Sally Newcombe from San Diego," he added, reading the name badge. "American Cyanamid—what kind of work do you do?"

Sally smiled as only Sally could smile. "Electrochemical analysis," she said, hoping this might be a blind spot for an organic chemist. "Trace metals, mostly, zinc, rhodium, platinum—you know."

He didn't, particularly, but seemed willing to overlook the fact. "Your party just get in tonight?"

"*I* just got in," Sally said with a rueful smile, "and I'm my party, I'm afraid." She looked helpless and bewildered as only Sally could. "I'm just very new at these meetings, you see, I don't know a soul in the place."

"That's easy to handle." Shipman introduced himself. "Now you know one soul. You're all checked in and everything? Registered—yes, of course. Well, you've started off right. I owe you something, after knocking you down. A drink maybe? There's a lounge across the lobby with a pretty good band. What say?"

"Sounds lovely," Sally said, "but first I should really, um . . ."

"So should I," Tom glanced over his shoulder. "In fact, I've got some bodyguards to shake off, they're afraid I might give away state secrets. Why not meet me over there in twenty minutes?"

He was actually quite a bit longer than that, and Sally was beginning to think she'd lost him when he finally reappeared and joined her at the table she'd selected toward the rear of the lounge. "Sorry to hold you up," he said. "They really *did* want to hear me snoring."

"Who did?"

"My bodyguards."

Sally laughed. "I thought you were joking."

"No joking about it," Tom said soberly.

"Those must be some state secrets you're packing around."

He grimaced. "Sealey is a drug company, and drug companies steal from each other. First job I ever had, the first thing they wanted to teach me was how to steal from the next company's lab. You never know who's safe."

"Even electrochemical analysts?"

He grinned. "For you, I'll take my chances."

The band came on and they finished a drink and had another, and listened to the music, and talked about a dozen different things. At close quarters he seemed far younger, and more attractive, and more responsive than her initial impression had conveyed; he had a boyish grin and an openness of appreciation and a certain sense of candor about him that struck her as immensely refreshing. For a forty-two-year-old entrenched lifelong bachelor, Sally decided, he was one hell of a lot smoother than she had anticipated—but there was nothing remotely furtive about his attention. She didn't have to do a damned thing but lean toward him now and then while he was talking over the band and he was all there, willing but not crowding her. With an inquiring tilt of his head he led her to the dance floor and made the transition from the conversational to the physical with a quiet assertiveness. She could, of course, have walked away, although she had no intention whatever of doing so. What startled her was that she truly didn't want to.

Back at their table he ordered some nibblies and they talked with more intimacy and less testing. Most of the talk, she found, revolved around her and her background, and she had to tiptoe, wishing she had improvised more detail. When she led him, he talked a bit about himself, too, steering rather clear of matters of work and employment, but three or four times there was a reference to Sealey and his connections there, each reference sharply edged with bitterness.

Finally Sally bit the bullet. "Tom—were those *really* bodyguards you were having dinner with?"

"Three of them were." He sat closer, placed an arm on her shoulders. "If they knew that I was not quietly holed up in my room right now, they would be down here in three minutes flat, sitting at the next table over there and conveying to me ever-so-subtly that if I didn't get up and walk out of here very quickly, they would soon carry me out, kicking and screaming if necessary."

"You mean they're not really chemists?"

"No, my dear, whatever they may be, they most certainly are not really chemists."

"But *why?*"

"I make antibiotics. Or at least I did. I was pretty good at it, and I've got an awful lot of useful information in my head. Not that anybody around Sealey Labs is letting me use it right now."

"I take it you're having a fight with Sealey."

"Wouldn't you fight if you came to work one morning and found a padlock on your lab door? I've been engaged in a major research and development program there. It's been an exciting scene, and unlike most R&D programs, this one has paid off in *answers*. Without exaggerating too much, I made one of the most important antibiotic breakthroughs of the last twenty years in that lab, a breakthrough that could save a whole lot of lives right now, today, if they'd follow through on it. And then, as soon as I had it nailed down to the floor, they slammed a padlock on my door and put me out to pasture. No reasons, no explanations. Now, how would you feel, in my shoes?"

Sally turned her head and kissed him gently. "I think I'd feel lousy. And mad. I've never heard of such a thing. But can't you just quit? Go somewhere else?"

"I'm locked into an ironclad contract."

"I always thought contracts could be broken."

"Sealey Labs has some—odd—business connections. I don't think I'd be around very long if I just quit and went somewhere else."

"Oh, Tom. You must have gotten onto something very important." She looked at him sharply. "You aren't involved with that new 3147 drug I was hearing about on the TV?"

Tom hesitated. "You might say I'm involved. But why talk about that? Let's talk about you. Tell me what it's like in San Diego."

He flagged the waitress for more drinks and they leaned back together to listen to the band, returned to dance very close, on the tiny dance floor, then back to their table, necking playfully at first, then more firmly and seriously, Tom's urgency growing steadily, her own response not in the least feigned until finally she touched his thigh and looked at him with eyebrows raised, and they rose and went out of the lounge together.

They went to the elevators arm in arm and without discussion he guided her to his room. He was an ardent, hungry lover, perhaps not overly skilled, but Sally made up for that in spades. Ultimately, when he had fallen asleep in her arms, she gently disengaged herself and lay flat on her back in the darkened room reasonably sated, thinking very clearly—it was a time when she always thought most clearly—and began sifting away at the pieces of the puzzle, picking at them and picking at them in her mind. And suddenly then, in the clearest simplicity, she saw what the picture had to be, hideous as it was.

Jesus, she thought.

It took quite a lot to make Sally Grinstone feel sick, but suddenly she found herself feeling sick. She tried to twist it around, add it up differently, but there wasn't any way. The pieces fit too well. They fit everything that had happened in Colorado, and everything she'd heard about Savannah too. It wasn't a question of what had happened, anymore. It was merely a question of *why.*

She looked over at Tom Shipman, his profile clear in the dim city skyglow from the window. Christ. So here she was. So now what? For a moment she felt an overwhelming urge to bolt—get up and slap on her dress and grab her handbag and get out of there, but she fought it down and just lay there shivering in the dark. *No good to bolt, not until you know the why of it all, straight from the horse's mouth. But how, exactly, do you swing that, from here? He might be as bad as his bodyguards, Sal. He might just kill you, if he saw a threat. But then again, he might not. They've hurt him badly. He's naïve, hungry for understanding, angry, and they've got him right by the ego. Maybe if you hit him with it right between the eyes, he might open up. It might just work.* She sighed, rubbed her forehead with a hand. *You're going to have to gamble, that's all. You're not going to win if you don't take the risk. . . .*

After a while she got up, went into the john, leaving the door ajar. She ran some water and bathed her face. Flushed the toilet a couple of times. Dropped the toilet seat with a whack. It was three A.M.

Back in the room she groped in the dark for the ice bucket, found ice cubes still floating, with the bottle of McNaughton's sitting on the dresser. She made herself a drink, ice and lots of whiskey and nothing else, clinking the ice cubes vigorously. Then she sat on her side of the bed, lit a smoke and sipped the drink, making small irregular visceral noises as she swallowed. Swished the bed clothes. Shifted position and then sipped again, more noisily.

After a while it got through and he stirred. "Mm?"

"Nothing, sweet. I just can't sleep."

He moved closer, wakening. She bent over and kissed him, first gently, then voluptuously, let him nuzzle a very handy breast. When she was certain arousal had begun she reached down to aid him, and then took over completely. With her own body available to his hands and lips, she began doing things that made him catch his breath and kept on doing them until he was totally ready for relief, and then even longer until, when she finally relented and yielded he was urgent as a wild man.

Then, when he had fallen back, still enfolding her in his arms, she said, "Tommy?"

"Mmm?"

"I'm scared."

He raised his head. "Of *me?*"

"*For* you, and what's going to happen."

"What do you think is going to happen?"

"Something bad, if you don't do something." She turned in his arms. "You were lying to me about the Sealey thing. It's something much worse than you said. You said they'd padlocked your lab on you, and that was true, but then you said the drug you'd developed was 3147, and that wasn't true—"

Tom sat bolt upright, peering at her. "What are you talking about? What do you care about that?"

"I care a lot about it. It *wasn't* true, was it?"

The man snapped the bedside lamp on, stared down at her accusingly. "Who are you, anyway? Why are you asking me this?"

"Tommy, I can't tell you, but I've got to know the truth. It's terribly important."

"Why?" Tom Shipman was still staring at her. "You're no lab tech from Cyanamid, you're one of those damned weasels that—" He broke off, looked around him frantically, as if he expected the door to burst open any minute.

Sally caught his eyes and held them. "Tom, listen to me. I promise you *I am not an industrial spy.* I can't tell you who I am right now, but believe me, all this wasn't any act tonight, and I am one hundred percent on *your side.* You've just got to trust me a minute and tell me some things I have to know. Those Sealey people have torn you to pieces—"

"*That's* true, but just the same—"

"And you'd like to put them where they belong."

"You bet I would, but—"

"Then just answer some things yes or no, nobody can blame you for that. You said Sealey padlocked your lab after you'd made a major antibiotic breakthrough—right?"

"That's right."

"That breakthrough was a totally new drug."

"That's right."

"But it wasn't 3147."

The man hesitated, then shook his head. "No."

"You'd developed 3147 months ago, hadn't you?"

"Two years ago."

"And they'd already done a lot of preliminary testing on it, hadn't they?"

"Yes."

"They knew it was active against plague?"

"Moderately active. Nothing to write home about, but it had some antiplague activity. But why are you asking all these—"

"Shush. Just answer me. They also knew 3147 was toxic."

"Not for certain, at least in humans. They'd never run clinical tests. But they were pretty sure."

"And then you came up with a totally new drug, your breakthrough drug, and it was a different story."

"Yes. God, yes."

"What was so different about it?"

Suddenly the bitterness and outrage exploded in Tom Shipman's face and voice. "It was a beautiful drug, a simply *beautiful* drug. It had everything that 3147 *didn't* have. 3147 was a mess in a dozen ways—hard to make, only moderately effective, toxic as hell, unstable on the shelf. The new one was an absolute beauty. It hit plague like a sledgehammer, it was easy to produce in quantity, it was utterly shelf-stable, even under field conditions, and you could eat it like popcorn without any side effects at all—"

"And that was the drug they sent to Fort Collins for testing, wasn't it?"

"That was the drug. Not much of it, just a little bit, for testing. And it proved out just as good as we thought it would on the new plague bug."

"But that wasn't the drug they sent down to Canon City, was it?"

"No. They sent 3147 to Canon City."

"But they didn't *tell* anybody it was a different drug," Sally said. "They told them it was the same drug they'd tested in Fort Collins."

"That's—right."

"And meanwhile they locked up your good breakthrough drug behind padlocks and put you out to pasture with bodyguards on you."

Tom nodded.

"But *why?*"

Tom Shipman crossed the room and poured whiskey in a glass, drank half of it neat. "Because they were in business," he said in a strangled voice, "and they couldn't make a nickel on my new drug. It was too bloody simple for them to be able to box it in. It was based on ordinary tetracycline, the cheapest, most plentiful, easiest-to-make antibiotic in the world. All I had to do was use simple reagents to break one little radical off the basic tetracycline molecule and add two acid radicals in the right places. Anybody with a little tetracycline and some vinegar and a crock-pot could make my new drug in his own kitchen—*anybody at all.* You could cover it with patents until the cows came home, but any little minor-league drug house in the *world* with any wit could jump the patent, and mass-produce the stuff for half a cent a dose. Which meant it wasn't worth a dime to Sealey Labs, Inc."

"All the same, it could stop plague," Sally said.

"Oh, yes—like nothing else on earth. But for *free?*" Tom made a face and poured more whiskey. "Now, 3147 was a different story. It wasn't half the drug, it might cripple people who took it, but it had one big advantage: it was complex and expensive to make. Any drug houses big enough to gear up for it and jump the patents wouldn't dare because it would be easy to spot them and sue them for their skins—and Sealey could charge a king's ransom for it if the demand was high enough. And Sealey sniffed plague in the wind and saw a multi-billion-dollar windfall to be made on 3147 if they could just work things right and bury my new drug deep enough." He looked bitterly at Sally.

"And they deliberately, consciously pulled this fraud in full knowledge that we were in the midst of a murderous plague epidemic? Tom, that's monstrous!"

"Well, they didn't actually know that when they made the decision. Some Sealey Labs people—Mancini and Lunch—were out in person in Colorado while the drugs were being tested. They didn't recognize what the plague was going to do, way back then. They thought it was a little, limited spread of a few cases, there in Canon City, and that 3147 would cover the ground and then be available for other little flare-ups they thought might occur. Mancini decided on the switch in drugs then and there, that early. It was still a monstrous decision, but it didn't seem quite as monstrous then as it does now. And at first, this thing in Savannah was just taken for another small outbreak, and they got in deeper. And then, by the time we *knew* what this plague was going to do, they were trapped on the ice floe moving out to sea with no way to get back to the mainland without litigation and penalties that would destroy them. By then they were trapped and couldn't—or wouldn't—change a thing. So there, Miss Whoever-You-Are, you've got the whole story."

Sally Grinstone made herself a drink and, for the first time in her adult memory, didn't like the taste of it. What was more, for the first time in her reporting career she had a story wrapped up tight and somehow didn't feel like heading for the nearest telephone at a dead run. Instead, they sat there, two people as different as two people could be, Insatiable Sally from Philadelphia and an angry little chemist from Indianapolis, sipping drinks in silence, neither one moving to do or say anything. After a long, long time Sally said, "They can't get away with it."

"You just sit back and watch them," Tom said.

"I mean they can't be *allowed* to. This plague—have you been following the news? It isn't going to go away."

"I know."

"It's tearing Savannah to pieces right now. It's going to move on and tear a lot of other places to pieces too, if it isn't stopped."

"Yes."

"It's going to kill people, thousands, maybe millions, before it's over, if your drug stays buried in that vault back there."

"Yes."

"So what are you going to do about it?"

"What can I do? If you're even halfway right about the plague, I'm not going to be around for very long. They can't afford to have me talking. They'd kill me right now if they walked in and found you here. I've never doubted it would come to that, sooner or later."

"You mean you're just sitting here waiting for them to shoot you?"

"I don't see that I have much choice."

Sally swung on him fiercely. "Of course you've got a choice—as long as you're still breathing. My *God,* Tom, you're practically a National Resource—you've *got* to stay around! Don't you see that?" She paced up and down, so agitated she could hardly speak. "Look, you idiot—what would happen if you just walked out of this place right now? Took a cab to the airport and flew someplace, anyplace, as long as it wasn't Indianapolis? What would happen if you went someplace where you couldn't be found, and got hold of some tetracycline and some vinegar and a crock-pot and went to work on your own? And then while you're safe and secure where nobody can find you and producing your simple little drug like mad, I'll personally be blasting the bejesus out of Sealey Labs, spreading the whole rotten story from one end of the country to the other. I can do it, believe me! That's my business. Don't think for a minute I can't. You want a choice, what's wrong with that, for openers?"

He smiled wearily. "And what do I do for money?" he said. "I've got forty dollars in my wallet. They've got my credit cards in a vault—"

"So you stop in the first city you come to and report them stolen and get new ones—except you don't waste the time. I've got some money, I've got a million credit cards. I'll go with you, help you find a place to work. Help do the legwork. Scrounge up the vinegar. Find some way to get the stuff distributed when you get it made. I can be a pretty good organizer when I want to be, I've got all kinds of resources to draw on—"

"And why are you getting into all this?"

"Maybe because I've got a hunch we're all going to need Tom Shipman very badly before too long," Sally Grinstone said. "Maybe just a crass, selfish desire on my part to stay very close to that crock-pot and the stuff coming out of it." She sipped her drink again, and then turned to him, her green eyes the most serious he yet had seen them. "Tom, honey, don't you understand? I have a very bad feeling about what's on the move, outside here. I hear hoofbeats in the distance, getting closer. We don't need to worry about what Sealey might do. I think if *we* don't do something and do it *now,* very soon the two of us are going to be dead, dead, dead, right along with a whole lot of other people, regardless of what Sealey might do."

"But what you're suggesting—" Tom spread his hands. "It's crazy. Like howling at the wind."

"It's something," Sally said. "That could be better than nothing."

Tom shook his head, walked to the window, and stared out in silence at the dark street. Sally watched him for a while. "Well?" she said finally.

He shook his head again. "It's crazy."

"Well, God damn it, you can stay here and get shot if you want to," Sally said angrily, "but I'm not going to. I'm a reporter, and I've got a story to report." She started dressing, retrieved her bag from the floor, paused to rake at her hair with a comb and dab at her face in the mirror. As she started for the door, Tom stirred, turned toward her. "Sally?"

"That's the name. Watch for the byline."

"You were really—serious—about the—vinegar and the crock-pot?"

"All the way."

"You know if they caught us, they'd kill both of us."

"First they'd have to find us."

Tom Shipman was silent for a long moment. Then he took a breath like a sigh. "Okay," he said. "Let's pack and go."

43

On the evening of the night that Savannah died, Jack Cheney and Carlos Quintana had met for a late working dinner in the little Chinese restaurant on Lafayette Street, just about the only public eating house that still remained functioning in the Old City, and since they were the sole patrons in the place that evening, the chef had brought out an endless succession of Cantonese delicacies for them to sample, one by one, steaming and fragrant, and generously pushed together two adjacent tables for them on which to spread out their charts and city maps and reports and papers and other paraphernalia. Since neither of them had eaten more than half-sandwiches at any time during the past three days, they were both famished by the time they arrived, and devoured the food as fast as it came out of the kitchen, and talked with their mouths full and dripped soy sauce all over their charts and maps, but this didn't really matter. They hardly knew they were eating, much less dripping soy sauce, and the maps and charts didn't make much sense anyway.

"Figures," Carlos said between gulps. "Have you got any figures on those close-in sections that Dingman had his crew working on yesterday?"

"Figures." Jack searched for a computer readout sheet. "Here are some figures, but I don't think they really mean very much. The data aren't complete, some stuff missing altogether, and some very sketchy so the projections are just as much garbage as the input."

"Well, that figures," Carlos said, and then winced at the inadvertent pun. "Let's see what you do have, all the same."

It had been a day quite indistinguishable from any one of the last six or eight as the situation in the city had deteriorated around them. There was nothing to indicate that this particular night would be different in any particular way from the night before or the night before that, only a steady deepening of the inferno atmosphere in the hot city streets and a tightening of the pressure on the two men and the frightful catch-up-from-behind battle they were trying to direct. The exodus from the city had continued to expand, filling major streets with long wandering files of people, children, animals, carts and rattletraps, blocking traffic on arterials to the point that simple travel from any Point A to any other Point B had become problematical if not impossible. For a full week past the air had been filled with the frantic siren wails of official vehicles of one sort or another trying desperately to get someplace or another fast and generally failing to get there at all; the streets shook from periodic explosions somewhere in the distance, explosions never identified with any specific place or event but steadily increasing in frequency all the same; looting and the roaming of street gangs seemingly motivated by free-floating anger and little else had accelerated with each passing day, first confined to late-night hours, moving into dawn and dusk and finally into broad daylight, preying on whatever stores were there and handy or whatever people wandered by and leaving largely untouched only the health workers identified by their Red Cross armbands. Aside from the wandering refugees, those who moved about at all moved *fast* on foot, lending a sense of frenetic urgency to the overall scene, recognized as urgency about essentially nothing by only a few.

Through it all Carlos and Jack Cheney had been doing the best they could do the best they could do it with the army of workers they still had rallied around them. The supplies had arrived at the beginning of the week, as promised—vaccine and antibiotic—airlifted by army helicopter to the abandoned construction site of a new hotel on the riverfront near Factor's Walk Warehouse 14 and then transported by van to the warehouse itself. There was not as much vaccine in that first shipment as promised, nor as much antibiotic either, there had been a certain inevitable element of attrition en route, but there was enough for them to start working pending the arrival of more—and two days later a small amount more actually did materialize.

By the time the drugs were on hand, Jack and Carlos had completed their field plan for distribution of the precious cargo, subject only to the amount actually available, and they had moved with all the speed their Shoeleather army was capable of. The first of the new vaccine, of course, went to the Shoeleather people themselves—the medical and nursing personnel and CDC and public-health field workers of all sorts, then to police and other civil-control authorities, to sanitation workers, waterworks personnel and other vital public servants, then finally to food distributors and others who came in necessary contact with the largest numbers of people. Next, with the vaccine remaining from the first shipment, the public-health field workers began vaccinating, en bloc, all of the uninfected people they could find in selected sectors of the city which had demonstrated the lowest infection rate, with preference given to families where infection had not yet struck at all. It made a certain medical sense to try to block the spread of disease into as-yet-uncontaminated areas as an early step in the battle, they knew, but it did not make political sense, since it could easily be construed that they seemed to be favoring the well-to-do suburban areas and avoiding the hardest-hit ghetto areas. For this and other reasons, pains were taken to avoid public discussion of the overall battle plan and to use the public media to direct people to vaccination centers on an apparently random basis: people living on certain streets between specified perimeter avenues were simply instructed to report to such and such a location on such and such a day for protective shots, and that was that. This pattern angered people who misinterpreted it, or seemed always to be missed, especially as word spread that new supplies of medicine and vaccine were coming into the city in enormous quantities, but compliance was high in the areas selected for coverage.

Unfortunately, steadily increasing civil disorder complicated things immensely. "This whole area here is closed for now," Jack would say, pointing to a section on a large street map. "I can't send workers in there even with two or three squad cars for escort. Snipers all over the place, and street gangs roaming around smashing in windows and trashing stores and residential buildings. They work in threes and fours, sometimes on motorcycles, move in fast, hit and run. They'd just as soon hit a squad car as a fat lady in a wheelchair. Not all black, either, lots of them are white, victimizing black neighborhoods. In some places, all the police can do is box them in—there's no way to go in and get them."

For all this, the work of distributing vaccine and drugs had gone on. In some sections field workers would hide out with tenement families overnight in order to work two or three days straight, especially in areas that were hard to reach and dangerous to try to go home from. With the progressive breakdown in sanitary disposal because of street bombings and barricades, the stench of death was heavy in all parts of the city— "But you get used to that, after a while," Jack said. "Something in the brain seems to shut down and you don't even notice it. . . ."

Carlos spread his hands wearily. "I know it's not nice, clean work—but at least we're getting there."

"Well, maybe, inch by inch," Jack said dubiously, "but I can't prove it with figures. If we could only have had this stuff a month ago, it could have been different. Now we can only hope to slow it down a little before the whole city explodes. Which it may just do, if this goes on much longer. Don't ask me *how,* exactly—armed warfare in the streets? Hell, it's coming to that already. The police are moaning that they're getting no help, they can't understand why the army doesn't send in paratroops to occupy the place and restore order." Jack gave a bitter laugh. "It's no mystery to me, to send an army into the heart of a plague spot is an excellent way of getting rid of an army, any idiot can figure that out. But the police can't hold down insurrection unaided, so maybe it'll be insurrection. Get a real wild-eyed panic going, mass riots, and there won't be much need for you or me or the Public Health Service."

"But all this aside, Jack, we're still *getting* somewhere," Carlos said again, almost pleading.

"Well, sure. As far as curbing the spread of infection is concerned, every day we work has got to be better than the last. But then we have little items like this." Jack dug an Atlanta newspaper out of his briefcase. "Did you see this?"

It was a lower-right front-page headline story, copyrighted by the Philadelphia *Inquirer:*

DRUG FRAUD CHARGED

In Washington today officials of the Food and Drug Administration charged an Indianapolis pharmaceutical manufacturer with conspiracy to suppress a new wonder drug which might have saved hundreds of lives during the plague outbreak in Canon City, Colorado, last month if it had been available to fight the deadly infection.

In a complaint filed with the Justice Department, the FDA charged that Sealey Laboratories, a major supplier of antiplague medications, fraudulently substituted large quantities of a less effective, more toxic and highly experimental drug in place of a safer and more powerful agent during the recent Colorado plague battle. According to reliable sources the substituted drug, known only by the code number 3147, was substituted because the company feared it could not protect its patent rights on the more effective drug.

In Indianapolis, John Mancini, Vice-President in charge of production at Sealey Laboratories, categorically denied the charges, citing Sealey's long history of public service in the pharmaceutical industry. . . .

It was all there, the whole story, from beginning to end. Carlos read it through slowly, including details on the back page, then read it again twice more before pushing it aside with a sigh.

"So that's the story," he murmured.

"Well, of course, it's nothing but an irresponsible heap of crap," Jack said, running his hand through his sandy hair. "Isn't it?"

Carlos shook his head slowly. "I'm afraid it isn't any such thing. I know the woman who tested the first drug in Fort Collins, and she isn't one to get excited about nothing. The drug she tested was great—but the drug they supplied us in Canon City wasn't. It could have been a ringer. I also know this reporter's work, and she doesn't write fairy tales. She got her facts from somebody who *knew,* and they're just liable to stand up in court."

"Then what are we supposed to do with this 3147 we've got?"

"If it's helping at all, we'll use it, of course. I'll double-check with Ted, but that's what he's going to say. What else have we got? The side effects are nasty, but not as nasty as dying. So we'll use it and pray. And remember, my friend, even you just admitted that we're getting somewhere, however slow. Before the 3147, we weren't. So let's wrap things up here and get busy before, as you so neatly put it, the whole damned place explodes."

It was just past ten o'clock and quite dark outside when they paid their bill and stepped out onto the street. At first they thought a storm had come up as a gust of disturbingly hot air struck them in the face—a hot, dry gust totally unlike the steamy breeze that had kept them both perspiring all day. They looked at each other and then, at the same moment, saw the unnatural pinkish skyglow in the southern sky and an even redder glare to the west and much closer, like some kind of aurora gone mad. Momentarily Carlos saw a tongue of yellow lick up into the red and fall back again and suddenly the air was dense with woodsmoke.

People were running on the street across from them. A group came around the corner past them and Carlos caught someone's sleeve. "What's going on over there? What's burning?"

A large man paused, gestured to the west. "The DeSoto Hilton. A bunch broke in and trashed the lobby and then torched the place. They're shooting the firemen tryin' to get close to it, and there's people up near the top that can't get down. Whole east side of Forsythe Park is burning too, and the big houses over on Bull Street—"

The man broke away, and now there were sirens on all sides of them, distant and nearby. Three squad cars roared up Lafayette Street and took the corner south onto Bull with screeching tires. Jack stared at Carlos in dismay. "God, this whole town could go up," he said. "I'd better get over to the Big Hospital—"

Carlos nodded. "And fast, too. But stay wide of Liberty Street, you're bound to get caught in a jam."

"You'd better come too."

"Maybe later. Right now I've got to get to my office and try to find out where my field people are."

Jack darted across the street and through Lafayette Plaza at a run. Carlos watched him a minute, then headed down the street toward the CDC office, watching the glare from the DeSoto Hilton rise and rise. People were running in both directions now to no apparent purpose. At one point Carlos saw a half-dozen men rushing down the opposite side of the street carrying planks and poles and at least one rifle, but he bowed his head and walked swiftly on, keeping to the shadows, and the group went on past without seeming to notice him. He tried to plot the shortest distance possible to the office, taking to alleys and deliveryways between the fine old mansions of the area. Just two blocks from the office building he came out on the street at the very corner of Roanoke Plaza—and then he stopped short, staring in disbelief.

The great mansions surrounding the plaza were ablaze on all sides, some just beginning to burn, others veritable columns of flame. The plaza itself formed a vortex, a chimney of superheated air sucking smoke and flame into the center and hurling it skyward, the foliage on the fine old live-oak trees flaring like a million torches. Cars were stalled on the streets, their tires popped by the intense heat. Two people suddenly burst from one of them and tried to make it at a dead run across the plaza. They stopped a third of the way across, tried to turn back, went down with their clothes blazing and very suddenly were no longer moving.

Carlos felt his face blistering and backed away from the inferno, looked for dark streets and cooler air. After twenty minutes of floundering up alleys and through backyards he finally found his own headquarters building. Lights were blazing in every room, but the building was empty. People had been there, all right; a telephone lay off the hook on a desk, emitting a loud bzzz-bzzz-bzzz-bzzz, and files were torn open and papers scattered all over the floor, but not a single soul there now—

Somewhere outside there were a series of explosions that jarred the very floor under his feet. Carlos sat down, trying to get his mind to focus on what was happening. Instinct screamed at him to get down to a basement room and stand by a phone in case some of his people called in. *And probably fry,* he reflected, *if that fire moves in this direction. And what good would that do, anyway? What will I tell anybody? People will already be looking for any safe exit they can find, wherever they are. And if this fire is really widespread, there won't be any telephone very long anyway. Or any power.* As if to punctuate his very thought, the room suddenly went dark. The lights flickered back on for one abortive moment and then went out altogether.

Well, there was no point standing here in darkness, waiting for the worst. Suddenly he was thinking of Warehouse 14, stacked full of precious vaccine and other supplies, with fire moving north toward the riverfront, and he knew what he had to do. At least the vaccine and antibiotics had to be salvaged—but how? Hell, if he could reach the warehouse he could *carry* the vaccine out. Carry it where? Who could say where? Into the river, if necessary.

With a course of action in mind, he ducked back out to the street. There was supposed to be a squad car assigned to this headquarters in case he or somebody else needed to get somewhere fast. It hadn't been there when he arrived, but he might just possibly snag one going by. On the sidewalk a hot stiff breeze struck his face, and he could see that the conflagration from Roanoke Plaza was spreading. Other sections of red in the sky suggested more fires, and the DeSoto Hilton tower was visible from where he stood as a ghastly pillar of fire. He waited ten minutes before he saw a squad car approach an intersection near enough for him to whistle and flag it. Carlos identified himself. "I've got to get to Warehouse 14, try to get the plague vaccine and drugs to a safer place," he told the driver. "Can you help?"

"The streets are alive down there, Doc. People've gone crazy in this town."

"I've got to get that stuff out of there, one way or another."

"Well, climb in. We can make a try."

The officer had a riot gun and a huge .38 pistol on the seat next to him, canisters of tear gas on the floor, one obviously leaking because the cop was weeping and Carlos was too in half a minute. They were just pulling away from the curb when a group of dark men materialized out of nowhere. One of them used a long two-by-four to smash out the squad car's right headlight with an enormous thudding blow. Another fired a shotgun blast, shattering the middle of the windshield. The cop slammed down the accelerator and the motor roared, but the group was too well organized; there was oil under the rear wheels already and somebody was busy slashing the front ones. The cop shoved the pistol into Carlos's hand. "Use it, man!" he said and shoved the riot gun through the hole in the sagging windshield, fired four shells blind and point-blank. Then the left side window exploded inward under a smashing blow, and black hands reached in and dragged the cop out through it bodily. Somebody else was beating in the hood and roof and Carlos, the pistol lost on the floor somewhere, was hauled out by his collar.

Once out of the car, he staggered for footing, looking for some direction to run, but he didn't have time. He caught a flash of the two-by-four plank swinging at him broadside, felt it crash into the side of his head, and that was all. He didn't even feel his knees give.

He didn't know when it was that he recovered consciousness. It seemed like hours later, but his cheap watch had been smashed when he had fallen. Someone had torn the diamond-braided wedding ring off his finger and his pants were torn half off, his wallet gone. The side of his head was screamingly painful as he lurched to his feet, and he couldn't see too well out of one eye. Worse than that, he couldn't think, and *knew* he couldn't think. He couldn't place where he was, or when it was, or what was happening except that buildings were burning on all sides, and he knew he had to do something about some vaccine while there was still time. . . .

That one thing flared into focus: the vaccine in Warehouse 14. That was urgent. He had to get there before the fire did. It made no sense, and he *knew* it made no sense, but some ingrained, dogged fatalism took control and he turned and stumbled down the street.

He could already see that the fire in Roanoke Plaza had spread: it looked like the whole restored Old Section of antebellum mansions and plazas was one vast, roaring conflagration now. He staggered down the street, heading vaguely toward Factor's Walk and the river and then saw flames to the east in that direction too: the farther waterfront warehouses were burning too, with flames driven west up River Street toward him by an active offshore wind. Fragments of flaming debris flew past him in the air; breathing was hot and difficult. Presently he stopped to tear off his necktie and rip open the neck of his shirt. A moment later he pulled off his jacket, looked about foolishly for some safe place to leave it. Then he saw a woman lying dead in the gutter, faceup, eyes wide open and staring at the smoke-filled sky, and he dropped the jacket over her face, and blocked it instantly, and went on.

The vaccine is all that's left, he thought. There were people moving out of buildings now and then, washcloths over their mouths, forearms over their eyes, but what Carlos saw were the rats, a veritable river of rats streaming from the buildings, up from the waterfront, under his feet, clinging briefly to his trouser legs, then moving on, silent as death they moved, silent as the death they sought to evade.

Somewhere ahead he saw Warehouse 14, or thought he saw it, down two levels on Factor's Walk, and he started to run. There was a narrow stone walkway down along a closer warehouse, the easiest way to reach it, if he could just get to the top of the stair. *Well, Monique, we'll try, won't we?* He tore off his sweat-soaked shirt to cover his nose and mouth and bolted past the nearer warehouse to reach the stair—

With a dull boom like the blast of a ruptured gas tank the nearer warehouse burst into flame, burning on all of its floors at once. The wave of exploding, searing gas struck Carlos and knocked him flat on the cobblestone pavement. He struggled to his knees, gasping for air, engulfed in fleeing rats. He focused his mind on the vaccine, and tried to rise, but now he knew with a terrible certainty that he was not going to reach the vaccine, and it really didn't matter, anyway. Savannah was dying, and so was he. *Ave Maria*—he fought to get to his feet, moved his hand to cross himself—*Madre de Dios.* A slight shift of wind, a blast of hot and poisonous gas and Carlos Quintana collapsed among the few rats still able to flee, and his lips stopped moving in the middle of the prayer.

He died at three minutes past midnight on the night Savannah died, and was cremated ten minutes later, and nobody knew for four full months exactly what had happened to him.

44

Requiem for Savannah, Pearl of the South Atlantic Seaboard, loveliest of the antebellum cities of the South. Destroyed by fire in a single night, but not by General Sherman. Three-quarters of the central city razed in eight hours. In the words of the Chief of the Chatham County Fire Department, widely quoted later: "I can fight fire. I can't fight God."

Statistics gathered and published later, when no one had any reason to care anymore: Dead of plague in Savannah: 35,400; dead of fire and insurrection: 85,143. An odd figure, that last one, for a footnote to history.

On the night the fire was finally curbed, the President of the United States on national television made a moving speech in honor of "those valiant dead who fell in the City of Savannah, and those valiant living who remain in the health-protection corps throughout the nation, and who pledge to you tonight that the disaster that struck in Savannah will never happen again. I can tell you the plague is curbed there, now, and we are prepared—I repeat, we are fully prepared—to curb it wherever else it may rear its foul head. As your President, I solemnly pledge to you—"

On the CBS-TV news network, perhaps without precedent in history, the President's message to the nation was interrupted at this point with an urgent bulletin. "Just moments ago, CBS news has learned from the Centers for Disease Control headquarters in Atlanta that major outbreaks of plague of the same sort that laid waste to Savannah, Georgia, have been confirmed in Charleston, South Carolina; Atlanta; Canton, Ohio; Washington, D.C.; Chicago; New York City; Seattle; and San Francisco. Residents of these cities and others are urged to remain tuned to CBS-TV for the latest bulletins and instructions from your local Public Health Services."

Hail and farewell, Savannah.

PART IV

THE FIRE STORM

45

In the cool dampness of the late November dawn Dr. Ted Bettendorf let himself into his second-story office at CDC-Atlanta and deposited his topcoat and muffler in the little corner closet. Chilly, these early mornings, *a warning,* he thought, *of another unseasonably wet, cold winter.* The office was spacious but untidy, the wall shelves piled high with jumbles of books and journals, the desk stacked with unfinished business and the nightly collection of dispatches, the newly installed eight-line telephone and the vital intercom to Mandy's desk outside—*God, how he was leaning on Mandy these days!* Through the window he could see the familiar view of this charming section of Atlanta, the huge old trees dipping their branches in early winter greenery. It was barely past 5:00 A.M., an hour before Mandy would be coming in, at least an hour before the first calls from the West Coast would be coming through, but for Ted Bettendorf it was the one quiet hour he could count on all day, an hour before the murderous pressure began once again, an hour between the nightmares of the slow-passing night and the raging nightmares of the day about to begin. . . .

He sat at the desk, pushed the dispatches aside and took out a yellow legal pad. For a while he just stared at it, deliberately forcing the present out of his mind, fleeing back to the historical past he loved so dearly. Presently he began to write.

According to the account of Giovanni of Montealbano, in the Year of our Lord 1357 the city of Tekirdağ on the western shore of the Sea of Marmara, between the Aegean and the Black Sea, had been spared the terrible plague that had ravaged other eastern Mediterranean lands; but rather than rejoicing in their good fortune, the people of Tekirdağ lived each passing day in fear and trembling lest the plague should even then appear. Because of the terror in which they dwelt, the people closed the harbor—their major source of commerce—and fortified the city, allowing no ship to enter there, and catapulted huge fireballs aboard any ship which defied them and ventured too close to their shores.

Most ships went away. But one day three Arab ships from Rashīd appeared and begged safe harbor, and were denied. Now there was plague on those three ships, with many of their crew dead or dying; and being turned away from every harbor in their course, their food and water were gone and some among them were starving and dying of thirst. Thus the three ships risked the fireballs to approach the harbor and beg that casks of water and food be set adrift to float out to them on the receding tide—but the people of Tekirdağ, fearing the air surrounding the ships to be unclean, answered their pleadings with fire and burned two of the ships, and all aboard were burned alive or drowned.

Then the Master of the third ship, when he saw this, was seized with anger, and ordered his own catapults to be manned, and ordered his ship to be brought about and driven deep into the harbor; and he filled his catapults with newly-plague-dead corpses, together with multitudes of rats that were gnawing on them, and hurled them over the city walls, as many as a hundred corpses, before fire destroyed his ship too.

And then it was, according to the account of Giovanni of Montealbano, that plague struck the people of Tekirdağ with unheard-of ferocity, and within a month the living city was reduced to a tomb. . . .

The first light of a wintry sun came through the office window, and Ted left his writing to stare out at the street below. *And so The Plague made its slow steady way across Asia Minor and Europe in the Year of Our Lord 1357,* he thought. There had been no hurry about it, in those long-dead days; it moved sluggishly but implacably. Only in the coastal cities did it strike swiftly. Farther inland, it inched along from farm to farm, following the cow paths and rutted mud roads, from one tiny village to the next, from one baronial castle to the next—never moving more swiftly than a horseman could gallop. It had taken months and years—decades—for that plague to sweep across the populated world. *Ample time for men to have stopped it, even in those days,* Ted mused, *if only they'd had some inkling how. But not today: Today we have a different sort of plague, and time is running out.*

The tall, gray-haired man sighed and walked back to his desk. More and more these days he found himself thinking about those ancient plagues, and the dreadful ironies of the past and present. Even when they *had* known how to slow it down, it hadn't done them any good. Like that little town in Tuscany, back in the mid-1600s—as early as then, level-headed public-health authorities had had some ideas about plague that had been close to the target. They'd isolated the sickest ones. They had sent out orders barring large public meetings and fairs, ordering people to stay in their homes, even to avoid daily attendance at church—and then sent out an emissary to see to it that the orders were followed. An exercise in futility, of course, because the orders were simply ignored. The priest demanded church attendance in defiance of the authorities. The people went to the fair in the neighboring town whether the emissary liked it or not, and the emissary found himself enmeshed in the solution of a long series of deliberately created petty squabbles, ridiculous court cases and night brigandries instead of enforcing orders to save people from the plague. *Bloody-minded people, as the British would say, mule-stubborn to the point of self-destruction in the face of a terrible disaster, going out of their way to defeat the public-health authorities and everyone else around, themselves included, because things were not going precisely to their liking. It was the pattern in those days long past, and the pattern repeated in Savannah, and the ever-growing pattern everywhere in these terrible weeks since Savannah.*

Certainly these days he felt strangely akin to that hapless emissary of three and a half centuries ago. He needed this one hour of peace and solitude each morning in order to face it at all. Where order and obedience and tight organization were needed, he spent endless days squabbling over legalities, as order disintegrated, obedience was ignored and organization became totally impossible. Each day brought fourteen to sixteen hours of pressure, fielding disaster messages from bloody-minded people, taking reports, relaying orders, solving fights, suggesting approaches, sometimes begging, sometimes blackmailing, sometimes shouting and screaming until Mandy said, "You're getting loud, Boss," and he calmed it down and got a new grip on himself and started over. Each day brought long hours on the telephone to Washington, witnessing the steady growth of panic there, the slow but clearly perceptible crumbling of authority, with the higher-level public-health authorities there wrangling constantly with Senators and Congressmen and whole brigades of White House aides, trying to maintain some semblance of order, some sense of balance, while whole echelons of national leadership steadily faltered and floundered, losing direction, losing control, subtly retreating day by day from an earlier stance of keeping things firmly in hand, with directives and decisions coming forth as needed, and moving steadily day by day, toward a new stance of merely wanting desperately to be bailed out. Ted Bettendorf watched it happening, a little more each day, the whole vast juggernaut of national leadership painfully grinding to a halt and turning more and more to *him* as the man who was expected to do the bailing. Well, an hour of solitude, early in the morning, was not too much to ask. One hour each morning could restore the soul and build up the strength to face another murderous day which would, he knew before it even started, somehow manage to sink to a slightly lower level of effectiveness than the day before or the day before that.

This morning, like every other morning, Ted thought again of Carlos, with the now-familiar wave of pain and bitterness that came with it. Like having his own right arm torn off at the shoulder, losing Carlos, such a needless, useless waste, and so much of it Ted's own fault. He should have hauled Carlos out of that snake pit weeks before the end; he'd known beyond doubt that he was going to need him a million other places, that the battle was lost there anyway. Hell, Carlos himself should have seen the handwriting and hauled himself out of there while there was still time—but that had never been Carlos's style. He had never been able to see the danger anywhere he went, only the challenge, the work that had to be done. He would never have left except under duress as long as anyone else was still fighting down there. The truth was, of course, that *none* of his people had left in time, not one of them that Ted had any knowledge of. Two hundred and forty-seven good people lost in a single hideous night, never heard from again, their bodies never even identified, consumed in the pillar of fire that consumed the city of Savannah. Missing and presumed dead.

The thought of them was torment enough to Ted—but even worse was the thought that always followed: that Carlos and all the others might well have died fighting a war already long lost before they ever got to Savannah. *And when, precisely, might the war have been irrevocably lost?* It was a terrible question to ask in the quiet of one's mind, an unthinkable question in this grim business of disease-fighting; one simply could not allow oneself to consider that the war might ever be lost, when your whole purpose for being here was to see that it was not. *And yet—and yet—* He glanced at the desk full of dispatches, one single night's listings of American cities and towns newly afflicted, never mind all the afflicted cities and towns elsewhere in the world, and his mind came back to the unthinkable question again as he groped helplessly for origins: at what precise point, back along the trail, had the war already been irrevocably lost?

Maybe before we even knew it had started, he thought. *Maybe as early as that. Maybe the very day that cursed girl walked up that cursed mountain trail, the war was already lost. Maybe even then.* Or maybe just a few hours later, when that boy in Seattle unwittingly administered the death blow. The boy had come down the mountain, already deathly sick, delirious, confused, out of contact with reality, wanting only to get home. An airplane ticket in his pocket. Hours spent in Sea-Tac airport, waiting for a flight, more hours on the plane itself, coughing the air full of bloody corruption. And how many others had been in that airport that day, in contact with the boy? Maybe a thousand? And how many on that plane? Maybe a hundred? And how many of them infected? Perhaps two dozen? With how many final destinations? Ten, perhaps, or fifteen? Including one or two, perhaps, coming to rest in New York, or London, or Moscow, or Tel Aviv—or in Savannah? And at each destination, how many had met and greeted those infected ones as they stepped off their planes? And scattered to what other distant places? Who could say when the war had been irrevocably lost?

And so, Ted thought, they had won the Battle of Canon City, a proud and decisive victory, except that the war had already leaped beyond them, like a metastatic cancer, the original dirty thing already spread to a dozen distant sites and organs, each to become a source of further spread—and the dispatches came in. Today half a dozen new cities and towns on the list, tomorrow dozens more, next month thousands. And slowly, slowly, everything they had to fight with falling apart—

The intercom chirped and Dr. Ted Bettendorf stirred himself, shaking the horror from his head, and flipping the switch. "Mandy? Yes, I'm here. What's the lineup?"

"They're starting early, Boss. Four people on hold already. There's the Mayor of St. Louis demanding special courier service on that vaccine you ordered for them yesterday, and a very angry Mr. Mancini from Sealey Labs about some things you said at the press conference yesterday, and you're supposed to stand by with a clear line at eight A.M. for a conference call from HHS, and—"

Ted Bettendorf took a deep breath and punched the button for line one.

46

"Harry, did you get those oil drums like you said you were going to?" Amy Slencik fixed her husband with a no-nonsense look through her gray-tinted glasses.

"Yeah, I threw six of them in the back of the pickup last night," Harry said. "Old Peachy ain't gonna be happy when he finds them gone, but I got them, all right."

"Well, you just back the pickup into the garage and keep your mouth shut," Amy said. "Peachy'll never know who took 'em, and we can haul them over to the cabin this weekend." She looked around at the small group of people gathered in her tiny Bozeman living room that evening—Mel Tapper, who lived on the little five-acre farm behind their place on Grizzly Creek; Doc Chamberlain, who was living year-round now just down the creek from them; Rod Kelley, with the cattle ranch right below Doc's place; Mel's huge son Tom, looking like some rawboned modern-day Paul Bunyan in his heavy beard and his Tractor Town baseball cap; her own two strapping sons Garth and Elmer, with their two pregnant wives whispering to each other in the background; and an uncomfortable-looking Harry sitting off to the right of her. "If we're going to store gas, we've got to have oil cans to store it in," she said, "and I say we've got to start storing gas—five gallons extra for the cans every time anybody hits the gas station. I'm telling you guys, if we're going to make our move out there at the creek, we'd better do it now, because tomorrow's liable to be too late. This plague thing hasn't hit Bozeman yet, but it's going to, sure as God makes the moon come up. It's all over the place down in Wyoming, from what I hear, and lots of people down there are doing just what we're planning to do—the ones that are lucky enough, that is."

"You mean holing up and hiding," Mel Tapper said glumly.

"Well, you can call it whatever you want to, Mel," Amy said impatiently. "I call it covering ourselves, and covering our kids, while we've got the chance. Between us we've got the land and the resources to make it work, if we move fast enough. Self-sufficiency is what we need—just as much self-sufficiency as we can manage, so that we don't need anything from anybody, and we don't owe anybody anything, and we can stay clear of anybody carrying a lot of bugs around with them. But I think we've got to move, because we haven't got much time left."

"You're sure right about that," Ben Chamberlain spoke up, a little unexpectedly, since he hadn't had much to say about the whole idea so far. "If we're going to do anything at all, we'd better fish or cut bait. I'm not so sure the whole thing is going to hang together—I'm not even sure it's legal—but I guess we can fight that out when the time comes."

"Why wouldn't it be legal?" Amy demanded. "What's illegal about people pooling their land and their labor and setting up a little freehold for themselves and their kids, way out of harm's way? We own the land, don't we? Free and clear? No mortgages, nobody else's fingers on it? Mel?"

"Mine's bought and paid for. Deed's in the box in the bank."

"Your taxes all paid up?"

"Every year."

"All right, Mel's got five acres nobody can take away from him. Good rich soil for hay, grain or vegetables. Good possibilities for irrigation as long as the creek runs, and it doesn't show any sign of going dry that I can see. Mel's got two horses that could drag a plow if they had to, and chickens, and two pigs and all Martha's goats, and God, do those goats make more goats. What's more, Mel's a crack shot with that old open-sight .30-.30 of his. I don't know how he ever hits anything with it, but he's the best darned still-hunter in this part of the state, and you all know it. If we end up having to poach some venison, Mel can do it up brown."

Amy sat back and looked around the room defiantly. "So Mel's got plenty to offer, and a wife and a boy to take care of. Harry and I are in the same boat: resources to offer, and a family to protect. We've got nine acres between Mel's farm and the creek, easy to clear of brush and plow and plant and irrigate. We've got Harry's backhoe and loader and drag blade to do heavy work, if we can lay in enough diesel fuel to run them. We've got a good stand of fir timber up the hill there, as well as cottonwood till hell won't have it, down on the creek bottom for firewood. Harry can wire anything that needs wiring and fix any piece of machinery that lets out a squeak, and Mel can too—between them they can keep things running. And we've got two boys with strong backs and pregnant wives. If it was just me and Harry alone, I guess we could take our chances in town, but we sure do want to see those grandchildren. We want these kids of ours to have something left when it's all over."

Amy took off her glasses and polished them on her shirttail. "Then there's Ben here—he's got more to offer than anybody. Ben, you've got sixteen acres of good arable land on the creek, enough to produce a surplus of food and run a few head of cattle for meat and milk as well. I could grow more spuds on half an acre of that south meadow of yours than we could eat in ten years. You've also got timber and cover for birds. And best of all, you're a doctor—you could keep us all alive. You can treat glanders, can't you?"

"Glanders." Ben scratched his chin. "I reckon I could if I had to."

"Horses get glanders," Amy said firmly.

"And people get plague."

"Only they don't have to," Amy said. "That's the whole idea of having our own safe spot. We're not going to get the plague—if there's some kind of medicine to get, Ben can get it for us. And we've got a place we can keep together when everything else falls apart. We've got everything we need, right out there on Grizzly Creek with our thirty-one acres of pooled land and the work each one can contribute. It's a perfect Freehold, everything we all need to take care of ourselves and our families. And if Rod Kelley wants to come in with us with his grazing land down the creek, he's got another one hundred sixty acres right there. Of course, that's mostly desert, but he knows stock-raising and you can sure graze steers on that land if you can get water to it. With that, we could have enough beef to sell or trade for anything we need. It's a natural-made Freehold—and if it comes to that, we've got enough artillery to hang onto it, too."

Yes, Ben thought, *we've sure got the artillery.* It was not like the bunches of crazies he'd been reading about down in California, with their stockpiles of submachine guns and automatic rifles and bazookas and mortars and Christ only knew what else—but they had enough iron there on the creek to keep the peace. He alone had his Browning .270 bolt-action rifle, high muzzle velocity and flat trajectory, drop a running bull elk at 450 yards, and his wife's old Remington .30-.06 with a Weaver scope that she'd used when she was still alive. And his Winchester twelve-gauge shotgun, clean pump action, and his wife's Ithaca twenty-gauge. The old World War I Enfield .30-.06 that had been gathering dust in the storeroom all these years, and the snub-nose .38 five-shooter pistol he'd hardly ever fired except once in a while at a stray grouse. Harry and Amy and their boys all had their hunting weapons, and certainly Mel did, including that damned old muzzle-loader of his that sounded like a cannon going off and nearly broke your shoulder every time you fired it. . . .

Yes, we've got the artillery. That's not the question. Ben stared thoughtfully at the small, wiry, sharp-nosed woman across the room, with her sly gray eyes behind those gray-tinted glasses. Amy Hyatt Slencik, must be about forty-five now, he figured, if she hadn't been lying on her last birthday. How long had it been since he'd first set eyes on her? Twenty-three years? Twenty-four? Something like that. That was about when she and Harry had first come out to Grizzly Creek, looking for some cheap bottomland to build a summer cabin on, to get away from the Bozeman heat. Young things, then, with the two boys still just babies. Harry was the same now as he was then—big, friendly, easygoing, generous to a fault. But Amy—how she'd changed since those days!

Ben Chamberlain had pieced the story together, even as he'd watched her changing. Amy Hyatt had been a Missoula girl to start with, only child of a good, solid, upper-middle-class family, at least to all outward appearances. George Hyatt had owned and run the big hardware store there in Missoula and built himself a small fortune from it in spite of a lot of heavy drinking right from the first. They had a big white middle-western house with heavy summer curtains on a tree-shaded street in the fashionable part of town, and two cars and a boat, and Amy had had everything she could ever have wanted, including a lively Appaloosa pony they'd boarded out at a nearby rancher's place. Until she was sixteen years old Amy Hyatt was a pampered, protected baby, friendly with her little clique of girl friends, imperious with the boys, a middling good scholar, with camps and riding school to while away the summer months.

Then the halcyon days of Amy Hyatt had come crashing to a halt in the course of a single year. First her mother had the stroke, a bad one but not quite bad enough, and Amy discovered the facts about living with and caring for a hemiplegic. Then the tax man nailed her father on a foolish Caribbean Island tax dodge he'd been playing for half a dozen years, unknown to anyone but a half-wit Missoula lawyer, and stripped him of every penny he had. George Hyatt crawled into the bottle then and never came out again until he died of cirrhosis two years later, leaving Amy to tend her mother and run the hardware store as well.

It was a staggering burden. The girl bent her back and took it, and toughened to the load, but she hardened, too. It was that summer at age seventeen that she'd met Harry Slencik, come over from Bozeman as ramrod for the construction company that won the bid to underground all the light wires in Missoula's historic downtown section. Harry was big, bland-faced, good-natured—and adoring when it came to Amy. She was a real beauty in those days, a lithe, blond-haired girl, laughing and sly of humor when she could find a few hours free, and sharp enough to recognize a good solid workingman when he came walking down the pike. She loved to square dance and square dance they did, she and Harry, all summer long . . . but then those long, feverish evenings parked in Harry's pickup after the dances finally caught up with her. Harry married her the week after the doctor confirmed the baby—people still did that sort of thing in those days—and moved into the big white house for the rest of his stay in Missoula. With patient thoroughness he helped her inventory the store and sell it for enough to place Mamma in the best nursing home in Missoula for all the years that were necessary, and by the time snow flew that fall he packed the pickup with all it would carry and took his pregnant bride back home with him to Bozeman.

It hadn't been the richest life they'd had together, at first. A second baby boy followed fast on the first, healthy kids that ate a lot and grew like jungle cats. The work was neither steady nor plentiful, for many years, and when the work *was* there Harry wasn't one to crowd the boss for money or privilege. Harry had a lot of rough edges on him that wouldn't wear off, and Amy henpecked him, and slowly, slowly, the sly humor began to sour slightly and take on an edge of malice. Later, when Harry started his own construction outfit, and made it go, and started bringing some money in, Amy was happier, perhaps, but didn't change back; the cutting edge was there to stay.

Dr. Ben Chamberlain had sold them a chunk of some family land he had on Grizzly Creek in the mountain foothills seventy miles from Bozeman, nothing worth a whole lot, just cottonwood bottoms and half-desert hills with some small stands of fir and pine. He watched

Harry build the cabin with his own hands, and take to firewood-sawing all day when he needed to get away from Amy. Ben had watched the kids grow up, those two hulking, muscle-bound boys; he was spending more and more time at his own place down the creek since his Emmie had died from the breast cancer, and he kept an eye on Amy and Harry's place when they weren't there. They had been good neighbors to Ben, over the years; there was nothing Harry couldn't fix or wire or screw together for him; Amy baked him cakes and fed him lasagna; they gathered sometimes for evening drinks and talked incessantly about hunting; and the friendship of proximity grew over the years—and bit by bit, the older man had watched Amy change.

Now, in the little living room, listening to her sharp voice and watching her sharp eyes and seeing her beat her little fist into her little palm, it struck him just how very much she really *had* changed. She could bring a whole whale of a lot to this Freehold she was talking about if she wanted to. She was tough, physically strong, hard-minded. *As an organizer, an administrator, she could keep things on the track,* Ben thought. *There'd be no coyotes in the chickens when she was around. But she'd have to come down a long notch or two if anybody was going to be able to live with her for any length of time. If the Freehold was to have any chance at all,* he thought, *somebody would have to teach her how to shut up and give in once in a while. . . .*

Well, it wouldn't be Harry that brought her down, that was sure, and it certainly wasn't going to be Mel Tapper or Rod Kelley, either. So that left *him.*

47

Inevitably, as the gray fall rolled into bitter winter, chaos deepened in Ted Bettendorf's Atlanta office. As the fire storm raged across the land, the urgent demands on the tall, gray-haired man climbed exponentially as the effective options for action plummeted. From one of the few vantage points from which the whole picture could be viewed at once, Ted himself saw the ever-expanding disaster through a wide-angle lens, and with each passing day he saw progressively less that could be done to stop it.

As might have been expected, the blossoming plague struck the major cities earliest and hardest, and one by one Ted saw them stagger and fall. The factors of inevitability were all in place, waiting: the huge numbers of people packed into small areas, impossible to isolate; the staggering insistent demands for vaccine and medication, undersupplied; social and health institutions, never too efficient at best in their gangling, rambling bureaucracies, ultimately impossible to keep functioning; the government, at all levels, already so acutely overdrawn in the huge cities, becoming impossible to maintain; law enforcement and police protection already staggering under their normal loads, becoming impossible to provide—the slow death of the cities was as inevitable and predictable during that terrible fall and winter as the ultimate burning of Savannah had been during the late summer. Ted Bettendorf knew that, as he fielded the increasingly urgent and impossible telephone calls from his headquarters in Atlanta or traveled out for on-site inspections and consultations in the failing cities, but by sheer force of will he refused to think about it or acknowledge it. If he had acknowledged it even for a moment, he might have been forced, in the cold light of inevitability and helplessness, to say, "Sorry, but we've written off all of the major cities and the hundred and fifty million people living there, so don't call back," and turned his attention to the ones that were left—but of course he could not have said such a monstrous thing, nor even thought about saying it, so instead he ignored the inevitable. Others in authority in the dying cities ignored it or confronted it as their individual natures inclined them, and one by one the major cities met the plague in their own distinctive ways.

As Ted observed it, it came to New York like the slow, crushing grip of angina, a deep-seated painful pressure, first irritating, then acute, then unbearable, relentlessly spreading and spreading and spreading. When it first appeared in the teeming ghetto rooms of Harlem and the decaying tenement towers of the Lower East Side and the grubby flats of the Village and the sprawling slum ruins of Brooklyn, it was only dimly recognized. That fall was cold and rainy in New York and everybody stayed indoors, fearful of a hungry, frigid winter to come. Health Department bulletins of warning, of precautions to be taken, of signs to watch for, of things to do, as always in New York, fell on hundreds of thousands of deaf ears. Interests were too narrow. Misery was already too deep. TV bulletins were ignored, snapped off in midstream in favor of the soap operas and the game shows and the oblivion of primetime entertainments. These were people who didn't know what Savannah was, or where, people who didn't listen, couldn't or wouldn't comprehend. Many couldn't even understand the language—and how could *they* respond?

Soon plague was spreading through the crowded, steaming subways, packed with coughing, spitting people feverish to reach home. People left work and never were seen again. In a sudden wave, within a single week, everybody seemed to be sick with something, and plague was there for certain, finally and reluctantly identified by the labs, as the health establishment struggled helplessly to fight it. Official cries went out for the vaccine, and for city-wide supplies of Sealey 3147—but not until demand had far outstripped supply. The city needed a river of vaccine and received a trickle as the CDC tried to juggle consignments and batch after batch was sucked away to a thousand other places. When a planeload finally did arrive at JFK in the dark of a cold, rainy night, already too late to stem the raging epidemic, it was hijacked into a semi trailer waiting at the loading dock and vanished into the Northeast somewhere—it certainly never reached the warehouse in downtown Manhattan prepared to receive and distribute it.

The crushing pain turned to agony with the first winter storm to strike the city, first a mass of cold, wet air sweeping up from the Gulf and dropping fourteen inches of snow on Manhattan in twelve hours, then an icy blast from the Arctic, rolling down from Montreal, dropping temperatures to -15° F, in New York, ten degrees colder in Westchester and Jersey. Supplies into the city, already hamstrung by truck drivers too sick to drive and others afraid to come anywhere near the plague spot, now slowed to critical. Fuel supplies began sagging, rationing pleas were ignored. Snow removal faltered—no one could get anywhere, and even those who did couldn't find what they wanted when they got there. A sad little emergency team tried valiantly for forty-eight hours to enforce a city ordinance to hold home and office thermostats down to fifty degrees, but panic and a very real fear of freezing to death met them at every hand, and the enforcement team gave up.

Then the garbage collectors struck, a wildcat affair; their contract was not up for another eight months but the opportunity was too good to miss. They couldn't move their trucks until snow removal had cleared the streets, they said. There were too many dead bodies turning up in the garbage, they said, and they were sanitation engineers, not morticians. A third of them were too sick or terrified to come to work anyway, which put more of a load on the dwindling number that were still able and willing, and you couldn't expect them to work like that without more money, lots more money, now, not eight months later. Day followed week of futile talks, threats, name-calling and sympathy strikes, as the garbage piled up on the sidewalks, steaming from its own fermentation in the frigid air, and the rats, knowing a good thing when they saw it, came up out of the sewers in regular battalions. There came a day when the chief Sanitation Workers' Union negotiator met with the Mayor and other city officials around a long table in a downtown building, the union man's eyes bright with fever, coughing blood into his handkerchief and chilling violently in his seat, explaining desperately that the men weren't going back to work without more money (more coughing, more blood), there was no way anyone could *make* them go back to work, a whole lot of them weren't going back to work at all, money or no money, anywhere, period, because they were sick and dying, and so was their negotiator, and there you were, boys, that was the whole picture. . . .

Little by little, New York City suffocated, strangling from its own size and complexity and the gradual day-by-day breakdown of supply and service and maintenance in an ever-expanding chain reaction more grisly and deadly and stultifying than any uranium fission bomb. Contrary to early predictions, New York City did not explode, as Savannah had. Instead, it slowly, slowly imploded, gradually collapsing under the weight of its own offal until one day it was no longer a functioning city on any level at all, merely a vast, hopeless quagmire of dying people.

The Kansas Cities of Missouri and Kansas faced the crisis with more style, if with even less wisdom. Those unequal cities standing like Great Claus and Little Claus at the confluence of the Kansas and Missouri rivers were blessed by a long, warm Indian summer that extended into late November. The million-odd people in their combined metropolitan areas were far more homogeneous than those in New York—at least they all spoke roughly the same language. More important, the plague came more insidiously there than in the eastern cities, nibbling at the edges of each social group like hors d'oeuvres before the devouring feast began. It took a while for the people there to fully realize how terribly dreadful the crisis was going to be.

In fact, given reasonable leadership from the respective city fathers and guidance from the local Public Health Services and the Centers for Disease Control, the Kansas City metropolis on both sides of the state line might actually have had a fighting chance to withstand the onslaught when it came, had it not been for a sequence of the most astoundingly obtuse political decisions ever taken in the long, spotty political history of the region. As it happened, Kansas City, Missouri, actually had a fairly adequate supply of the new vaccine, as well as a reasonable stockpile of Sealey 3147, on hand in the city at the time the first bite of the plague was really felt there. The shipments had come in late September as part of a nationwide pro rata distribution of then-existing supplies of vaccine and antibiotic to the major cities, undertaken as part of a presidential executive order at the persistent urging of Ted Bettendorf, and had been completed before other mutually exclusive executive orders began curtailing the air traffic that made such rapid shipments possible. What was more, the Kansas City public-health authorities, in cooperation with CDC field workers, had actually developed workable blueprints for a rudimentary emergency action plan to swing into effect whenever it became clear that plague was indeed hitting that metropolis: traffic and police control plans, hospital utilization plans, medication distribution plans, block-by-block isolation plans, sane quarantine regulations—in total, one of the best-conceived and earliest-developed citywide defense programs to be worked out in any major city in the country since the burning of Savannah. Indeed, the whole Kansas City complex might conceivably have weathered the storm for a while—except that the whole action plan fell apart before it ever got instituted.

What happened was horrible in its very simplicity. When the vaccine and antibiotic shipments arrived, with distribution jointly entrusted to the governing authorities of the two major metropolitan segments of the city—the Missouri city and the city across the state line in Kansas—disagreements between the two governing bodies immediately appeared. Those two governments had seldom—if ever—agreed on anything whatever in the past, and the imminent crisis did not make them any better bedfellows. In fact, the two communities reached real agreement on one single point alone: that distribution of supplies to the *other* community should take place only after prudent and ample provision had been made for the protection of the entire governmental and health preservation organization of the first community—and since possession was indeed nine-tenths of the law, the "first community" was defined by its governing body as the community which managed to obtain actual physical possession of the whole metropolitan shipment of vaccine and antibiotic. And an early, frantic and very secret cashing in of political credits speedily greased the shipping skids so that the entire consignment arrived by air on the Missouri side of the line.

The city fathers there lost no time making prudent and entirely ample provision for the protection of themselves, their wives, their children, their nephews, their closest and most profitable business friends, their most reliable supporters in the second echelon of government, their most reliable supporters in the third, fourth and fifth echelons of government, including all *their* wives, children, nephews and close and profitable business friends, and so on into the night. All this was accomplished with positively breathtaking efficiency, amid a succession of highly secret and totally illegal meetings, and with the quiet collusion of certain highly placed commissioners and subcommissioners of public health on the Missouri side of the river, within hours of the time the consignment of medicinals touched ground, and a full week before CDC personnel and the actual working crew of the Missouri-side Public Health Department even knew the consignment had been shipped. During that time not a single carton of vaccine nor case of antibiotic crossed the state line into Kansas.

When at last a by-then-much-depleted supply of medicinals was finally released for distribution to public-health and CDC authorities on the Kansas side, virtually none of it actually reached its target. Distressed as they were at Missouri's rape of the shipment, the city fathers in Kansas said nothing; their police simply appropriated every bit of the consignment that crossed the river, quietly and efficiently, the moment it hit high ground and delivered it to City Hall. Of this supply, officials and subofficials on the Kansas side made prudent and extremely ample provision for their own protection in the same pattern as had occurred in Missouri. Thus, like wheat shipments to India since time immemorial, seven-tenths of the entire consignment vanished from the docks before anyone knew it had arrived, and only three-tenths ultimately sifted down to the hands of the public-health and CDC workers and finally, to the doctors and other health workers designated by the blueprint action plan to distribute it. Many of those people, angered in their turn by the city fathers' actions and panicking at the sudden appearance of the disease itself on all sides of them, used the materials available quite arbitrarily to protect themselves, their families, their office workers, their receptionists, their administrative personnel, their switchboard operators and billing clerks, selected business friends and finally, certain favored patients and their families. What little of the material sifted through *that* enormous sieve fell, for the most part, into the gentle hands of the most powerful Mafia family between Chicago and Houston and became available, as the city fell into increasingly extreme straits of illness, not for the free distribution intended, but for sale to the highest bidders. . . .

It was an example of greed and unenlightened self-interest of staggering proportions. It all happened *fast* and in secret, before Kansas City's most wide-eyed news hawks tumbled onto it—and when they did, suppression of news was ready and waiting on either side of the river. The Kansas City *Star* broke the first story on the Rape of the Shipment, with screamer headlines and promises of details to follow—but details did not follow, because the Commissioner of Public Utilities, on his own recognizance, cut off the power to the newspaper's press with one flip of an enormous switch and then posted armed guards around the switch to see that it stayed flipped. TV news reporters, never famed for their follow-up capacity under the best of circumstances, emitted a single loud scream in concert and then were drowned out by endless hours of solemn denials by trusted city officials.

Of course, such a story could not long stay hidden. Very soon the people of both cities became acutely aware of increasing disease and death in their midst, at precisely the same time they became aware that virtually all of their public-health protection had been betrayed by their community leaders in the course of a single week. Public outrage began as a murmur, blossomed into a rumble and then a roar. One morning a crowd of eighty thousand people converged on City Hall on the Missouri side, many of them armed and all of them howling for blood and heads on stakes; denied and turned away by an embattled police force, they dispersed through the downtown area, smashing department-store windows, looting shelves, raging into office suites and rending and tearing everything in sight. It took police two days to clear mobs out of the downtown shambles, with eight hundred dead, fully half of them police—but the looting spread and continued in widespread outlying areas of the city. Cars were dumped on their sides to blockade streets, windows were shattered, bombs exploded, small fires raged.

Ted Bettendorf believed every word of the accounts that came to him from CDC field workers: Kansas City was a city gone mad, enraged at betrayal in a place long familiar with the finer points of political betrayal. Governmental controls collapsed altogether as the angry mobs grew and officials were searched out and besieged in their houses, defending their doorsteps from pillagers and watching their families dragged away before their eyes. Utilities fell apart, electricity and communications were virtually obliterated. For days the city convulsed with a rage of street fighting. Functioning automobiles for escape came suddenly into demand, and street thieves came into their own, stealing first hubcaps, then tires, then wheels, and then whole engines out of cars that anyone was foolish enough to leave parked and unguarded for more than half an hour at a time. And then, as the real depth of the plague began to rack the city, now totally helpless and defenseless, protective fiefdoms sprang up from block to block to guard what was left to be guarded. Cellars were converted into hospices for the dying, barricades blocked two-thirds of the city streets, nine-tenths of the stores and most of the richer homes were looted and ransacked, the dead were burned on street corners in ever-increasing numbers and finally the ice-cold winter came as a frigid blessing because it kept down the stench. In a different way and much faster than New York, Kansas City also died.

In Chicago the plague itself struck more swiftly and widely than perhaps anywhere else in the country. In early October, multiple mini-epidemics sprang up simultaneously in various areas of the city, most of them ultimately traced to air travelers from the West and South, until all possible track of them was inevitably lost. Multiple nameless prediagnosis contacts, including a dozen-odd black families that had evacuated, already ill, from Savannah to Chicago, vanished into the fastnesses of the city slums, never to be heard from again except through outbreaks of the infection they carried. On-hand supplies of vaccine and Sealey 3147 were quickly exhausted protecting essential hospital and public-health personnel, while urgent appeals for more took their place at the bottom of the growing stack on Ted Bettendorf's desk in Atlanta. With incredible swiftness the infection spread, with first hundreds and then thousands of new cases appearing daily. In the deep urban tenements the Horseman could almost have been seen galloping from block to block, had any alert epidemiologist had the time or facilities to tabulate the wildfire spread; in the middle-class tracts and wealthy suburbs the firestorm burned less flagrantly, perhaps, but no less fast. In the endless flatlands of Chicago, of all places, the ground had been prepared for uncontrolled spread of pneumonic plague by an immediately prior epidemic of A/Montreal influenza which had struck the city unseasonably and hard in late September and left 400,000 people near prostration from a three-week illness *before* the plague appeared.

In Chicago, the spreading illness produced a confrontation between citizens and authority of a different order of magnitude than was witnessed elsewhere that early in the fire storm—a confrontation between huge masses of people determined to go elsewhere and a military authority empaneled and determined to keep them where they were. As the total inability of health authorities either to treat the infection or control its spread became increasingly evident, vast squadrons of people, both the quick and the dying, began a mass exodus to the south and west of the city in a hapless, hopeless search for open country, help, food, warmth and succor of some sort. Hundreds, thousands, tens of thousands began flooding the major expressways, open, pulsating arteries hemorrhaging people into the countryside, people with small possessions on their backs, dull eyes, coughs and high fevers, all afoot or on bicycles, since auto traffic was quickly and totally choked off by the sheer mass of moving bodies. In a matter of days those tens of thousands became hundreds of thousands, leaving their dead where they dropped, moving as relentlessly and mindlessly as a staggering army of human ants down the freeways and across the countryside. . . .

Local authorities quickly made the bold decision that these masses must not be allowed to leave the city—they faced certain chaos and slaughter to the south and west in a countryside that did not want them. But stopping them and turning them back was something else altogether. A National Guard militia composed of a few hundred exceedingly green, inept and combat-innocent farm boys flown in from southern parts of the state to barricade the expressways found themselves immediately stripped of clothing, shoes, arms, supplies and even underwear almost the instant that they took up their positions. As swiftly as possible, which was not quite swiftly enough, federal authorities then declared martial law for all of metropolitan Chicago and surrounding areas, and army and marine units moved in, complete with tanks, field artillery and quite a considerable air force of transports and helicopters with orders to stop the outflow. Yet not even the leaders of these units, much less the troops themselves, had any stomach for mass slaughter of helpless people. Rubber bullets and riot-squad attacks merely pushed masses of people from Point A temporarily over to Point B and then back to Point A again; tear gas produced instant chaos wherever it was used, effectively halting all motion whatever and reducing an advancing mass of people to a blinded, weeping *milling* mass of people—but a mass of people who were *not going back where they had come from* and couldn't even if they had wanted to because of the further masses of people piling in behind them. Tank commanders refused to send their tanks rolling north through masses of people moving south, and those foolish enough to try soon found the masses of people separating around them like buffalo and then engulfing them in a sea of bodies—and what tank commander wanted his troops in that close contact with *that* infected sea of bodies? The intent was sound enough, but the task was impossible; a solid line of D8 bulldozers forming an unbroken arc 150 miles long might have stopped those people from moving forward, perhaps even moved them back a few hundred yards, but presently the people would simply have climbed over the bulldozers. In the end, the total net effect of this military adventure in confronting people and stopping them from going where they wanted to go (or thought they did) was hopelessly perverse: a containing arc of militia and machinery and vehicles and helicopters all slowly *retreating* to the south and west in the face of the oncoming horde, with no alternative to retreat other than chopping the horde down like wheat on the prairie, with lots more wheat where that came from.

As it was in New York and Kansas City and Chicago, so it was in the other cities, minor variations from one to another but the same major theme. As the fire storm raged on, government institutions and public-health facilities grew steadily less able to cope with, much less contain, the holocaust. In fairness, of course, the day-by-day disintegration of the government and authority could not be blamed solely on the ineptitude or venality or incapacity of national or local leaders. The President proved no better nor worse a crisis leader than any other President in recent history would have been; he was not stupid, nor blind, nor even overly concerned with the political implications of what he did. If anything, he rose far above his capacity in facing the fire storm and did as much as any other human being in his position might have done. Behind and about him, tens of thousands of others in high places in government worked valiantly and did the very best they knew how to do to preserve the reins of control. In the final tally there were far more heroes than cowards in those ranks.

The problem was, very simply, that the best those leaders knew how to do fell far short of what needed to be done, and the tools that were needed were not there. No government in modern history had ever faced a disaster of the magnitude and suddenness of this one, whether economic, medical or military. The great, crushing depression of the 1930s had taken *years* to mature to its most dismal depths. Later, in the midst of the most terrible war in all history, it had taken six full months after the bombing of Pearl Harbor before the country was fully mobilized to fight back, despite three full years of advance warning; by then the enemy had achieved their empire, and it took four long, bloody years to wrench it back—but the first six months did not see the total disintegration of the nation. It merely made the fight longer and harder and more costly.

But even that disastrous war was of a different nature entirely from the present fire storm. In this case there wasn't any six months in which to mobilize. Within a couple of months or so after Savannah the major cities were buried in corpses, and the wherewithal to fight simply didn't exist. A year before the storm began, a total of twenty-three cases of plague had been reported in the entire year, confined to eight western states, all but six cases bubonic and flea-borne in nature. In all common sense, there had been nothing to be prepared and mobilized *for* until Pamela Tate was carried down the mountain, and within days all rational efforts at mobilization were already running frantically merely to catch up with a disaster far out of control. What was worse, for mobilization to be possible at all, the gears of national commerce, health controls and communications would all have had to mesh perfectly—but as the storm spread, the gears failed to mesh in too many areas at once, and quickly ground themselves to powder. Nothing of any significance could be accomplished because *nothing really continued working enough of the time in enough places at once.* Highway shipping could not accomplish anything when cross-country truckers fell sick at the wheel halfway to their destinations, or refused to drive their trucks into plague-stricken cities or simply walked away, leaving their vehicles planted on the highways. Without effective medications the medical establishment was reduced to the prayers, promises and post-mortems of a bygone age. Locally operated public utilities worked valiantly to keep such basics as heat, light and electricity going part of the time in most places, shoring up areas that broke down as best they could, but all too soon generating capacities began to crumble from lack of coal and oil immediately at hand to power the generators.

Telephone communications worked better than most things, at first, with at least the main trunk lines functioning to most areas part of the time and with overloaded satellite facilities pressed to the utmost—yet in counterpoint to this, the postal system ceased to work at all except on the most local, hand-delivery levels—and who wanted to do the hand-delivering? Checks that were mailed never arrived; heaps and mountains of mail piled up in central dispatching offices and overflowed into the streets; orders for goods and cash were never confirmed if they were ever received; nobody got paid. Normal commercial air traffic ground to a halt, amid a massive confusion of counterdirections, impaled on the horns of dilemma—the acute, agonizing need for fast transport of people and knowhow and materiel on the one hand, and the acute, agonizing knowledge that airplanes were spreading the disease worldwide on the other hand, so that the Horseman had leaped cities and countrysides and borders and oceans long before he was even recognized. . . .

And so it was, Ted Bettendorf reflected, that hell followed after Him Who Rode. Paralysis spread hand in hand with plague; first the cities and then the towns and villages and hamlets were stricken in the ever-growing fire storm, and the nation headed into a dreadful winter without food or fuel or medicine or leadership enough to go on for six more weeks, and no idea on God's green earth where any of those things were going to come from. . . .

48

In a ruined industrial-warehouse area on the outskirts of Wichita, Sally Grinstone wrestled the wheel of the old Dodge van to avoid the larger potholes and craters in the street, cursing under her breath as she steered the rig around heaps of rubble, expecting a tire to go at any minute. It was late afternoon and she was heading straight into a baleful yellow-brown sun still trying to burn through the lead-gray overcast of a wintry Kansas sky. She shivered despite the soiled down jacket she was wearing and glanced approvingly at the wrapped-up gin bottle jouncing on the seat beside her. Sally at heart was a creature of the warm countries, the lands of few clothes and many palm trees, the sun-drenched swimming pools of Florida and New Orleans and The Coast; she had nothing but dread for what that lead-gray Kansas sky might hold in store when the white stuff started coming down, with an icy northern wind behind it—*Ugh. Going to need that gin bottle, especially with the work we've got lined up. . . .*

She eased the rig around the fallen brick wall of a burned-out warehouse. It was the most inauspicious-looking vehicle imaginable, a big, boxy, mud-brown van, top-heavy and awkward, with one side panel crunched in as though it had been stepped on by an enormous foot. Not the sort of rig that anybody was likely to stop and hassle, she had thought, which was exactly why she and Tom had stolen it, if you could call it stealing. They'd seen it standing abandoned on a street in Des Moines one day, forlorn and wrecky-looking, the crunched side panel forced open, windshield smashed with a rock, tires so lousy nobody'd stolen the wheels. Sally had crawled in under the dashboard upside down and hot-wired the thing to get it going while Tom stood chickie against cops and looters, looking acutely embarrassed, and then gaped as Sally left her little red Fiat sitting with the keys in the ignition in the exact same spot as they drove away in the van. "Fair enough trade," she'd said. "Nobody could use this wreck but us; they'll take *that* little bomber apart right down to the chassis and make a fortune selling the parts."

Now Sally watched the rearview mirror, a line of worry creasing her baby face. A blue Ford pickup was about two blocks behind her, pacing her rather too neatly; she was sure she had seen it a couple of times earlier. She hit a pothole and heard a sloshing sound in the back of the van, glanced over her shoulder at the half-dozen acid carboys riding back there in their wood packing frames—the object of this trip in the first place. It had taken her two days to track down a supplier and some highly ingenuous lying to explain just what she wanted with them. *Maybe they didn't believe me that women use the stuff in shampoo,* she thought, glancing again at the pickup in the rearview. But Tom had said he needed acetic acid, reagent grade, and innocently left it up to her to get some, and that was what she had done—

She took a sudden left and stamped hard on the gas pedal, running the van down the obstacle course of a little side street as fast as she dared. The pickup passed on its way behind her without even slowing, and she breathed easier. A real nervous pain, she thought, this business of back and fill and dodge, you just couldn't trust anything or anybody, the number of weird people running around was just incredible, almost to the point that anybody seen wandering the streets afoot or on wheel was by definition weird until proven otherwise—

The street she had turned into was really just an alley with brick-walled buildings tight on either side and trash and rubble strewn everywhere. Twice she had to get out and move overturned garbage cans to get through the single block to the next avenue—and then, just as she reached it, the blue Ford pickup swerved in from the other end and decisively forced her into the right-hand wall. A swarthy man leaped out with a shotgun in his hands, and the shotgun was trained on her.

For a moment Sally just froze. Then, very deliberately, she uncapped the gin bottle, took a long pull and rolled down the window. "Okay, dummy, what's your trouble?" she demanded.

The man was short and fat, either Mexican or Indian, with a long, droopy black mustache and a face like a discontented spaniel. He motioned to her with one hand. "Hop out," he said.

The shotgun drooped as she hopped, gin bottle under her arm. She squinted hard at him as she climbed down. *Definitely Indian,* she thought. "You'd better push the safety on that thing," she said, "before you shoot your foot off." The man's face darkened, but she heard the click of the safety.

He pointed a finger toward the back of the van. "What you got in there?" he said.

"Vinegar," Sally said.

"Vinegar?" His mouth tightened. "Open it up," he said.

She threw the side door open and the man peered inside. Then he moved closer, frowning, and sniffed. "My God, it *is* vinegar," he said.

"Thirty bloody gallons of it," Sally affirmed. "Good and strong. You wanted some vinegar, dummy, you got it."

The fat man edged away from the van—and from her. "What you doin' with all that vinegar?"

"I mix it with my gin," she said evenly. She offered him the bottle. "Have some?"

He shook his head quickly and edged away another step. "Stomach wouldn't take it."

"Well, then, I suppose you're going to rape me," Sally said impatiently. She glanced at her watch. "Where? Hood of your pickup? Let's get on with it—"

"*Jesus,* lady, who said anything about rape?" The man was in full retreat now, his spaniel face a study in distress.

"Well, hell's fire, man, if you don't want my vinegar and you don't want my gin and you don't want to rape me, why are we hanging around? Get that junker out of there so I can go home." She started climbing back into the van, then paused to peer at the shotgun. "You ever actually shoot that thing?"

"Once or twice."

"You want a job as a bodyguard?"

"Jesus, lady, you don't need no bodyguard."

"Maybe not—but I sure could use a runner. I've got errands to run all over this broken-down town, and this hijack-the-woman-driver crap gets old, believe me. Yesterday it was a cop in uniform—how about that? So maybe you'd like to run errands."

The fat man eyed her nervously. "What's in it for me?"

"Maybe some food and a place to hang out, if you're worth it. And some medicine to keep bad things away. What's your name?"

"Willie."

"No, I mean your *real* name."

"Dog Runs Quickly."

"There, you see? So give me an address or phone number. I'll send for you if I need you."

She left him scratching his head as she turned the van out of the alley, then wove through a series of back streets, caught a broader avenue going south and then turned into a concrete drive beside a ragtag-looking, gray-green, two-story building and stopped to activate the gate in a chain link fence. The fenced-in yard to the south of the building was filled with loading pallets and a totally demolished forklift; beyond the yard was a huge black building marked SKINNER IRON WORKS. Muffler City and a very dead-looking plumbing and heating wholesale place were just across the street.

She backed into the loading dock of the gray-green building. Two sides were covered with faded aluminum sheeting, with the north and south elevations of both stories mostly painted-over windows. Several that were smashed had been boarded over with fresh-looking plywood—*Good, Tom got that lower one closed up, finally.* She killed the ignition, got out and walked up a ramp to a door on the loading platform. A faded sign on the door said INTERNATIONAL PHARMACALS, WHOLESALE.

They had spent the better part of three weeks searching four different cities before finally settling on this place, staying in the cheapest motels they could find and living on Egg McMuffins and gin while they searched. In St. Louis Sally had pulled the one trick she'd never pulled before on an editor: wired for a huge cash advance on the promise of a red-hot story, and then simply vanished into the sunset in her little Fiat with Tom Shipman in the passenger seat beside her, still wondering dazedly what exactly he was doing there. Sally wondered half the time, too; aside from his obvious and undeniable expertise in chemistry, she had never encountered quite such a totally inept human being. Tom Shipman would lose every motel key she gave him, get lost walking around the block, agonize for twenty minutes over what kind of hamburger he should order and wear the same shirt for seven days end-running until Sally couldn't stand it anymore and said, "God, Tom, that thing will never wash; burn it and we'll buy you another one." By common agreement they headed vaguely north and west from St. Louis, mostly because east seemed to be where more trouble lay. They had stopped for a day in Lincoln, Nebraska, while she had rapped out the entire story of the Sealey drug switch and telephoned it to the paper (not the story they had sent her funds for, but enough to hold them, she figured—enough indeed) and then wired for (and waited interminably to receive) all the cash she could muster from her several bank accounts, together with the couple of thousand Tom had stashed away—but all that money was for capital, not spending, and they lived on dirty socks and fingernails as they groped their way westward looking for precisely the place they needed to set up their bizarre operation.

Tom was, at least, quite clear and succinct about what it was, exactly, that they needed. The idea of trying to build the sheer physical plant for any kind of serious pharmaceutical manufacturing venture from the ground up was clearly insane. True, he *had* told Sally Grinstone that his "pneumomycin" drug could be made in a bathtub out of ordinary tetracycline, vinegar and a few other reagents, and in point of fact, it *could* be—but the claim was perhaps a bit of an oversimplification all the same; along with the quantities of his "pneumomycin" one might precipitate out of such a bathtub slurry, one might also find a number of other things one would rather not offer to unsuspecting patients. A simple chemical process that could be carried to completion on a kitchen stove was one thing; preparing and packaging a large quantity of a reasonably pure drug in a form suitable for human consumption was something else. An abandoned truck-tire warehouse wouldn't do as a site for manufacture and packaging. Even the most pristine of headquarters would require an impossibly long time and far, far too much capital to start up even minimal production unless it offered certain basic rudiments of equipment and facilities. Tom recognized as starkly as Sally that time was both their enemy and their ally; if they were to do anything effective at all, they could take time to do it right without fear of interference, but they had to do it fast, in a matter of weeks, not months. Sometime next year would be altogether too late.

In short, they needed some base of operations that was already plausibly equipped for production of some reasonably similar pharmaceutical product. "We can't build it from scratch, but we can convert, maybe very quickly," Tom said. "Anyplace with water baths and incubators and clean vats and working space and processing and packing equipment would do."

"We could go to Rahway, New Jersey, and take over Merck and Company," Sally said dryly.

"We don't need Merck and Company," Tom said. "Even Sealey labs was a little fly-by-night subcontracting outfit pressing aspirin tablets for Rexall until they hired some good research chemists and got Mancini running the business end. There are literally thousands of little plants of the sort that Sealey Labs used to be, cranking out vitamins or antihistamines or even tetracycline with enough quality control to sell their stuff cheap, at wholesale, to the big outfits that can charge a mint for their brand names. Hell, *none* of the big companies could make a dime producing their own standard tetracycline-type drugs after the patents ran out or the government got their thumbs in. They had to buy them very, very cheap from producers who could make them very, very cheap, here or abroad. Thousands of little plants scattered all over—and with the plague hitting the cities the way it is, lots of those places must be closed down by now, at least temporarily. We might even find warehouse lots of finished tetracycline sitting around waiting to be moved, with nobody to move it, if we're lucky. . . ."

They weren't *that* lucky, but they were lucky enough, and they had Sally, to boot. All that Sally had needed was a place to start; rooting out information was her stock-in-trade. Some data came from ordinary library sources, some from business indexes, some from drug-company contacts that owed Sally favors, or leads that Tom could dredge up out of his memory. They spent days, weeks, fighting failing telephone service and waiting endlessly for returned calls, nine-tenths of which never came. They focused their attention on the general area of the central and southern Midwest, partly because they were already there, partly because highway traffic was still functioning to some degree in that part of the country, and especially because most of the medium-sized cities, except for the Kansas City complex and the St. Louis area, which was suddenly reeling from its first wave of the fire storm, hadn't really been hit yet. They spent eighteen-hour days, first one place, then another, looking, telephoning, Sally's fantastic organizational mind tabulating and filing reams of data as they gathered it, Tom ruminating for hours and then coming up with ingenious suggestions that Sally soon learned to listen to because more often than not they were almost directly on target.

And as they moved in on the problem, trying to bring their focus down to serious prospects, Tom did one other thing that even he didn't know he was any good at: bit by bit, clearly and simply, in veritable chemical baby talk, he told Sally how antibiotics were made, from the ground up—the nature of the compounds, where they came from orginally, why and how they could work to destroy pathogenic bacteria and stop a wildfire infection in its tracks and how bacteria developed resistance, so that a good antibiotic presently became not so good and then rather poor and ultimately virtually useless against a certain species of organism. He explained to her how the search for new compounds went on, what particular scientific concepts had led him to his "pneumomycin" discovery to begin with, some of the truly weird problems he had encountered here and there in his research.

Sally listened and Sally learned. She couldn't follow all the chemical terminology, precisely, but she had enough background to get the broad picture. She was startled—and appalled—to learn that Tom had already worked out the chemistry for some seven other relatively simple tetracycline-conversion compounds in addition to the "pneumomycin" he had actually developed, every one of which he had some reason to believe might be biologically active against the mutated plague organism, but that Sealey had simply jerked the purse strings shut and told him to forget about them. "Not economically feasible," they had told him. "Anybody in the world could jump our patents on these things without even turning over in bed. What we need is something complex, not something simple. . . ."

Along with the chemistry, Tom also outlined for Sally some of the realities and necessities involved in production, quality control, *in vitro* biological testing, *in vivo* testing and clinical trials of a drug such as his "pneumomycin" before one would ordinarily seek to make it available for general use—("Of course, we don't ordinarily have a wildfire plague slicing through the population, either," he pointed out, "and because in fact we *do,* and since this is a rump operation we're talking about, completely outside of any laws or regulations, those rules are going to be bent all out of shape, but it's good to know what the rules are, and why, all the same")—right down to such mundane practicalities as how you get all that loose powder stuffed into all those little capsules so that there is almost precisely 250 milligrams of antibiotic in each capsule without having to weigh each one, and what you do to control the unpleasant smell of the stuff, and what solubility qualities both the capsule and the contents have to have so that the drug doesn't just go in one end and out the other, and how long you can store the finished drug on a shelf before it begins spontaneously disintegrating and losing its potency—and through it all, in a remarkably short time, Sally Grinstone began to grasp at least in vague outline the sheer magnitude of the task they were setting out to accomplish and to recognize how, just conceivably, *something* might be done fast enough and efficiently enough to actually end up doing some good somewhere—

In the end, the real gold mine was delivered to them almost intact by a young stockbroker in a Wall Street office who had had quite a steamy affair with Sally Grinstone not too many months before, and hadn't begun to forget it, there was a special Grinstone crease in his brain three inches deep, and he wasn't all that busy selling stocks these days anyway because the Market was closed more than it was open and it took him all day to get to work and all day to get back home again to his wife and kiddies, but he was a specialist in drug-industry stocks and had his finger on such information as precisely what companies were thriving these days and what companies weren't. "All we need is a plant with just the kinds of equipment and heat controls and outfittings that I've mentioned," Sally told him urgently. "It's got to be a basically operational plant, but shut down, at least temporarily, and we don't want to buy, we just want to lease it as is, and everything in it needs to be in working order, just like I told you—what's that, Pete?"

"Sal, I said what in hell are you going to do with a chemical factory way out in central Kansas or someplace?"

"My hair's getting dirty, Pete. I'm going to make shampoo."

"You wouldn't pull my leg, would you, Sal?"

"Not yours, Pete. Not if there was anything else to pull. . . ."

Long pause. "You're not planning some acid or coke operation that's liable to get me nailed to the wall like Nell's ass?"

'Pete, baby, those days are truly over. This is for real. It's straight as an arrow, and it's urgent. Now, no more fun and games. Can you help me or can't you?"

Pete said, "Get back to you," and presently he did. It took him about eight hours, but he brought the goods with him. "You've got about eight choices in Kansas, Nebraska and Texas," he said, "but the best deal all around for your specs is a place in south Wichita, an International Pharmacals plant that's been closed down since last spring. They're manufacturers and wholesalers, with their main plant and headquarters in Chicago. They were using the Wichita place for ampicillin and some kind of time-release antihistamine. Closed it down as marginal when the interest rates got back up there into the clouds last year. Yes, yes, they'll lease, I didn't talk bucks, but I told them you were pure and clean, and they might just listen to a minimal, *very* minimal, offer just to have somebody in there, considering what's happening to empty buildings in some of those cities these days. There's a man in Wichita you can contact. . . ."

Now, as Sally walked inside from the loading dock, the pervading stench of the place hit her like a physical blow, an acrid mixture of rotting mold, acid and old garbage. The first time they'd walked in, she'd thought she could never stand it, that awful smell, but soon, she discovered—just as Tom had promised—after a few minutes something happened to her olfactory nerve endings, they just rolled over on their backs or something, some patch of cortex in her brain got overloaded and cut out altogether and the smell was gone, or seemed to be, until the next time she walked outdoors and found out what good clean dust-filled Wichita air smelled like again. Now she saw Tom up on a walkway working on the pilot line he'd been setting up, and she hooted at him. "I'm back," she said.

"Great. You get that carboy of acetic?"

"I got half a dozen while I was there."

He stopped halfway down the stairs. "God, Sally. I can only use one."

"If you need one now, you're going to need five more later."

"Yeah. I suppose so." He sounded gray, depressed, very tired. "Well, I'll haul them in after a bit."

"How's it going up there?"

He motioned her to come up. The area he'd converted into a pilot line was completely enclosed in glass; she knew vaguely that the things inside included a precipitating pan, a centrifuge, vacuum drying oven, and an automatic belt. Up near the end, where Tom led her, she could see a brightly lighted vault with a large stainless-steel receiving pan. In the pan, just beginning to accumulate, was a steady sifting of a fluffy-looking pale green powder.

She stared as if suddenly confronted with something she had insisted she believed in for months but never really had until this very instant. She pointed toward the pan. "That's it?"

"That's it. No fanfare. Just some green powder."

She whirled, hugged him, nearly lifted him off his feet. "Tom, that's great. I can hardly believe it. I just can't believe it. . . ."

"I'm not so sure I can either," he said, gently disengaging her. "I just don't know."

She realized then how *very* gray and tired he looked. "You must be half dead," she said. "You've been at this for three straight weeks, and you haven't been sleeping worth a curse. But now it's *here*."

"I know." He turned away from the glass encasement. "Trouble is, I keep wondering, so what? Up to now, just getting it set up and getting a pilot line running has been *doing* something, without much time to think. But then this morning it hit me: this is ridiculous. What are we *doing* here?"

"We're making some stuff that will kill plague bugs."

He made a vague gesture. "I suppose. At least we think that's what this is—testing it is something else, that comes next. So it tests out, and we've got a few thousand milligrams. But so what? Have you read a paper lately, looked at the TV? You know what's happening in Chicago? Atlanta? All these other places? What are these few thousand milligrams going to do when the full wave hits St. Louis or Des Moines or Wichita? What's this little bit of fluff going to do? The answer is: not very much. We're really just fooling around."

"If we can make this much, we can make a lot more."

"Sure, but how much more? How fast? And then what can we do with it? This fire storm is moving too fast, out there—what kind of dent are we going to make in it? It's silly. It's worse than silly, it's a travesty. We're keeping ourselves busy spinning our wheels and that's about all."

Sally stared through the plate glass at the accumulating tray of powder. Then she turned to Tom. "You really don't get it, do you?" she said. "You just don't see the point at all. You get hit with the sheer enormity of the thing, all of a sudden, and you're just like everybody else: you stand there and wring your hands. You're stone blind, Tom. You don't see how great that little bit of stuff is, sifting down into that pan *right now.*"

"What's so great about a stick in the wind?"

"Well, let me ask *you* something. Is that stuff in that pan right now enough to keep you alive for one week when the plague gets here?"

"That's about it."

"So you call it a stick in the wind, but I say that's one person kept alive for one week. Okay, is there enough already there for me, too?"

"I suppose."

"Then that's two of us kept alive for one week. Maybe that doesn't matter a whole lot, but I say *that's two better than none.* If we make enough to protect two more, then that's *four* better than none. *Christ,* Tom, somebody's got to start somewhere, and I don't think too many people are starting anything anywhere. So what are you planning to do, just lie down and die? Quit and give up before we even get started? Sit down and fold your hands and wait for it to come eat us alive? Well, if that's *your* answer, I can't fight you, but let me tell you something. *I* never sat down and folded my hands in all my life, and I'm not starting now. The day *I* drop dead from this damned thing, I'm going to be *fighting.*"

She turned and started down the stairs, kicked a carton out of her way with a vicious swipe, stamped back to the living quarters they'd set up in the rear of the main factory and began smashing bottles.

Tom followed her down, alarmed, when the bottle-smashing suddenly stopped. She had an old suitcase out on the bed and was tossing blouses and pantyhose into it. "Sally, listen, for God's sake! I didn't mean I was planning to quit, or anything like that. I know how much you've given up coming this far—"

She whirled on him like a furious kewpie doll. "Listen, you dummy, I haven't given up one goddamned thing coming this far. It just dawned on me sometime back that you couldn't fight plague by writing newspaper stories, that's all. Anyway, I already tried that. I wrote that blast about Sealey and the drug-juggling, and look what it accomplished: not one damned thing. Oh, it took care of John Mancini and Hiram Lunch, all right—they got chopped down by machine-gun fire that day when a mob of angry people who read the story converged on the Sealey Plant in Indianapolis and burnt half of it to the ground. Sliced them right in half, I heard, so at least the story accomplished *that.* But for the long run, not much more. I thought that publicity blast would nail Sealey Labs to the door like a deer skin, just sink 'em in the sea. Well, it didn't, and the fire wasn't more than a fleabite to them. The Justice Department can't even decide whether to convene a grand jury or not, and don't worry, they're not going to decide. Nobody that I can see is going to do *anything* about Sealey Labs, they're too bloody busy trying to figure out what to do about Chicago. And meanwhile, Sealey Labs is busy producing a lousy drug in trickle quantities for whatever the traffic will bear, which is quite a hell of a lot, from the last quotes I've heard, and most of the people that go blind or shaky from taking it aren't going to complain because there's nobody to complain to and they're just happy to be alive, and Sealey has got *your* drug locked up in their vault, or so they think, they sure are not making it, and it just makes me blind with fury to sit around and watch this. So I'm *doing* something, *anything,* I don't care what, as long as it's something. And I thought you were doing something too."

"I am. I will. I promise." Tom looked at her, stricken. "Sal, stop packing that damned bag. I don't know what I'd do if you took off now."

"Took *off?* She followed his eyes to the suitcase and then suddenly her face melted and she was in his arms, hugging him to her fiercely, her face buried in his neck. "Oh, Tommy, you dummy, you dum-dum-*dummy,* can't I get a little pissed off at you when you're so stupid and blind and gray and won't think? I'm not *leaving.* I've got to take a little trip, that's all. I've got to get you back on the track and *working* first, but then I've got to get away and do *my* part of it—but I'm not taking off. I need you more than you need me. Times like these, *everybody* needs *somebody,* even somebody stupid and blind. Nobody just takes off. But dummy, you've got to get off this gloomy kick and get working, that's all. Quit worrying about sticks in the wind, just do what you can do as fast as you can, and I'll do what *I* can. You keep that fluffy green powder coming down into the pan, and tell me what you need, and I'll get it. Just start building that stockpile up—"

"But I need a million things," Tom said, "and I need them all *now*. I need help, just plain *hands,* if I'm going to turn that pilot line into production. I need help with the quality control. I need lab animals for testing, some really sophisticated lab equipment, a million other things. I need a hot lab with some live plague cultures and a microbiologist to work with them, somebody who really knows what he's doing with those bugs. You don't just make stuff like this in the kitchen and turn it loose on people."

"Well, maybe you *do,* right now," Sally said. "Maybe for now we've got to do things all the wrong way because we haven't time or facilities to do them right. But remember, that green powder had some testing at Fort Collins. Maybe we're going to have to count on that. And maybe I've got to go recruiting, get you some people—I've got some ideas." She told him about the spaniel-faced Indian with the shortgun. "You've got to grab what comes to hand and try to work with it," she said. "He may turn out to be a thief and nothing more, but maybe not—his heart wasn't in it, and he had kind eyes." She sat down on the bed. "Well, he might be a start. I haven't just been lying on my back wagging my tail all this time, I've been thinking about what we might do when the pilot line was finished and the stuff started coming down into the pan, and I've got some ideas. First we cover ourselves and anybody that's helping us—we don't need testing for that, and if we go, it all goes. Then we've got to find someplace, some small place, for a *real* test. We'll need help, we'll need cooperation, we'll be illegal as hell, we may have to fight our way through mobs, but if we can get this stuff moving, somehow, and stop the damned thing cold in one small place, *just one*—God, Tom, can't you see what that would mean?" She kissed him and gave him a shove. "Now go unload that van before somebody steals it. I've got to go see a couple of doctors in a little burg up north of here, and I'd just as soon get up there before it starts snowing. I'll just be gone a day or so. And meanwhile, for the help you're talking about, I think I know what our next step has got to be—and I think you're going to like it."

49

Harry Slencik was driving his old red pickup out the Grizzly Creek road, coming back from Bozeman with another ten cases of coffee for the hoard, when he saw the light flickering down on the creek in a brushy area just below Ben Chamberlain's place, It was almost seven in the evening, and daylight was failing rapidly.

Harry pulled his pickup over, snapped out his lights and peered through the brush. A campfire—he could see somebody moving. Too late for hunters, the season was over. There was an old logging road that went in to the creek a short way back, and he *thought* he'd seen fresh tire tracks. . . .

Harry pulled his shotgun off the gun rack and stepped down to the road. He loaded a shell into the chamber of the gun with a loud clack and pushed two more into the magazine. Then he walked back to the logging road. His flashlight picked up the tire tracks; a little farther on it glinted on the side of a small camper backed into the brush. Wyoming plates, and Harry made the connection. Someplace down there—was it Laramie?—had been hit real bad with plague, just about wiped out the town. This could be somebody that got out of there.

Up ahead a campfire was flaring, throwing mottled yellow light through the brush. For a moment he thought he heard a woman's voice. Then he stepped into the open along the creek, shotgun resting in the crook of his arm. He pushed his ten-gallon hat back on his head and cleared his throat.

A man was leaning over tending the fire. He leaped back and turned to face Harry. Behind him a woman sat on a rock clutching an old Pendleton shirt around her shoulders; she was shivering in the chill evening air. Beside her, two small children were wrapped in sleeping bags with just their noses sticking out. Harry saw no weapon, and relaxed his grip on the shotgun a little. "Nice evening," he said.

The man by the fire nodded. "Yeah." There was a long pause. "We were, ah, just fixing up a little supper. Ran out of bottled gas for the stove in the camper. You probably saw it sittin' there, back in the brush." He paused again. "Care to join us?"

"No, the wife'll have something ready when I get home, up the road a bit." Harry studied the people closely. The man was about thirty-five, Harry judged, short and stocky, solidly built, with a pointed nose and a shock of black hair over his eyes. The woman might have been pretty once; right now she looked utterly exhausted, dull-eyed and pallid. They both looked cold and hungry and tired, but otherwise healthy enough. "You just come up from Wyoming?" Harry said.

"Yeah. From Casper, before the trouble hit there."

"That's right, I heard about Casper. Laramie too. Both of them damned near wiped out."

"True, but Laramie got it first. Some people must have brought it up from Colorado. We got nervous a month or so ago, figured Casper was going to be next—just about any town could get hit—so we stuffed everything we could into the camper and got out of there."

"Just been roughin' it ever since, huh?" Harry said.

"You might say that." The man tossed more driftwood onto the fire.

"Well, better not plan to stick around here," Harry said. "Cook up your supper, sure, but when you finish that, you'd better move on."

"Wouldn't hurt to let us sleep a few hours, would it?"

"It don't think we'd like that. Makes the wife kind of nervous."

The man glanced at the woman behind him. "You own this land?" he asked Harry.

"Me and a few neighbors. We didn't like the looks of Bozeman too much, and we've got a pretty good chunk of land between us up here along the creek, so we kinda went together on it. We figure we can make out."

"It's a nice place."

"Right. No sick people around. Plan to keep it that way, too, so we can't welcome strangers."

"I see." The man gave a bitter laugh. "Especially strangers that just came up from Casper, where everybody dropped dead last week. Look, I already told you—we got out of there three weeks before it hit. We had no contact at all—"

"Well, better safe than sorry."

"I suppose you've got a point." The man pulled a grill out of a pack sitting nearby, carefully set it up over the fire, supported by rocks on either side. "By the way, I'm Dan Potter. This is my wife Ellen."

Harry nodded, but he didn't move forward to shake hands. "Harry Slencik," he said.

The man regarded him gravely. "Just out of curiosity, Mr. Slencik, how long do you people plan to stay out here? Just this fall? Going back to town for the winter? Or next spring?"

Harry shook his head. "We're not so damned sure there's going to be any town left to go back to," he said. "Nor any country left, either, for that matter. So this is where we are, and this is where we're stayin'."

"Sort of an independent Freehold kind of thing," Potter said.

"You could call it that."

"I guess there's a whole lot of them popping up, here and there. People get together, pool their land and resources, everybody contributes something important, like that. I suppose you plan to be, um, sort of self-sustaining."

"You got the idea," Harry said. "Completely self-sustaining."

"So you'll have gardens and grain and hayfields, run some stock, that sort of thing," Potter was watching Harry closely. "Lot of work to be done."

"Three or four of us got pretty good backs," Harry said. "We'll manage."

"I didn't mean just strong backs," Potter said. He chewed on his lower lip for a minute. "Pretty dry country around here. You're going to have to irrigate to grow anything."

"We know that. We've got the pumps and pipes all set up."

"Gasoline pumps, I suppose?"

"No way. Electric."

"So what do you do when the power goes off?"

Harry laughed. "We're way ahead of you, man. We've got two big gasoline generators, turn out enough power to light up this whole valley."

"Well, that's great, you're all set up." Potter dipped a pot into the creek, set it on the grill and began cutting up potatoes into it. "So what do you do when the gas runs out? Way things are going, one day the man ain't going to bring any more, sure as God made little apples."

Harry stirred uneasily. "So maybe we convert the generator to steam and burn wood," he said. "But that's a long time ahead. Hell, we can haul the water by hand then if we have to."

"For irrigation? Great system. They've been doing that in India for four thousand years. And look at India. And you've got to irrigate how many acres?"

"About sixty."

"Wow." Dan Potter pursed his lips, threw some beef bones into the pot and started stirring. Suddenly he turned to Harry. "Listen, Mr. Slencik, let me talk straight out for a minute. We're none of us sick, or anything, but I'm sure as hell in trouble. I need someplace to go. I've got a wife and two kids here and they're getting hungry and we're about to the end of our rope. We can't keep moving on much longer. But I know we can't just come and freeload someplace, either. If I want a place to stay, I've got to be able to earn my keep, right?"

"That figures."

"Okay, now let me tell you something. I can give you people something you need, if you can let us stick around."

Harry tipped his hat back. "You can give us four more mouths to feed, all right. Why do we need that?"

"Because you're going to be stone dead for irrigation water to feed anybody by next spring, and that's going to be the end of your little Freehold, unless you find a way around it."

"We could have some problems. We know that. So what can *you* do about it?"

"Maybe a whole lot. When we first drove in here today, I walked up the road to the dead end. I saw what you've got going here. I saw how much water you were going to need. I also took a rough guess at the drop in the creek through your land, and I knew right then I could solve your water problem for you."

Harry Slencik frowned. "Like how, exactly?"

"Falling water is energy," Potter said. He pointed to the creek. "See that pool out there? See that big rock at the edge with the water running over it and dropping into the next pool? Go stick your hand in the stream down below that rock. Go ahead, try it."

Harry walked over to the creek and reached down below the rock. The water struck his outstretched palm, spreading his fingers and splashing all over.

"Feel it push?" Potter said. "That water's heavy, and when it's running downhill naturally like that, you can use the weight. Listen to me: I can build you a ramjet pump on this creek that won't take any outside power whatever to run, just the energy of the falling water. No electricity, no gasoline—ever. It'll deliver enough to irrigate your sixty acres till your back teeth are floating, push water uphill if you want, put it exactly where you want it when you want it, and never cost a penny. I can engineer a whole system of pipes and valves and ditches for you, and then I can maintain it, so you've always got water—including all the household water you can use. And I can build it so it won't ever freeze up, too."

Harry stared at the man for a long while. "You never told me your line of work, Dan."

"Engineering," Dan Potter said. "Hydraulic engineering. I can't make dandelions grow, but I can sure build water systems, and when I build 'em, they *work.* You want references, you're out of luck, but I can *show* you what I can do quick enough."

"And you could build that kind of a system here?"

"No sweat."

"I suppose you'd need a lot of materials."

"A little plastic pipe. Some two-by-sixes. Couple of hardware-store valves. A good set of tools to work with. Beyond that, I could improvise a whole lot of it." Potter checked his dinner, decided it was ready to eat. His wife was getting out plates and cups. "Of course, you might just want to take your chances with those gas generators."

Harry set his hat squarely on his head and sat down on a rock. "Go ahead and eat," he said. "Maybe when you finish we can drive up to the place and talk a little bit."

50

For Frank Barrington the trip back from Laramie to Fort Collins was long, miserable and gray—as gray as the desolated place he had left behind him. The old Jeep was leaking oil badly, so he had to stop every sixty miles or so to fill up the crankcase, and as he drove south into Colorado he had hit a cold November drizzle that wouldn't stop. For having been away for just seven days, he was missing Monique achingly, not even a single phone contact in all that time, with the Laramie telephone system a hopeless tangle—one whole solid day wasted just trying to get a single call through to CDC in Atlanta, for God's sake—and through it all, the nagging fear that the devastation that had taken him to Laramie in the first place might have moved south to Fort Collins before he got back. The whole trip to Laramie had been Roger Salmon's idea, and a good enough idea, too—that he and a few already up there might somehow draw a line and break the onrushing wave. It hadn't worked, of course, the wave had moved too fast and far for any line to hold. A week of hard, horrid work and nothing to show. . . .

The drizzle turned to downpour as he finally hit the outskirts of Fort Collins. He drove straight to Barnaby's Grill, left the Jeep in ankle-deep mud in the parking lot out back, and leaned into the rain to get inside. It was almost nine P.M., but Monique wasn't there yet; he took the booth they especially liked in the rear corner, brushed the rain out of his hair and settled back to wait.

When she finally came in she looked absolutely awful—gray-faced, bone tired, her eyes dull. She leaned across the booth to kiss him and he caught the inevitable whiff of lab disinfectant that she couldn't ever seem to scrub off anymore. "God, it's good to see you," she said, collapsing in the booth across from him. "It seems like six months."

"I know." He frowned in alarm. There were lines of weariness around her eyes and mouth, all signs of the old familiar sparkle gone. "What's been happening?" he said. "You look like you've been whipped."

"You're not so far off." A shrug of one shoulder, just a tired hint of the old, wry smile. Drinks came and she put down half her Scotch and water neat. "This is getting to be the only good part of the day, anymore." She looked up then. "So how was Laramie?"

"Dead on its feet," Frank said. "I might just as well have stayed here. The ranchers all are boarded up on their ranches eating their cows, and the people in the town are dead or dying fast. The ones that can still move are packing out any way they can. Don't ask me where they're going. *They* sure don't know, and there's an awful lot of that country with nothing in it."

Monique shrugged. "At least you helped some, maybe."

"Precious little. There was nothing we could do. Not enough vaccine to cover the medical workers, much less anybody else, and the 3147 we were promised there never turned up. When I finally got through to Ted Bettendorf in Atlanta, he figured that hell was likely to freeze before *anything* got to Laramie, including any more manpower to help. Everything available is going to the big cities. Tough luck, Laramie."

"Oh, God." Monique shook her head. "Where's the man's head? Atlanta is doing everything just exactly backwards. They're going to lose the cities anyway, they already *know* that, there's not one thing on God's earth they can do for the cities—and they still keep dumping everything they've got into the cities. It's the Laramies and Fort Collinses and all the other little isolated places where they could really help if they only would—"

"It's not Ted's fault," Frank said. "He tries to be evenhanded, but the pressure is impossible. All he can do, in the end, is what the administration tells him to do, the best he knows how. The administration sets the policies, and the pressure all comes from the cities."

"Pressure from whom?" Monique's voice was bitter. "From dead people? And what administration policies? The administration doesn't have any policies. The administration is quietly disintegrating, that's what the administration is doing. Frank, CDC should be making its own policies and telling the administration to go chase itself—but it's not. Ted should have grabbed the rudder months ago, but he's just dithering." She sighed. "You don't know what a mess it is, out there. Listen, a month ago I needed emergency authorization to break some very secret codes we have sequestered in the vaults here at the lab—some top-secret biological warfare codes—to get some data I needed desperately to do some gene-splicing work on a new vaccine. Well, those codes are potentially very dangerous. You don't break them unless you have to have them, and they aren't supposed to be broken without specific written authorization from the Joint Chiefs of Staff countersigned by the President himself. So I wired my request and justification to Ted Bettendorf in Atlanta on a crash-emergency-must-do-now basis, and he got it onto the Telex to Washington within minutes with his must-approve authorization—and do you know what happened? It sat on some bureaucrat's desk for three solid weeks without so much as an acknowledgement despite three-times-a-day telephone calls for immediate action, and when Ted finally bludgeoned his way through to the President personally, all the President could do was moan and wring his hands about the terrible things that were happening in Pittsburgh, and demand that Ted do something to get some extra drug shipments out there. It seemed that some minor functionary in HHS hadn't assigned my request sufficient priority to get it anywhere near the Joint Chiefs, to say nothing of the President, so there it sat on the bottom of the pile on some desk in Washington."

"And you're still *waiting?*"

"Don't be ridiculous. I gave them four days, and when I didn't have an answer by then I broke the codes without authority and started work. I daresay they could put me in jail if they wanted to, but I don't think that they're going to put me in jail. They need the vaccine." She looked up as Barnaby brought the steaks and potatoes. "Not that breaking the code did me any good. The gene-splicing technique isn't working. These are weird bacteria. I'm getting a vaccine, but it's taking six weeks or more to build up a very low level of immunity."

"In other words . . ."

"Forget it. It was a good try, but it's not going to solve any problem whatsoever. We need a vaccine that works *fast,* and we haven't got one. Right now I'm just playing around, trying DNA recombinations in old strains of *Yersinia,* but I haven't even got the *antigens* identified." She fluttered her hands. "I don't really even know what I'm doing. Nothing is working, not even things I'm absolutely sure *have* to work according to all the experience I've ever had. I don't even know why I'm hanging around anymore. Maybe we should just get out of here. Go find a ranch somewhere with some good strong fences and some cows to eat."

Frank took a bite of his steak. "Funny you should mention that," he said thoughtfully. "I had a visitor yesterday. A man flew all the way from San Francisco out to Laramie, of all places, just to talk to me. He didn't say how he knew I was in Laramie, but he did. And he came to make me an offer I almost can't refuse."

Monique put her fork down. "A job offer?"

"Right."

"What man was this?"

"An old friend of mine, used to be in the Forest Service. Name of Shel Siegler. Deschutes National Forest, working out of Bend, Oregon, when I talked with him last summer—just after Pam went. Only he's not working for the Forest Service anymore, not by a long way. A very sharp fellow, Shel, the sort of guy who always ends up on top. Quite a joker, too, but yesterday he wasn't joking."

"Who is he working for now?"

Frank looked at her. "For Lord Chauncey Sparrow, once and future King of Mendocino County, California, and all points north, south and east that he thinks he can lay his hands on."

"Oh, Frank. Good Lord."

"Listen, kid, Shel had a very well-thought-out, legitimate proposal to make. They've got almost a thousand people up there, dug into the mountains and armed like Cuba. They've got four years' worth of food and water and ammo, and lots of plans for expansion, along with quite a few delusions of grandeur. They want an epidemiologist who knows the wilderness, knows how to move around in the bush, travel cross-country, high country, any kind of country. They want somebody with plague experience—somebody who knows what to look out for, to spot trouble *coming* and warn them so they can stop it before it gets to them. Shel thinks I'm the man for the job. He wants me to come out there and look the scene over, see what I think of it."

Monique's eyes were huge with horror. "Frank, those people are crazy. I mean *crazy.*"

"Of course they are."

"When they get hit with it—and they will surely get hit—they'll go down just like Laramie did."

"Of course they will." Frank took another bite of steak.

"So what are you *talking* about? Honey, if you're ass enough to go out there and 'look the scene over,' as you put it, you'll never come back. They won't let you."

"Of course they won't," Frank said. "Matter of fact, in order to present me with a convincing argument to induce me to take the job, Shel was forced to tell me a whole lot of things that would make it politically inconvenient—to them—for me to refuse their offer. If I do, it will unfortunately become necessary for them to shut me up. Just quietly shoot me. Some sort of bizarre accident. To get down to specifics, I now have about twenty-four hours left in which to say yes."

"Frank, you *can't* go out there and leave me here—"

"No chance of that, kid." Frank gave a harsh laugh. "I couldn't do that even if I'd consider it, which I wouldn't. Fact is, you are very much a part of their bargain. These people are *organized.* They want a vaccine, and they want an effective antibiotic. They've checked you out from top to bottom, honey. You've been on their grab list for quite some time. They'll provide you with a fully equipped lab, better than the one you've got right here, dug down deep into a mountainside and secure as a tomb. You just give them your list of specifications, and then all you have to do is go to work and make them an effective vaccine and a magic-bullet antibiotic, real fast. They feel certain that with the proper incentives, you'll find a way to come through."

"They're insane."

"Of course they are—but there's a wild sort of rationale behind it all. Right now, Lord Chauncey merely wants his group to survive the plague. Then later on he plans to end up controlling all of California,

Oregon, Washington, British Columbia, Idaho, Montana, Nevada and Arizona. The entire Fraser, Columbia, Snake and Colorado river drainages, to be specific. The Mormons can have Utah as long as they pay him rent. But first he's got to survive. To survive, he's decided he needs both of us, badly. He has some, uh, commensurate rewards in mind for us, also."

"You mean like not shooting you, right yet."

"That's one."

Monique pushed her unfinished steak aside and sat in gloomy silence for a while. "So what are you going to tell them, Frank?"

"What *can* I tell them? I just don't know. I mean, I really don't. But I tell them nothing, without you. That comes first."

"You think this is survival?"

"Of course not. Maybe in the short run, but not for very long. I mean, suppose these thousand-odd people *do* survive in the short run. Suppose they fight off all challengers—and there are a dozen other Lord Chaunceys running around loose in those hills, all of them armed just as well as he is. But suppose he wins. He ends up with total control of a third of a continent of dead land with a few thousand demented survivors wandering around. So what does he have? He can't govern; he can't protect all that space; he can't provide necessary services for anybody. All he can do is seize and exploit. Very, very soon he personally would be shot and gutted out like a hog and his head put on a stake, and somebody else would take over for a few weeks, and then somebody else, and so on into the next century. You call this survival? I'm not so sure. But then, what else do you see coming down the pike, besides the Horseman?"

"Suppose I told you there was something else," Monique said slowly. "An alternative."

"Like what?"

"Buy me another drink, and get yourself one too. Happens that I had a call from an old friend today, too, and she made us an offer we almost can't refuse."

"What old friend?"

"Sally Grinstone. That odd little person from the Philadelphia *Inquirer* who came out here and picked our brains one night about Sealey 3147 and why it looked so good in the lab and then turned out a little different in the field. Remember her?"

"Yeah. The kewpie doll with the ponytail. Funny kid, really."

"Well, there's been no dust gathering on Sally Grinstone since the night she was here. She took what she learned from us, and then went and did her homework, including some intensive dirt-digging, and found out just why Sealey 3147 worked so well in the lab and then turned out so bad in the field."

Frank nodded. "I remember some articles. A big newspaper series on it. Sealey switched drugs on us because they couldn't make any money on the good one."

"That was Sally."

"Then I heard that some Select Congressional Committee was going to investigate Sealey for fraud or something—and that was the last I heard. They're probably still at it."

"No, they haven't even got a committee together yet. And meanwhile, Sealey is sending this carefully controlled dribble of S-3147 out into the market at highwaymen's prices, and a lot of people who take it are going blind and Parkinsonian, but the FDA figures that may be better than being dead, so under the circumstances they're looking the other way. All perfectly legal, special investigative drug permits and all that to protect Sealey, of course." Monique sipped her drink. "Well, what you didn't read in the paper was that before that story broke, the little chemist at Sealey Labs who was busy developing the *good* drug that we tested disappeared under mysterious circumstances from a Chemical Society conclave in St. Louis, which is something scientists don't generally do—just gone like the month of May. Sally Grinstone also dropped out of sight about the same time; her muckraking articles won some kind of prize, and all of a sudden the *Inquirer* couldn't find her to make the award. And that is *very* strange, for a crack investigative journalist from a top national newspaper to just disappear—"

"You talking about foul play?" Frank said.

Monique gave a brittle laugh. "There would have been, all right, if Sealey had had their way, but they didn't move in on the little chemist quite fast enough, and they didn't count on the very extraordinary persuasive powers of Sally Grinstone—or else they couldn't believe that anybody would have the almighty nerve to snatch that chemist right out from under their noses. There wasn't any foul play. Sally Grinstone *told* me all of this, in person, over the telephone last night. She talked for nearly three hours, and Sally is alive and well, believe me. So is the little chemist, Tom Shipman. Alive and raring to go."

"Raring to go *where?* What are these people *doing?*"

"Trying like hell to stay under cover, for one thing, until they have some kind of reliable protection—if they ever achieve that. But what they're *doing* is setting up shop in an old chemical plant on the wrong side of Wichita and starting to make the antibiotic we tested here in the lab before Canon City. They're already making it by the pound, Frank. They think they can make it by the ton. Sally says you can make a utility grade of the stuff in your bathtub if you have some ordinary tetracycline and some acetic acid and a couple-three other reagents. It's a simple radical substitution and then a precipitation process. Dry it, stuff it in capsules, mix it with simple syrup, stir the powder in coffee if you want to, it doesn't matter. She's talking about mass production and mass distribution and to hell with the FDA; the FDA people are barely hanging onto their desks as it is."

Frank whistled and pushed his dinner plate away. "These people are crazy, too," he said.

"Yes. But not quite as crazy as your King of California."

"There's no way they can get anywhere at all, honey."

"In ordinary times, of course not, but these are not ordinary times. These are times when you start doing anything you can do, however crazy, if you've got wit enough, and don't worry about what happens next because there isn't liable to be any next." Monique's voice was thin and strained, close to tears.

Frank reached across the table, took one of her thin hands in both of his big paws. "Okay, let's back up a minute. Whatever they're doing, and whatever the odds, I guess that's *their* business. But why was Sally calling *you?*"

"They want us in Wichita. Both of us. Shipman has six other models of the drug he thinks might be more effective than what he's making, but he's just a chemist. He needs a microbiologist, a very capable microbiologist who is also an expert at working with *Yersinia.* That's me. He also needs a really top-notch genetic engineer to find a way to get the wrong radical into this bug so he can model the antibiotic to the bug, and maybe make a really effective vaccine as a spinoff. He thinks maybe I can recruit somebody like that, if I can't do it myself. That's the scientific and manufacturing side. Then there's the supply and distribution side. From what Sally remembers of you, she's got the idea that you might just be big enough and tough enough and maybe smart enough to move in on that end of it. They want to get a shipment to some little town up in Nebraska as fast as they can—don't ask me why—and they've got a drop for the stuff lined up undercover with a couple of doctors and some public-health man up there. If that works, whatever it is they're setting up, then they plan to spread out. They need unmarked trucks or cars, drivers, somebody with savvy to set them up, route them, troubleshoot them—"

"You mean somebody to ramrod the operation and ride shotgun, both."

"Well, she thinks if you knew which end of the rifle to put the shell in, it might be a very definite plus."

"Wow." Frank sat staring at Monique. "If I'm getting the picture anywhere near right—oh, boy. Look, if that little chemist of hers is actually cranking out a good, solid antibiotic that *works* from some little rump laboratory and they're planning to go outside the law to distribute it—my God. Half the people left in the country are going to want to get their hands on it—and I'm supposed to ride shotgun? I wouldn't last six weeks. Hell, kid, I might not even last six *days*."

"They've got to have somebody, and have him fast."

"Oh, yes. They surely do. Wow. Talk about suicide." Frank finished his drink at a gulp and pushed himself up from the booth. "Come on, kid, it's getting late. We'd better get home. I've got to do some thinking before I tackle this one."

The rain had stopped and a few stars shimmered in the cold night air. Frank turned the Jeep out into the thin traffic. They drove in silence. "You'd be a lot safer right where you are here in Collins," he said finally.

"Nothing's going to happen here at Collins," Monique said. "I feel it in my bones. The government's falling apart and so is the CDC. All I'm doing here is frittering away precious time."

"Then we'd both be far safer with the King of California. What this Grinstone babe is talking about is sudden death. With Lord Chauncey we might at least survive for a while."

"Maybe. But Frank, Sally Grinstone is trying to *do* something about this mess. Something that could *help*."

"I just don't know." He turned up the canyon road toward the little three-room house they were using now, parked on the hill half a block away for a downhill start to spare his tired battery. He put his arm around her thin waist as they walked together up toward the house, felt her shiver. "Why don't we just sleep on it, for now? We've got till tomorrow to decide."

He let them into the overheated living room—it was either bake or freeze in there with the wood stove going, nothing in between. He took Monique's coat, slipped off his own jacket, and started into the bedroom with her behind him.

One step inside the room, he realized too late that there shouldn't have been a light on. The window was open, the casing forced. A small wiry man was crouching across the room, the bed between them, with a very small black pistol pointed straight at Frank's chest.

Frank tried to stop Monique but he was too late, she was already in the bedroom beside him, hand to mouth, stifling a cry.

"Hold it right there," the man said. "One move, I kill." Cold little ferret eyes, a prow of a nose, thin lips pulled back from crooked yellow teeth. *Like a river rat.* "The little lady first. The earrings, over here on the bed."

She took them off, tossed them to the far end of the bed as Frank stirred. "Don't move, Frank," she said quietly. "Give him whatever he wants."

"Now the rings. Both your watches. Same place."

Frank tugged off the black onyx in cheap gold that he wore, tossed it over, along with his Omega. Monique followed suit.

"Now the little lady's jewelry. Where is it?"

"Top right dresser drawer," she said, "right there by your hand. "No, Frank, *please.* It doesn't matter."

The man pawed open the jewel box, scattered the contents with a finger. He spat on the floor. "Junk. Where's the good stuff?"

"Tear the place apart," Frank said. "You won't find any. That's it." He watched the gun, dead steady in the man's hand.

"Nothing in here?" The man pulled a black case from Frank's side of the drawer, flipped it open, tossed cheap cufflinks and tietacks onto the dresser top. "Junk, all junk. Ah, hold it a minute. Well, well. What have we here?"

He picked up the small white pasteboard jeweler's box, pried the lid off with his thumb, set it on the dresser. Lifted a thin silvery necklace chain, held it up, saw the tiny star sapphire at the end. "Now that's more like it. That's nice."

Frank leaped across the bed like a cat, driving head and shoulder into the man's belly, crushing him into the dresser front. The gun fired twice, muffled sounds. Frank grappled, grabbed the gun arm with both hands, slapped the hand against the dresser and saw the gun go flying. Small thin armbones snapped; the man let out a cry. Frank wrenched the other arm up behind the man's back, pressed his body very close, then brought his right paw up under the shoulder and around under the chin in a deadly reverse half nelson. Began pressing the chin back. . . .

"Frank, stop!" Monique had the gun in hand, aiming at nothing. "It won't do any good. Let him go."

Frank eased his grip, drove his left fist hard into the man's belly. Then he brought his hand down to his shirtfront and ripped off the greasy clothes, kept ripping until the man was naked except for shreds of undershorts. "You come back again, I kill," Frank told him hoarsely. Then he shoved him bodily out the window. There was a groan, a scrambling sound and then silence. Frank stood straight and turned around. His left shoulder was aching, with warm wetness soaking through his shirt.

"Frank, you've been shot!"

"So I have." He ripped his shirt from his shoulder, moved the arm. "Got the deltoid and some skin, that's all, no bone. The other one went through the ceiling. Just nicked my ear. The bastard." He reached down, picked up the necklace with the little sapphire. "Blood on it again." He looked at Monique. "Sorry, kid, but I just couldn't let him have this."

He sat down on the bed, shaking now, sat patiently while Monique scrubbed the superficial shoulder wound, applied a pressure dressing, fussed and fiddled getting his huge arm into a sling. "Come on, Florence, for god's sake. I'm going to make it."

"You're sure the bullet's out?"

"No, but we'll go find out. And call the cops, I suppose. Not that there's much point to it."

"Let's go right now, then."

"Not until you make your other call," Frank said. He tossed the sapphire necklace in his hand and then dropped it into his shirt pocket. "Call your friend Sally Grinstone and tell her she's got a couple of recruits."

51

In Brookdale, Connecticut, Carmen Dillman watched her husband eating his breakfast across from her in the breakfast nook, slowly and methodically, munch, munch, sip, munch, munch, sip, his eyes turned to the window, staring out at the bleak, dead winter backyard of their comfortable home. Once there had been a respectable garden out there, climbing roses along the side fence, cut back and mulched with straw by this time of year, the mums also covered, only the neatly planted evergreens showing color—a respectable garden. Now mostly weeds and junk scattered around after just one summer's neglect. Not much time last summer for gardening, nor much reason. Too many other unpleasant things going on, not much entertaining, hardly opened the barbecue. And not much likely to be done with it next spring, either, she thought, as far as she was concerned.

Munch, munch, sip, taking far more time on breakfast than he ought to on a Tuesday morning, damn him. Same old breakfast every morning, two sausage patties, two eggs soft-boiled on a split English muffin, grapefruit juice, coffee. Every damned morning of his life. Let her make hot cakes once a month and he'd bitch about it all morning and then make two sausage patties, two boiled eggs on a split English muffin, et cetera for lunch. Carmen looked more sharply at him. Definitely getting a little more gray now, Jack Dillman was, definitely getting more paunchy, the faint yellow galley pallor of a Connecticut sunless winter spreading out under that last Florida tan, giving his face a vaguely jaundiced look. Heavy night's stubble still on his jowls, like a smudge of fireplace ash. Not that she was such a great sight herself. She was wearing paint-smeared jeans and blue workshirt, black hair pulled back in a bun, her least fetching of all possible hairdos. Without morning makeup she looked every bit of age forty-one going on thirty-nine; the little wrinkles on her lower cheeks and neck that would soon be screaming for face-lift, skin wrinkling a bit on the hands, too, little crows' feet at the eyes, the once-teasing sparkle and flash in those dark brown eyes now turned to a wary coldness. *The King and Queen at breakfast,* she reflected. Only thing missing was the morning *Times,* always used to be the morning *Times* at breakfast, too, but nowadays it only turned up on the porch one or two days a week and the man's telephone never answered when you called to complain.

Jack poured himself more coffee, stared out the window as if he had all day to drink it. Not a word yet this morning except a grunt when she nearly tripped over him in the kitchen earlier. Well, it had been a nasty fight last night, an awful fight, the worst they'd had for months. Their fights had taken an ugly turn lately. Somehow she couldn't quite sense when to quit anymore, when to stop goading him, a skill she'd had down to a fine art years ago, except now all of a sudden her timing seemed to be off or something. She wasn't reading the signals right anymore, and Jack—of all people—was beginning to slug back, like last night, leaving her feeling depressed and gray and half sleepless all night instead of exhilarated. And oddly enough, there was no mention from him about just bagging it, this time. Strange. Didn't hardly seem fair to start changing the rules at this point, but somehow, she'd been sensing recently, a lot of things were changing. And now the inevitable long, silent breakfast. If he didn't get moving pretty soon, he'd miss the only train that made sense for him to take anymore. . . .

Jack finally finished his coffee, stood up with a last look out the window, refilled his cup from the pot on the table and started for the stairs. "I'll be up in the study," he said.

She looked up sharply. "Aren't you going down to the city today?"

"Nope."

"But you always go to the city on Tuesdays."

"Not anymore, I don't. Not after last week."

"Didn't you finish that Upjohn layout last night?"

"Yep. It worked out just fine."

"So how are they going to use it here in Brookdale, Connecticut?"

Jack shrugged. "Let the mailman do the walking. Let them send a courier up for it if they want to. They don't need it today anyway. And if they have any questions when they do get it, the telephone's still working. Part of the time."

Carmen frowned. "Jack, is that smart? They aren't going to like it, getting a layout in the mail. And you know you need a day a week in the city, anyway." She spread her hands, sensing that her voice was a little too strident. "I mean, the contacts you make, your lunches with Ed or Barry or Jocelyn—"

Jack turned and stared at her. "You got some kind of plans that I'm queering somehow?"

"Well, of course not. I mean, nothing special. I was going out later, down to have coffee with Edna maybe, do a little shopping. . . ." Her voice trailed off.

"Well, don't change your plans on my account. I'll be up in the study all day, starting the sketches for the new Northwest Rockwell campaign, just working up some ideas. Business ideas." He paused. "Fact is, I'm not going down to New York anymore, period, whether I need to or not. You catch the news last night? This whole last week or two? The place is a sewer. It's falling to pieces. Nothing works anymore, not even the elevators. Do you have any idea how many people are sick in just Manhattan alone right now? Well, neither do I, and nobody's saying, but a whole lot of people aren't turning up for work. And as for deliberately, voluntarily going down there when I don't have to—well, no more of that, thank you. Not after last week."

"What happened last week?"

"You've forgotten already? I told you all about it."

"You didn't tell me a thing. You were just very late getting home that night, was all I knew."

"Well, maybe I *didn't* tell you. I was just very lucky to get down there at all, and even luckier to get back home again. I nearly got killed down there."

"Killed! Jack, what on earth *happened?*"

He spread his hands. "It's not just a nice, quiet train ride anymore, baby. Last week there was a truck turned over on the tracks just above Van Cortlandt Park, and when the train stopped we had a little boarding party of thugs. Then the cops came and there was a big shoot-out right there on the train. They finally got us all out of the train, at least, and onto the street—in the middle of the Bronx. I grabbed a cab with four other people, and we had a couple more impromptu hijacking attempts on the way down. The man next to me got shot right through the window, this guy on the street just stuck his arm in and blasted away. So then we had to make a hospital stop for the poor guy, and if you think *that* wasn't a mess, one man merely shot in the neck and bleeding all over—they nearly laughed us into the East River. There was a line of sick people four deep and six blocks long outside that hospital emergency room, and you think *they* liked us driving up and trying to shove this guy in first—we left him on the sidewalk and got out of there. We had to, by then they were trying to turn the taxi over."

Jack took a deep breath. "So I finally got downtown by one-thirty, too late for lunch with Jocelyn, but that didn't matter because Jocelyn hadn't been to the office all week anyway. Neither had half of her graphic-arts department, so I might as well have mailed the stuff in the first place. The only one there to go over the layout with me was Mooney, so Christ only knows what's going to go back to the client. By three-thirty I figured I'd better get a train out of town if I was going to, but there was some kind of riot going on in Grand Central, something about trainmen striking in sympathy with the sanitation workers. I just went down to the platform and sat in the train for three hours—it seemed safer than standing around up in the station—and I figured the train was going to go somewhere sooner or later, or else it wasn't and I wasn't going anywhere anyway. So it finally took off and made it to Stamford before something broke down, and we got to sit there for another hour before the man came by and told us it was going to be buses or cabs. I stood up on a bus all the way to New Haven and then took a cab from there. I think it was the only cab still operating there, and I had a regular fistfight to get into it, I mean I had to slug my way through a crowd. So I got back here about eleven-thirty and you were already in bed so I figured why disturb you." He looked at her oddly. "I'm sure I told you all this. You just weren't listening. Anyway, I decided that was my last trip to New York for a while. Just a little bit more than I want to put up with."

He turned and went on up the stairs to the big north-facing sky-lighted studio, sipping coffee as he went. He sat down in the soft swivel chair in front of the huge drafting board, brought the Luxor lamp around behind his shoulder and switched it on. A big, comfortable room, bright without glare, the place where he had been doing his work for —Lord, how many years now? He couldn't even remember. Everything about the room reflected Jack Dillman's personality: neat, quiet, meticulous to the point of obsession. The drafting board itself, built for comfort and ease; the soldierly rows of paint jars and brushes, oils and solvents, pencils fresh-sharpened, inking pens, nibs cleaned and set in the graduated holders. A wall full of references and catalogues on orderly shelves to the left, within easy reach. The big north window looking out onto the cul-de-sac occupied by two or three other prosperous, expansive exurban homes much like this one. Green lawns, broad driveways leading to double garages.

It was a pleasant, quiet, secluded place to live and work, and he'd done very well indeed by the standards of his friends and neighbors in Brookdale, Connecticut. A topflight commercial artist, heavily in demand, his fees escalating far beyond reach of inflation every year. He could have done twice as well, probably, if he'd stayed with Milk and Sanders and worked his way up the ladder in a major ad agency like that. But that would have meant living in the city, and spending half his work time cutting throats, and he prized the freelance scene far more than money could spell out, and he'd done just fine with it, really. *Not much sweat to stay on top, considering the crop of wobbly-kneed young punks coming up in the field,* he thought. *Expecting it all to fall in their laps, mistaking their marijuana highs for creative inspiration, unaware of what "have it by yesterday" means to a harried ad exec, just unable to hack the pressure, unable to produce the steady, solid, reliable work, always right on target, always there and more than just presentable and always on time when the name of the game is "do it fast and do it right"*—that was where Jack had always had them whipped. Who, for God's sake, wanted to mess around with some kid who was liable to try to paint a four-page layout with his toes, when they already *knew* what Jack Dillman would do without any wet-nursing and turn it in yesterday too. Of course, he was getting a little paunchy now, drinking too much every night, smoking too much all the time, never getting any exercise. Short of breath at funny times, a little aching chest pain now and then when he had to sprint for a train—but then, there wasn't going to be any train anymore now, at least not for a while. That last trip had scared him shitless, and life was too short—

He looked up, suddenly, and saw Carmen standing at the studio door, watching him strangely—Christ, had he been muttering to himself? "Just getting down to work," he said.

"You really *didn't* tell me, Jack," Carmen said.

"You mean about the trip last week? Oh, well. I thought I did."

"You didn't say a word about it. I wish you had." She hesitated, as though debating taking that one forbidden step across the threshold into the studio. "I hear a lot of people are getting sick in Bridgeport and Westport now. Big TV interview the other morning with the Fairfield County Public Health Department, a big appeal for cooperation and staying calm. It was scary."

"It's scary, all right. And it's going to come. The Public Health people aren't going to stop it."

"Jack—what are we going to do when it gets *here?*"

He shrugged. "What else? Just sweat it out, I suppose, Just plant our feet in the ground right here and sweat it out."

"Seems like—" She broke off and shook her head. "Well, I'm not going to worry. I'm going to change my clothes and go shopping."

"Sure thing," Jack said. As she started back down the stairs, Jack got up and closed the door firmly, went back to his chair, brought out a big sketch pad. He sat staring out the window for a long while, soft-lead pencil in hand. Then he began sketching rapidly.

52

At CDC in Atlanta, Mandy was just putting down the telephone when Dr. Ted Bettendorf headed out of his office for a five-minute sandwich in the commissary. "Now *that's* interesting," she said, giving him an odd look. "I think that's a call you'd better return yourself."

Ted stopped in midstride; Mandy never bothered him with trifles these days. "How so?"

"Damnedest thing I ever heard. That was a Perry Haglund. He's one of our Shoeleather Boys in Lincoln, Nebraska. That is, he *was* one of our EIS people in Lincoln until Lincoln got hit and he packed up and went back home to Willow Grove, Nebraska, allegedly to help out there if the plague came, but more likely to get out of Lincoln."

Ted motioned her to follow him. "Come talk while I eat. Why should I call somebody in Willow Grove, Nebraska, when I've got exactly four minutes to eat in before I have to come back here and spend an hour of delight with a team from Sealey Labs? Wait a minute—*Haglund*. Rings a bell. Used to be in Lincoln, you say? You're right. A good guy, had some public-health background. And he was one of the crew that helped Carlos in Canon City."

Mandy nodded. "You've got him. I don't know how good a guy he is; after Haglund ran for home we lost seven CDC people in Lincoln in one fast week waiting for your Mr. Mancini to produce, but maybe his conscience is bothering him now or something—"

"So what did he want?" Ted pushed open the commissary door, stood aside for Mandy.

"He just wanted us to know that a couple of weird con artists are trying to set up some kind of phony drug sale in Willow Grove, Nebraska, and he's been rung in on it, and he wants to know what he should do."

"Phony drug sale?"

"Some kind of homemade antibiotic."

"In Willow Grove, Nebraska?"

"Right."

Ted wolfed down half a sandwich. "I would laugh, except I don't think you think I should laugh." He looked at her. "Look, I'm trying to goose Sealey Labs into to springing enough 3147 to help get the city of Pittsburgh off the ropes, and you want me to worry about somebody peddling snake oil somewhere in Nebraska. Why?"

Mandy shrugged. "According to this Haglund guy, these people are operating very strangely. So far, Willow Grove has had no plague, but they don't think it's going to be long before they have it. Willow Grove is a county seat, about twenty thousand people, but there are a whole bunch of little nearby towns where everybody's kind of holed up, following Haglund's advice about no public meetings, no church services, everybody stay home and eat out of the freezer and so on. So this woman turned up from somewhere down in Kansas and went straight to the local doctors, there are two of them, pretty sharp guys, and she also went to Haglund as the nearest semblance of a public-health officer around, and she set them up that she has a way to keep Willow Grove and all those other little towns free of plague."

"By magic or by willpower?" Ted said.

"She says her partner is whomping up some new antibiotic that's supposed to stop the plague in its tracks. They want to supply Willow Grove with all they can use—before the plague gets there."

"I see," Ted said. "And what's the asking price on this new antibiotic?"

"They don't want to sell it. They just want to trade it for all the plain tetracycline these doctors and the local pharmacies can lay their hands on."

Ted scowled. "Well, that's a new wrinkle. But it's still just a con, Mandy. Or else they're a couple of nuts."

"Maybe so. They're sure claiming the world for the new drug—and nobody has any except them."

"I see. And they want to run a nice little clinical test on Willow Grove, Nebraska—is that it?"

Mandy leaned toward him. "Ted, that's *exactly* it. Haglund called because that was *exactly what they told the doctors.* But they also told them that it had *already been tested.* In our own CDC facility at Fort Collins. They say it's the drug that Sealey buried and ran 3147 in as a ringer. The exact same drug. And these people say they can make it in quantity."

"And kill everybody in Willow Grove, Nebraska. God! Remember that guy peddling the fake vaccine to half the people of Joplin, Missouri? You know what happened to all *those* people—" Bettendorf stood up very suddenly. "Look, maybe I'd better do something. Let's get back to a phone. I can damned well check with Fort Collins and find out why nobody around there denied that newspaper exposé about a phony drug switch after the first tests—Monique Jenrette did the testing, she should know, and she's still out there."

Back at the office, he turned to the girl. "Where's this Haglund's number? Okay, fine, let's hope a couple of trunks are open all the way. It should be eleven in Colorado. You get me Fort Collins and get Monique on the line for me first. Just Monique, nobody else. Then you go downstairs and stall Sealey Labs. I'll come rescue you as soon as I can."

Back in his inner sanctum, Ted tried to clear his head, bring back in focus that newspaper story that had raised such a fuss. Sealey and Mancini had denied it fiercely, but Fort Collins had never denied it, and then he had simply lost track of following it up. He was not a superstitious man and he seldom paid attention to hunches, but something crawling up his spine was telling him very loudly that there was something more to this odd story than a couple of snake-oil peddlers trying to make a fast buck out in the ding-weeds. If some kind of kitchen-stove outfit was busy making some kind of rump drug that might wipe out twenty thousand people, and were dragging Fort Collins CDC into it as their backup—well, CDC's rep was not faring too well anywhere at all these days, and a bad grassroots scandal could be a terrible albatross—

The phone buzzed. Ted grabbed it. "Monique? Ted Bettendorf in Atlanta—"

He heard Mandy's voice. "Sorry, Ted, you're not going to get Monique. She's not there anymore."

"Not *there!*"

"She hasn't turned up for a week, they say, and they went out to her place and she's nowhere around. It looks like she and her boyfriend have just quietly packed up and gone west. Or some other direction."

"Okay, go on downstairs and hold the fort. I'll be along in a minute." He dropped the phone on the hook and sank into his desk chair, shaking his head. Monique just bagging it at a time like this? *Monique?* He couldn't believe it. Monique was too solid—and the boyfriend she was with was solid too—or at least Carlos had once thought so. For a moment he had a shaky feeling, as though stable underpinnings were shifting subtly, as though stability were an illusion and *nothing* was holding still—but it passed in a wave. Tired, he was getting tired, too tired. He took out the telephone memo Mandy had handed him, then reached for his private line and slowly began dialing Perry Haglund's number.

53

It was almost pitch dark on Grizzly Creek when Ben Chamberlain got back to his house and found a note pinned to his back door, written in Amy Slencik's spidery hand: BEN—DROP OVER AFTER DINNER. WE'VE GOT TO TALK.

The old doctor tucked the note in his pocket and let himself in with a sigh. He saw that there was a huge new camper parked out behind his barn this evening, a great big thing covered with mud. Also two big motorbikes that hadn't been there that morning. Amy must have brought them down here to park during the day, and then stopped by to leave him the note.

He looked at it again, then crumpled it up and tossed it in the fireplace. *So this is going to be it,* he thought gloomily. *Well, better now and get it over with than sometime later in the dead of winter.* He'd known it was coming all along; he'd felt it in the air around Amy, getting thicker every day as the wind got colder and the daylight shorter. Hell, it was really his own damned fault, he should have brought it right out front and center long ago, but she'd never really said anything specific yet and he was getting too old to go hunting up confrontations.

Methodically he stuffed his wood stove full of cottonwood and opened the draft, then just as methodically started laying a new fire in the fireplace. Going to be cold tonight, colder than last night. He'd been outside working all day, finally getting all his perennials and the smaller trees mulched and piled high with straw, and none too soon, either. There'd be snow flying pretty soon now, and then the bitter arctic cold. Across the creek, all afternoon, he'd put the finishing touches on the big half-acre garden plot he'd plowed up in what used to be his private deer-and-elk pasture, tilling in the goat manure for the last time and then mulching the whole thing with leaf mold he'd collected all summer. *Old Ben's secret garden,* he'd thought wryly. Hadn't mentioned it much to anybody, but next summer it would grow potatoes and carrots and peas and tomatoes galore—if he was still around after the cold died out of the ground.

Couldn't knock the approaching winter, though. It ought to help protect them, these next few dangerous months. Traditionally, throughout the centuries, cold weather had always slowed the plague, from everything he'd ever read; now he wondered vaguely why. Rats holing up and not coming out so much? Fleas not so active? Trouble was, from all the reports he'd been hearing, it wasn't working that way this time. So much of it was pneumonic, a staggering eighty percent of it, from one CDC report he'd read, so much direct human-to-human infection, and you couldn't keep human beings from huddling together in the cold with fuel deliveries canceled, power stations failing. Here on the creek they could hope the cold might help them *here* in this little Freehold of theirs, if they played their cards right—but his notion of playing the cards was different from Amy's, and now finally the crunch was coming. . . .

The old man cooked up some dinner, frying some fresh sausage and boiling some fettucini, homemade stuff he'd hand ground out of cracked wheat and bran and mixed up with one of his duck eggs. It turned out to be pretty pasty, thick and coarse, kind of falling apart instead of hanging together like the old semolina stuff used to do. *But edible, at least, and it certainly does fill you up. Probably good for my bowel, too.* He chuckled at himself as he sat down to eat. Even now he knew perfectly well, deep down, that all this back-to-nature do-it-yourself effort was pure sophistry as far as he was concerned, nothing but an intellectual challenge that he played around with the way you'd play around with a hobby. Sure, now he knew that he could make his own cracked-wheat fettucini—and eat it—but he also knew that he didn't really believe in it.

And that, of course, was his problem around here right from the start. He didn't really believe in the Freehold, either. Never had. And the thought came, unbidden: *If only Emmie were still here.* Then at least he wouldn't have to go it alone.

Later, when he made his way over to the Slenciks' cabin, he found the place oppressively warm, with a huge tamarack fire crackling in the fireplace and that goddamned wood cookstove of Amy's throwing heat like a blast furnace. Mel Tapper was there, looking gloomy, and Kelley, the rancher, and Dan Potter, which surprised Ben a little; the little hydraulic engineer was pretty new here to be sitting in the Inner Council. Harry Slencik poured Ben a good slug of McNaughton's and gave him a big friendly grin. "You look like you need something to warm you up," he said."

"Kinda chilly out there," Ben acknowleged.

"Yes, and it's going to get a whole lot chillier," Amy said, looking up through those big gray-tinted glasses.

So here we go. Ben took the whiskey neat. "So what's the problem?"

He knew that tact was not her long suit, but never before had she been so totally blunt. "The problem is this immigration wave we're having around here," Amy said. "The time has come that it's got to stop before we're up to the neck in stray people."

Ben grimaced. "There's not really that many. We've been through all this before. Another couple turn up today?"

"They sure did. In a Road Schooner half a block long. You know where they blew in from? *North Dakota,* that's where."

Ben shrugged. "Good a place to come from as any, I guess."

Amy looked up. "Yeah, well, these folks got four kids and Grandma in that rig with them, and they all eat. The guy is too crippled up with arthritis to work at anything, and the woman doesn't look like she'd know how to do the dinner dishes. There's not one damned thing they've got to offer us here but more mouths to feed, and the one thing they just ran out of in that rig of theirs is food. Oh, and then there's the two bikers that came in this afternoon. You haven't seen them yet, either. They're fresh up from the Bay Area, and they're a couple of *real* beauties. Flies in the sugar bowl, two by two. They've got a poodle as big as a horse that rides sidecar with them, and it also eats. Ben, this has just got to stop; if we don't all catch the plague from them, we're going to be starving to death instead."

"They won't bring us plague if we just follow the protocol we've set up," Ben said. "Keep your gate locked so they don't drive into the main compounds. Mask and gown when you go out to meet them, simple isolation technique just like I've shown everybody. Send them down to the quarantine spot on the creek and I'll see to it that they keep separate from the others down there for the critical period. Four days will tell us whether they're clean or not, and meanwhile we can assess them, set up work assignments, figure out where to plant them—"

"Ben, it isn't going to *work,*" Amy broke in. "Something's going to slip through our guard, it just isn't that controllable, you yourself admit that."

"It's the best we can do."

"But we don't *need* these people! And I say they're going to kill us. Listen, this new crowd cracked it today, as far as I'm concerned. Harry and I went into Bozeman this morning, regular supply run, and we heard that people are getting sick in Bozeman. Four cases in one week, all in different parts of town. Doc Smythe thinks he's got them isolated and contained, but nobody is sure where it came from, and all they need is about ten more cases and they won't be able to contain it because that burns out the available vaccine and drugs. People are packing up and leaving already, and if some of them head where I think they're going to head for, we haven't seen *nothing* on Grizzly Creek—and they're going to bring the infection here with them."

Ben stood up and poured himself some more whiskey. He looked at Amy and then at the others. "Okay, now everybody listen to me real carefully, because I'm going to tell you the bad news. I don't care if nobody else came up this road all winter, it wouldn't matter a whit. No matter *what* we do, we're not going to keep plague out of this Freehold."

"Like hell we're not," Amy snapped. "That's why we've got the Freehold, and that's why we've got to control it. Look, I'm not worried about *me,* for God's sake. I'm just an old woman—or at least I sure feel like one, these days. I'm not worried about Harry, or Mel here, or even you, Ben. We've all had our turn, and if something hits us, then something hits us. But I've got two boys with wives that are pregnant, and I sure do want to see those babies safe. Mel's got his son, and Kelley's got his daughters, and we've got to keep this Freehold safe for *them,* not for the whole wide world. And the only way to keep it safe is to keep plague out of here, and we can't do that if we don't keep people out."

Ben shook his head. "Sorry, Amy, but you're dead wrong. I'm telling you, no matter what we do, it's going to hit here, sooner or later. We can't keep it out. We can't make it through the winter totally isolated. We can't fight a war to keep people away from here, and we can't stop the wind from blowing over the hill."

"It's *people* who are going to bring it, not the wind," Amy said. "And we can shoot people dead to keep them out if we have to."

For a moment the room was still. Mel Tapper shuffled his feet as if embarrassed, his craggy features working. The other men stared fixedly at the fire. Finally Ben Chamberlain sighed. "Well, I'm sorry, Amy. Maybe you can shoot people dead to keep them out, or think you can, but I sure can't. And if somebody's sick and needs help, I can't throw them out of here on their asses in the middle of November, either. I've spent most of my life trying to help sick people get well, trying to put broken bodies back together again, and I'm too old by now to start killing them with bullets or neglect. I don't know what's happening in Bozeman. I'm not going in there to find out, either. The damned thing is going to hit there sooner or later if it hasn't already, and there's not much any of us can do to help anybody back in town. But we can sure take in the ones that turn up here, and do the best we can with what we've got."

Harry Slencik shook his head. "Look, Ben, you've got Amy all wrong. She's not seriously planning to shoot anybody, for God's sake. And she's not going to drive anybody out that's already here, leastwise not if they're trying to pack their own weight a little bit. We're not going to drive Dan Potter here away—he's been working a miracle with this water system of his—it's already delivering permanent house water for year round, and it's almost set up to irrigate the whole valley when the ground melts next spring. And how many others have we got in here now besides ourselves, including kids? Maybe twenty, twenty-five. Well, we can squeeze by with that and keep the place safe too. But we can't just be sitting ducks for anybody that wanders in and decides they like it here. Amy's dead right about that. Sooner or later somebody's going to bring something bad in with them, and what do we do then? We've got to keep the ones out that don't have to stay. Like this family with the four kids and Grandma. They're not in any real, immediate trouble. They're just plain squatters."

"They've got to go somewhere," Ben said mildly.

"Sure they do—but it's a big world. They don't have to pick us to squat on, and we don't have let 'em. If they're out of food, that's all right, we can help 'em out. We can give 'em a ham and a pound of cornmeal and pack 'em out of here tonight. Tell 'em we're sorry, but they've got to move on, and that's that. And while we're at it, we can sure manage to live without those faggots and their dog, too."

"They've also got to go somewhere," Ben said.

"Well, not here," Harry said. "You've just got to listen to reason, Ben. We're not going to go fighting any wars with anybody, but if we have to make a little show of, like, hostility or something to keep more people from pilin' in here, then we're just going to have to do it. The way I see it, it's getting pretty close to being them or us."

"I see," the old doctor said.

"You can understand that, can't you?"

"I take your point, Harry." Ben looked around the room. "What about you other folks?"

Mel Tapper shuffled his feet. "I—I guess I've got to go along with Amy and Harry, Ben." Across the room the rancher nodded vigorous agreement. "Damn right," he said. "It's private land. We've all sweat for it. We can keep it private."

"Potter? How about you? You don't have any land, you came in here like a plucked chicken. What do you think?"

The little engineer grimaced, glanced at Amy. "Hell, Doc, I can't really say much. But I do think everybody ought to contribute *something,* at least. Keep as tight a ship as possible."

"I see." Ben Chamberlain scratched his chin. "Well, like I say, I take your point. But I've got a point too, and I guess I might as well make it. In four short months this epidemic has already brought misery and nightmare and death to millions of people in this country, all over the world, and I don't think we've seen the half of it yet. So far, by the grace of God, we've all stayed clean as an elk's horns, we haven't even been touched, but that's not going to last, and I'm sorry, but just watching our own asses here on the Freehold is not going to work. Before it's all over there's going to be grief and suffering enough for every soul around, and I for one am not going to add to the total. When the crunch comes here, people are going to need *people* more than anything else. The only thing people are going to be able to do that'll amount to a damn is help other people as much as they can and do the best they can, and that's all." He set his glass down, put on his cap and zipped up his windbreaker. "Well, that's all I've got to say, so take it easy. Thanks for the drinks, Harry."

"Well, sure, but hold it, Ben. We've got some other things to talk over while everybody's here."

"Not me, Harry. I'm all talked out."

"What do you mean?"

"Look, I can't fight you people—but I damned well don't have to stay with you, either. I'll mark my corners down the creek here and put up a little fence line tomorrow, and I'll take care not to be trespassing on any private land. Best you folks do the same."

He walked out into the darkness, stepped down off Harry's back porch in the darkness, and started on down the path along the creek toward his own place. He walked it firm-footed in the pitch dark, the path he'd walked down in the dark a thousand times before in those last twenty years; he knew every dip and rise, every bit of brush that slapped his face as he walked. For almost a full minute he heard only the sound of his own footfalls, the grumping of a nearby owl and the ever-present gurgle of the creek. Then he heard Harry's door crash open behind him and heard Amy screaming at him: "Ben! Come back here!"

He kept on walking. She shouted his name again, and a moment later he heard her coming after him, still shouting, crashing a short cut through the brush to cut him off, her voice rising to a wail as she came. She caught up as he reached the last turn down toward the creek; now, in the starlight he could make out her slim form and her ghostly face as she broke out of the brush into the path, clutched at his arm, tried to haul him around. "Ben! For God's sake, come back! You can't walk out on us now—"

"Sorry, girl, but I can. And I have to."

He tried to shake loose, but she held on, turned him to her, clung to him with amazing strength. "You can't go now, Ben, you can't leave us now, after all these years! We can't let you go—"

"I have to. You leave me no choice."

"You don't either have to! Please, Ben, you didn't hear me right—"

"I heard you, and I can't buy it."

"Then I'll take it back. Maybe I was wrong, all wrong. We can do it different, do it your way if that's how it has to be."

"I can't fight you, Amy."

"You won't have to fight me, I promise! I thought I was right but maybe I wasn't. Either way, you've got to come back. You *need* us, Ben, and God knows how bad we need you." Her voice was crumbling now and he felt her wet face on his neck as she clung to him. "*I* need you. Oh, God, Ben, I'm *scared.* I'm so scared I don't know what I'm doing half the time, and Harry's scared too and he doesn't know what to do. None of us know what to do."

"I don't know, either," the old man said, "and I'm just as scared as you are. All I know is what I can't make myself do."

"That's all right, you won't have to. We'll do it your way and take it the way it comes."

"You'll say that loud and clear to the crowd back there?"

"I'll say it."

Very gently he disengaged her, supported her shoulder and turned back up the path with her. "Then we'd better get back," he said, "before you catch your death out here."

54

And as the winter deepened, the fire storm flared hotter and faster through the cities and countryside, leaving a deepening, paralyzing desolation in its wake. No major population center in the country escaped, although plans and preparations and defenses were hastily and desperately erected; in the end there was no way a population center *could* escape, for there was no way that movement of people could be stopped, and in those places like Pittsburgh and Dallas where city ordinances and state emergency orders and state militia movements and police firepower were all made part of the defense effort, to block the movement of people and attempt isolation, the fire storm licked into those cities anyway, leaping firebreaks in ways that no one could possibly foresee, through loopholes no one could plug, and the fiercest and sternest of martial-law measures quickly crumbled. One by one the cities took the bow-shock of the fire storm, and set their emergency plans and defense measures and desperation contingencies into motion, and fought back fiercely, and slowed the fury not one whit, and became overwhelmed, and gradually came unraveled like all the rest. In extreme cases like Spokane, bridges across rivers were actually blasted out and major throughways blown apart in hopes of isolating one part of a city from another, but there were all those side streets and water craft and back roads and country lanes to watch, and who would watch the watchers?

One thing seemed certain: the advancing winter did nothing significant to quiet the advancing plague storm. No one had really expected it to when it became blindingly clear that the mutant strain of *Yersinia* involved was spreading far more predominantly by respiratory contact than through the classic vector of the infected flea. Perhaps, during those winter months, the fire burned more swiftly in the great southern cities—New Orleans or Houston or Phoenix—than in those in the north. But who really could say? One terrible problem was that no one could really say much of anything about *any* affected area because solid statistical and epidemiological data was virtually nonexistent. Who had time to count the dead? Who had time to tabulate figures? Who could rely with any confidence on such figures as might happen to be available? There were more important and urgent things to do. Whatever figures did appear, here and there, had to be the sheerest blind guesses; who could calmly sit back and separate the plague-dead from those dead from conflagration or civil disturbance or riot or martial confrontations? Indeed, who could care? What *use* was such information? The dead were very dead. The sick of one day from whatever cause, or the wounded, or the hypothermically exposed, or the starving, were likely to be the dead of the next day, and did tables of figures matter? Most authorities ultimately thought not and soon stopped trying to compile them.

For those few people in government, or in the CDC or in the public-health offices, or in the military, who had access to some sort of an overview of what was happening, piecemeal as it might be—people like Ted Bettendorf, for instance—certain patterns of events could be perceived occurring in the great population centers. In place after place, again and again, effective public-health defenses were mustered and maintained control for a brief while; but in every instance, again and again, despite what anybody did, that control ultimately faltered; slipped away and finally crumbled.

It was not the fault of the health workers that this happened—Ted knew that better than anyone. Indeed, if there was major heroism to chronicle during those winter months of the fire storm, it was in the stubborn, determined efforts of individual nurses, doctors, public-health officials, epidemiologists, aides, orderlies and other health workers. Time after time, these people fought down to the line and beyond, did their work with or without protection, the best they could, long after it became obvious that they were losing beyond hope, their front lines broken, their flanks eaten away. Of course some quit and ran; some vanished into the woodwork; not a few sickened and died; but most held on, trying to do *something,* far beyond reasonable limits. It was not here that breakdowns came, but in all too many places elsewhere.

The first and most pernicious breakdown, in almost every instance, was in communications at all levels. In city after city, at the approach of the Horseman, local telephone communications fell into chaos. Contingency plans crumbled within twenty-four hours; switchboards were tied into knots, backed up for days. Everyone was on the telephone at once, jamming and overloading every circuit. Within hours it was impossible to prioritize local and distant calls, simply because every single caller regarded his call as first priority, whether it was to call out the fire squad or to check on Aunt Mabel, and there was no one with wisdom and authority to slash through the urgency and panic and say, "These calls must go through, these must wait, these you forget about." By and large, major trunk lines or satellite connections were kept open, at least part of the time, sometimes too open. In cities like New York it became easier to direct-dial Hong Kong than to get through to a party six blocks across town. Calls placed to a local hospital in Scranton mysteriously reached Sioux City, Iowa. Thus in most communities, large and small, and more so in the larger than in the smaller, the telephone as an instrument of communication or defense became virtually useless within hours or days. Only the person with endless time, endless patience or endless determination could get through to anybody.

Public communications media fared as badly or worse. Endless power failures slowed newspaper printing to sporadic outbursts, and distribution was impossible. Such news as there was was garbled, unedited, unverified, and usually self-contradictory. Television and radio—the anchor in the chain of public notices and the transmission of directives, orders, advice and vital information, upon which virtually every preplanned contingency program depended to get the right word to the people fast—became an outright laughing stock. Directives and advice that were three days old were broadcast and rebroadcast mindlessly in the absence of anything new to say. Unverified reports fed sensationalism and panic, and became the order of the day. And for all their lifelong dependence on television and radio for input, people were not totally stupid: they very quickly learned that even when some TV news announcer told them something in utmost urgency and earnestness, it was probably either two days out of date or totally false; radio announcers talked nonsense to fill time and competed for listeners with "on-the-spot reports" of things that never happened anywhere, or were grossly misinterpreted. In the end, almost always, the sets got turned off, or simply babbled endlessly in the night. Local mimeographed or photocopied newssheets were far more likely to have *valid* news, and these appeared by the millions in city blocks or residential areas, handed out free by small running boys or tacked up on telephone poles to gather graffiti.

With communications unreliable or nonexistent, there was no way to get health information distributed. Clinics and hospitals became mob scenes; officials with bullhorns would broadcast information and directions from emergency-room roofs to mobs piling in below, usually blaring out directions people didn't want to hear, such as Go Home, Listen to Your Radio for Word of Medications, Boil All Your Dishes and Clothes, Stay Away from Crowds, Stay Home—unpopular, those bullhorns. Ambulances in full siren inched through crowds of people who imagined, almost always incorrectly, that they contained precious medical supplies. . . .

Not only could the health services not function well—and public power services only sporadically—but food supplies also began to falter. Ancient cities such as Rome and Constantinople were limited in their ultimate size and population by the length of time it took to bring fresh food from the countryside into the heart of the city. No such problem had existed in modern cities, with trucks and freight cars following fast, established delivery routes. But as supplies in the countryside dried up and as trainmen and truckers parked their trains and cabs outside "dangerous" areas and refused to move into the cities, food began to vanish. People with well-stocked shelves and freezers and refrigerators managed to eat—until the power went off long enough for the frozen food to melt and spoil . . . (attempts were made to distribute such food while it was still good, some successfully, some not). . . . When cooking power failed, people ate their food raw, and when fresh foods dwindled they ate dried macaroni and chewed uncooked rice, soaked overnight into a soggy sort of softness.

And throughout it all, worse some places than others, there was the panic, the looting, the rioting, the burning (though not so much burning, so often—Savannah had been a dreadful lesson that hit home to most people), the slow strangulation and crumbling of the great and small population centers, and—ever-present—the gathering heaps of dead and the clustering of the dying for warmth and comfort and sharing of misery.

In multitudes of places, for multitudes of people, it was a winter of nightmare and horror—yet somehow, in some places, good spirits hung on for dear life. Sometimes good things happened that might never have happened otherwise, and heroism in small, increasingly meaningful things, appeared in strange places. If too many people surpassed themselves in compounding the growing misery around them, in venality and cruelty and sheer blind raw selfishness, other people far surpassed themselves, rose far above themselves, in selfless acts and kindness to others and compassion.

55

Siddie Harper's turf was unpromising land for heroism. Through the endless, broken slum streets of Chicago's South Side the Horseman had taken his hideous toll with the sureness of a surgeon's blade in the face of little or no opposition at all. Unlike so many other major-city slums, there had been no rioting there to speak of, little violence, little looting, little response that could be characterized precisely as panic. It seemed, in many ways, that the scourge had sliced its way through tens of thousands there like a knife through softened butter. Partly, of course, it was the long, long tradition of submission to utter grinding poverty so characteristic there, basically unrelieved in the slightest by the welfare checks or the child-support money or the food stamps nobody could buy or the huge, ineffective health-care institutions nobody would trust or the vast, towering, barren, strife-torn urban renewal projects erected there to rot or the endless preachings of the endless Jesse Jacksons. The yawning gulf of poverty there, entirely comparable to the barrios of Rio or the drought-starved Sahel, sucked them all in and gulped them down without the faintest residual trace that they had ever come and gone, despite all the publicity and the political posturings, leaving tens and tens of thousands no better off and probably worse, with little will or human spirit left to fight anything with anything.

Even more, there was the very swiftness with which the fire storm had struck south-side Chicago, a devastating blow that had moved through the tenements and sewers and alleyways like a demon, numbing all facilities at once, offering no chance for recovery, too vast and relentless for anyone even to imagine where or how to start fighting. And the early, bitter winter that struck the northern-tier states merely contributed a little bit more than usual to the agony, with icy Canadian winds slicing down off Lake Michigan and snow at two-foot depth by early October. Rat-borne plagues of the past had always been slowed in winter, but not this man-borne plague. Inevitably the power outages and fuel-delivery failures and street blockings and commerical stoppages that plagued all of Chicago came first and worst on the South Side and were repaired last, which meant not repaired for weeks at a time as the death count mounted and the people there, for the most part, bowed their heads with almost inaudible wailing and waited with folded hands for any delivery at all.

Sidonia Harper was never one to have much use for folded hands, but then, one might have thought that Siddie had little choice in the matter. Sidonia had sat helplessly and watched her mother die in their little second-floor cold-water tenement flat during the first tidal wave of plague that hit Chicago. There was nothing she could do but sit and watch as her mother, already sick and dispirited, crippled with arthritis, abandoned by her only serious consort four years before in the wake of Sidonia's accident, losing her four boys to drugs or prison or the rolling mills in Gary, barely able to keep Siddie and her younger sister alive, became suddenly and violently ill one night, and abruptly ceased breathing three days later. Her mother had been unwilling, or unable, even to try to travel to the nearest hospital facility twenty blocks away (not that it would have done her any good) and Sidonia was certainly not in a position to drag her. Siddie had nursed her as best she could, understanding all too well exactly what was going on in that tenement block where everyone, *everyone,* suddenly seemed to be getting sick at the same time. Siddie understood, all right; she had a very good mind and a TV set for a teacher. She had done all the right things for her mother the best that she could do them from her wheelchair, and—maybe fortunately for Siddie—it made her postpone thinking or paying attention to anything else, for a while. It was not until her mother was finally breathing no more and the truck had finally, finally come to take her away, that Sidonia had realized in a wave of absolute horror that the tenements on her block had become for the most part empty, and that death and her eight-year-old sister were the only companions she had left.

They waited for days for something to happen, with Siddie's sister in abject terror, unwilling to go out on the street to try to get food until Siddie had soothed and assured and calmed her for hours, and then returning more terrified than before she had gone out; and Siddie, of course, could not go out at all. She had not been out of that second-story flat except rarely at any time during the four years since the terrible hot summer night when a wild-eyed boy she had known and teased at school had broken in the door of the place and brushed her mother aside and backed the fourteen-year-old girl out onto the fire escape to rape her and was stripping her clothes off her when the fire-escape railing gave and Siddie plunged two stories down to the concrete alleyway below and broke her back in three places. After the short hospital visit to make sure she was going to live at all, she had returned home to endless months in traction in the tenement flat as an ill-nourished body slowly, slowly allowed broken bones to heal—but the torn spinal cord would not heal.

Time had ceased to exist for Siddie Harper for part of that four years as her broken body matured and her mind changed. For a while girl friends came by, but they were aliens to Siddie, talking about their "men" and their pushers and their johns, and presently they stopped coming by. Broken bodies made them feel uneasy and so did Siddie's head—she seemed far too old and thought about far too many weird things that didn't really fit *anything* the others knew. They were lonely years, but something happened in Siddie's mind to make the loneliness not too bad; of all people on the block she was the only one who waited for the bookmobile week after week, who wondered about things outside the block, who read and who taught herself to do many little things no one else knew that she *could* do when there was so much she couldn't. She had lived on a timeless island, served and maintained and changing until the sudden, terrible fire storm struck and her mother was gone and Tessie, her sister, was terrified.

She helped Tessie, then, showed her how to do things, instructed her where to go to get what was needed in spite of her fear and the terrible things happening outside as the fire storm raged. Siddie was by no means helpless; she could get around well enough in the old beat-up wheelchair the state had provided (the state had actually paid for a brand-new chair with all the special features, but the one that had finally arrived at the second-story flat was an old, used, decrepit model with sharp angles and rusty swivels and the stuffing hanging out of the seat). Things would have been much easier for Siddie if her mother could have found—and paid for—a first-floor flat, as the visiting nurse had urged on one of her three visits, but the hard work of searching for a ground-floor place, and the ever-climbing rentals quoted for such flats whenever anybody heard about the wheelchair and smelled welfare money defeated *that;* so Siddie seldom got downstairs. But she managed just the same. Though her legs had withered, her arms and shoulders and pectorals and wrists and hands had become powerful from constantly manipulating her chair, as was the case with so many paraplegics, and she became very capable in many ways. So it was, after Mamma died, that she had been able to show her little sister what to do, and used her strong arms to comfort her, and wheeled herself around the flat to manage the cleaning and the simple cooking that sustained them. As long as they were well, they managed—but then the inevitable day had come when Siddie realized that Tessie was suddenly ill, gray and coughing and shivering violently in the cold flat, and that she herself had suddenly become feverish too, with angry, painful swellings appearing under her arms, and a vicious cough that would not stop.

Like Mamma before her, Tessie also had died, though not quite so quickly. Some person from some clinic, spurred perhaps by some quixotic urge to help the handicapped, had come by with a small bottle of capsules for the girls to use if they got too sick, and Tessie ate the capsules and they seemed to help somewhat, she seemed to improve for a little, but Siddie just got sicker, doing her best to help the child until one evening her sister's breathing stopped and she knew she was comforting the dead and she herself was so sick she could barely ease the body to the floor and move it into the bedroom alcove; then she just sat there, watching over her dead sister, totally alone, waiting for her own time to come, if it was going to.

By some miracle of justice Sidonia Harper did not die. She was terribly ill, with draining sores and pain that was unbearable, and no one coming, delirium that wiped out days and made the nights endless; but she did not die, and then one morning—who could say how much later?—she had opened her eyes and her head was clear, and she was aware that her clothing stank until she got it stripped off, wheeling her chair around to hide from the icy blast from a window that had somehow gotten broken, and bathed herself from the washbowl, aware suddenly that she was desperately, unspeakably hungry. Cupboards were bare, milk rotting in the refrigerator, a handful of oatmeal and nothing else. Somewhere nearby a child was crying endlessly, somewhere else in the building, but when she tried a hoarse cry out the window herself, there was no response, and when she looked down at the alleyway and the street beyond she saw no people, no traffic.

No food. Nobody to help her. It was then that she knew with utter clarity that somehow she had to get downstairs.

She thought about it for a full day and night, trying to think out ways to make the unthinkable possible. For the past four years her major terror had been a fear of heights and falling; she had nightmares about falling, and woke up screaming. But now, alone, fear of falling or not, there was no other choice but to get herself down those stairs.

It took her most of another day to work up the nerve to actually try it. First she wheeled herself down the dark hall from the door of the flat to the top of the stairs, a yawning gulf stretching down and down to a landing and a wall, then farther on down the other way to the first-floor hallway. For a moment she panicked at the very sight of that gaping chasm; she pounded on the floor with the heavy cane she used to hook things to her, screamed out for help again and again, but no answer came. The place seemed empty, deserted. She considered trying to do it by brute strength alone, clinging to the banister with one arm and scratching at the wall with the other hand as she eased the chair down, but she knew she didn't dare. She was far too weak for that; she knew the agony of overtaxed muscles too well. She wheeled herself back into the flat, found an old piece of clothesline rope under the sink. Back at the top of the stairs she turned the chair, disengaged the left arm of it, tossed it down with a clatter, then seized the banister and slid herself off the chair onto the floor. She could ease herself down the stairs all right, that was no problem, but without the chair at the bottom she couldn't do anything once she was down there; the chair had to go first.

She tied the clothesline securely to the banister at the top, tied the other end around the axle of the chair. Seizing the banister with her left arm, she clutched the rope in her right hand, gently pushed the chair to the stairtop and over. It started down, bump, bump, bump, faster, the rope sizzling through her hand until she howled from the burn and let it go. The chair leaped downward, banging on each third step, came to the end of the rope in midair halfway down, snapped the rope and crashed down into the wall at the landing.

Siddie eased herself down, step by step. Eased down, rested. The strength she was used to wasn't there, and she wasn't thinking clearly; she was a third of the way down before she realized she had left the upper half of the rope tied to the banister above, and painfully had to work her way back up to retrieve it. Finally down at the landing, she tied the broken rope back together, then dragged her legs along to the chair, finding only that its back was bent from its upside-down collision with the wall.

This time she was more careful. She wound three turns of rope around the cane and wedged the cane into a banister spoke to control the rope's slide as the chair went down. She rested for an hour, dozing part of the time, before she dared try it, but it went smoothly, especially because at the last minute she wrapped her hand in her T-shirt tail before clutching the rope. Halfway down, the chair stopped and she followed, reached it, tore the tail off her T-shirt to tie the wheel to the banister before climbing back up to untie the rope. Long minutes later she had repeated the process, and the chair came to rest on the first-floor hallway.

The outside door hung open on one hinge—and that left seven steps to go, down the outside stoop onto the street. She was exhausted now, tired beyond words, no longer able to face the ordeal of hitching herself up and down stairs to get ropes. The seven stairs didn't look too steep, and suddenly something in her mind said *To hell with it all, I've got to get down there NOW,* and she acted on it. She grabbed the iron rail and hoisted herself into the chair, replaced the left arm, then clutched the railing and started easing the chair down. She controlled it for three steps before the strength of her arm gave and she and the chair plunged down to the street, lurched to the right as a wheel gave and bent when they hit the bottom, banged down the curb into the street, across to the other side, struck the other curb and threw Sidonia off, skidding on her face on the sidewalk as the chair turned over twenty feet away, the unbent wheel spinning and spinning in the air like a crazy thing.

Five minutes later she opened her eyes, realizing she was still alive and miraculously unhurt except for scrapes and bruises. She tested the limbs she could move. Only then did she become aware of the perfectly enormous human figure towering over her.

56

Frank Barrington liked Dr. Sam MacIvers from the moment he saw him on that sunny winter morning in Willow Grove, Nebraska. The dour little sandy-haired man, senior physician of the two-man Willow Grove Family Medical Clinic, was not really all that senior—maybe forty-four or forty-five, Frank thought—but he had that certain wiry agelessness about him, the look of having stood out in the wind and weather too long, so common to many Scots. MacIvers had a long crooked nose and a face like a prune, which could wrinkle into a wry smile once in a while, and a pair of tired gray eyes that looked as if they might have been watching far too many less than pleasant things for far too many years at far too close quarters. *No flies sitting on this one,* Frank thought, five minutes after he met him, *and if I'm going to have to have some people on my side up here, this man looks like a mighty good one for openers.* And aside from first impressions, there was something else that Frank liked: there was no possible doubt, after the first ten minutes together, that Dr. Sam MacIvers saw with utter bleak certainty just exactly what was coming down the pike toward Willow Grove, Nebraska, and was damned well ready to do anything necessary to stop it.

Frank had driven up from Wichita that morning on frigid, snow-packed roads through endless miles of flat winter-stubbled wheat country, the monotony of the trip broken only on occasion when the road dipped down into small creek or river valleys, probably verdant enough in summer but now lined with tall, skeletal leafless trees and small towns that looked battened down for a long, cold winter, lights on behind frosty windows in the late morning dawn, woodsmoke curling from chimneys and rich in the air. Willow Grove lay in one such river valley, bigger and more sprawly than other towns, a pretty place as the sun broke through, many evergreens planted among the stark elms and oaks and sycamores.

Frank found the small, neat clinic building with no trouble, following Sally Grinstone's directions. He paused with MacIvers just long enough for a fast cup of coffee before they took off together in the doctor's well-worn Chevy. "I'm free for the day," MacIvers told him, "as long as I stop at the hospital and check an OB who may be going to do something. So you tell me what you want to see."

"Everything," Frank said. "The lay of the town, where things are, the medical facilities, the countryside around. The broad geography, so I can snoop myself later. Things like what the school gymnasium looks like and where the telephone office is and where the power company keeps their boom trucks—"

"Yes, if you're going to be the commissar of this little operation, I guess you'll need to know where things are located."

"Aren't we going to pick up the public-health man first?"

"You mean Perry Haglund?" MacIvers frowned. "That was the plan, but he called me an hour ago and said he couldn't make it."

"I see," Frank said. "That's not so good. Maybe we can catch him later in the day."

"Afraid not. He said he'd be out of town for a couple of days. He didn't say where. I'll just have to brief him when he gets back."

It was a typical southern Nebraska town, flat as a pancake except for the little dip down to the river, a major Main Street on the old highway, now broken up in the main shopping area to form a grid of one-way streets and angle parking, some care in the planning, pleasant-looking even in winter. The usual roadside sprawl at either end, and the inevitable grain elevators standing like giant sentinels—"the Nebraska Rockies," MacIvers called them. Neatly kept homes on the side streets, some looking very old, and a couple of 1910-vintage buildings downtown, restored and well kept. A look of quiet prosperity about the place. Kids on bicycles, pickup trucks parked in driveways alongside the little Toyotas and other compacts. Not many Cadillacs or Lincolns that Frank could see, and that added up, too. *Too damn smart to buy Cadillacs,* he thought, *or too tight.* "Any sign of infection yet?" he asked the doctor.

"Not yet, and it's not that we haven't been watching, either. The usual round of bronchitis and flu for this time of year, and a couple of cases of measles that we don't like to see, mostly in the older school kids. We thought we had that stopped. As far as plague is concerned, we've just been dead lucky, so far. Of course, this isn't exactly a world trade center, it's pretty dead during the winter. Not much traffic in and out. No place much to go, except for vacations to Mexico, and there hasn't been any enthusiasm for that this year, believe me."

"How many people?"

"Around twenty thousand in the town, another ten thousand out in the county and on the farms. Willow Grove is the major grain center for the region, but then we have the little satellite towns scattered around—Plunkett and Metuskie and Dust Bin—that's no joke, there *is* a place called Dust Bin—and Wattsville, and Oberon down in Kansas. They account for another few thousand people all together."

"Sounds very workable. People know each other, I suppose? And work together?"

"Pretty much, and pretty well." The doctor swung past a school, took Frank in to see the gym and meet the principal. "Matter of fact, everybody knows most everybody, and there's been a very positive response to the meetings we've been holding—lots of families represented by somebody. In town we're getting the block watches set up, like Sally Grinstone suggested, somebody on every block responsible for people counts and reporting what's going on, so we should be able to get a picture of what's happening twice a day. See that church over there kitty-corner from the clinic? Big parish hall there is a natural storage and distribution center for your pneumomycin. People can get in and out without a lot of mingling, and it's within reach of everybody. We've got your tetracycline stored in there—you can take it on back with you if you want to." MacIvers looked at Frank. "I just wish you'd let us start stockpiling the stuff now instead of waiting until the ax drops."

Frank shook his head. "We just don't have it ready yet," he said, as earnestly as he could. It was a lie, and he found himself feeling bad lying to this little doctor, so he suddenly decided to level. "But that's not really the problem. The truth is, it's an arbitrary matter of policy that we've had to decide on for right now. Doc, you're smart enough to see the situation. We are totally extra-legal, and our necks are out there through the noose individually and personally. We're trying to do something that's absolutely insupportable, medically speaking, and totally unjustifiable as far as any constituted authority is concerned. We've got to test the efficacy of a brand-new drug very quickly on a whole lot of people who are getting sick, and right now Willow Grove, Nebraska, turns out to be our guinea pig. If some higher authority comes in and cuts us off here, we're *cut off,* and we're the only source for the finished drug, right now. We're trying something wild and crazy, and it's sink or swim, and to our minds, that means we've got to keep it a hundred percent under our own control. If we win on this, and get a really definitive profile of disease control in Willow Grove, it'll be the first place since Canon City that we've stopped this damned thing, and we'll all smell sweet, and the end will justify the means. At the very worst, we're pretty sure it won't *hurt* anybody, and you must be sold on that, too, or you wouldn't be playing games with us at all—"

"We're playing games with you because there's no other ball game in sight," the doctor cut in. "I don't think Perry Haglund is really sold, he seems to keep tossing up horror-story scenarios for us to bat down, but my partner and I don't foresee any horror story much worse than what's going to happen when that Horseman finally rides into Willow Grove unless we can do something to stop him. We just wish to hell you'd let us get ahead of him, that's all."

"Well, you think it through, Doc," Frank said. "Suppose you stockpiled the stuff now, right here in town. Everybody would know it, and you know what would happen then. You'd be on the dime, subjectively involved right up to the neck, and I don't think there'd be a way in the world you could keep from putting the whole damned town on the stuff before the infection even turned up. You'd just inevitably jump the gun. And if you did that, and then nobody got sick, *what would we learn?* Nothing. Not one damned thing of any use to anybody."

"What you're saying is that we've got to have some corpses."

"I'm just repeating it. Sally already told you that."

"Sounds an awful lot like playing God," MacIvers said.

"Yes, and it's not fun. But it's the only game we can see that has a dream of winning. We had to make some rules, so that's how we're going to play it."

The doctor took a deep breath. "Okay, Commissar," he said. He grinned crookedly at Frank. "At least I know one thing for sure: you really *were* at Canon City; I checked that out three ways. So let's make Willow Grove Canon City number two. Okay, the parish hall is the stockpile, and maybe a good central headquarters, but the clinic has got better communications. You can check that out and see what you think a little later when you meet my partner Whitey Fox. Right now let's get over to the hospital; you can look around while I see if that OB of mine is ready to sprout or not. . . ."

57

In Brookdale, Connecticut, the call came late in the afternoon when Jack Dillman was just climbing out of the shower, and Carmen took it down below. A moment later she called up the stairs. "Jack, can you get it? It's Hal Parker."

That wimp, Jack thought. *That fucking bastard is going to pull it again.* He took his time drying off, then walked to the phone beside his drawing board, still covered with the half-finished layout he was no longer working on because there was no way at *all* to deliver it anymore, and probably nobody to pay for it, either. "Yeah?"

"Jack, buddy. Hal here." The same bluff, hearty voice he always used, as rich and vibrant as Hal himself was confidently handsome.

"What's your problem, Hal?"

"Buddy, I need a favor. Somebody to cover for me tonight." He faked a cough and somehow made the voice less vibrant. "Must have picked up a flu bug or something, it's really got me down and out today. How about you picking up for me tonight? I'll take your turn Friday in trade."

Jack hesitated just long enough. "Boy, Hal, I dunno. I had some work planned tonight—"

"Buddy, you know I wouldn't ask you if it wasn't desperate, but I tried Vince and Angelo and practically everybody else I could think of and they're all boxed in. I'll be okay to cover for you Friday, don't worry."

You bet your ass you will, you prick. You'll be all taken care of by morning. "Well," Jack said, "I suppose I can cover. But, look—you want Carmen to drive tonight, too, in Ellen's place?"

"Huh? Oh, no. No. That won't be necessary. Ellen's fine. She'll go ahead and drive."

"Okay, just thought I'd check," Jack said. "I'll meet Bud down at the Tav at eight-thirty."

"That's great, buddy, great. I owe you one. You know I'd do the same for you."

Yeah, I know what you'd do for me, Jack thought as he set the phone down. *I'm not stone blind. And with me out of the house from 8:30 until 5:00 A.M., and your Ellen out driving until at least 1:00 A.M., you'll have plenty of time to do it for me, too, old buddy. Where's it going to be, your place or ours? Probably ours, Ellen might stop at your place any old time to take a quick pee.*

He walked downstairs and met Carmen coming out of the kitchen with the martini tray. "What was that all about?" she said.

"What would you guess?" He took a martini. That was what got him the most, he thought, the sheer indignity of it, all the pukey little lies he was supposed to swallow. "He's got the flu tonight, he says. He wants me to cover his watch for him."

"Really? I hope it isn't—something bad."

"Don't worry about it, dear. His blood alcohol's too high for anything to grow in there."

"Did he want me to drive in Ellen's place, too?"

Jack looked at her. "He didn't say anything about that."

Carmen turned away and set the tray down in the living room. "Seems to me this is the third time he's pulled this since you guys started these night watches."

"The fourth time, to be exact. One time it was a bad cold or something, and then there was a lodge meeting, except that I heard later there wasn't any lodge meeting that night. I forget what the other excuse was."

"Well, you didn't have to say yes," Carmen said. "You could have told him to shove it if you didn't like it."

"Yeah sure, but somebody's got to take the watch, and if old Hal isn't going to show up, somebody's got to show up for him." *And anyway, it wouldn't do any good to refuse; he'd just find some other way to shove it, big virile Hal Parker. . . .* Jack gulped down his martini without tasting it, drank another standing, staring out the front window. Then he went to the front closet and took the old M-1 out of its rack, his old rifle from Korea, tested the action out of easy habit. He took a couple of filled clips off the shelf and stuck them in his pocket. At least he knew how to shoot the damned thing, more than you could say for some of the others on these patrols. He'd never bought a smaller or lighter rifle, never bought any other firearm, for that matter. He'd had to drag this one out of the attic and spend a day cleaning it when the watches had started. Actually, he'd always been pretty fiercely antigun in his thinking, right in the midst of a whole bunch of gun nuts living in this small community, arguing endlessly against their silly cant. IF YOU OUTLAW GUNS, ONLY OUTLAWS WILL HAVE GUNS. Didn't sound so silly anymore, with what had been going on these past two or three months. He was glad he had this baby now. Probably couldn't actually make himself shoot anybody with it, but then so far they hadn't really had to. "We'll, I'd better get a little nap if I'm going to be out all night," he said. "Wake me up for dinner about eight."

He sprawled out on the daybed in the TV room and closed his eyes, but he couldn't relax as his anger and frustration mounted at the cheap baldness of this pukey little affair, his own self-disgust at having played along with it. He might just as well have invited the bastard in for cocktails first. Of course he didn't have any real proof—he'd very carefully never looked too closely for proof. Maybe it was all in his head. Maybe he was just one more burnt-out exurban jackass with paranoid delusions about his still-beautiful, still-painfully-passionate wife. But there were so many things, the little things, the way the bastard kept pawing her at cocktail parties and her playing the innocent coquette, making sure Jack didn't fail to notice. The way they'd disappear from the crowd for a half-hour at a time. The time she'd spend away from home, "having coffee" with somebody, "shopping," even now when there wasn't anything to speak of to shop for. And old Hal, with his big, bearish Ivy League good looks, and all that family money so he only had to play at making a living, two half-days a week in the office, and all that time on his hands, and all that booze. . . .

And tonight—*Yes, tonight. The same old story. But then again, maybe not. Maybe tonight is the time to split it open like a rotten melon. Everybody else in town must already know—why not just bring it all out in the open?* Before, the thought of doing that had been repugnant, better just not to look, but now the pain was getting to be too much to take. *Why not tonight? Why not just leave old Bud safe and sound at the Tav for half an hour in the middle of things this evening and drive up to the house about midnight?* He figured Hal would probably park his big blue Chrysler wagon in that half-hidden slot between the big tree and the fence, invisible from the street, he'd have to nose into the driveway to see it—and also block it. And then—well, he had a screamer in his car, too, that would bring all the lights on and the neighbors out in a hurry. . . . That was what this watch system was supposed to be all about, wasn't it? To drive thieves out into the open—wasn't it?

That, of course, had been exactly the point when Jack himself had first suggested the watch system two months ago. The plague itself hadn't really hit Brookdale, Connecticut, yet, even though it was savaging Boston and New Haven and outlying places like Guilford;

Brookdale was more self-contained, more of a total bedroom community, and the very few suspicious cases that had turned up so far had been hustled away fast to the big county hospital. Somehow, too, affluent Brookdale seemed to have a reasonable supply of S-3147 stockpiled at the Public Health Service offices, enough to treat contacts and suspected contacts, at least so far. Not inexpensive stuff, that drug, two thousand bucks for a four-day course for one person, and nobody seemed to know how Brookdale happened to have supplies on hand when a place like New Haven just plain didn't and couldn't get it—but then, this was not something one asked too many questions about, was it? When one happened to be a solid citizen in Brookdale? No, not really.

The trouble was that if plague itself had not been hitting comfortable, affluent Brookdale, other unpleasant things had. Packs of midnight raiders had begun assaulting the residential community, first in isolated incidents, then with accelerating frequency. Men and sometimes women began turning up here and there at secluded homes at two in the morning, heads covered with nylon stocking masks, well armed, kicking in doors, holding the husbands at gunpoint, gang-raping the mothers and daughters, stripping the houses of jewelry and money and blank checks and stereos and TVs and liquor and any guns that happened to be around. Not many places, at first, one here, one there, but then more and more, bolder, more atrocious, shooting the ones who resisted, hitting harder and more viciously every week. The police did their best to cope—but Brookdale's small police force was spread pretty thin anyway, and were hard to contact in a hurry when telephones were out half the time, or wires were cut—

At first people thought the bombers were Brookdale's own kids running wild on some kind of hideous break-loose lark—Brookdale had a singularly wild crowd of kids in high school and just out, home and hanging around, with colleges slamming their doors as fast as they could on all sides—kids who didn't care to account for their time, with lots of parents who just didn't care or had given up trying long since. But soon a large network of parents, cooperating and communicating with each other as the raids became more frequent and closer to home, found they couldn't pin things down to *their* kids, at least not with any consistency; *their* hellers, it developed, were mostly just getting off at local coke and pot parties where nobody was going anywhere much except sprawled out on the floor with the music going and all those cool vibes. These raiders were coming in from outside—

somewhere—who could know where? Brookdale was just a nice, juicy, defenseless target, like some other affluent communities in the area. . . .

Things had begun getting really raw when some of the raiders coming in obviously had the Horseman's hoofprints all over them in black and blue, coughing and spitting blood on their victims. The rawness intensified when they came into closer neighborhoods, when people could hear the carnage going on in the house next door and didn't dare do a thing, terrified to unbolt a door until they heard rubber squealing on the streets as the dog packs took off. It was about then that Jack Dillman and Angelo Curccio and Bud Elvin and a few others decided that Brookdale couldn't remain a juicy, defenseless target anymore, especially with the local police walking one by one through the town-council meetings demanding more money as hazard pay and threatening to strike, and no help from other towns because they were having their own problems—

It started off with block watches: porch lights and floodlights on, everybody supplied with screamers, *everybody* pledged to turn out at any hour, in case of trouble, everybody to watch everybody else's house throughout the night on regular shifts, to start a screamer going if they saw anything whatsoever that was suspicious. Firearms were voted down at first—Christ, somebody'd shoot some neighbor's ass off for sure—but in the first week they trapped three gangs by turning quiet little murderous raids into block-wide melees, blocking escape routes with cars sideways across streets and somebody snaking out to slash getaway tires and taking baseball bats and spading forks to the raiders until the cops came and hauled them away.

The effect was electrifying: the raids dropped sharply in frequency by the second week, and the raiders tended to bolt the minute the screamers went off. But the system didn't help the more isolated homes too much, and people were getting tired and going to sleep on watch. Fewer people could cover more territory, Jack pointed out at a meeting of twenty or thirty townspeople, if cars would just patrol all night and the drivers trigger screamers whenever they saw trouble. One person could cover several residential blocks effectively, and people living there would recognize which cars were theirs and which weren't. Some merchants from the neat shopping plaza downtown were at that meeting, and appealed for some citizen help patrolling the shops and stores—there had been looting, break-ins, trashing, and they didn't have any way to work all day and stand watch all night.

Ultimately it was decided that wives could do the driving, they'd be safe enough in cars as long as everybody responded to a screamer alarm in any neighborhood. They could take half-night shifts on regular rotation, eight-thirty to one, one to five, while the men with firearms could foot-patrol the business district on all-night shifts, in pairs, spread out so that each participating man drew the duty one night out of seven.

Some opted out, calling it an invitation to suicide, calling it vigilantism, but as the break-ins continued it made a certain sense to keep live male bodies, armed or not as they wished, highly visible on the downtown streets. The one place everybody sweated out was the huge Betterway supermarket down in the shopping mall; already a couple of small raids had resulted in smashed windows, and this was the one viable food-supply center for the whole town. It had constant trouble keeping stocked, but what was there was all there was, and Jake Sugarman, the manager, was breaking rules and letting people low on funds run up tabs, at least on cheap meats and staples, and people knew that store had to be kept going—especially with all the empty stores down in Westchester and Dutchess and the southern Connecticut counties.

So the watch patrols began, with Jack Dillman suddenly finding himself a leader and organizer and coordinator, such an unaccustomed role that he hardly knew what to do with it, but he worked to put it together. He and several others were formally deputized, and patrols walked the streets, and the women drove the neighborhoods and an uneasy peace settled on Brookdale. Except there was not all that much peace in some quarters, because tonight Jack Dillman would be taking patrol out of turn so that the man he was covering for could come over and tumble his wife. . . . *But why not split it open, tonight?*

At eight-thirty sharp Jack pulled his car into the bank parking lot, down at the edge of the shopping mall. He shoved a clip of shells into his M-1 and double-checked the safety. Then he cut across the corner of the green to the Village Tav. Bud Elvin, small, wiry and fortyish, was standing outside with a small .30-.30 carbine slung over his shoulder, talking to one of the local police. "You the lucky one again tonight, huh?" he greeted Jack.

"Yeah. I get all the luck. Didn't Hal call you?"

"Nah. But *that* don't surprise me."

"How did things go last night?" Jack asked the cop.

"Quiet. Been quiet all week." The cop grinned. "I think the sports are scared one of you guys is going to trip over his rifle and shoot somebody. This place has been like a morgue."

"Well, that's just what we have in mind," Jack said. "Anything special tonight?"

"Keep a close eye on the drugstore," the cop said. "Kennie reported a couple of strangers in there this afternoon, man and a woman, trying to pass some bad drug paper. He thought they might be just casing the place, scouting for somebody. So pay attention over there. And over at the Betterway, of course."

"Yeah, there's some good news, at any rate," Bud said. "Somehow Sugarman sprung a couple of fresh shipments loose from somewhere, last couple of days. Half a semi-load of side beef and pork came in yesterday from a packer out in Ohio, and new produce the day before, and flour and macaroni this afternoon. Jake was walking on air."

The cop got into his squad car, and Jack and Bud started off on foot. It was going to be a long one, Jack reflected, not a whole lot to watch for, really, until midnight, with the Betterway and the drugstore both open until eight, Clancy's Bar until ten, the Tav and a couple of the other watering holes even later. *If things stay quiet like this, maybe we can shove the starting time to 10:30 or 11:00, give a guy a little sleep,* he thought. They crossed the green, made the circuit of the Betterway with its big parking lot on three sides, its loading docks and the truck ramps down to basement storage around at the rear. Bud wasn't exactly the most scintillating company, hardly said a word from one hour to the next after his limited supply of small talk was exhausted and his two rancid jokes from the latest *Hustler* told. They circled their assigned blocks, keeping themselves highly visible under the bright parking lights in the Betterway store lot and the town streetlights elsewhere. Now and then they glimpsed other pairs patrolling other streets, once in a while walked down to confer. Ten-thirty came, then 11:30, and Bud was yawning; Jack was just getting more and more tense. Finally, a little after midnight he could stand it no longer. "I've got to take a quick check on something," he told Bud. "Take me a half an hour. We've seen no strange people or cars around. Why don't you go into the Tav for a quick beer? I'll be right back."

His hands were trembling as he let himself into his car, wheeled it down to the end of the business section, then up the winding wooded road toward the Heights and home. The drive took exactly eight minutes. He hesitated as he turned into the little three-house cul-de-sac to be sure a driver wasn't already swinging around there. Then he turned into his own driveway, cutting his lights.

58

The figure towering over Siddie Harper was a perfectly huge man, six feet eight at least, with shoulders as broad as a barn, enormous arms, hands like sledgehammers, thick-fingered, short-thumbed. He was bareheaded and dressed in assorted filthy rags leaving half of his vast expanse of chest bare. He was just standing there, staring down at her for a long while, and then he crouched down, reaching for her with those massive hands. "Hurt?" he said.

Siddie shrank away as he came for her until she saw the docile eyes and smooth, unlined baby face of the never-bright. He touched her scraped face with a thick finger, looked at the streak of blood. "Hurt?" he said again.

"No, not bad. Just a scrape." She edged back, still unsure. "Who're you?"

"Joey." He stared at her stupidly. "Not hurt?"

"No, no, but look, can you get me that chair?"

"Chair?"

"Over there." She pointed to the overturned wheelchair on the sidewalk. "Bring it over."

"Wheels!" the huge man walked over, picked up the chair like a toy. He spun one wheel and grinned, then tried the other, which jammed. "Won't go round."

"It's bent. Try to unbend it."

"Unbend?"

"Twist it straight, Joey, so it'll go around."

He turned the heavy chair over in his hands, grabbed the bent wheel and pressed it against his knee. It bent back straight like a cold licorice whip. "Goes around now."

She could see that the axle was bent too, but maybe that didn't matter. "Joey, put me in the chair. I can't get into it. My legs don't work."

He blinked at her. "Don't work? Hurt?"

"Yes, they're hurt. Just lift me up and put me in it."

"Lift up." He grinned. He knelt, picked her up like a rag doll, lifted her with surprising gentleness.

"In the chair, Joey."

"Yeah. In the chair." He got her into it, watched as she inspected the wheels, turned them, rolled the chair ahead a few feet and then rolled it back. Something went clank-clank underneath it as it rolled, but at least it *went.* "Well, thanks, Joey. Thanks a lot. Listen, do you know . . ." She paused, saw the big man wasn't tracking her, just watching her. "That store in the next block—you know?"

"Back there?"

"That's right. Is it still open?"

"Open?"

"Is the man still there?"

He shook his head. "All broke up. Nothin' there."

She looked at him, an idea formulating. She had to find food somewhere, get back home. There was still Tessie in a crumpled heap in the blankets in the other room. "Let's go see the store. You come along."

Joey followed her as she maneuvered the chair along the sidewalk. It was like one of the old Frankenstein movies she'd seen on the late show, with the monster following Igor like a huge, dangerous puppy. Maybe nobody'd bother her if Joey came along. Joey didn't seem to mind. Joey didn't seem to have anything to do. She questioned him, probing a little. Like probing a vast, soggy sponge. Joey didn't know where he lived except somewhere near the El. Joey didn't know how he'd gotten here or what he was doing here. Just wandering, eating garbage out of cans in alleys when he could find it. Too big for anybody to argue with or fight with. She couldn't tell if he'd always been dim or if something terrible had just recently happened to his mind—he couldn't tell her. He said he was forty-one, but he looked ageless as cast iron. He said he hadn't been sick, but he couldn't really remember. He couldn't put sentences together too well, and it was slow getting through, but there was *something* up there, not too capable but willing enough, and childlike and needing—

Joey was right about one thing—the little grocery store was a wreck, window smashed, door hanging open—but it hadn't been completely emptied. Some canned goods still sat here and there on the shelves—a few soups, canned vegetables and fruit, tomato juice—things nobody had wanted. "And cocoa!" Siddie cried, tossing one-pound cans to Joey. "Man once lived for a week on just cocoa, somewhere out west. I read about it somewhere. How much can you carry, Joey?"

"Carry?"

"Bags. Food." She got him to stacking cans of food and cocoa into grocery bags. "What about out back?" She pointed and Joey emerged from the rear with a fifty-pound bag of flour on his shoulder. Meanwhile Siddie found a pencil and began scribbling a list of things taken on a grocery bag, every item accounted for. "There's nobody here to make a deal with, but we don't steal. Maybe somebody'll come back." Before they packed out, with Joey laden like a pack mule, she made him drag some moldy wallboard from the back to block up the broken window and to get the door carefully closed. "Maybe nobody'll bother with it, and we can come back. Now let's get out of here."

Joey followed her, wonderingly, as she wheeled the banged-up chair back down the street. It was already getting dark and bitter cold, and she could hear the child crying again as they approached the building. At the stoop she made Joey set down the food. "Now you've got to help me upstairs again, somehow, I don't know how—"

"Upstairs?"

"Up." She pointed at the stairs, jabbed at the second-story window with her finger. "Maybe you can just drag it up—oh, Christ."

He wasn't tracking, just staring at the stairs and her in the wheelchair. Then suddenly he reached down and picked her up, chair and all, turned around and started up the stairs. She clutched one chair arm and threw her other arm around his heavy neck, felt his muscles strain to lift the chair high enough to clear the steps. He didn't pause until he reached the second-story landing and he wasn't even panting.

"Great," Siddie said. "That was great, I just hope you don't get mad at me. Now go back down and bring up the food." She pointed down the stairs again. "Down."

The man regarded her, utterly crestfallen. "I gotta go?"

"Not away, Joey, just bring the food up. The bags."

She was afraid he might forget and just wander off when he got down there, and he did get sidetracked for ten minutes watching a big yellow tomcat near the garbage cans in the alley, but finally she heard him plodding back up, thump—thump—thump, coming down the hall and dumping the bags on the kitchen table. He looked around the place like a child in wonderland as Sidonia followed him around in the chair. Then he saw the child's body in the bedroom corner in the blankets and he began crying. "It's okay, Joey. She won't hurt you. Won't hurt anybody, but she's got to go out of here, down to the street. I don't even know if there's a truck anymore." She got a wet washcloth, made him bend down and tied it across his mouth. "Keep it on. Take her down across the street. That's all we can do. Then come back."

After three repetitions he got it, lifted the body in a blanket like a sack of oats, and headed down. Siddie got a gas flame going on the stove—thank Jesus the supply was back on, at least for a while. When Joey came back she showed him the big copper clothes boiler. "Put water in it and put it on the stove. You've got to take a bath."

"Bath?"

"Wash all over. In the tub. Get the crud off, get Tessie's bugs off. I'll boil your clothes while you're at it."

It took forever, herding him into a tub with enough hot water poured in to take the chill off the tap water, getting his ragged clothes and Tessie's blankets into the boiler, digging a set of her biggest brother's pants and shirts out of a closet for Joey to put on, big enough that Joey only split one seam getting into them, and through it all the sound of the child crying, intermittently. She was exhausted, her body still wracked with the infection, but some ideas were formulating in her mind. Most everybody seemed gone from the building, or not showing, but there were some signs of life she had seen from out on the street. She knew *she* needed help—she was a prisoner up here without help—but there had to be other people around somewhere who needed help too. Maybe sick or getting sick, maybe dying, but if they could work together, they didn't have to be sick or dying alone in some icy room somewhere with the windows broken out. There could be safety in numbers—it might be easier to find something to eat together instead of each one grubbing for himself—and some body warmth in numbers too, mattresses and blankets to be pooled—certainly something better than crawling under front doorsteps to sleep and eating out of garbage cans like Joey had been doing. Of course they said it was trouble to be around too many people—one person gave it to another—but if they were all sick already anyway, what difference would it make? She wasn't sure, but she had a hunch that now that she was recovering she couldn't catch it again; if she'd been going to die from it, it already would have happened. There must be others who'd recovered, she'd heard about one or two before she got sick. She couldn't run up and down those stairs, go out and get things, but she and others that had recovered could at least help the sick ones. . . . *Somebody's got to do something, you can't just sit here and watch everybody die and not try to help—*

The crying started again, and she motioned to Joey. "You hear it?" He listened blankly and then nodded as if only now aware. "A baby. Downstairs somewhere, or maybe next door. Maybe all alone. Go look, Joey."

"Look?"

"Find the baby. Go down and look. Bring it back if nobody's with it; person can't leave a baby alone. You go, and I'll start cooking some—"

Joey was shaking his head, looking fearfully at the door into the hall. "Don't wanna go. Dark down there."

"Nothing's going to hurt you, Joey. Go look. Here." She dug under the wheelchair seat and brought out one of her most prized possessions, a little pocket flashlight. "Use this, then it won't be dark. But you bring it back, you hear?"

It didn't take him long; in ten minutes he was back carrying a year-old baby boy over his shoulder, bare naked and filthy, blue with cold and wailing, but breathing well and not coughing. Siddie already had some thin oatmeal cooking on the stove with some cocoa mixed in. She held the baby tight against her, got Joey to wrap a robe around her and sat hugging the child until it began to get warm, cooing to it and rocking it and presently feeding it a little of the porridge until it stopped crying and finally went to sleep.

With the baby sleeping on a blanket, Siddie directed Joey to get some boards over the broken window to keep the cold out, and she lit the oven to make some heat and cooked something up for the huge man and herself, opened some cans, made a pan bread and some cocoa. Joey kept eating as long as she kept cooking, he must have been starved, but hungry as she had felt, she didn't have any appetite after the first few bites; she was almost too tired to swallow. Just as well, for now, but that would change soon enough and she'd be famished like Joey—

There were footfalls on the stairs while they were eating, voices in the hall, and then the door suddenly banged open. Two men came in, not really men, they looked about fourteen, but obviously scavengers, bundled up in brand-new looted sweaters and hats with the tags still hanging on them. They stepped to either side of the door, leaving it open behind them. Sidonia turned her chair to face them. "What you men want?" she said. "We got nothing here."

"You got eats," the smaller one said. "Bags full. We seen you come out of the store. Seen the big guy haul 'em up. We'll take 'em."

"Oh, you think you will?" Siddie laughed as Joey slowly rose to his feet. Face-to-face with the huge man in the confines of the small room, the boys looked at each other and began edging toward the escapeway. Siddie laughed again. "Is that all you big men got to do with yourselves, going around robbing cripples and half-wits? What you gonna do when we say no, cut us up? Well, not from me you don't steal. Get out of here!"

"You don't need all them eats," the smaller one said, almost wheedling. "Bags full of 'em."

"We'll share with civilized folk, not with thieves. Now get out, the two of you, before I tell Joey here to fix you both. You hungry and want to act like civilized folk, you can come back and knock on that door, nice-like, and I'll cook you some eats."

The boys departed down the hall, but they didn't go far; she heard them shuffling and debating, start down the stairs, start back, stop.

She held her breath, looked at Joey, who looked back at her, not tracking at all. It was all bluff, she had no idea in the world that she could get Joey to attack the pair or even defend himself if attacked. *Probably not. He's shivering like a puppy.* But then after a long while the smaller boy came back up the hall and peeked in the door. "We're hungry," he said. "You cook us some eats?"

They came in and sat down on the floor, as far away from Joey as possible, while Siddie got busy. They were hungry, all right. With the menace gone out of them, they were just hungry kids. The big one didn't talk much, but the smaller one warmed up as his belly got full. They were brothers, lived just up in the next block; they knew about Siddie and her wheelchair from before. After the first wave hit, they'd teamed up and went "store-jobbin'," came back one night to find their mother and sisters gone, they didn't know where, maybe south, a lot of people were trying to go south for a while until too many got sick. For over a week now they'd been wandering, making it pretty much like Joey had, they weren't really big enough or strong enough to be effective bombers and none of the bigger guys wanted them around.

"You can sleep here if you want," Siddie told them when they finished eating, "there's blankets in the other room. But tomorrow you've got to do something for me. Go check all of this building and the other buildings on the block. Find out who's still here, who's sick, who needs help, and come back and tell me. You got legs and I haven't, you gotta be my legs tomorrow and my eyes too." She looked up. "No stealing, either. You go like civilized folk, just find out. Everybody's got a little food or blankets or clothes tucked away, and a lot don't need 'em anymore, and some got more need than others. We can bring the sick ones here, take care of them and maybe get some well, but nobody should have to die alone. . . ."

She went to sleep in her chair that night, too exhausted to shift herself out and not willing to wake Joey up once he went to sleep. She'd slept in her chair a lot, she didn't care. Tomorrow she'd get Joey to heat water for her and get a bath, boil her own clothes. She got the baby changed when it woke up, fed it a little more, then pulled off her clothes and wrapped up with the robe over her shoulders. She saw Joey was awake, watching her, but he didn't move.

Later she woke up with cold winter moonlight coming through the good window. Joey was up, moving around in the dark, back and forth, back and forth. "Joey?"

In the dim light he stopped by her chair, knelt down beside her and took her shoulders in his huge paws. It seemed like his face was wet. "Siddie help Joey?" he said, his voice cracking. He touched her body almost delicately.

"I can't, that way, Joey. I can't move my legs right. Maybe when I get stronger I can find a way."

"Siddie get stronger."

"Can't get much weaker. Bound to get stronger, with a little time." She reached out, pulled his head to her breast, cuddled him like the baby. "You can wait a while?"

He nodded. "Wait a while. Sure." He remained kneeling, hugging her for a long moment, then looked up. "Siddie take care of Joey?"

It was a different question, totally different, the cry of a helpless child. "You bet, Joey," she said softly. "We'll manage, one way or another. Cripples got to help each other, don't they?"

59

Back in Wichita, very late that night, Sally Grinstone was far from pleased when Frank told her he'd gone the straight route with Sam MacIvers. "Trouble with you, Frank, you're just too goddam honest," she said as he munched away at fried potatoes and pork chops and she drank gin and orange juice. "I'm very nervous about giving too much away at this point. I wish I could tell you what I'm nervous about, but I can't. Just one of old Sally's famous hunches, I guess."

Somewhere up on the second story of the big building Frank could hear voices arguing vigorously—Tom Shipman and Monique, having at it as usual, something that sounded very technical, unaware that he was back. "I figured it was the least I could do," Frank said. "And there isn't any doubt that those doctors are with us."

"Oh, they're with us, all right. Trouble is, they're only with us *second.* First of all, they're part and parcel of that community, that's *got* to be their first concern, and there's the rub. If they decide to second-guess us on the timing, or spring it to the wrong people . . ." She sighed. "I suppose you had to give them our location and telephone contact too."

"Just to MacIvers, and I made him swear he wouldn't share it with anybody. I also warned him not to cry wolf, told him we'd bag the whole thing if he pulled that on us. He sees the picture. And I only gave him Running Dog's number and address, not ours. The Dog can come flag us if word comes through."

"Well, that's all right, if that fat little bastard will just hang around for a while. I don't know what I'd do without him, but you never know what he's going to be coming up with next." Sally had contacted Dog Runs Quickly two days after her first encounter with him, and the spaniel-eyed fat man with the drooping mustache had soon become Sally's eyes and ears and feet. Despite appearances, Running Dog had proved uncommonly bright, perceptive and canny, possessed of a fascinating capacity to fade in and out of scenes with startling swiftness, entirely apt to turn up right at your shoulder when you thought he had to be five miles away on an errand. Fast on his feet, that man, and very quiet; once she had gotten him moving she couldn't slow him down, and the nickname, which he first applied to himself, perfectly deadpan, stuck. He was only five feet two, round as a pumpkin and capable of eating more food than three normal people combined; Sally once ruminated aloud that maybe it was his thyroid but she was not about to check and find out. With security an ever-increasing concern, Dog's quicksilver ability to be all places at all times, to see and hear everything and know everything that was happening within a two-mile radius had proven absolutely indispensable.

"Yes," Sally agreed, "Dog will certainly flag us if he gets a message from Willow Grove. Meanwhile, I don't worry about our doctor friends one-tenth as much as I worry about this public-health chap Haglund. He should have been there with bells on today. In a half-assed way, he is our CDC representative in Willow Grove, Nebraska, our sole and single and absolutely only claim to legitimacy. So you went up there specifically to review the setup and the plan, and make sure everybody understood what was going to happen, and really essentially to cock the hammer for the trigger-pull—and Haglund is out of town for two days. What other business forced him to be out of town at this particular time? What other business could be more important?"

"There wasn't any 'other business,'" Frank said around a mouthful of potatoes. "And he wasn't out of town, either. I saw him walking out of the Willow Grove Public Health office at three in the afternoon while I was driving around doing some last-minute geographicals before heading home. I recognized his face—he was one of the ones at Canon City."

"Oh, boy." Sally shook her head and took a belt of her gin. "Did he see you?"

"I don't think so. But he was headed for the hospital; I followed him a little way. He seemed to be in quite a hurry."

"Well, I don't like this," Sally said heavily. "I believe in my hunches, and I have a very bad hunch that when the time comes, we're never going to get this stuff up to that town—we're going to be intercepted and busted."

"On what grounds?"

"We're *illegal,* and from CDC's point of view, maybe very dangerous. I rang Haglund in because he and the doctors were all they have up there, and he understood epidemiology, and I would have sworn I had him sold—but maybe I didn't. Maybe he turned right around and got on the horn."

"To where?"

"Atlanta, maybe. Or the state bulls. Or Christ knows to where;

anywhere that we wouldn't want. We could get busted right out of orbit at the wrong time and the whole thing could go down the drain."

Frank Barrington scratched his chin. "Maybe you're just begging trouble," he said finally. "Maybe Haglund was genuinely busy with something, maybe actually out of town in the morning. *I* don't know. But as for moving the stuff north, there's more than one way to skin a cat. If worst comes to worst, we can pull the old poacher's trick for getting the dead elk down the mountain."

"What's that?"

"He knows the terrain and all the roads, and he knows where the warden is going to try to stop him if somebody's blown the whistle on him. So he never goes up the mountain alone. His buddy takes a second rig, and they fill one rig with firewood and his buddy takes it down through the checkpoint first. If it's all clear, his buddy comes back and they go on down together. If it's not clear, he goes through the checkpoint and right on home. Then when buddy-boy doesn't come back, the poacher ditches the elk and the tarps and comes down with a load of firewood himself and smiles sweetly at the warden and then comes back with his buddy at three A.M.—or else he goes down some other way, some long, hard, back road, figuring there's only so much of that warden to spread around."

Sally looked thoughtful. "I suppose you could take Running Dog to ride shotgun for you."

"Not shotgun, not if we're worried about state police. Just interference."

"And then sprout wings and fly at the right time, I suppose."

Frank grinned. "If we have to, we can get resourceful. But we'll get that stuff through there."

After a while Sally went back to her staging plans, and Monique and Tom apparently reached agreement upstairs, they were now talking quietly and using the blackboard, and Frank went to bed. There were lots of things to be done tomorrow, and the next day, and the next. They really needed at least two more weeks before they were ready to deal with Willow Grove, three would be better, but the word coming in on TV and radio, when there was any word, was that little places like Willow Grove all over the Midwest and South were getting hit fast, without warning, one by one, no rhyme nor reason why. There would be no guessing in advance when the call might come. All they could do was pray for three weeks.

They didn't get their three weeks. The word came from Willow Grove exactly eight days later.

60

The porch and yard lights were blazing, as they should have been, when Jack Dillman turned into the drive, but the house itself was totally dark. He edged forward until he could see the concealed parking slot. No blue Chrysler station wagon. No car at all except Carmen's little Honda sitting where it belonged in the carport.

Slowly Jack backed out of the drive, eased his car around the cul-de-sac and out onto the street. He had been so certain, so absolutely certain that now he felt a wave of total confusion. *If Hal had come over at all, he'd still be here, he wouldn't have wasted four good hours. And she wouldn't have been idiot enough to go walking someplace—and they wouldn't have driven anyplace, not with safe harbor right here. Ergo. . . .*

He turned down the hill, driving faster now and inexplicably uneasy. He really hadn't had any business leaving old Bud holding the bag, even in the safety of the Tav. He hadn't had any business leaving the patrol at all. He parked by the bank again, started running across toward the Tav and then stopped sharply. The lights were off, the place totally dark. Half a block down the street he saw Bud's car parked at the curb on the town-green side of the street, under a streetlight. Someone behind the wheel. *They must have closed up and tossed him out,* Jack thought. *But why so early?*

He hesitated, M-1 in his hand. Something about the tableau—the dark building fronts across the street, the empty green, the lone car parked with the figure behind the wheel, something about it was wrong. Something in Jack's mind shrieked *Take cover!* and he moved, sprinting for the building fronts across the street. In the same split second there was a flash of light and a cracking report from a low building rooftop to his left. Something hit the curb behind where he had been and whined away in ricochet. Two more cracks as he ducked across the street; he saw a chunk fly out of a telephone post. Then he hit the storefront, flattened to it, looking back for any sign of his assailant. "Bud!" he screamed. "Don't get out. Get down!" He heard a clear echo of his words in the empty night.

Silence. Nothing moved. In a burst of motion he pelted down the street toward Bud's car, hugging the storefronts. A little short of the car he stopped. He could see, now: the glass of the driver's window showed a ragged hole and the figure was slumped forward, angling across the steering wheel.

He had just hit the trigger to his screamer when he heard the roaring sound, felt the ground shake as the two huge semi trailers roared down the street. The first turned into the Betterway store lot, roared across and swung to a stop directly in front of the big windows. The second truck halted with a squeal of air brakes a few storefronts back and Jack saw the figure of the rooftop sniper leap for the top of the semi. It was a long jump; the leaper caught with just one foot, sprawled on the truck top, rifle still in hand.

For Jack Dillman, thirty-year-old reactions moved him, rescued him. Without conscious thought he was on one knee in a doorway, sighting, squeezing the trigger, seeing the man on the truck roof topple to the street as the heavy rifle slammed Jack's shoulder. Jack dove for the shelter of Bud's car, caught the fallen man with another shell as he grappled for his rifle. Then the truck moved forward, its New York plates clear in the streetlight. Jack fired at the windshield point-blank, saw a chunk of it fall away, and then the truck swerved into the Betterway lot and roared across it, around the back toward the loading docks.

Many things happened at once, then. The first truck's rear doors burst open and people poured out—five, six, seven, it looked like. There was an earsplitting crash of glass as the front window of the store went. At the same time, down the block, another screamer went off and then another, and somewhere farther away sirens were sounding. Off to Jack's right a rifle cracked, followed by the crash of broken glass—a near-miss that went into the store. The shot was suddenly answered by a rattle of submachine gun fire from the truck—and the night air exploded into a barrage.

The raiders had been ready. The first out had gone into the store and started loading; now half a dozen more poured out and deployed themselves with the truck for cover, commanding a wide semicircle across the store parking lot and the green. At the far side of the green a police car roared down a side street, skidded to a halt amid a spray of bullets and backed abruptly into a protected alleyway to unload three uniformed men.

From his vantage point, Jack could see the trouble all too clearly. The thing had been planned beautifully; the front truck all but hid the storefront, providing access to the interior for the loading crew and protection for their covering firepower. The truck was doubtless armored—he'd heard accounts of this; it could take a bazooka shell to punch a hole in it, and with snipers and machine gunners protected, the police and townspeople couldn't get close. A pitched battle going on, all kinds of sound and fury in front of the store—but the heavy loading was going on in *back* at the loading docks where the second truck had gone, where the side meat and flour and sugar and macaroni was stored and where nobody was interfering. When *that* truck got full it would move out and plow through anything that got in its way, leaving the front truck to follow with rear-guard protection, carrying whatever incidental things there had been time to load into it.

There had to be a tip-off somewhere, Jack thought. This was one of the gangs from the south, working out of the Bronx or Yonkers, hitting stores like clockwork. It wasn't coincidence that they had turned up here tonight just after two days' worth of food shipment had come in. Somebody tipped them—*and they were going to get away with it if somebody didn't get back of that store and cripple that truck. . . .*

There was a little time—you don't fill a whole semi full of meat and flour in fifteen minutes. He was safe enough crouched in the doorway with Bud's car for cover, but he was a wide-open target if he moved. The street lighting and the big parking-lot floods had been to the town's advantage before, illuminating the downtown area so the watchers could spot trouble—but now that light was keeping him from where he wanted to go. In the floodlights, he was dead. If he could douse them, he might possibly get back to cripple that truck. . . .

He had fired four shells from an eight-round clip. He had two more clips in his pocket—why the extra he didn't know. He crouched back in his hidey-hole, sighted the streetlight above him and fired.

He'd been a top marksman in Korea, and those reflexes carve a crease in the brain that doesn't go away. He was back thirty years—and the light went out. He turned to the first side parking-lot light. Pop! It was gone too. Then to his amazement, two more went, with two sharp reports from his right. He had a friend. . . .

In the relative darkness he ran an evasive pattern back up the sidewalk toward where those reports had come from. Then he heard a voice: "Jack! In here!"

It was Angelo Curccio in a store doorway at the far corner of the green. Jack ducked in, backed against the door. "You're a good shot, Angelo."

"Yeah. So I discover."

"There's nobody in the back. They're making a big fuss out front."

"Yeah. I know."

"That ain't no accident."

"I know."

"You got shells? Let's get the rest of those damned lights."

Two minutes later their side of the Betterway parking lot was dark. "What do you have in mind, Jack?"

"We've got to kill that truck or it's going to take away three months' food. Let's work around."

Together they worked to the right, around against storefronts until they could see the rear loading area of the store. The fire barrage went on in front. Then Angelo stopped. "Hey. Wait a minute."

Jack stared across at the rear loading area. There wasn't one truck. There were two, side by side. "That delivery this afternoon—looks like the truck didn't leave, and we didn't notice it. They could have been loading all evening, and nobody saw them. They could be ready to bolt."

"Yeah." Angelo leaned alongside Jack to peer. "Then we gotta cripple both trucks. How?"

"Front axle. Tires. That's the only thing that will stop them. They'll run rims on the rear. Let's go."

They started across the darkened lot toward the trucks in a broken field pattern, crouching low, heading for the side of the building, where they would be momentarily out of sight. Men were still loading the truck nearest the loading dock, totally oblivious to anything but their work. Jack didn't see any gunmen covering the trucks under the huge spotlight over the loading dock, but he saw the light. No chance to get near the trucks with that light blazing away. The light had to go. But there was another obstacle before they could reach the loading docks: a small-truck ramp leading down to a basement unloading area, for bread trucks and beer trucks to get in and out fast when a semi was occupying the loading dock for half a day. If they went out around the ramp, they'd be wide open to fire, no cover of *any* sort. If they went down into it, they'd have cover at least momentarily and they'd be closer, able to see better to make a rush. . . .

He felt Angelo's hand on his shoulder, a hoarse whisper in his ear. "We're going to have to rush them to get those front tires. There's no other way."

"I know."

"If you could get down into that ramp, you could cover me. Then I could rush, get both trucks fast and keep on going. There's cars for cover on the other side."

"It could work if I could douse that big light," Jack said. "I'll kill it if I can, and run for the ramp. Then you go."

He edged to the corner of the building, rifle at ready. For an instant it seemed to him he was transported in time, slipped a cog back to thirty years earlier in a little town in North Korea, when he and another Angelo and a dozen other men were moving from building to building in pitch-darkness, facing sniper fire they could only pin down by the muzzle flares of their rifles, trying for an ammo truck that had to be blown. They'd gotten the ammo truck at the cost of four men, and then been pinned down in bombed-out rubble for three days before their backup finally came in. There'd been a big floodlight there, too, guarding the approach to where the ammo truck was housed. He'd taken that light. . . .

He stepped out from the corner, flinching at the light hitting his face, took fast aim and blew the light. Then he ducked and ran at top speed, low to the ground, for the ramp. He heard a rattle of fire as he reached it, heard slugs thunking the corner of the building, and dove headfirst into the slot of the ramp, rolling downward as he landed, right back onto his feet, his heart hammering. He froze, listening. No more fire, but they had the corner pinned; Angelo would have to wait a little. Angelo had *better* wait.

Jack glanced down the ramp, checking for a possible escapeway, and realized suddenly that there was a car parked there, not two feet down the ramp from where he'd landed. He peered through the darkness, caught the shadow of the grillwork. He knew that car, a big Chrysler wagon. For an instant he thought someone was in it and ducked down, but one step and one quick glance told him different. Nobody in it—but it was packed to the roof, fairly stuffed full with flour sacks, rice sacks, large irregular lumps that looked like sides of beef. . . .

The discovery had taken only seconds, but it was enough. Jack raised his head over the far edge of the ramp, searching the gloom around the trucks for some shadowy movement. The men loading were cursing the darkness now and flashlights were appearing. He thought he saw a dark form around the rear corner of the outermost truck, but he couldn't be sure, and then it seemed to be gone. He brought the M-1 up, rested the barrel on the edge of the ramp. *Okay, Angelo. Any time now. Go!*

He heard footfalls and Angelo went, a gray blur in the darkness, out around the end of the ramp toward the trucks. Jack saw the dark form reappear at the corner of the truck and he fired instantly, saw the form crumble, his rifle going off in the air as he hit the ground. Then Angelo was between the trucks. Another black form moved; Jack saw a muzzle flare at the same time he felt a heavy blow to his right shoulder. He got two more shells off, then heard more rifle shots echoing from the loading dock, near the front of the trucks, but he couldn't get his arm to move to his pocket to get his other clip of shells. Vaguely he could hear somebody bellowing, *"Let's get this mother moving,"* vaguely heard truck motors starting up, saw one truck move and then veer insanely left into the very path of the other, the cab listing badly. And Jack was talking to his arm, repeating the words, "Let's get this mother moving," but his arm wouldn't move. Once again he saw the wagon parked down the ramp, realized his vulnerability, and groped with his left arm for a grip, hauled himself out of the ramp, out of the direct path of the car and onto the tarmac of the parking lot. And then suddenly everything was dim and spinning and he saw himself turning a giant cartwheel as he went over on his face on the pavement, and that was all he saw or heard.

Sometime later there were bright lights and voices and movement. A spotlight from the fire-station aid car was in his eyes and two men, vaguely familiar, were trying to hoist his considerable bulk onto a stretcher. His right shoulder was throbbing violently and his hand was still numb, but he could move the fingers and the arm again. The men moved back when they saw him trying to struggle up onto his left elbow, move his right arm. "I think you just fainted or something," one of them told him. "The slug went through high in the biceps and under your shoulder. Must have hit a rib and ricocheted behind. Tore up some muscle and gave your brachial plexus quite a jolt but it didn't get bone, or anything vital. Lucky."

"Angelo?"

The man shook his head. "Truck got him when they tried to take off. Creamed him. They didn't get the rig out of the lot, but they got Angelo. Bastards."

"What about *them?*"

"Got fifteen of them down at the station. Four took off on foot, but they won't get far. Now we've got to get you down and X ray that shoulder—"

"Hold it." Jack struggled upright, peered around at the people milling around the parking lot, patrol cars here and there, the ramp. The Chrysler wagon was gone. "Where's a cop? I've got to tell him something."

"The Sergeant was here a minute ago." The man gave a shrill whistle, motioned to somebody, and a cop loomed out of the dark, crouched down by Jack. "Look, there was a station wagon down that ramp," Jack told him. "It was Hal Parker's. Now it's gone."

"Yeah, a couple of guys saw it go, just after Angelo hit the truck. He must have gone for more ammo or something, he was on patrol."

"No. That wagon was full of food. I saw it. And he wasn't on patrol. I took his place."

The Sergeant frowned. "Then what was his wagon doing here? I don't follow."

"Don't even try. Just check out his basement good and fast and see what you find."

The officer stood up, hesitated, looked back down at Jack. "You sure it was his?"

"It was his. Hidden down the ramp, there, packed full of food. Look, somebody had to tip that gang, Sergeant—they didn't just happen by—and somebody got paid off. He drove in early, they loaded him, and he took off when he thought he had a chance. All the action was supposed to stay out front—and I wasn't supposed to be telling anybody anything, either."

Later, in the emergency room, Carmen was waiting when he came out of X ray, arm splinted, walking unsteadily. She was wearing an old bathrobe and pink slippers. She caught his arm and steadied him, warm pressure in her grip. "You goddam fool. Come sit down someplace before you go over on your face." Not harshly. She guided him like a mother guiding a blind child.

"Just a little brush fire, kid."

"Yes, so I heard. We've got a town full of heroes. That crowd has been hitting stores all over the East. Five in one week."

He sat down, still holding her hand. He looked up at her. "And I was wrong."

"This time, yes." She gave him a weak smile.

"He had it double-loaded. He was sure I'd be nailed."

"I know. The putrescent bastard. But you weren't, and that's what matters to me."

"He did have a little motivation," Jack said.

"I know—but not anymore. Jack, let's go home. We can take care of that shoulder there."

"Is that what you want?"

"Yes. That's what I really want."

PART V

WILLOW GROVE, NEBRASKA

61

In Wichita it was just after midnight when Frank Barrington was jarred awake by somebody shaking his shoulder. He saw Running Dog's sad spaniel eyes and drooping mustache in the flashlight beam. "Okay, Frank. Time to head north."

"MacIvers? When'd he call?"

"Midnight. Ten minutes ago."

The Indian retired to the little kitchen to heat up coffee. Frank shook Monique awake, then pulled on warm clothes and went out for coffee too, cradling the heavy mug in his cold hands. Tom Shipman and Sally came down from their sleeping loft. Sally looked small and untidy and childlike. She also looked frightened. "This is going to put you in Willow Grove about five-thirty A.M.," she said. "Why's he calling so late? Why not six hours ago—or in the morning so you could drive in daylight?"

"Beats me," Frank said. "Did he have any message?"

Running Dog shook his head. "He just said to make tracks, now was the time."

"Then I guess that's the message. Well, the van's loaded, and you've got extra gas in the pickup. We'd better move out. It's going to be a long, cold trip, I think."

Monique set her coffee cup down, looking huge and bear-like in her goosedown jacket and trousers. "Are you still sure you want me to go along? I've got cultures growing—"

"Tom knows what they are, doesn't he? He and Sally can tend them for you for the time being. We're going to need a competent microbiologist where we're going, and I don't think we'll find any in Willow

Grove, Nebraska. Anyway, if you think I'm going up there without you, you're out of your wits. We've got a hell of a lot riding on this little deal. I'm going to need all the help I can get."

"You think there's going to be trouble tonight?" Sally said.

"I sure do."

"Well, whatever happens, for God's sake don't let that cargo get away from you. This thing has got to work. If that stuff doesn't get to Willow Grove, we might as well fold up and go home."

"Don't worry, Sal. The stuff is going to get there, and it's going to work. It just may not be all hearts and flowers along the way, that's all."

Outside it was an even four degrees below zero. Frank checked signals with Running Dog for a final time. Then he and Monique climbed into the van, Running Dog into the pickup. The van was packed to the roof with cases of Tom's antibiotic; the whole vehicle smelled like rotting hay. They wove through the dark city and headed north on I-235, the pickup in the lead. At the interchange they caught I-35 West and moved up across flat country, the van lagging just enough to keep Dog's taillights in view. There was an icy wind coming out of the northwest, and the fields were still spotted with patches of last week's snow, but the highway was bare and dry.

At Salina they stopped for coffee, then headed due west on I-70. It was a desolate drive through desolate country, flat, flat, flat, the only sign of life the occasional barnyard light of a distant farm, a rare truck blaring past in the night. Frank drove in silence, felt Monique curl up against his shoulder and presently begin snoring softly. Frank was feeling as bleak as the countryside, a sense of desperate grayness growing in his mind. It was all very fine to assure Sally that the goods would be delivered, but the one significant thing that Dr. Sam MacIvers *hadn't* told Running Dog over the phone was that everything was clear.

So what can they do? Frank thought. *We aren't running contraband. This stuff doesn't carry a dangerous-drug classification. Unapproved and totally illegal to use, maybe, but not dangerous. Until it's actually distributed, we've broken no laws, and with a licensed physician actually doing the prescribing and dispensing, they'd need a court injunction and some muscle for enforcement to stop us.* So he kept telling himself, but it didn't make him feel any better. Actually, if they got their hands on the stuff—whoever or whatever "they" might be—they could do any damned thing they chose to, and there was the rub.

Anything anybody did to delay things at this point would be absolutely fatal. MacIvers's call meant that plague was in Willow Grove, Nebraska, *now.* If their plans to stop it and turn it back were blocked, Willow Grove, Nebraska, was dead in the water, and the Shipman antibiotic along with it.

At a place called Wa Keeney, Kansas, they stopped for gas and coffee and a final warming-up. Frank asked Dog if he needed some rest from driving, but the man shook his head. "Might as well just plow on through and get there," he said. "We turn north through Wheatville, right? Any particular place you're looking for trouble?"

"If somebody's really trying to nail us," Frank said, "it'll probably be right at the Nebraska border, just north of French River—but we'll make our move about ten miles this side of the town just in case." He opened up a map, pointed with a huge finger. "This little road off to the left—there's a big white barn and some willow trees right at the junction. We'll stop there. You go on. Just play it cool—you know what to do."

Wheatville, Kansas, didn't amount to a great deal: a couple of stores, a gas station, a grain elevator, all dark and deserted. They drove on north to the junction with State Route 603, then north again across more undulating country. It was nearly 4:00 A.M. Presently the pickup slowed as a white barn and willow trees appeared at a country road turnoff up ahead. Dog winked his taillights twice and drove on through, disappearing over a slight rise in the land. Frank eased the van off onto the shoulder, idled the motor and sank back with a sigh. "Well, kid, now we find out."

"Dog's going on to Willow Grove?"

"Right. There's no reason he should be detained—nobody knows him, and the pickup's empty—but he's got good eyes even if he isn't stopped. If everything's clear right through to the clinic in Willow Grove, he should be back here to give us the word within an hour and a half, even allowing time for a flat tire."

"And if everything isn't clear?"

"Then he won't be back. No news will be bad news."

"So what do we do in that case?"

Frank grinned. "You just keep your eyes open. We're going to get this stuff to Willow Grove whether he comes back or not. It's just a matter of how. For the time being, we just wait—but not out here on the highway."

He turned the van up the country road past the barn. All that could be seen in the darkness was the hard-frozen lane in the headlights and two or three distant farm lights. In a mile or so the road rose, then dipped down a gulley to follow a small stream, with willows and elms crowding in on either side. They followed the creek for a couple of miles. Then the road turned back up onto the rise again. Monique saw a fence and an open gate flash into view, then some ramshackle abandoned farm buildings in the headlights. Frank drove the van to the edge of a large open barnyard and killed the motor and the lights. "Good place to wait," he said laconically. "Not much traffic."

Cold began seeping into the van the moment the engine stopped. Frank pulled Monique over to him, kissed her and pulled a big puffy sleeping bag around them. They sat in silence for a long while. Icy stars glinted like cold sparks in the black sky. Now and then Frank snapped on the dashboard lights to check his watch.

"Frank?"

"Mmmm?"

"You don't really think Running Dog is coming back, do you?"

"Nope."

"Why not?"

He sighed. "I had a long talk with MacIvers on the phone about a week ago. He was almost certain that Haglund, the public-health man, had something up his sleeve. Seemed to him that Haglund was bad-mouthing the plan to everybody in sight, especially some of the town fathers, consulting a lot with the local police, doing his best to get people nervous about it. Haglund insisted he was with us, but all he seemed to talk about was how maybe he could spring some vaccine loose from somewhere in time to do some good, and that was really all he wanted to plan on. Trouble was, no vaccine was turning up. Well, I *saw* Haglund when I took my trip up there. I *know* he was at Canon City, and I'm almost certain he was one of the CDC people there. I'd cover any bet you could name that he's been on the line to somebody in Atlanta about what we're planning here, and that they don't like it."

"How can you be so sure?" Monique frowned. "If they took it seriously, it would get to Ted Bettendorf. He's reasonable enough—and right now he might be glad for any help he could get anywhere."

"Then why hasn't MacIvers heard from him? Had some offer of cooperation? Honey, you know CDC better than I do, but nice guy or not, Bettendorf could never go for this. At the very best he'd have to assume we were ignorant meddlers, and at the worst, bloodthirsty profiteers with a dangerous product to sell."

"But we're not either one."

"We know that, but CDC doesn't. They could feel obliged to block us any way they could, using local police or state patrol or even federal men if there's any office functioning out here anymore. Even if they thought Tom's drug might be worth something, they couldn't let us do what we're planning. We're not working through them, and we're totally outside the Food and Drug regulations. We're just not doing it the right way."

"But *God,* Frank! If something can help, how can there be any *wrong* way? CDC has put all their money on the cities and lost every dime. The FDA is dead at the switch—the only move they've made *at all* in the last six months has been to give the go-ahead to the wrong people to distribute the wrong drug. Other than that they haven't done anything but sit there fibrillating and getting in the way. I *know,* I was so close to it at Fort Collins I wanted to sit down and cry. So we're trying to do something in a different way. Trying to move *around* them and make something work. How can that be wrong?"

Frank shrugged. "By definition, pushing a wildcat drug in the middle of a plague is *wrong,* honey. Ask any epidemiologist. Hell, suppose *you* were responsible and you heard about something like this—you'd try to stop it too. You couldn't risk having some irresponsible idiot, however well meaning, piling dead on top of dead. Of course, we *know* the stuff we've got is good—or at least we think we do, and unlike some other nuts who might be operating, we've got some reasonably solid reasons to think we're right. But they aren't going to take our word for that. We're going to have to make an end run clear around them and make Tom's stuff work in the field, under fire, in order to prove we're right."

Monique was silent for a long while, staring out at the icy darkness. "You didn't tell Sally and Tom about this little phone talk with MacIvers," she said at length.

"There didn't seem to be any point," Frank said. "Sally's jittery enough as it is. She's totally exhausted, and there's nothing more she can do at all until we see what happens at Willow Grove, and she's frantic enough to climb walls. But for planning and organizing the next step, if there is a next step, Sally Grinstone is our ace in the hole. We can't afford to have her falling apart at this point."

"I'm not hanging together so well myself," Monique said sourly.

"Ah, but you've done this kind of battle before, you see. Sally hasn't. And that makes all the difference. Anyway, you're not going to have to hold yourself together too much longer. My watch says Dog is already overdue."

"So what do we do now?"

"Give him another hour."

"And then what? Frank, you're not seriously going to try to plow through a roadblock with this stuff!"

He grinned at her. "You just watch," he said.

They waited—thirty minutes, forty minutes, a full hour. From time to time Frank got out, walked around the van, stamping his feet. Monique watched him through the windshield. Then in the darkness she saw him stop, cock his head to one side as though watching the sky. A moment later Monique sensed an almost subliminal vibration that gradually emerged into a crescendo rumble and then the familiar chuff-chuff-chuff of a chopper's rotor.

Frank fairly leaped back into the car and pulled the headlight switch on. "Here comes our end run," he said. "Grab that other flashlight on the dash and come on out."

A moment later Frank picked up the chopper in his flashlight beam, wig-wagged it and stepped back as the little craft swooped down, hovered, and then touched ground on its own landing lights. The instant the rotor stopped a door popped open and a lean young man in dungarees hopped down. "Barrington?"

"Right."

"Your canine friend made it in, all right, but he didn't want to come back. They've got the highway blocked at the border. Sam says there's no time to screw around—I'm supposed to bring you and the cargo both."

"Better take a look at the cargo first," Frank said. "You're Dr. Fox?"

"That's me."

"What's the score in town?"

The young doctor paused and looked at him. "You mean the clinical picture? Lousy. Two confirmed cases yesterday morning, seven more identified for sure by last evening, and Sam has been up all night. I'd say maybe twenty-five cases with at least two hundred contacts. Except for that bastard Haglund we'd have called twelve hours earlier." Fox stuck his head in the van along with a flashlight and whistled. "Good God, how much have you got here?"

"About thirty thousand individual doses," Frank said.

"Wow. Maybe I can get it all crammed in and still lift, but I can't take you."

"Just take the drug and jump. We'll get there on our own."

It took precisely ten minutes to unload the van and cram the chopper full of cartons. The young doctor grinned and climbed aboard, waving them back from the rotor and slamming the door. A moment later he lifted and headed in a long sweep north. Frank gave Monique a hug as the chuff-chuff-chuff faded into the darkness. "Okay, kid, hop in," he said. "Let's go give those border cops a look at an empty van."

62

When they finally arrived at the Family Health Clinic in Willow Grove a little after 7:00 A.M., the parking lot looked like a major disaster scene, crowded with local squad cars, state patrol cars, an Aid Car from the fire station and half a dozen other vehicles, including Running Dog's pickup.

Their trip across the border had not been totally uneventful. They had been flagged down by State Patrolmen a hundred yards north of the border, invited to step out into the biting cold while their identification was examined, their persons and the van thoroughly searched by a couple of very unenthusiastic officers. One of them even got down on the frozen pavement and examined the van's undercarriage with a big flashlight, while the other quizzed them about their origins and destinations, questions that Frank answered as noncommittally as possible with as much patience and forbearance as possible. "They said it would probably come through in a van," the first one muttered, climbing back to his feet, "but there's no goddam dope or anything in this rig." Frank and Monique had climbed into the car again and started the motor while the two police continued to confer interminably, one shrugging his shoulders and the other spreading his hands until finally, with most obvious total reluctance, one of them motioned them on and they drove on north.

Inside the clinic building the waiting room and reception desk were both jammed with people. Dr. Sam MacIvers, looking sour as vinegar, was hunched over the reception desk talking on the telephone; young

Dr. Whitey Fox, still in dungarees, was at another phone. Police and civilian-clothed people milled around the waiting room, drinking coffee; in the far corner Frank saw Running Dog's fat form sprawled in a chair, sleeping. Near the center of the room was the man Frank recognized as Perry Haglund, short and chubby and red-faced, talking intently and gesticulating with vehemence to a town policeman with sergeants' stripes on his sleeve. But the center of attention seemed to be a tall, gray-haired man at the side of the room, surrounded by several others—a round-shouldered tired-looking hawk of a man with lines of infinite weariness on his face. Frank heard Monique's sudden intake of breath beside him as she saw the man standing there, and then the man looked up and saw her and raised his head sharply, staring at her. "Good God, it's Monique," he bellowed, striding across the room to her. "I've been trying to track you down for weeks. What in the name of God are you doing here?"

"I'd ask you the same, except I already know," Monique said. "Frank, this is Dr. Ted Bettendorf, Carlos's old boss, head of the Uncommon Diseases Section of CDC in Atlanta. Ted, this is Frank—"

"—Barrington," Bettendorf interrupted. "That's got to be it. You were with Carlos in Canon City. I never got out there—you guys were sure you had it whipped right there. Oh, boy. And then there was Savannah, and Carlos was gone, and we've never stopped running since. . . ." His voice trailed off and he looked at Monique again as if trying to focus on her face and not quite making it. "But why here? What are you doing here? We're trying to stop these idiot doctors from using a batch of bathtub antibiotic that hasn't had the breath of a clinical test, and it's gotten here somehow, but we can't even get our hands on a sample of the damned stuff, and then *you* walk in, of all people—"

Across the room Sam MacIvers reared his head back and clapped a hand over the telephone mouthpiece. "Hey, would you people mind *canning* it over there? I've got a sick woman on this telephone. Frank, glad you're here. Get the other line, will you? Everything you can learn, write it down." The doctor turned back to the phone again as if the rest of the room had ceased to exist. "Okay, Janie, give me that again, we've got a bunch of people interfering with us right now. You say his fever is a hundred and three since he woke up? Chest tight and he's coughing. No blood? Good. Now listen, this is important. First thing is don't panic—you're going to have to hang together and lay down some law. Don't let him go to work, don't even let him get out of bed, have you got that? None of you even go out the door, and don't let anybody in. Get your husband water or juice to drink, make sure there's some ventilation. We'll get some medicine over to you just as fast as we can with a sheet of instructions for using it. You and Shari right along with Pete, start it as soon as you get it. Yeah, one of the Scouts will bring it over. *Don't ask him in the house—just nobody in or out of the house,* and I'm not kidding—"

Frank caught the other telephone jangling on the reception desk. There was a frantic woman's voice on the line. "Dr. Sam, this is Susan Lemmon. I don't know what's going on, but Jake and I went bowling last night, you know, the Blue Devils' tournament, and this morning we're both sick as dogs, he can hardly breathe and I feel like somebody's been beating me with hammers—Dr. MacIvers?"

"I'm one of the doctor's aides," Frank said. "He's on another phone. I'll tell him if you'll tell me—how long since you thought something was wrong?"

"He started coughing about three in the morning and couldn't stop, and I nearly fell on my face when I got out of bed, and I'm scared to death it's this plague—"

"If it is, we'll get you treated," Frank said, "but first we need information." He scribbled as she gave him her name, address, telephone number—"Dr. Sam knows where it is." He passed on the basics he and MacIvers had worked out, simple short instructions, brief enough to take only a couple of minutes on the telephone, simple enough that they didn't need repeating. Then: "Now this is very important, Mrs. Lemmon. How many people were bowling with you last night?"

"Gee, there were—there must have been eight couples in the tournament and quite a few others along to watch—"

"Okay, Dr. Sam needs to know who they were. Just give me their names." Frank scribbled furiously on a scratch pad as the woman started listing names, phone numbers when she knew them offhand. The list lengthened—eighteen, nineteen, twenty people including the ones who were running the bowling alley. Frank got them all down. "Now, listen," he said. "Do you feel up to doing some telephoning? I mean right now—good. Call as many of these people as you can possibly reach, right now. Tell them that they may have had contact with plague last night through you and your husband. Tell them you've already called the doctor so that they don't need to, but they're in danger. Tell them Dr. Sam wants them all to cancel whatever plans they have and *all stay home,* not go anywhere, not let anybody in except their own family, until he or Dr. Fox contacts them. We're going to try to get them medicine to prevent the infection—yes, for all of them that you know you contacted. We'll get back to them in a few hours, but you can help them protect themselves and others by staying home if you call now. . . ."

He was sweating by the time he hung up, saw Dr. MacIvers momentarily off the phone, looking at him. "Somebody else?" the doctor said. Frank nodded, handed Sam the data sheet. Sam whistled. "Twenty of them. Oh, brother. And that's not even thinking about contacts earlier in the day—you think they're not infective until they're symptomatic?"

"They're infective by droplet contact as soon as the bug's in their lungs," Frank said, "which could be up to eight or ten hours before they actually become aware of symptoms, or as little as three or four hours. Maybe these other bowlers are infected, maybe not. We can only watch and see." He looked up at the doctor's gray face. "You got the medicine cached away?"

"Ten different places, and so far not many people know where the places are. The stuff is secure enough for a few hours, but we've got to start moving."

"So what about distribution?"

"Here comes a major part of the team right now." He nodded toward a youth coming in the door, about seventeen years old, tall and gangling, and Frank blinked in momentary disbelief—he was dressed, of all things, in full Boy Scout uniform with a red-white-and-blue ribbon and a dangling medal on his chest. Sam motioned him over. "Tim, meet Frank Barrington—he's had experience with plague and he's going to help direct this campaign. Anything he tells you is just as if I told you. Frank, meet Tim Larramee. He's one of five new Eagles, we installed them at our big Court of Honor last month, and all five of them are going to help with distribution of the medicine. How many men have you gotten organized, Tim?"

"Let's see," the youth said, "there's thirteen from my troop, if Johnny Berger's mother lets him do it, and twenty-one from Troop 235, and fourteen from Troop 406—"

Frank whistled. "Forty-eight runners! You *said* you thought you could count on them, but I didn't really believe you."

Sam MacIvers's dried-prune face cracked into a grin. "My Baker Street Irregulars," he said. "Some of them horse around a lot, like any bunch of Scouts you ever saw, but when the chips are really down, they come through. And they've all got feet, and they've all got bikes, a few of the older ones have cars. If we can use the Eagles and older boys for sort of whippers-in, the bunch of them can keep the medicine moving right to people's doors, where it's needed when it's needed, man the CB radios and carry messages when the telephone company switchboard gets overloaded—they're going to be a major resource. They're all going to wear uniforms, at least neckerchiefs and caps if they don't have anything else, and that's going to be their passports. Not one person in this town is going to interfere with a Scout in uniform—"

"Not even these cops and patrolmen?" Frank said, gesturing.

MacIvers looked pained. "Listen, these police are scared shitless already. They've got word from this Bettendorf fellow and a couple of FBI people who came with him that we're moving a dangerous drug and that they have to root out where we've got it hidden and confiscate it, I mean, big federal authority is leaning hard on them right now, and if we hadn't jumped the stuff over them at the border we might be having to fight for it right now or just plain do without—but they know that there's plague in this town now and it's moving fast, Sergeant Davis's own daughter was one of the first to turn up with it, and they're scared, man. Most of the police are local people, even the State Patrolmen, and they don't know this Bettendorf from God's left thumb, but they know *me* from way back, and *I'm* telling them that this medicine is the only thing that's going to save this town if anything does, and if they can't help right now they can at least stay out of the road. They don't figure Whitey and I are lying to them, and *they* don't want to be the ones to be staring the people of this town in the eyes if they've interfered with our supply and distribution of the medicine and then their own townspeople and families start dropping dead like cordwood. Right now they're just in the process of discovering that they're right in the middle of a real crisis instead of lining up with the Good Guys, and this Bettendorf is the one that put them there, and if they look just a little bit shocky, that's what they are. So they're milling around right now watching the town's Boy Scouts move into real action while they're standing here with their thumbs up their asses, and you can figure out how long *that's* going to last. They're not going to interfere with me and the Scouts, and it won't be too many hours before they're digging in and helping too."

The doctor broke off and turned to the uniformed youth at his elbow. "Tim, here's the first list of names and addresses. Dr. Fox will take you to the place where the medicine is and fill up bottles and put names on them and give you mimeographed instruction sheets. You get the first ten guys over to that place to start running the bottles to people. Make sure they understand about wearing the face masks, and just hand the bottles and the instructions in the door and take off—no more contact with the people than is absolutely necessary. Meanwhile get the rest of the Eagles over here so they're ready to help direct traffic." He caught Whitey Fox's eye and motioned him over. "Whitey, we've got to start moving on this. Take Tim here over to the Grange Hall. He's got the first distribution list." MacIvers took a deep breath. "Meanwhile, I think it's about time we confronted this Bettendorf chap and got him out of our hair. Do you know him?"

Frank shook his head. "Not directly, but Monique does—and it doesn't look like she's making any headway. . . ." He had noticed the two of them in heated conflict across the room, Bettendorf shaking his head and gesticulating angrily, Monique talking to him quietly but doggedly. "Well," MacIvers said, "he's been badgering me to talk to him since ten o'clock last night when he flew in from Lincoln with the agents, but I've been too damned busy. So let's give him a chance."

The skinny little doctor pushed through the waiting-room crowd, with Frank at his heels. He had to tilt his head back to look up into the gray-haired man's face. "So you're Dr. Bettendorf," MacIvers said before the older man could open his mouth. "From Atlanta, Georgia, out here to pay us a visit. Centers for Disease Control. Great. I'm Sam MacIvers, general family practice, nothing fancy, from Willow Grove, Nebraska, where some of our people have gotten sick and started to die of plague, and I live here, and these people are my responsibility, so you'll excuse me if I make this as brief as possible—"

"Look here, Dr. MacIvers—"

"Hold it. We've got some cops in here so nervous already that they're going to start shooting the lights out if we give them anything more to worry about. Since we're going to argue for a while, I suggest we go back where we can have a little privacy. Flag down your aides and let's all go back to room number three."

While Bettendorf corralled his FBI men, Frank grabbed Monique's arm. "What was he saying to you?" he asked.

She was white-faced, almost in tears. "He's not buying it, Frank. He's going to stop us. He's going to shut us down if he has to bring the army in here to do it."

"What army?"

"He's talking about troops stationed in Lincoln. To say nothing about the National Guard units in Omaha—"

"And they're going to volunteer to come into a plague town? He's dreaming. And what would they do if they came here? Bomb the place out in order to save it? At the very worst it's going to take him hours to mobilize any kind of force, and that's going to give us the jump on him. And anyway, I don't believe it."

"He *means* it, Frank."

"Well, I don't think he can do it."

They crowded back into the little examining room, MacIvers and Frank and Monique, Bettendorf and two very beefy, hard-eyed gentlemen in dark business suits, with Perry Haglund wiggling in just before the door was closed. "Okay, Dr. MacIvers, now I'm going to talk a minute," Bettendorf began before the little doctor could start. "I represent the U.S. Public Health Service and the Centers for Disease Control on the national level, and that means I represent the *enforcement* arm of the CDC, if necessary, and I'm telling you that you don't have the authority to use an unknown, untested drug in this city, and I'm going to stop you if I have to. There are procedures to be followed in situations like this—"

"Yeah, I know all about your procedures," MacIvers said. "And we're all very impressed with the way your CDC has been dealing with this murderous thing. That's why we plan to do things a little bit different here."

"My God, man, we've been doing the best we can do! We're in the middle of the most vicious worldwide pandemic of plague in all history—"

"That's not news to me, Dr. Bettendorf. I've been on the telephone all night, and we have plague here in this town right now, and you're the man our good friend Haglund over here was going to contact three weeks ago to bring in vaccine. Now where's our vaccine?"

"There isn't any vaccine anywhere in the country. There hasn't been for six weeks. Every supply in the country has been exhausted, and there won't be any more for ten days, maybe more. I assure you that we'll get you some off the top when we have it."

"Well, ten days is too long. You may be managing things on the national level, but I'm managing things here in Willow Grove, Nebraska, where we've got plague *right now,* and we're going to do something about it right now."

"You don't have authority to do what you're planning."

"I have a license to practice medicine in the state of Nebraska, and that includes the authority to prescribe medicine as I see fit."

"You don't know this medicine."

"Well, I do," Monique snapped. "You're the one who doesn't know the medicine, Ted—"

"You have a series of preliminary tests on rats," Bettendorf said wearily. "You don't really know what this may do to people. Look, Doctor, you don't *need* to take this risk. With proper public-health measures taken now under Mr. Haglund's guidance, rigid isolation, sane protective measures, with vaccine arriving within ten days or sooner if I can possibly expedite it, *your town can survive this attack.*"

"What survival rates do you have for isolated rural communities the size of Willow Grove without any defenses?"

"I would hope forty percent of the population would make it."

"Good Christ. You call that *survival?* And what towns do you know that are doing that well? I mean which specific communities where?"

"Look, I don't have precise data right here in my hands."

"Well, the question was rhetorical anyway," MacIvers said. "You're simply wasting my time here, Dr. Bettendorf. I'm supposed to stand around and watch eighteen thousand people in this county die? You'll have to shoot me first. Now stand aside, I've got some productive work to do."

"I will bring force in here if I have to," Bettendorf said angrily. "I give you my word I'll give you all the help I possibly can, all the manpower I can muster, all the guidance, but if you start dispensing a potentially dangerous drug, I will be obliged to stop you—"

Frank Barrington cleared his throat. "Dr. Bettendorf, I don't think you quite took the doctor's meaning. He's through talking, now, and I, for one, am through listening. In terms of practicality, you and your people are outnumbered in this town right now about five thousand to one. You aren't going to call in any force from anywhere unless you get to a telephone or a radio, and if Dr. MacIvers doesn't want you to get to a telephone or a radio, there is a crowd of local police out there who are probably going to see to it that you don't get to a telephone or a radio. So much for force. Now, if you actually want to *help* in this situation, there are three things you could do. First off, you could get on your plane and go back home to Atlanta. Now, that would really help, and then when we find out what happens here using Tom Shipman's drug, we'll give you a jingle. Or if you insist on hanging around, you can go sit and sulk in a motel room and stay out of people's way and see what happens in the next few days with your own eyes. Or if you *really* want to help, you can rustle up a few competent people, just a few, to run statistics for us so that we won't have to work all day and then stay up all night every night trying to figure out where we're getting. Now, those are your three choices. Which is it going to be?"

Bettendorf looked at them, and finally looked at Monique. "You are really going along with this?" he said.

"Every inch of the way," she said. "I helped get us to this point, and I am most assuredly not quitting."

"What you don't seem to realize is that you could be slaughtering more people than you helped. We're the only ones who are *equipped*—"

"And what *you* don't seem to realize," Frank said, "is that the roof has fallen in on this country, and when the roof really falls in, the ones who survive are the ones who help themselves. We've decided that we're going to help ourselves here—and maybe test a way to help a whole lot of other people who are left too. Now you'd better make up your mind what *you're* going to do."

Bettendorf stood for a moment with his jaw clenched. He took a deep breath and opened his mouth as if to speak, then closed it again. Finally he looked at one of the FBI men. "Jackson," he said quietly, "if Dr. MacIvers will give you permission, get to a telephone and get Cooper from Omaha out here with some statisticians, and then see about getting some computer facilities here in town connected with our network—Dr. MacIvers will find you space. Then we'll handle the statistical end. As for you people"—he looked up at Frank and Monique—"let me tell you, by Christ, that whatever goes on in this town in the next few days, I am going to be here to see that it's documented from here to Guinea and back. And may Carlos Quintana rest in peace."

63

When the plague finally came to Brookdale, Connecticut, late in January in the midst of an unseasonable midwinter thaw, three doctors from the town and fourteen nurses and aides from the Brookdale Community Hospital were among the first to go, which effectively cut the heart out of any organized community medical resistance to the onslaught. The fact that one of the doctors was also the Chief Public Health Officer in the town really didn't make much difference; there was no wherewithal with which to mount a public-health battle anyway. No vaccine had been available anywhere on the northeast seaboard for weeks, and the tiny supply once kept on hand in the Brookdale Hospital dispensary for the inevitable emergency had long since been commandeered for use in the hard-hit metropolitan areas around New Haven and Westchester County. Supplies of the Sealey antibiotic were available in various distant warehouses, but reliable shipment of anything anywhere in the East had disintegrated to the point of the ridiculous. Even public-health education efforts, planned with considerable care in Brookdale, couldn't be carried out. The public power grid was operating only sporadically, a few indeterminate hours a day; when telephone switchboards were open at all, they were clogged; newspaper distribution had ceased about the time the last remnants of postal service had creaked to a halt, and even mimeographed handbills prepared as a last resort had no one to deliver them and sat in stacks at the few places in town where anyone congregated at all: the Betterway supermarket, the local newsstands, the county courthouse and the coal yard.

Thus when it came, hard and sure and swift and seemingly in the course of a single night, many people of Brookdale reacted rather like trapdoor spiders, crawling inside their domiciles and pulling the lid shut after them. Some packed up and left in the night, but there was a sense of futility to it: where was there to leave to? Boston was a sinkhole; Albany and other upstate New York cities and their environs were as dead as New York City to the south; the smaller New England semirural towns and cities were being hit too, despite sometimes violent or heroic attempts to isolate themselves, and Montreal was reeling from the impact of plague which seemed to have moved eastward from Toronto and Ottawa.

Of course, some people in Brookdale had made some tentative preparations, despite a certain pervading sense of unreality about the whole thing. After the aborted raid on the Betterway store, some people, at least, began laying in some kind of stockpiles of staples, whenever they could be found from whatever source—rice, flour, sugar, coffee. Tastes and judgments varied; one family with four children filled their basement with cartons of Froot Loops and nondairy creamer (partly, perhaps, because there was a considerable oversupply available); one man somehow obtained an entire side of beef at God only knew what cost in money and integrity, cut the entire thing into two-inch cubes and had his wife home-can the whole thing. Certainly the raid on the Betterway had shocked people into a realization that something real and frightful and very deadly was going on even before the plague itself hit. There was not going to be business as usual tomorrow or perhaps ever; the nightly armed patrols lost the patina of fun-and-games-and-camaraderie with which many had participated in the beginning and became a deadly serious matter of halting any unidentified person or vehicle in the community, simply shooting the tires out from under unrecognized cars that did not stop and possibly shooting the occupants as well, and now and then somebody didn't come home from patrol.

Of all the people in Brookdale, Carmen Dillman was perhaps the most curiously transformed by the Betterway supermarket raid and the slow community disintegration that followed. First and foremost she had had Jack on her hands, and Jack had turned out to be no mean medical challenge. His wound did not heal well. A piece of shirt carried into the wound by the bullet and undetected by the emergency-room doctors sat festering and the wound in his chest and armpit abscessed. For weeks it had healed and drained, healed and drained; for weeks he had been toxic, devoid of appetite, unable to hold down much that he ate, running fevers daily to 103 degrees and losing weight and strength until he was gaunt and frail as a scarecrow. Carmen nursed him diligently, applying hot epsom-salt soaks until Jack wanted to scream, inserting sterile drains at the doctor's telephoned directions, tearing up Jack's old flannel shirts for dressing materials and boiling them sterile whenever they were changed, so that during whatever hours the power happened to be on the whole house smelled like a cross between an abbatoir and a Chinese laundry. During this period Jack seemed to sleep interminably; he was hardly awake and stirring for more than three hours in the morning before he dozed off in whatever chair he was sitting in, napped in the afternoon, napped in the evening, slept like an exhausted dog all night.

And during these times when the telephone was also out, so that she could not keep in touch with her various "spies" around the community, Carmen spent long silent hours over coffee at the breakfast table in the kitchen, staring out at the wasteland of the backyard. Something about the raid and Jack's part in it and his wounding and Hal Parker and the whole nauseating mess had come suddenly into focus for Carmen Dillman, and she found herself looking back on the wasteland of their lives together, all those long wasteland years, dragging a veritable Marley's chain of cruelties and infidelities and hatreds and missed opportunities, many of the links—not all, but too many—of her own forging, and it was not entirely with self-pity that she regarded the stultifying barrenness of those years, those desert years.

And now, with Jack sick almost to death, she began glimpsing for the first time perhaps in her life the meaning of an actual loving relationship with another human being; she saw infection whittling away at a person she had scorned and belittled for decades who suddenly was very dear to her in ways she had never imagined possible. Mysteriously, as she changed dressings and tried to fix food that Jack could or would try to gag down, they found themselves talking; she found a wry, almost whimsical humor in her husband, so subtle sometimes as to be almost indistinguishable, yet present just the same, and, amazingly, an unbelievably powerful sustaining force for him, time and again helping to pull him out of pain, helping him rally from a bad spell as if solely to have a chance to pass on something bizarrely funny that had come into his mind a few moments before. Then, at one point, the abscess became almost the size of an orange under his arm, and there was a crisis of pain and fever; he lost the use of the arm again, indicating pressure on the brachial plexus, according to the doctor on the phone, who promised to come over and try to install a drain when he had a chance—but never had a chance. One evening while Carmen was applying the hot wet dressings, the swollen, inflamed area opened quite spontaneously and drained copiously and, unbelievably, a still-recognizable chunk of embedded torn shirt came out in the drainage, and by morning the fever was down to ninety-nine degrees and Jack, for the first time in weeks, found himself halfway hungry for some breakfast. . . .

All this, fortunately, came before the onslaught of plague began in Brookdale. With Jack suddenly less of a worry, Carmen began turning more and more of her awesome energies to getting ready—and, as his strength increased and his capability grew, nagging Jack to get ready too. "It's going to be us against it, buddy," she told him. "There's nobody going to help—but when it comes, it's going to have its work cut out for it, because we're going to beat it, you and me, or go down trying. None of this wailing and gnashing of teeth like I hear from Nancy Tollman every time she talks to me, the idiot. None of that for me."

Good as her word, she started out by learning what she could. They had actually accumulated a huge library over the years, with all kinds of books, including medical references, that Jack had used from time to time. She read everything about plague she could find in the house from the Merck Manual to Defoe's *Journal of the Plague Years* to articles in an assortment of family medical encyclopedias and a dozen other references. Of course they all talked about rats and fleas and didn't say anything much about direct respiratory convection of the organism—but then one night when power was on she caught a rerun of a PBS plague special on TV—she'd seen it once before way last October, with that blonde biologist Monica Jan-somebody from the CDC lab somewhere in Colorado patiently explaining how this plague microorganism (the woman said "mahcro-awg'nism") was a virulent mutant form that liked lung tissue better than anything, a different kind of plague bacterium than had ever been seen before—and there were charts of how the current plague could jump over the man-flea-rat-man cycle and go straight from man to man (or woman) and how it grew faster than most—time-lapse microphotographs of the organism actually growing in lab cultures of lung-tissue cells—and the measures one could take in the home to protect oneself and prevent contact and prevent spread if one followed the rules of sterile and isolation techniques to the very letter—and how with these simple home measures, together with the ample supplies of effective antibiotics and new forms of vaccines available through your local state and county Public Health Service offices or your doctor's offices, this epidemic of a dangerous disease could readily be contained and controlled and wiped out. . . .

Well, so much for the miracles of modern medical science, Carmen thought sourly, that little blonde may have known her mahcro-awg'-nisms but she sure didn't have the rest of the scenario straight. Carmen had heard the broadcast, or part of it, those long months back and tuned it out for the latest "Sour Apples" show, but she listened intently to the rerun—the two-thirds of it that played before the power went out for the day—and then caught it again two or three more times at odd hours. She doubted from what she'd heard that there were going to be any antibiotics or vaccines around when the ax dropped, but that business of sterile techniques and isolation and simple measures in the home began to sound plausible and not even all that difficult, once you understood what you were doing.

When Jack was on his feet enough to be left alone, Carmen went out to stockpile things. While other people stockpiled Froot Loops, she stockpiled Clorox, gallons upon gallons of Clorox. She stockpiled cheap kitchen rubber gloves and ripped up old bathrobes to make face masks and set up a changing room in the back entry so that clothes worn outside wouldn't come inside and kept a kettle of water ready on the fireplace hearth so that they could burn the furniture, if need be, to boil water.

She discovered to her horror that there really were rats in the basement, they got into one flour sack and a bag of oatmeal, so she dressed up in clothes soaked in Clorox until she looked like a one-woman decontamination crew and moved all the untouched stockpiled food into the kitchen, and then put the contaminated flour in bowls mixed half-and-half with plaster of Paris and left them for the rats; she'd read about that once in some country journal she'd subscribed to. Then she nailed the cellar door shut and enlisted Jack in the enormous task of decontaminating the house—with Clorox. That operation nearly killed them both; they scrubbed walls and ceilings down with Clorox, soaked down chairs and sofas and mattresses with Clorox, tore carpets up and hurled them into a heap in the backyard ("Millie says fleas just *live and breed* in carpets") and mopped the bare floors down with Clorox, running outdoors gasping for air, their eyes streaming because the whole place reeked with Clorox, until finally Carmen declared the place adequately decontaminated. And when the day finally came that one sick patient unexpectedly contaminated the whole Community Hospital and plague began in earnest, Jack and Carmen Dillman were as well prepared as anybody in Brookdale, Connecticut.

The Horseman rode the streets of Brookdale with typical swiftness. One day there were people still to be seen occasionally on the streets, the next day, no one. From Jack's upstairs study window they could see many of the homes around, see candle lights at night when the power was off, saw the candle lights going out one by one, as night followed night. A man down the cul-de-sac, Jerry Berman, Millie Berman's husband, was out back one night digging a hole by flashlight, and no one answered the Bermans' phone anymore even when the phone was functioning, and two nights later there were no candles burning in the Bermans' house. Only the silent echo of hoofbeats past the Bermans' house, around the cul-de-sac, down the next street—

Carmen heard rats gnawing on the fourth and fifth evening, found a hole in the floor almost big enough for one to squeeze through, fought down a wave of hysteria as she stared in the flashlight beam at the corner of the kitchen floor and saw a hairy nose and yellow teeth sticking through, working furiously. She cut up a tin can, spread it out flat and nailed it down over the hole, then spent the night searching for other weak spots. Each one that appeared, she plugged, poured a gallon of Clorox down one hole—they didn't seem to like Clorox—and then she and Jack made a twice-daily inspection of every inch of floorspace and Carmen's fright and revulsion gave way to anger—"The bastards," she went around muttering, "the dirty, slimy, nauseating bastards. . . ."

They marked days on the calendar, and waited. The phone was out more and more, Carmen could get through to her "spy" network only rarely and then presently not at all. They ate oatmeal and biscuits or bread baked in the fireplace in a reflector oven Jack ingeniously devised from a couple of plywood scraps and some aluminum foil; it caught fire one night, but only one corner burned before they rescued it. Carmen set out other rations like Captain Bligh in the lifeboat—half a can of tuna one night, a can of so-called beef stew (lots of stew and little beef) another. They filled the bathtub with drinking water when water would run from the faucets, at least a couple of hours a day, and they took sponge baths out of a common saucepan of water heated on the fire.

On the eighth day the unseasonable thaw came to an abrupt end with a screaming blizzard down from Canada, dumping eleven inches of snow on the ground in seven hours, heaping in drifts around the houses, and that night the temperature dropped through the floor, icy, brittle, pipe-bursting cold. For most of the next day they made do huddling in blankets and sleeping bags, running the furnace for an hour at a time just to take the edge off—no response from the oil man for four days—but by evening Jack said he'd had enough and went to the changing room, dropped his inside clothes inside the entry, got on his outside clothes and waded through drifts to the dwindling supply of cordwood stacked in the locked tool shed against the house, brought some in for the fireplace after changing out of outside clothes and sloshing down with Clorox. He didn't notice Carmen shivering violently, wrapped in a blanket in the middle of the living-room floor, until he had a fire built. "Jesus, you *are* cold," he said, looking at her blue lips. "Well, the fire will help, and I'll give the furnace a goose too."

"I don't think it's that," Carmen said.

"Come on, you just got overchilled—"

"I'm not cold. I'm burning up," she said through chattering teeth. "You'd better get a mask on and some gloves and get some water on to boil your clothes. This started about an hour ago, and I'm already aching all over."

Silently Jack went to the bathroom, got the thermometer. "A hundred and four," he said.

"That's what I thought." Her voice was very small. "Jack, you mustn't come near me."

"Sorry, kid. I'm not running from you, plague or no plague. For once we're in this together."

"Then get me some aspirin. I've got to stop this shaking."

After the aspirin he pulled her over to the fire, wrapped her in more blankets, sat and held her as she shook. There seemed nothing else to do; no doctor was going to help; they had done everything reasonable that they could do. Yet something now was tugging at Jack's mind. *No help but what we have in the house. Not much in the house but a little stored food—and Clorox.* And yet—and yet—*something* like a fishhook in his mind. "Carmen, honey? You remember back when you were such a pillhoarder?"

"Hmmm?"

"Back ten years ago when you were going to the doctor all the time? Before you got disgusted with doctors altogether?"

"Yes. I remember. Why?"

"And you'd never finish a prescription but you'd never throw the pills away? While you were having all those damned bladder infections? What did you do with all those pills? It seemed to me you had *boxes* of them."

She looked at him, her teeth still chattering. "*I* don't know. I suppose they're still up in the linen closet, I had some boxes there once. But they'd all be out of date—"

He was running up the stairs to the master bathroom, grabbing a flashlight on the way, tearing open the linen-closet door, tossing towels and washcloths and sheets and pillowcases in a flurry around him. Back on one of the shelves, way back, long forgotten, two large pasteboard boxes—full of pill bottles. He took them out, shook them out on the bed. All dated ten, eleven, twelve years ago. Some with the names on them, some without. White pills, gray-and-white capsules, blue-and-yellow capsules, red-and green-coated pills. A bottle of pills marked *V-Cillin K,* probably no help if the books were right. A large bottle of white capsules with a gray stripe with *CHLOROMYCETIN 250 mg* typed on the label—he remembered something about that, she had had this fierce bladder infection and nothing else had worked and Doc Jensen had finally ordered up something like this, but he'd so thoroughly scared the shit out of her about how dangerous they were, how they might depress her bone marrow and all sorts of horrible things that she hadn't taken a one of them. . . .

He gathered up pill bottles in both hands and went on downstairs. She had stopped chilling now and was drowsy. "Armpits sore as hell, and down between my legs—God, they hurt," she said.

"But you're not coughing."

"No—I'm breathing all right. What's—what's all this you've got?"

"Pills," Jack said.

"Don't be silly, we can't take those. We don't know what they are."

"Does it matter?" Jack said. "Maybe something in here will help some, I don't know. Don't care, either. They can't any more than kill us, and you can only die once. What you've got is going to get worse if we sit here, and we *know* it can kill us. If we're going to die of plague, we might as well die eating pills." He got some water and returned to her side. "Here, this one for your bladder—two four times a day, it says, and there's enough here for both of us for two days. Might as well pile another one on while we're at it, and vitamins—hell, vitamins can't hurt us. . . ." He counted out pills, dumped about nine of them in her hand. "Here you go. Down the hatch."

She gulped them down. He took largely the same things himself and swallowed them. Watched her closely, then after a while checked his own pulse thoughtfully. "Nothing happened yet."

He wrapped up in a blanket and sat down Indian fashion beside her. She stared up at him, wonderingly. "We really going to keep on taking those things?"

"Bet your ass we are. Every four hours. When the chips are down, kid, you gotta use whatever you've got. If those don't help, you got a lot more of them upstairs to try—"

Suddenly she was laughing, roaring with laughter in spite of herself, tears rolling down her face. "Oh, Jack, you crazy idiot," she said. "Did I ever tell you what a silly nut you are?"

"I'm crazy as a fox," he said, pulling her to him and holding her close. "You sleep now, while you can. Just close your eyes and let me be crazy. It's just like you've been saying right along—we're going to beat this thing, or we're going to die trying. . . ."

64

In Willow Grove, Nebraska, Ted Bettendorf did what he said he would: he really did back off and leave them alone. He flew in two medical statisticians and a small Hewlett Packard computer from what was left of the public-health operation in Omaha, which was not much, and set up shop in the basement of the First Methodist Church just across the street from the Willow Grove Family Health Clinic. Sunday services didn't interfere; on the first afternoon Sam MacIvers had buttonholed the Reverend Dr. Paul McFarland and said, "Sorry, Paul, but there won't be any Sunday services for the duration; have your people do their praying at home—but for God's sake see that they *do* some praying at home." (Unfortunately, the good Dr. McFarland took MacIvers's admonition perhaps more literally than intended and, ignoring all embargoes to the contrary, made daily rounds of his parishioners to make certain they did their praying at home, neglecting either to call his own burgeoning symptoms to anyone's attention or take the capsules MacIvers had forced on him, and falling dead of plague on the fourth day, bringing his short-lived emergency ministry to an untimely halt; at which news Dr. Sam MacIvers almost muttered, "So much for praying" within somebody's earshot, but bit his tongue in time and didn't.) The basement of the church was an excellent place for Bettendorf and Co. to work, since figures could flow across from the clinic on an hourly basis as they came in, and twice a day Frank Barrington or Sam MacIvers or Monique could run across to pick up printouts to study. From the beginning, Bettendorf directed the statistical work, but offered the emergency workers not a single word of advice. "If you people are running the show," he said stonily to Frank the second day, "then you're running the show. All I am is an innocent bystander. A very *interested* bystander, I assure you, but a bystander just the same. You want rope to hang with, you've got it. . . ."

The basic idea they pursued seemed sound enough. In a community like Willow Grove and its surrounding villages, with their aggregate of thirty-thousand-odd people, communications could be maintained one way or another—by local radio run by gasoline generators, by local TV, by mimeographed handbills, by runners where necessary, leaving the telephone lines open for vital messages that *had* to get through. Nobody had to check on Aunt Mabel because after that first day Aunt Mabel was home where she belonged and didn't go out again until she was told to. There were neighbors to keep an eye on Aunt Mabel and see that she was doing okay without exposing either her *or* the watchful neighbors to more than minimal risk. Nobody *had* to use the telephone except for certain specific things, and the switchboard *had* to be kept open for those specific calls—and miraculously enough, in Willow Grove, Nebraska, in direct confrontation with the long-ingrained American instinct to get on the phone the moment anything interesting or out of the way happened, most people did *not* get on the phone, and the telephone switchboard remained mostly open and functional for vital emergency use most of the time.

If that, in itself, was the First Miracle of Willow Grove, it was only the first of many. The message that went out to thirty thousand people by way of every communication channel that anyone could dream up was a marvel of bald simplicity, calm enough but deadly serious, as bluntly devoid of euphemism and false cajolery and political puffery and ambiguity as Frank Barrington and Dr. Sam MacIvers and half a dozen others (including Sally Grinstone, who had actually written the draft text weeks before) could make it: *Every soul in this town is in mortal peril; this plague will give you no warning; it moves like the wind and it kills quickly. Unless you are specifically called upon for help, freeze in your tracks. Stay home. Keep your family home. Don't visit anybody. Don't go anywhere. If you see anybody wandering around without Scout neckerchiefs or red armbands, call the police and report them—they may inadvertently kill you if you don't. If you develop fever, nausea, pain, coughing, bruises or anything else that doesn't seem right, call any of seven medical numbers and report it without a minute's delay. Medicine will be brought to you with instructions for use. Use it as directed because it may be the only thing that can save your life. In addition, if you develop symptoms, report the names of anyone you contacted face-to-face within thirty-six hours previously, and then try to phone them and tell them you are sick and they should contact a medical number themselves. If you need food, water, help, call the same medical numbers; otherwise stay off the phone. Above all else, stay home, stay home, stay home—help will come to you.*

Nobody can give orders like that to thirty thousand people and expect all of them to obey and get things straight and do what they are told for long—but the message hung together well for seventy-two hours, and that was the Second Miracle of Willow Grove, Nebraska. That was long enough to get the organization working. Seventy-two precious hours to get telephones manned, to get vital functions organized, to find out what they were starting with, how deep the knife had already plunged. Within twenty-four hours there were 103 known or suspected cases, 4 known deaths, over 1,000 identified contacts. By seventy-two hours known or suspected cases had risen to 430, with almost 100 dead but another 100 not yet dead that should have been, and the contacts fell sharply by proportion, only another 900 contacts. Initial plans to try to isolate known cases in the high-school gymnasium were debated and redebated and discarded—treat them in their homes, treat *everybody in each afflicted home,* treat every reachable contact as soon as the fact of contact became known, and treat each contact of the contact if the contact became ill, with full therapeutic doses of the Shipman drug. The Scouts were tireless, moving packets of capsules through town on foot or bicycle, sticking them in doors and turning and bolting like the devil was nipping at their heels. Within forty-eight hours, with people largely off the street, all the local police and the fire-department volunteers had joined the distribution team getting medicine, messages and supplies where they were needed and when. One phenomenon, miraculous in itself, went totally unremarked until much, much later because everyone had simply taken it for granted: there were no gangs roaming the streets of Willow Grove, no looting, no violence, hardly even a parking violation. Nobody thought this was particularly remarkable.

By the fourth day the numbers of afflicted were still rising inexorably—the sick, the dead, the contacts—but not on the deadly curve that had become the nightmare of every health official in the nation. On the fifth morning Ted Bettendorf met Frank with hands shaking so hard he could barely hang onto the printout sheets, and looked at Frank with an odd light in his eyes. "Something's happening," he said hoarsely. "I've been working at it all night long and something statistically significant is going on. That drug is doing something the Sealey drug has never done. . . ."

Frank, red-eyed and bleary, just blinked at him and looked at the readout, looked at the curves, and grunted. "Our control of things is also beginning to fall apart," he said. "You can only hold people rigid for so long, and it all begins to unravel. Tomorrow is going to be a bad day. . . ."

It was. An upsurge in new cases, the highest number for one twenty-four-hour period yet, and an alarming rise in the contact curve. People who hadn't been hit were getting bold. They were getting bored, going next door to talk to the neighbors, thinking things weren't really that bad, gravitating back toward normalcy. Several shopkeepers opened their stores, defied the police to send them home, claiming the whole thing was blown up out of proportion. They found out, soon enough, but by then others were breaking discipline. Another day, another big rise in new cases and a doubling of contacts. Running Dog was dispatched south for another vanload of medicine—with all highways rigidly blocked around the plague town, there wasn't enough gasoline left to take a chopper down for it.

Monique took the Community Hospital pathology department for her lab, handled all the samples for culture and identification, directed the hospital lab people in keeping running checks on blood pictures and liver-function and renal-function tests on people taking the drug. The drug was working, there were no side effects except a little diarrhea here or there—but the toll kept mounting.

Had the Horseman faltered momentarily after the first onslaught? Had he paused before unexpected resistance, a barrier he hadn't met before? Had he slowed to reconnoiter, regroup his hellish forces, seek another route, a weaker place to break through to ride and ride? Was there something new in the wind, something different that some vast, malignant, animate sensing mechanism detected? Surely there was a sense of silence and suspended animation, a deathlike winter stillness like a pall of malice hanging over the empty streets of Willow Grove, Nebraska. . . .

Council of war on the eighth day in the basement of the First Methodist Church. Sam MacIvers and Whitey Fox were there, looking gray and weary and vastly dispirited. Avis Rupert was there, the large, quiet, motherly, incredibly competent head nurse from the Community Hospital who almost single-handedly had been fielding the telephone advice on home care of the sick and exposed, encouraging, supportive, compassionate, sympathetic as the situation demanded, Sam MacIvers's good right arm and merely one of the many townspeople who had risen far above themselves to meet the crisis. Frank and Monique were there, and Ted Bettendorf and the statisticians and a very quiet, thoroughly chastened Perry Haglund.

Ted Bettendorf was not silent now; he had abandoned his cold silent observer status completely by the fifth day and joined in wholeheartedly, which was just as well because it was really he, with his figures and computer readouts and analyses, who held the key to what was actually happening in Willow Grove. Now, meeting the grim, silent faces around him, he started out without preamble. "Something is going on here," he said, "beyond any doubt in the world, something different than anything we've seen anywhere—but I'm not at all sure what it is. Monique, have you found any change in the organism turning up here?"

"None. At least none that I can detect."

"Could you detect it if it were there, with the facilities you've got available?"

Cautiously: "I—I think I could. There are good enough culture facilities, I've got a really quite good Hot Lab, for field conditions; I've been able to do a lot of things that should have showed up changes if the bug were different, and I haven't seen them." She hesitated "On top of that, I don't *feel* anything different with these bugs. That's not very scientific, but I've quit fighting it. I've been living cheek by jowl with these organisms for six solid months now without a break, and I swear to God I *feel* them. I *sense* them, and I don't sense anything different here than anywhere else before, and I think I would. The organisms are the same."

"Then we have to rule that out," Bettendorf said. "But we're seeing funny patterns just the same. I'll tell you this: we're using one whale of a good drug—*Christ,* I wish we'd had it six months ago. It's so much faster and more effective than the 3147 that I can't believe it—but it's here on the curves. We're getting far higher rates of recoveries among proven, massively symptomatic plague victims than we've ever gotten anywhere since this started. It's also highly effective at blocking the organism among contacts, once you've tracked them down and stuffed the pills in their mouths. About twenty percent of the people on full therapeutic doses get the trots from it, but we can live with that. We may have some pseudomembranous enterocolitis turning up, too, but we can also live with that. What we can't foresee is long-term or late side effects, and I'm now forced to agree with you that we've just got to live with that—"

"The dead ones don't have to worry about long-term side effects," Frank said.

"That is very true—and by now the dead in this community would be overwhelming without that medicine. The trouble is that there are still too many dead, and I don't know why. It isn't your approach or your epidemiology—so far the organization of everything has been beautiful; control is unraveling now, but we have to expect that, because people are going to behave like people. The trouble is that a certain small amount of unraveling of social controls at this point shouldn't matter that much; with this drug and this degree of organization we should have the cutting edge turned by now—and we don't. We're doing far better here than you were doing at this point in Canon City, Frank—believe me, I'm not being critical—but for some reason it's not cutting it. Put it this way, very simply: we're containing it better than any other place I know of, but we are not controlling it, and we are most certainly not stopping it. As far as I can see at this point, Willow Grove is losing this fight. It's losing it slower than other places by a factor of ten, but it's still losing."

"So what can we do?" Sam MacIvers blurted. "What should we be doing that we're not?"

"I don't know," Bettendorf said. "All I can tell you is what the picture is. Renew the efforts you're already making. Keep doing it, don't let down. Let's make another major fight to restore social control, keep it from unraveling. Maybe I'm getting a distorted picture. Maybe it's still just too early. Let's go on and review it again tomorrow and the next day, and the next. Maybe we'll see it turn. Or maybe we'll think of something. . . ."

That night Frank and Monique made love, the first time since they had left Wichita, slowly, sweetly, intensely passionately, even though both of them were close to exhaustion. Almost nostalgically, their lovemaking a bittersweet salute to things and times and events past, almost with a sense that there might never be another time. As their passion faded, sated, they lay in darkness holding each other closely, both awake, neither speaking, not expecting passion to arise again, not really wanting it to. In the darkness Monique lit one of her rare cigarettes; Frank saw the coal glow, saw the glow reflected in her eyes, gently kissed her naked breast, faintly pink in the glow. "You know what I wish?' she said finally. "More than anything else in the world? I so terribly wish we had Carlos here." She turned her head. "Not for loving, no, I don't mean that. Just to *be* here."

"I know," Frank said. "I've thought the same thing for a week."

"Carlos would see what's wrong. He'd know what to do. He'd find a key."

"Carlos was a great key-finder."

"He was a great man, in his funny way." Monique raised up on her elbow, looked at Frank's shadowy face, softened from its craggy norm by the darkness. "You know what I think Carlos would say? I think he'd take one hard look at what's happening here, and he'd say we're still just chasing it, not catching it. And you know, he'd be right.

That's all we're doing—chasing it. Reacting to what's already gone by. Cleaning up the mess after it's happened. Carlos always wanted to move in ahead, cut something off at the pass—"

Quite suddenly Frank Barrington was sitting up in bed, staring down at Monique. "Keep talking," he said. "Say that again, a different way."

"We're just running after this murderer, Frank. It acts, we react. We can never *re*act fast enough to stop it. We've somehow got to get ahead of it, ambush it, blast the pass full of rocks so it can't get through. . . ."

"Yes," Frank said. "Ambush it. Kid, maybe you've got the key. Maybe, if we move fast enough, you've got the key. . . ."

Five minutes later in the south side of Wichita Sally Grinstone was awakened by the jangling of a telephone.

65

The plague came to the Freehold on Grizzly Creek early in February, sweeping in on the wings of a late winter storm. Amy Slencik saw the boy late one afternoon, making his way down through the trees on Grizzly Ridge toward the creek, clothes ragged, long hair matted, filthy and stinking, barefoot on the crusted snow, pole over his shoulder with the faded bandana bag dangling from it. "I must have been dozing there in the chair by the window," she told Doc Chamberlain later, "and I looked up and there he was, stooping down to drink. I went to the door and shouted and he just ignored me, but the air smelled like a dead deer, and then he looked up at me, and God! that face—And then he waded the creek, barefoot in all that ice, and when he got to this side, right in front of me, he turned to the creek and . . ." She made a crude gesture and grimaced. "Well, he started down the path toward your place, and I grabbed the shotgun and ran after him, hollering, but when I got to the turn in the path, he was gone. I don't know, maybe I'm getting spooky or something. Maybe I just dreamed it all. . . ."

"Maybe," Doc Chamberlain said.

The storm hit that night, straight down from the north, loading the trees with snow and piling ten inches of it onto the roads and dumping so much into the creek that great blue clots of it floated downstream and hung up on snags. And then about four in the morning a woman started screaming in one of the big campers in the fifth circle and Elmer Slencik, Harry's older boy, plowed his way through the snow and storm to knock Doc out of bed and said, "It's Jennie Ozmovitch, Doc, her mom woke up and found her coughing and choking and she's spitting up blood all over the place," and Doc knew right then that it finally had come.

Every reasonable preparation he could think of had already been made, everything he could dredge up from his long experience dealing with infection and pneumonia and death. There were forty-odd families at the Freehold by then, mostly arrived in campers or trailers. Most had brought some food with them; most had had some money to help buy additional food and supplies, and despite Amy's misgivings they had managed to live much of the winter in reasonable peace and harmony without anybody bothering anybody too much. Mel Tapper's five acres and a big chunk of Kelly's west pasture had been devoted to camping space for them, and they had ultimately settled on small groupings of five or six rigs each, set out in rough circles to break the sometimes biting canyon wind, with buried water pipe going to each grouping and a big fire pit in the middle of each one, vaguely reminiscent of the rings of covered wagons set up to weather winter storms and Indian attacks on the prairies a century before. The men kept busy cutting and hauling firewood from up in the hills above Grizzly Ridge as long as the weather and gas for the chain saws and pickups held out, sparing the cottonwoods on the creek bottom near the Freehold as much as possible. The food wasn't much, but there was plenty of it, and fires to keep warm by, and people to talk to and an odd sense of shared hardship and shared waiting-out of crisis.

Doc had been the busiest one in the Freehold since his confrontation with Amy three months before. Quietly certain that plague would come sooner or later, one way or another, he had set about a series of preparations designed to deal with the problem as well as it could be dealt with when it arrived. He could see no reason to believe that any help would be available from anyone or anywhere when the chips were finally down. Harry Slencik, with the best and most powerful AM/FM receiver on Grizzly Creek, had spent many hours monitoring the increasingly fragmentary news of what was happening outside—the falling of the cities, the inexorable sweep of plague into and through the rural areas in all parts of the country, the slow disintegration of power grids and interstate shipping channels and fuel supplies and telephone service; the failure of delivery of a much-touted "new vaccine," at first because it was deemed too toxic and dangerous to use, and then when released anyway, was available largely in the wrong places at the wrong times; the demoralizing announcement, made post facto and without any preamble, that the top echelons of the federal administration and selected top political leaders had been transported by the Secret Service to whatever sterilized grottoes had been prepared to receive them in case of life-threatening national emergency or disaster, that they might survive to continue "leading the country," meanwhile leaving an unfortunate skeleton crew of underlings in the White House to "carry out executive orders" and sending the remainder of both houses of Congress scurrying for cover in their home districts—followed by the later news, largely unlamented by very many, that three-quarters of those who had descended to the sterilized grottoes, including the President, Vice-President and Speaker of the House, had perished soon upon arrival because, like medieval barons and kinglets who had pulled up the drawbridges and settled into the safety of their castles, they found they had taken plague into their grottoes with them. . . . From these tidbits scooped up by Harry Slencik from the airways in bits and pieces, Doc Chamberlain had come to realize quite clearly that whatever was to be done when plague came to the Freehold was going to be done by him and those he could teach. . . .

A lot depended upon doing things himself, fast, and on teaching as much as he could as quickly as he could to as many people as he could. But then, after all, that was how he had spent all those long years in practice, wasn't it? Doing and teaching? Carefully and patiently he had begun by explaining to people everything that he had been able to glean about this new mutant plague infection, what it did to people and *how* it did what it did. Carefully and patiently he started hammering home the basic ideas he knew the freeholders would need to know when the crunch finally came. He was convinced, he told them, that survival would depend not on drugs and medicines and vaccines and fancy medical miracles, but on simple, old-fashioned principles of isolation, disinfection and physiological support. Patiently he reiterated one simple fact that practically nobody in the Freehold had ever seriously thought about: that people had survived devastating, virulent infections and deadly pneumonias for centuries and millennia before the so-called miracle drugs were even dreamed of. True, not so many had survived, and survival had often meant weeks or even months of debilitating illness, but people had survived. Ancient Egyptian pharaohs had contracted crippling paralytic polio—and survived it. As far back as Hippocrates it has been known that people could survive deadly pneumococcal pneumonia. Women survived the dreadful ravages of childbed fever—not too many, perhaps, but at least some—before its causes were even suspected. And people had survived the vast pandemics of plague that had preceded this one, even back in the filth and ignorance of the Middle Ages—not too many, perhaps, but at least some.

Then he explained the changes that had come about from the great nineteenth-century discoveries of men like Louis Pasteur and Joseph Lister and Ignaz Semmelweis—names some of the Freeholders might have heard about once, but certainly hadn't thought about for years. There were ways of loading the dice against infection, of increasing survival by understanding the way infectious organisms passed from victim to victim, by isolating those infected, preventing spread by disinfection and giving support to the sick ones to give them a fighting chance to heal and survive. True enough, these things seemed stupidly simple, as he went over them, hardly what you would call the keen cutting edge of a modern medical campaign, but when there wasn't any cutting edge to use, you used what you could.

Certain key decisions fell to Ben alone, and he made them and then enforced them. It was Ben, for example, who decided on keeping the campers and trailer rigs in small, isolated groups, with at least 150 yards of clean air between the groups, with totally separate water supplies, latrines and cooking facilities. If one group got hit, he pointed out, maybe another wouldn't. It was Ben who had taken the two Slencik boys and a few others down to Kelley's place and completely cleaned and scrubbed down the enormous loft of a big hay barn, still fragrant from last year's hay, and built raised pallets and partitions out of two-by-fours and old shiplap siding lying around to create a crude twenty-five-bed infirmary to isolate and care for any who turned up actively infected. Cattle in the lower level would help keep the loft warm; snow on the roof would insulate; and he commandeered Dan Potter, the hydraulic engineer, into building a boiler and a network of steam pipes in the walls for further warmth.

It had been Ben Chamberlain who had made endless trips to Bozeman for odd and mysterious batches of supplies. On one trip he had brought back bolts of ticking and put the Freeholders, men and women alike, to work sewing them into mattresses and stuffing them with the cleanest wheat straw he could find within a fifty-mile radius, to make mattresses for the Sick Barn. He bought even more bolts of cheap cotton polyester yard goods, Woolworth prints and the like, the colors were wild and the storekeeper in Bozeman thought he was crazy as a loon—"Did you say twenty *bolts?*"—but that didn't bother Ben any, and again he put people to work cutting and sewing dozens of loose throw-over gownlike affairs with long sleeves and drawstrings at the necks and dozens more floppy surgical-type caps and masks. He scoured the town for surgical gloves, rubber kitchen gloves, rubber scrubbing gloves, *anything* that might work for isolation techniques, and had elastic banding put into the wrists for close fits. He bought and stored iodine, Clorox, chloride of lime, bichloride of mercury, Bard-Parker solution by the gallon, Pine-Sol by the five-gallon can and rubbing alcohol in whatever quantities he could drum up. He also saw that each group of campers had a big kettle or water boiler of some sort somewhere near the firepit, to be shifted onto the fire and filled at a moment's notice; and that each group had a fifty-gallon drum with a lid for discarding contaminated clothing; and that each had a big burning barrel.

Some of the people objected to "all this nonsense," of course, didn't feel like sewing up all these yard goods in a hurry, didn't see the point, but Amy Slencik, with Ben's full approval and blessing, laid down the law when necessary. "Ain't nobody around here going to freeload, everybody works, and if Doc Chamberlain says sew up them gowns, you'd better start sewing up a storm. I'm not too sure what he thinks he's doing, but you can bet your ass *he* does, and what he wants he gets, and if any of you don't feel like sitting down and working, you can pack up and leave any old time you want." Amy sewed with the rest, and Ben watched things piling up, and got them stored where he wanted them, and if there was a little bit of overkill mixed in with what he was doing, that was all right too. It'd keep their hands busy and their minds on *something,* by God, but that was just a side benefit—because when the Horseman finally came riding up Grizzly Creek—and Ben knew in his bones that the time would come—he intended to be as ready as he could get.

But if Amy helped prepare, and the others as well, the real heroes of the preparation were the two Slencik boys. They worked their hearts out helping Ben get ready. While Harry monitored the radio for news and Mel Tapper brought venison down from the hills, the boys manned the shovels and the hoes, the tractors, the plows, the posthole diggers, the trenching tools, the rock buckets, the hammers and saws, the paintbrushes, the pinch bars. From the beginning, with nothing even said, they became Ben Chamberlain's good right arms; what Ben proposed, the boys disposed—quietly, efficiently and well. Huge, fearsome-looking brutes, the two of them, with their solid legs and broad shoulders and shaggy, sandy beards, they looked like bouncers, but were actually the major getters-of-things-done. As their wives grew progressively larger and rounder, the boys worked harder and in the long run, made possible two-thirds of the things around the place that got managed, whether it was rebuilding the barn into a sick bay or amiably keeping the peace just by their huge presences at times when the peace might easily not have been kept at all. If the Freehold were ultimately to be of benefit to anyone, Ben realized, it would be the boys more than anyone else who had made it possible. . . .

When the blow finally came, it came hard and fast. Jennie Ozmovitch had pneumonic plague, no question about it. When Ben got the call early that stormy morning, he threw gown, cap, mask and gloves on over his winter clothes and drove over to Circle 5. The girl, about ten, was wheezing and coughing blood, fever and chills. It must have come with the last camper that had pulled in from somewhere down in Nebraska just three days before, part of the same circle, and sure enough, two others of them weren't feeling too well either, father and son in a family of five, running fevers, some vomiting in the night. Ben drove Jennie down to the Sick Barn after carefully examining her mother and father and brother, telling them what to watch out for, having them put clothing and bedding into the kettle to boil and dress in boilable gowns and gloves before scrubbing down the camper with Pine-Sol, every inch of floor and walls and ceiling, every dish. Later he hauled the father and son from the new rig down to the Sick Barn too, using only his old Bronco to do the hauling and having one of the Slencik boys stand by to swab down the inside of the vehicle when he came back.

By then it was dawn, and during the long day that followed, he swung his long-planned operation from the preparation to the active phase, personally and from a distance warning each family in each camper that plague was there, reinforcing orders previously only discussed in theory, setting up cooking and food-distribution arrangements and getting set to enforce strict isolation of each family in its own living quarters. About five that afternoon Elmer Slencik, who had drawn the short straw for the first twelve-hour watch at the Sick

Barn, sent word for Ben to come on the double, and at six-fifteen Jennie Ozmovitch was dead; she already had had a bad cold when the infection had struck, anemia and chronic malnourishment piled on top of that—nothing much to fight with—and Mel Tapper and Harry Slencik pitched in to the grimmest task of all, put off even by Ben until absolutely necessary: digging the wide, deep pit in the frozen, rocky earth at the far corner of Mel's pasture and lowering the girl's almost weightless body, covering it with quicklime from the barrel Ben had stored there and then with a thin layer of earth. They made it extra wide and extra deep at Ben's personal direction; there were going to be more where Jennie came from.

That evening Ben met at his place with Harry and Amy and Martha Tapper and Dan Potter after an evening inventory had shown two people in Circle 1 with slight fevers, but no other symptoms. "There can't be any possible mistake?" Amy said. "She couldn't have just had pneumonia?"

"No," Ben said. "It's here, beyond the slightest doubt."

"It must have been that last bunch that brought it," Amy said darkly.

"It doesn't matter," Ben said wearily. "Maybe it was them, maybe not. It could have been me on that last run I took to Bozeman—they've got it there now, too. It just doesn't matter, Amy. If it wasn't those people, it would be somebody else. So now the long winter begins. We've got to remember the rules if nobody else does: isolate; disinfect; support the sick ones. Get them down to the Sick Barn as soon as we're sure there's active infection. Thank God I got some oxygen last trip in, and some visqueen for tents. We'll have to use triage, save the oxygen for the strongest ones, the ones with the best chance of slugging it out. The other end of the triage is to keep the sickest and weakest down in the critical corner and just try to make them comfortable. It's going to be brutal, but we've got to do it. Martha, you've got to handle food for down there."

"Yes, and I'll see that the kettles keep boiling and help with the disinfecting," Amy said. "And I'll set up a schedule for the runners—we've got to have people to carry food, supplies, messages, from one place to another—"

Ben shook his head. "I don't want any more people moving *anywhere* than we absolutely have to. I'm going to be exposed anyway, I'll do as much of the moving and contacting as I can, as long as I can."

"Like hell you will, Ben," Amy said. "Of all the people around this whole place, you are the one single one that *isn't* expendable. We've got to have you directing things, not screwing around with details. You of all of us have got to stay clean, Ben. With you around, we've got a chance. If you go, we might as well just go howl at the moon. I'll take care of the runners."

The storm had ended, and that night the temperature sank like a stone, 10 degrees below zero next morning, and there it stayed. The Freehold valley was like a frozen, silent death camp. Eight o'clock inventory that morning found four more sick enough to be taken to the Sick Barn and two others to be rechecked later; all these were from Circle 3, untouched the day before. Heat tapes connected to Harry's gasoline generator and transformers kept the water lines open, but fire-watchers had to be appointed to keep the fire pits going; late winter cold snaps like this, Harry warned, could go on for days or weeks. On that second day Ben Chamberlain, having been up and moving forty-eight hours without a break, reached the end of his rope and turned direction over to Amy and Elmer, and went to bed. It was a long sleep, and just as well; it was his last unbroken sleep for a long time. When he woke up on whatever day it was—the third or fourth or fifth, he couldn't be sure—there was too much work piled up for any long sleep again. Day melted into day; it was an endless, exhausting, defeating Red Queen's race just trying to keep from falling farther and farther behind, and nobody had time or energy or interest to keep much of a diary. When things happened, as of course they did happen, they didn't happen on such-and-such a day at such-and-such an hour, they just happened one day, or one night, indistinguishable from any other, each as dread-filled and endless as the last.

One day—maybe the fifth or sixth—there were twelve people in the Sick Barn, three certainly and imminently going out, two almost certainly going very soon; four more had joined Jennie Ozmovitch in the cold comfort of the rocky pit—but Russ Jenkins, the father of the family from Nebraska, was still limping along, perhaps even getting a little better with the support of oxygen and intravenous fluids, and his son, beside him in the same partitioned cubicle, was doing much the same without oxygen. Two others were still breathing unsupported and not actually doing worse. Ben steadily made his twice-a-day inventory of all the campers and trailers, one job he would not let Amy delegate to herself. One day he found one more to send down to the

Sick Barn, a teen-age boy who was sick enough not to object; twelve hours later he found four more, and next day, another day, there were three.

One night, just as he was finishing his camper rounds with Circle 7 (every circle, of course, had been hit by now) a man came out, took him aside. "Doc, you'd better know. Some of the people are lying. Fran Solomon, over in that blue-and-white rig, won't report sick, but the women say she was coughing all night and has a terrible fever. She's got her baby with her, you know. She don't want to go to the Sick Barn. Scared to. Says nobody's ever coming back from there. . . ."

Ben sighed and said, "Just don't say anything for a half an hour and I'll try to take care of it, okay?" He'd had suspicions in two or three other places too. He drove down and saw Russ Jenkins in his Sick Barn cubicle. "You doing better, Russ?"

"Yeah, breathing better. Been off the oxygen for over a day now, too. Mighty weak, though."

Ben believed him; he looked like a walking corpse, but one side of his lungs, bubbling last night, was almost clear now. "You think maybe you could walk for about fifteen minutes, if I helped you?"

"Mebbe. I could try."

Ben bundled him up against the frigid night air and supported him out to the Bronco and then drove back to Circle 7. "That blue-and-white rig, woman named Fran. She's sick and won't go to the Sick Barn. Thinks everybody goes there is going to die. You go in and tell her, Russ. Tell her that you were dying, and you got better in the Sick Barn. Lie to her a little, tell her I said you could be out of there tomorrow and go back to your family. You can't, quite, not tomorrow, but tell her I said you could."

He helped Russ up to the door, and he went in. Low talking, a woman sobbing, denying, refusing. A minute or two later the man came back out. "No use, Doc. She's got her baby. She won't take her baby down there."

In desperation Ben turned to Amy. "Maybe you can woman-talk her," he said. "She's going to infect the baby and everybody else in the circle." Amy struggled into a boiled, frozen stiff gown and cap and mask and icy rubber scrub gloves and went into the rig; she was there almost fifteen minutes, but came out shaking her head.

"But damn it, what are we going to do with her?" Ben exploded, a week's frustration pouring out.

"I don't think we're going to do anything with her," Amy said with uncharacteristic gentleness. "Poor woman is sick, but it's *scared* to death she is, and not just for herself, for the baby. If she's not going to go, we can't make her. Mark the door or something and warn everybody that nobody goes near the rig except me. I'll dress up in this monkey suit and take care of her. We've got that extra kerosene heater over at our place—I'll bring that over, get some heat in there, and maybe I can get her to let me take care of the baby over at our place. But you can't make a woman like that do anything; she'd drive herself off down the road first, and we can't let her do that. . . ."

There wasn't any extra kerosene heater, Ben knew that, just the one in Amy and Harry's bedroom, but he acquiesced, and a day or so later Amy had the baby boy over at her kitchen table, a husky kid, no sign of sickness, and Fran Solomon was at least still breathing. . . .

Things like that happened. Unexpected things turned up. Ben learned you could set up the plans, but you couldn't make people follow them. He did his best, and day followed day, and new sick ones turned up every day, but there wasn't the wildfire through the Freehold that he had heard about in other communities; *something* they were doing was helping. Presently there were twenty-three dead by the grisly tally Amy kept on the kitchen calendar, the only record anybody was keeping—but five or six who had been deathly sick were recovering—make that seven, Teddy Bairn's fever just broke and he sweat so much he soaked through a six-inch-thick straw-and-ticking mattress and left a puddle on the floor under the shiplap pallet he was lying on, and that tight chest of his sure as hell was breaking up.

Another day, late in the afternoon, a woman from Circle 2 flagged Ben down as he headed into his cabin for a catnap. "Another rig came in this morning," she said, "a big thing down from Utah. Full of people. Turned around and got out of here like the devil was after them when they found out we'd been hit. You should have seem 'em run!"

"Yeah, I guess it figures," Ben said, looking down at the woman from the window of his Bronco. "Nobody wants to snuggle up too much to what we've got."

"Well, reason I stopped you—they talked a minute before they left. Said somebody somewhere down in Nebraska was experimenting with some new drug that really did wonders against plague. Lots of sick people getting well. Some kind of new wonder drug."

"Somewhere down in Nebraska, huh?" Ben said sourly. "Well, that figures too. It wouldn't be right around the corner here."

"Still, maybe you should look into it," the woman said. "Maybe we could get some of it."

"You know somebody here that wants to drive down to Nebraska?" Ben asked.

"Well, not me! At least I *know* what's going on here. . . ."

"Yeah. Well, you go home and take your vitamins, Becky, and let's not worry about some wonder drug down in Nebraska. Before this is over we're going to be hearing about more new wonder drugs turning up somewhere else than God made little apples. I don't think there's going to be any wonder drugs for us."

People stopped Ben to talk to him like that, everyplace he went. Talked about all kinds of crazy things sometimes, never any telling what was on their minds, and they had a lot of time for thinking about things. They'd stop Ben and talk to him, or come to his place and talk to him, when they wouldn't dare go near anybody else. He always took time to pause and listen and talk to them, too, and they didn't mind if he always took a mask out of his pocket and slipped it over his nose and mouth when anybody came near—in fact, it was a kind of reminder to them, when they tended to forget or get sloppy, and they'd go home and tell the others, "Don't forget those masks when you're near somebody. I was talking to Doc today, and he never forgets."

And then one day, another day, Harry Slencik came down the trail to Ben's place just at dark in the evening, just as Ben had pulled in and was getting himself something with rum and butter and brown sugar in it to warm him up after making his evening inventory out in the cold. It surprised Ben a little, seemed like he hadn't seen Harry except for a glimpse or two across a field for a week or more. Big, bland-faced Harry Slencik with his sweat-stained old cowboy hat cocked to one side as usual on his big head, and the usual big grin on his face; but that night when Ben greeted him and asked him in, it seemed as though Harry's big grin had some look of a skull about it. "Cold out there," Harry said, and looked over at Ben's rum-and-butter. "You got any more of that stuff around, why don't you buy me one?"

The big man walked over and sat down, warmed his hands by Ben's fireplace while Ben made the drink. Took a long pull, big smile gone, set the cup down on the hearth and just sat staring at the flickering light.

Ben sat down across from him. "Amy, Harry?"

Harry nodded. "She'd kill me if she knew I was down here; she says it's nothin', just a little chest cold, but it's not just a little chest cold. Coughing and feverish, threw up once this morning that I know of. She's been goin' too hard, hasn't been taking precautions, goin' into all those trailers, takin' care of that baby; I told her she shouldn't be doing all that, but hell, Ben I can't fight with Amy when she's got her mind made up, you know that."

"No, you don't get far fighting with Amy. But we'd better go up and see her."

Harry nodded again, stood up slowly. "Ben, listen. She don't want to go down to that barn down there, and I don't want her to. I'll put her to bed and take care of her, make sure nobody comes in and gets contaminated or nothin'."

"Harry, for Christ sake—"

"I know it ain't very smart, but that's what I want. We been in that cabin up there too long to go somewhere else now."

Well, Amy wasn't the only hardheaded one in the family, Ben thought, trudging up the path with Harry. He checked her over carefully, and after a sad little pro forma protest that everything was fine, she let him get her to bed, get some aspirin into her, get something cold on her forehead. He didn't put on mask or gown or gloves; there'd been too many things in the past, they'd all been together too long for that at this point, he wasn't going to look at this woman out of a big protective gown or over a cold muslin face mask, to *hell* with that. "Well, you're right," he said finally. "You've got a little bronchitis; what you need right now is some sleep and a little rest for a couple of days, and Harry'll see that you get it. But you've got to stay in bed—no going out, no seeing anybody. There are others can pick up the load. . . ." And Amy nodded weary agreement, no argument there, and turned her head, got comfortable with her wheezing and occasional burst of coughing and was sleeping, finally, before Ben clapped Harry on the shoulder and left. Back at his cabin he threw all his clothes into the big vat of Clorox and sloshed his hands and face and hair with Bard-Parker's, but his heart wasn't in it. It seemed, all of a sudden, that his heart wasn't in anything anymore. *At this point, who the hell cares? And what does it matter?*

Amy died about two the next afternoon, Lord only knew how long she'd been sick before even Harry noticed. Tears were freezing on Harry's cheeks as he and Ben and Mel Tapper put her down in the burial place just at dusk, and nobody said any words, it was just too bitter cold to stand out there talking. But—maybe it was an omen—that night the frigid, icy sky clouded over and the temperature outside rose thirty-five degrees overnight and next day a warm southerly breeze brought the mercury above freezing and somebody said something about it seeming almost springlike and after a while Ben Chamberlain found himself thinking that Amy or no Amy, maybe some of the Freehold would endure. . . .

66

"It's saturation bombing," Ted Bettendorf said when Frank collared him in the basement of the First Methodist Church in Willow Grove at two in the morning. "That's what it is, plain and simple."

"The air force would call it 'deep interdiction,' " Frank said. "Bombing and enfilading behind the enemy's lines."

"It's still saturation bombing," Bettendorf insisted, "and it's never worked in modern warfare that I know of on a tactical level. And with an *antibiotic?* I don't know that it's ever even been *tried.* Jesus!"

"Look, don't carry the analogy too far," Frank pleaded. "We're not talking about field warfare, and we're not talking about dropping antibiotic bombs—except figuratively."

"Yes, I know." Bettendorf paced the floor. "What you're actually talking about, specifically, is loading up the entire population in the area—every man, woman and child in Willow Grove, Nebraska, and its surrounding villages—with a full ten-day therapeutic dose of a new, completely untested antibiotic drug, including about seventy-five percent of that population that has no established evidence of infection whatever, nor even any established evidence of *contact* with the infection."

"Not yet," Frank said. "But what are the odds that any one of them is going to turn up with active infection, or have active exposure in the next ten days? You figure the odds. You've got the numbers from other similar communities. You know what the penetration curves are."

"It's insane," Bettendorf said.

"Different, maybe. Not insane. Look, the bald fact is that what we're doing now isn't working, even with a remarkably effective drug. That's what you were telling us in our little conference. We aren't stopping it. It's simply moving too fast. Monique hit the target right on the bull's-eye: we're always behind it, never quite catching up. We're merely *reacting to what it does*—and that's not enough. We've got to jump over it just like we had to jump over those state cops a week ago just to get the drug into town."

Bettendorf shook his head. "Frank, what you're proposing is scientifically insupportable. If we were to try it and it backfired, our asses would be hanging so far out in the wind there'd be nothing left of them."

"Seems to me that mine is already out there quite a ways," Frank pointed out. "So are a lot of other people's."

"That's true enough—including mine." Ted scratched his jaw. "Jesus. The CDC could be drummed right out of existence as a credible entity. But then, its credibility isn't all that high right now, as it is. And if something doesn't slow this plague down somehow, there's not going to be any CDC around very long to point fingers at—"

"Who's going to be pointing fingers, anyway?" Frank said.

"The entire scientific and medical community, for openers."

"Oh, come on, Ted. What scientific and medical community? There isn't any left, to speak of. It may be gone for good, as far as we know. All we have are a few remnants here and there, a few Whitey Foxes and Sam MacIvers slugging it out for their own immediate patients. And what do *they* have to offer? Precious little, I'd say."

The tall gray man paced some more, paused to sift some computer readouts through his fingers, shook his head. "Well, I still say it's insane," he said, "even if Monique *is* right on target. But suppose we tried it—would it even be practical? It would have to be all or nothing, you see. How many individual doses of that stuff did you bring up here to begin with—ten thousand or so? And you're already running low, just covering the ones we know are infected or exposed. Now you're talking about a gram of the stuff per day per person for ten days straight—and for how many people? About twenty-five or thirty thousand? That's well over *a million and a quarter doses* you're talking about, and to do what you want to do you'd need them here, right now, *today*. Where are you going to get them?"

"Well, in the first place, we don't need it all today," Frank said. "We only need about 120,000 doses the first day, along with some wild kind of distribution system, to buy us twenty-four hours. But in practical terms, I've already checked, and there are approximately 700,000 doses in all stockpiled right now in Wichita."

"In Wichita."

"That's right. I've also already talked to Sally, and by now"—Frank consulted his watch—"she will have stolen a truck—"

"Stolen a truck," Ted Bettendorf repeated.

"—stolen a truck and gotten it loaded with half the stockpile we have down there and be heading north, due to pull in here about eight hours from now if the truck she's stolen doesn't break down. No, you haven't met Sally Grinstone yet, but you will, you will. Sally is a very resourceful young woman, and she doesn't mind stealing trucks in the least when she figures she needs one. She'll only bring half of the stockpile with her, just on the off-chance that some vagrant idiot somewhere down in Kansas tried to hijack the truck somewhere along the way. Meanwhile, Running Dog—"

"That's the Indian?"

"—will bring the other half of the stockpile up in a different vehicle, following a different route and arriving a little later. While all this is going on, the rest of us are going to figure out how we can get the stuff spread out, with instructions, to thirty thousand people, preferably within the next twenty-four hours. . . ."

Ted Bettendorf reached for a chair and sat down, somewhat unsteadily. "I—I think I'm following you," he said carefully. "But you still are only accounting for three-fifths of the drug you're going to need."

"Right," Frank said. "That's where you come in. Tom Shipman and his rump factory for making this stuff is down in Wichita, and the only thing standing between us and the remaining two-fifths of the drug we need is enough tetracycline to make it with. The finished product may not come to us in the elegant form you'd like, all dosed out and stuffed in capsules—it may come up here in bulk, packed in drums, just a raw green powder mixed with excipient, and we may have to guess a little bit at the exact dosage, but if Tom can get enough tetracycline fast enough and the place down there doesn't catch fire, he should be able to produce in time."

The man from Atlanta suddenly stood up. "Yes," he said, "and it's time we're talking about, isn't it? If you need tetracycline somewhere in Wichita, you'd better tell me just where in Wichita you want it to appear, and then I'd better get on the telephone and start drumming it up for you. And you'd better get Sam MacIvers out of bed and start planning how you're going to distribute the stuff." He looked at Frank. "It may be insane and scientifically insupportable and we may all be dead men if this scheme doesn't work, but by hell, it's going to feel good to be doing *something* for a change. Even something as crazy as this."

Sally Grinstone pulled into town at ten in the morning in a twelve-ton dump truck marked Murphy's Sand and Gravel, its rear neatly packed with cartons and a tarp thrown over the top. She was covered with grease from head to toe—the muffler had fallen off halfway there and she'd had to crawl under the truck and wire it back on again—"All I needed was a ticket from some jackass for making too much noise"—so she didn't look too much like an angel of mercy, but 350,000 doses of the Shipman drug were delivered safe and sound in Willow Grove, Nebraska. Ted Bettendorf spent eight hours on the telephone, pausing only once to look at this grease-smeared truck thief of a female with a completely unreadable expression on his face; he had trouble getting through to much of anybody for most of the eight hours, and the ones he did get through to either didn't believe it was really Ted Bettendorf calling them from somewhere out in Sticksville, or thought he had taken leave of his wits, considering the requests, pleas and directives he came up with, but at the end of the time he sighed and rumpled his hair and said to Sally Grinstone, "Better phone your chemist friend down there and tell him to get ready, because he's about to be buried in tetracycline."

Meanwhile Frank and Monique, the two doctors and their office people, Sally Grinstone and Running Dog (when he finally arrived with his half of the stockpile) set about organizing the first stage of a truly prodigious distribution effort. Later on, nobody could possibly have said who did precisely what, who came up with what ideas, who manned the phones for what purpose, or who could take credit for any given thing that happened; it was totally impromptu, there were no guidelines to follow, and plans changed from hour to hour or even minute to minute, mostly in terms of implementing changes to speed things up.

The problem was simple enough, on the face of it: how to get three days' dosage of the drug into the hands of every breathing soul in Willow Grove and environs within twenty-four hours, even within twelve if possible, without exposing anyone to any unnecessary contact with anyone in the process—and identify for certain which people had the medicine in hand, with instructions, and which ones didn't. It was clear from the start that the people could not be allowed to come get the medicine—the medicine had to be taken to the people, and people had to be notified that it was coming and why. Sally took over liaison with the media, most notably the town's single radio station, providing a stream of messages to be poured out without even pauses for station identification—communiqués written by Sally, even identifying which streets and which blocks were being covered when, and repeating the most vital word: STAY HOME; WAIT; SOMEONE WILL BRING ENVELOPES WITH MEDICINE TO YOUR DOOR; READ THE DIRECTIONS AND THEN TAKE THE MEDICINE AS DIRECTED; YOUR LIFE MAY DEPEND UPON FOLLOWING INSTRUCTIONS EXACTLY.

Tim Larramee and the other Eagles mustered their Scouts and took over the waiting room of the clinic to help with the stupefyingly dull task of counting out twelve capsules and putting them in envelopes, one envelope for each citizen, stapling the envelopes shut and rubber-stamping them with directions made from one Scout's toy printing set; running to the stationers for staples and inking pads and more envelopes and still more envelopes. Once a supply of envelopes was ready the town police delivered Scouts and others willing to serve as delivery boys carrying boxes full of envelopes to block after block of homes, each delivery boy armed with a felt marker to leave a clearly marked X on each door where delivery had been made, along with the number of envelopes delivered to that house—"Use the red markers," Sally insisted; "we might as well make it symbolic while we're at it." By noon the first loads of envelopes were going out, and feedback said that most folks were getting the message, if not directly from the radio, then from the next-door neighbors who were, at Sally's broadcast suggestion, going out on their front porches and shouting next door or beating on a dishpan until somebody looked. By 5:00 P.M. most of the downtown residences had been covered and some of the more peripheral areas were being penetrated. Squad-car policemen not actually depositing Scouts on street corners were patrolling the streets themselves, looking for unmarked houses, delivering envelopes in person. By midnight, with virtually everyone involved facing exhaustion, the stockpiles of drug had dwindled sharply, and street maps were checked, and outlying village maps were checked, and there came a point of consensus that just about everybody had been covered who could be covered and there was nothing more now but to go home to bed . . .

That night in his mind's eye Ted Bettendorf saw the Horseman, riding the streets and byways of Willow Grove, Nebraska, pale and naked, bony legs clasping the flanks of his nightmare steed, pale as its rider, its shoulders pouring sweat, great nostrils flaring, fearsome eyes blazing with death, the great spiral horn spearing up from its heavy forehead. Silent hoofbeats clattered through the streets and alleys and across the rooftops, and behind the Horseman his ragged, filthy hell-child rode, clinging fiercely to his master. Was there something different tonight? The pale steed seemed nervous, pausing now and then, changing direction slightly at no urging from the Horseman, dancing a nervous death-dance at the street corners, looking, turning before dashing off. Did the beast sense something different tonight? Did the Horseman? No matter; still they rode through the frozen night.

. . . to bed, yes, but not to sleep. Long hours, wide-eyed, staring into the darkness. Too exhausted for talk, too much tension to sleep. A waking nightmare of waiting.

And at dawn, more waiting. Too early to know anything, far too soon. Frank and Monique found MacIvers pacing his waiting room at 7:00 A.M., already taking the day's calls. More new cases, ignoring all directions, waiting until seven to call the doctor. Contacts written down, medications confirmed; yes, keep taking them. Frank and Monique drank coffee in glum silence, hearing the doctor's gravelly voice. No point even looking for Bettendorf, he would have nothing to tell them. By noon MacIvers was showing signs of cracking, his voice tense as piano wire on the telephone, fairly snarling answers—Frank caught Monique's glance, nodded, took the little doctor's arm—"Come on. There's a little gas in the van. Let's take a ride."

They rode out to the edge of town, down along the river gorge, through the willows, the little city park, empty of people, up the grade on the other side. No words, and after a while Sam MacIvers turned his face to the window and covered his eyes with a hand and began crying, very quietly. Frank drove on out through the open fields of wheat stubble, let him get it over with, and presently he stopped. Sam turned back, looked out through the windshield. "Dumb country," he said gruffly. "Stupid country, some people think, even people who live here, but it's beautiful, beautiful. Made to support life. Good rich land, good people. Too many tornadoes in the summer, but that's all right, too, they pass."

Back in town, back at the clinic, Sam said, "Thanks," and Frank nodded, watched the little man sprawl out on a waiting-room couch and sleep like a baby for three hours while he manned the phone.

Later they went to find Bettendorf, but Ted just shook his head. "There's nothing yet," he said. "Too early; you want too much too soon. Sam called in his figures—the new cases are the same, perfectly flat curve. Not going up, that's something. Recovery curve is a little better, but it was getting better before we started this. When will we have a hint?" He shook his head. "I don't know. It takes twenty-four hours to establish an effective blood level; we have no real handle on the *in vivo* sensitivity of the bug. I can't tell you when. Maybe tomorrow . . ."

That night Frank slept, with nightmare dreams. Slept late, actually, had a long breakfast with Monique. Called in to confirm with the radio-station manager that the station was still broadcasting directions, reminding people to take their capsules, each mealtime and at bedtime, don't miss a dose. Call in if you didn't get the medication, call in if you dumped some down the toilet by accident. Stay home. Wait. The station manager sounded weary; yes, he'd been up all night, spelling the regular announcers and manning the phone. "Calls? God, yes, we've been getting calls—referred them all over to the clinic. Lots of them, last night; Dr. Fox was fielding them until four in the morning. Yes, mostly new cases, I guess."

No word from the basement of the First Methodist Church. No point dogging Bettendorf, Frank knew; he'd let them know when there was anything to know. It was as if, with enormous effort and every ounce of strength available, they had rolled the blunderbuss cannon to the top of the hill, given it the final push to get it over the hump and now could only watch, totally helpless, as it bounced and rattled and crashed its way down, watching in horror that it might veer from its path, strike a bump and shoot off course, and there would be nothing, not one thing in God's world, to steer it back if it did. . . .

The next day—the third—Sally Grinstone confronted Bettendorf in the church basement early in the morning. "We talk," she said.

Head shaking helplessly, Bettendorf spread his hand. "I can't tell you anything. We haven't even got the night's figures yet."

"Doesn't matter," Sally said. "If we lose this one we're washed up anyway, so we assume we're going to win and we plan for that, okay? Call it fantasy, call it wish fulfillment, I don't give a damn, we plan just the same. Tom Shipman called me earlier, and Dog is on his way south again—there's more drug to pick up. We're going to have Willow

Grove covered for ten days, by the skin of our teeth. But if we win here, one man working one little production line in Wichita isn't going to fill the bill. We're going to need factories churning out that stuff everywhere we can plant them, chemists to work them, personnel, plenty of raw materials. Priority lists of where it goes first, where next, where after that. Financing. Transport. Communications. There'll be nothing else in this country that matters but grinding this stuff out and dumping it down people's throats. Right?"

"Right. That, and vaccine to follow it up. If we win here. God, yes, if we *win*. . . .

"So we plan. We start now and pretend. Now I happen to have a rough flow sheet and a few ideas that I've been working out—" And Sally pulled out a sheaf of yellow legal-tablet sheets covered from top to bottom with her weird spidery scrawl and she began telling Ted Bettendorf in some small detail how *she* had figured out that it was going to have to work, after the battle of Willow Grove, Nebraska, was history.

One of the computer men tapped Ted on the shoulder some hours later. "Won't it keep?" Ted said irritably.

"No. Come take a look."

He took a look, a long, detailed look, checking and rechecking. The he tore sheets of readout from the machine and snatched the roughed-in graphs from the statistician's hand and ran for the door. "Keep writing," he shouted to Sally over his shoulder, "for Christ sake, keep writing, I'll be back in no time—"

—Plunged across the street at a dead run, papers flapping under his arm, realizing as he ran that they would already know, they would *have* to know, because the telephone calls would have dwindled to a standstill.

Frank was holding the door for him. "The new case curves?"

"They've fallen off the cliff. Not some little decline—they've sunk like a stone." Bettendorf looked at people standing frozen around the room.

"You mean we're winning," Dr. Sam MacIvers said hoarsely.

"We're not winning," Bettendorf said. "We've already won. We have already stopped it dead in its tracks. It's not going *anyplace* from here."

The Horseman felt the great beast shift under his bony body, felt the change, saw the horse throw back its head, rolling its wild eyes, rearing its forequarters with a whinnied scream of fear. A moment before, clear riding, but now, looming immediately ahead, a barrier, impenetrable, unscalable—

Flank it, flank it then! Something wrong here, to the right flank, away! The pell-mell clatter of hoofbeats, the Horseman peering ahead, something fogging his vision like mist in the cold night air. And again, looming up, the barrier. Left flank, swiftly! But again the barrier. On all three sides, a dead end, with an incomprehensible barrier and the sides closing in. No way to go—except back.

Then back, and be damned! The great beast whirled and plunged back the way they had come, head down, a great roaring gallop, echoing from the sides and the rear—but now, vision keen again, the Horseman saw what lay waiting this way, far in the distance but already looming up, soon to be upon them, the barrier closing off their retreat.

He seized the pale horse's mane, brought the beast to a halt, pawing the ground, stared around him. Something tore from his throat then, a scream of rage and frustration and unbridled malice. For one instant he was frozen there, straddling the beast, fist raised, and then the earth was parting beneath their feet and the only way was down.

Every time, throughout all history, the barriers had always been there, finally, sooner or later, and every time the Horseman had fallen short of his mission. This time, with new weapons and new speed, he had nearly made it; he had never been so close. Well, so it was, then. Another time would come in its season. And time, he knew, was on his side.

67

For Ted Bettendorf there was little time for rejoicing, far too little time for the staggering job ahead. There were resources to be mustered, and precious few sources to muster them from. Paradoxically, the mountain came to Mohammed; Atlanta was a corpse, whereas Willow Grove, Nebraska, was a living, breathing community. Those few that were left in Atlanta who could help him found themselves summarily shipped west. It may have seemed like going to Siberia, but then, as it were, Siberia was where the action was. Very swiftly Willow Grove was transformed, in its moment of glory, into a *de facto* national headquarters for the Centers for Disease Control. A team of excellent chemists, all high on Tom Shipman's want list, moved in to take over the operation in Wichita, buried under tons of tetracycline, and Shipman came north to rejoin Sally and take a desperately needed rest and put his head together with the others who had already formed such a spectacularly effective team. Bettendorf knew how badly he needed that team, and he was not taking any chances of it dispersing or losing momentum *now*. Within two weeks a second factory was established in Novato, California, and a third in Knoxville, while what was left of the Justice Department in what was left of Washington, D.C., started emergency injunction proceedings to condemn and then commandeer the Sealey Laboratories establishment in Indianapolis under martial law; arrest, convict and execute the members of the Sealey management responsible for the fraud, summary executions by burning becoming rather commonplace in areas of civil trouble or in cases perceived as profiteering, while a new production team got the new antibiotic pouring out of there on a proper scale under Tom Shipman's supervision. Meanwhile teams of sociologists, biomathematicians and statisticians began building a priority list of isolated, medium-sized rural communities for saturation bombing as soon as drug enough was available, while others scrambled frantically to establish transport and distribution teams so that not an hour was lost when the stockpiles began to build. And as winter moved into long, cold spring, the machinery slowly began turning.

In Brookdale, Connecticut, Carmen Dillman staged a slow recovery. There was a day when Jack Dillman was certain she was gone, and another day when he knew she would make it but didn't know when, and another day when he woke up and heard her banging pots in the kitchen, and an early spring sun was coming in the window, and she complained bitterly about the accumulated filth in the place. It was not until that day that either of them put their head outside their door, and then cautiously began exploring, and then, unbelieving, began searching, and discovered that they were two of seven people who remained in the entire community. Jack himself never did get sick, and he carefully never asked himself why. . . .

At the Grizzly Creek Freehold, as winter passed into spring, the toll was not as bad. Harry Slencik, of course, became desperately ill twelve hours after Amy was buried, and Ben fought a six-week battle over him; no one ever knew why he made it, and nobody ever asked; such questions were regarded as Bad Medicine at Grizzly Creek. Nor did anyone ask why or how Ben himself escaped, and he himself had no serious answers. What was clear was that the program he had conceived and executed at the Freehold helped cut the losses, however imperfect the program may have been. When it was finally over and supplies of the new drug finally reached Bozeman and surrounding areas, of the 163 people living at the Freehold when Jennie Ozmovitch took sick, 110 had become clinically ill; 62 of them had died and 48 walked out of the Sick Barn. And that, Ben Chamberlain thought, was not such a bad record.

It would be years, of course, before all the data would be collected; much inevitably would be lost, and in vast expanses of the world, even parts of the "civilized" world, no records were even kept. But in the continental States, as winter moved into spring and spring moved into summer, no one really terribly worried about the data; there was far too much to be done digging out of the chaos. It was enough for the country, one day in midsummer when some semblance of communications networks were being pieced back together again, that someone speculated in official tones that on that morning something on the order of seventeen million pairs of American eyes had greeted the dawn. Nobody really believed the figure; on the very face of it, it was really pretty unbelievable. And everybody was probably right, too.

It probably wasn't the right figure.